WHAT IT TAKES

THE WINDY HARBOR SERIES
BOOK 2

WILLOW ASTER

Willow Aster
www.willowaster.com

Copyright © 2026 by Willow Aster
ISBN-13: 978-1-964527-10-9

Cover by Kira Sabin
Photo by Wander Aguiar Photography
Map by Kira Sabin
Edited by Bill Siever and Christine Estevez
Formatted by Natalie Burtner

The Loon

Windhaven

The Rusty Trunk

Elm & Echo

COX TRADING POST

Cox Trading Post

WINDY FIT

What The Book?

Windy Fit

Kitty-Corner Cafe

The Cozy Palette

Lake Superior

Juju's House

The Hungry Walleye

Windy Harbor

NOTE TO READERS

A list of content warnings are on the next page, so skip that page if you'd rather not see them.

CONTENT WARNINGS

The content warnings for *What It Takes* are sexual content, profanity, cancer diagnosis and treatment, loss of parent in the past.

PROLOGUE
THE DAY WE ME

JULIANA

Past: Juju, age 5, Camden, age 7

I held the plate with both hands, but it was still wobbly. So heavy. My fingers hurt a little, but I could see the stand Daddy helped me make, and I wasn't far. I needed to get there before the tablecloth blew away. The paper sign that said "Cookies" was crooked, but it was okay. I thought I'd done a good job.

I took one slow step. And another.

Then…oh no, oh no.

The plate tilted and then *crashed*. Cookies fell in the grass, and a couple even rolled under the bush.

I froze. My eyes watered and my nose burned. I wanted to cry really bad. I'd worked so hard on those cookies. I stirred the dough with the big wooden spoon all by myself. Mommy let me use the oven with the timer and her oven mitts and even let me take the cookies out of the oven. They were supposed to be perfect for my first cookie stand in our new neighborhood.

Now they were ruined.

Before I had time to be too upset, tires squeaked on the sidewalk. A boy on a blue bike hopped off and tossed his bike on the grass. He had dark hair, and his eyes were bluer than his bike. He crouched down next to me.

"Are those the cookies for that stand over there?" he asked.

I nodded.

He started picking up cookies, brushing the grass off with his fingers. I watched as he held one up.

"Thirty-second rule. It's still good," he said and popped it in his mouth.

"Hey!" I said, forgetting that I wanted to cry. "My mom says that's not true."

His eyes widened. "Well, that's what we do at my house, and I'm not dead yet."

He laughed and then chewed the cookie, his face turning serious, and then a slow smile spread across his face. "Wow. These are really good. Did your mom make them?"

I straightened. "No, *I* made them. That'll be fifty cents."

His eyebrows lifted.

"I'm Camden," he said, stacking the cookies back on the plate. He reached into his pocket and pulled out a quarter.

"Does this work? Since I saved the cookies and all." He laughed.

"You can just keep it," I said. "Thanks for saving them."

"Thanks! And…you're welcome." He grinned.

He carried the plate to the stand and I followed, hurriedly dusting off a few strands of grass from the cookies.

"I'm seven," he said. "I make pancakes and scrambled

eggs. And Dad says my grilled hamburgers are better than his."

I grin. "I'm Juju. I'm five."

Camden blinked. "Oh. Five."

My head tilted. "What?"

He scratched the back of his neck. "My little sister's five. She still thinks unicorns are real, and she named her goldfish Ariel."

I frowned. I loved Ariel. And unicorns.

"Juju!" Jackson called.

"I'm at the cookie stand," I yelled back. To Camden, I said, "That's my brother. He's seven too. We like to ride bikes, and we play video games together every day. We climb trees…go swimming…"

I wanted Camden to know I was just as good a bike rider and video game player as my brother. And I didn't just sit inside with my Barbies, but I really liked them too. Well, maybe I wasn't as good as Jackson at all the bikes and games and tree stuff…I also couldn't do flips in the water like he could, but I bet I could soon.

"Cool," Camden said, and I got this warm feeling in my chest.

He showed me where his house was, and I showed him mine.

"That's why the cookie stand is here, right?" he said.

"Oh. Right," I said, my face feeling hot.

"And my brothers and I saw you moving in last week." He grinned and I relaxed.

"You have brothers *too*?"

"I have three brothers and one sister."

I wasn't sure I'd want more than one brother. Jackson was enough for me. I wouldn't mind a sister, though.

Jackson came around the side of the house, bouncing his basketball. He stopped when he saw Camden and me.

"Hey," he said.

"Hey," Camden said.

"This is Camden," I said. "He lives over there." I pointed at his house.

"I like basketball," Camden said.

Jackson lit up. "Yeah? Wanna play?" He motioned toward the hoop near the garage.

"Yeah!" Camden said.

And they took off.

I stared after them and kicked a rock. I liked basketball too, but they didn't even ask if I wanted to play. I kicked the rock all the way to my cookie stand and sat down on the chair, looking down the street to see if anyone was around who might want a cookie.

I sat there forever. And no one came. I was about to give up when a girl came running out of Camden's house. Her hair was like mine—bright and yellow. It was in a ponytail and it swished when she ran. When she saw me, she gave me a wide grin and ran over.

"Hi!" she said. "You're our new neighbor!"

"Yes!" I couldn't help but be excited because she looked so happy to see me.

She gasped when she looked down and saw the plate. "You have cookies!"

I handed her one without caring if she paid for it or not. She bit into it and her eyes got wide.

"Mmm! These are good." She chewed a little more. "I'm Marigold, but everyone calls me Goldie." She looked over my shoulder at Camden and Jackson playing. "That's my brother, and I have three other brothers too." She wrinkled her nose. "I wish there was another girl in there somewhere, but they're pretty nice too. Tully is my twin, Dylan is my little brother, and Noah is the oldest."

"Wow. A twin. My grandpa is a twin! Is it sad having the same birthday?"

She shook her head. "No, because Mom and Dad make it special for both of us. There are lots of twins at school, you'll see." Her head tilted. "You didn't tell me your name."

I grinned. "My name is Juliana, but everyone calls me Juju."

"We both have nicknames!" she said, laughing. "Do you like unicorns?"

"I love them!" I said so fast.

"Me too. My room is all unicorns. And Ariel. Do you like Ariel?"

"Your brother said you liked unicorns and Ariel." I nodded. "I do too. Ariel is the best princess. She sings the best songs."

Goldie smiled so big. "You should come over to my house, and we can watch Ariel with my unicorns."

"I can't wait!"

Maybe Camden didn't think being five was cool, but Goldie was the coolest five-year-old I'd ever met.

CHAPTER ONE

GRAND OPENING

CAMDEN

Present

It's a great day to be alive.

I'm completely stressed, running on fumes, and don't see sleep in my future for a long time, but it's the opening day of Elm & Echo, my new restaurant.

You only get one opening day.

My brain won't shut off. I went to bed at 2:30 and woke up at 4:30, my thoughts in a whirlwind. I've gone over every possible worst-case scenario in my mind and am hopefully equipped for whatever goes wrong.

Because something will definitely go wrong.

I moved back home to Minnesota recently. I wasn't sure I'd ever live here again—not because I don't love it, but because I'd found my place in Colorado. The restaurant I opened there is still thriving, but when I found out my dad had cancer and wanted my siblings and me to help him do an overhaul of the run-down resort next to our lake home, I got serious about making the move to be with my family. He's thinking about the legacy he wants to leave behind, and I'm thinking about being near him. I don't want to miss a single day with him.

Which is why, as soon as he texts his standard good morning to the family, I jump on it and pull up a separate thread with just the two of us.

> Are you up for coffee this morning? Get our day started out right before the craziness begins?

DAD

I'm always up for coffee with you, son.

> I'm at the restaurant already, but I can come back to the house. Or do you feel like getting out? I can have coffee ready at the restaurant in five minutes.

DAD

Choices, choices. Actually, I have a craving for one of Juju's scones. You up for going to the Kitty-Corner Cafe?

I groan internally. Juliana Fair, best friend to my sister Goldie, and the sister of *my* best friend Jackson, knows how to get under my skin. She owns the cafe in town, and it's excellent. The girl has been a phenomenal cook since the day I met her as a kid and ate her homemade chocolate chip cookies.

As a chef, I'm particular about all things food, but Juju has only gotten more skilled as the years have gone by. No one can cook like her.

We may butt heads, but I know an amazing scone when I

taste one…and the best grilled cheese sandwich I've ever had.

And I can't say no to my dad.

> I'll swing by to pick you up in twenty. Sound good?

DAD

Sounds perfect.

The Kitty-Corner Cafe is bustling when Dad and I walk in. The place is great, overflowing with charm. Juliana Fair stands behind the counter, looking all kinds of beautiful. Yes, as much as she can annoy me, I still think she's the most beautiful woman I've ever seen, which probably only serves to annoy me further. Long blonde hair, vivid green eyes, and pink lips, all a deceptive disguise for the venom this girl can spew.

At least when it comes to me.

There have been times over the course of our twenty-one-year history—we met when I was seven and she was five—when we've had a peace treaty between the two of us. The first day was such an example. I saved the day by salvaging the cookies that had fallen, and she looked at me like I was her knight in shining armor.

It all went downhill from there.

Today, she shoots me a withering glare and says, "I thought I wouldn't have to see you for a few more hours."

To which I say, "Today is your lucky day."

She rolls her eyes and continues helping Sandy, one of the locals, who looks back at my dad with interest.

"Everett, how are you?" she says. "How is that hotdish I sent over this week?"

My dad swallows hard and makes a point of not looking at me because he knows if he does, it's over. We won't be able to keep a straight face.

"Thanks again for that hotdish, Sandy. So thoughtful of you."

That hotdish is fucking awful. It's hard to make Tater Tot hotdish taste bad, but Sandy succeeds every time.

She beams at Dad, and I quietly chuckle next to him. My dad, ever the diplomat. When it's our turn at the counter, Juju gives Dad her warmest smile. That's the thing about her. I know she's capable of being kind, friendly, and even sweet, but with me, ninety percent of the time, she pulls out the rotten.

We won't think about the other ten percent.

I think she enjoys keeping me on a never-ending roller coaster.

"You're looking great this morning, Everett," she says. "What can I get for you?"

"And you're looking lovely this morning, Miss Juliana," he says. "I woke up thinking about your scones. And I'll have your light roast as well."

"Coming right up," she says.

"Uh, I didn't order yet," I say when she walks off to get my dad's order ready.

"Haven't you asked enough of me today?" she snaps.

I shake my head. "Really, Juju? Are we really gonna do this?"

She slams the plate down, and the scone almost falls off as she moves to pour my dad a cup of coffee.

"Sorry about that, Everett," she says.

"It's okay." He waves it off and grins, and she turns her attention to me.

"I don't know, Camden. I'm surprised you want any of my baked goods for your perfect restaurant, when it wasn't that long ago that you said Caribou's coffee is better."

I groan. "This again? Your specialty is baked goods. You don't have to have coffee down too."

She slides the coffee toward my dad and crosses her arms as she stares at me.

"My coffee is freaking delicious," she says, "and you know it."

"Well, I would prefer to deal with your bear claws, since that's all you seem to show me anyway."

She sputters, and I think maybe she growls too. I grin. I'd forgotten how fun she is to turn sideways.

She puts a bear claw on a plate and slams it in front of me.

"And a cup of your light roast too, please."

If fumes could come out of her head, I think they would be right now.

"Unbelievable," she says.

My dad is chuckling when we sit at the corner table.

"Why do you have to pick on that girl?" he says. "She's like family to us, and she has idolized you since the day you met."

I frown. "*Juju.* You're talking about Juliana? You're mistaken. We are like fire and ice. She hates me."

"Ah, son, for someone so smart, you sure can be dumb sometimes. Besides that, this little attitude you have when she's around, it's like you're a different person. As Goldie says, you're the nice one in the family."

I chuckle. "I don't know where Goldie gets that."

"She gets that because until she met Milo, she was also the sweet one, but he seemed to bring out the worst in her, the way Juju brings out the worst in you. I wonder what that's about. And look at where Goldie and Milo ended up." His grin widens.

"Don't start," I groan. "I haven't been in Windy Harbor a month and you're already matchmaking. You and Mom always had so much to say about me and Juju."

We both smile wistfully, thinking about my mom. I miss her every damn day.

I clear my throat. "Juju and I are not gonna happen. Did you see the way she flung that bear claw at me? She wished it was my balls on that plate."

I hear a gasp next to us, and Beverly and Carol are staring at us with wide eyes.

"Pardon my language," I say apologetically.

Beverly titters, and my dad is trying not to laugh when I look at him again.

"See what I mean?" he says under his breath. "Tully and Dylan…and even Noah, wouldn't have apologized."

I laugh. "Just because they're assholes doesn't make me the nice one."

He just looks at me like *Come on now*, and I grin as I enjoy my bear claw.

It's a fucking spectacular bear claw.

Before we leave, I tap on the counter, and Juju jumps. Her expression quickly turns from pleasant to volcanic.

"Please be on time with the desserts, Juliana. Today's a big day for me."

"I run my own business, Camden. I know how to be a professional."

I tilt my head and smile. "Great. Shouldn't be a problem then."

A few hours later, everything is in place. The tables are set. The sauces are ready. Everything is primed, and the staff are all in place. There's a level of high anticipation in the air.

But I'm waiting on one thing.

Or rather, one person.

Juliana fucking Fair.

"She was supposed to be here half an hour ago," I mutter, stalking past the kitchen doors. "I should've known she'd try to sabotage this."

Bobby, my new sous chef, looks at me in surprise. "Sabotage? Like she'd want to bring you down?"

"No," I admit. "She wouldn't go that far. She just really likes to irritate me."

And I seem to fall for it every time. I revert to my teenage years, when Juju and I started this bickering that is our new normal.

That's easier to deal with than the soft Juju who feels like my friend, because almost always, she turns on me.

A couple of weeks ago, when I asked her if she could make desserts for the restaurant until I could hire a new pastry chef, her eyes softened.

"I'd be honored," she said. "You know that I'm really proud of you, Camden…right? I think what you've done with the restaurant in Colorado is epic, and I know this new restaurant will knock it out of the park too."

"Thanks, Juju," I said, surprised.

Her mouth parted slightly, and I stepped toward her. I heard her breath hitch and could see the rise and fall of her chest.

"What is it?" I whispered.

"It's been a long time since you called me Juju," she whispered back.

"I always call you Juju in my head," I confessed.

We stared at each other for a long, weighty pause, and I could've sworn she wanted me to kiss her. She leaned in slightly, and her eyes dropped to my mouth.

And then her brother walked in, and we both took a step away from each other.

"My two favorite people. I'm shocked you're alone and not throwing dough at each other." Jackson laughed.

"Give it time and we'll be back at it," I teased, grinning at Juju.

Her jaw tightened, and the warmth left her eyes.

I fucking hated to see it go.

I wish I didn't always say the wrong thing when it came to her.

But this was us, a seesaw that never balanced.

The door flings open, and Juju rushes in.

Her hair is up, her cheeks flushed, either from the cold or because she knows I'll be ticked. She's pushing a cart loaded down with desserts.

"You're late."

"I'm here," she sings. "And I brought the pies and cheese-cakes you wanted…plus mousse cakes and bread pudding that I thought would fit nicely with your menu."

"I didn't ask for the mousse cakes or bread pudding. I asked you to be on time."

She stares at me indignantly. "I was doing something nice for you."

I exhale slowly. "I didn't ask you to be nice or to bring extra food that I may or may not be able to sell."

Her cheeks burn brighter. "You'll be glad you have them, you arrogant control freak."

"It's not about control," I say between gritted teeth. "It's about not having waste, and doing what you say you'll do."

"Trust me, if you let the good people of Windy Harbor know that my mousse cake or bread pudding is a surprise dessert for this evening, they will sell faster than you can plate them."

"That's not how restaurants work, Juliana. I've already printed the menu."

"So tell them it's a special that isn't on the menu," she grumbles. "Should I have brought store-bought cheesecakes instead?"

I take a step toward her. She does the same thing.

"Why are you always pushing?" I ask. "It's like you find a nerve and just poke, poke, poke."

"I can't help it that you're an uptight, bossy, overly sensitive, emotionally constipated man who—"

"I'm the uptight, bossy, overly sensitive, emotionally constipated one?" I yell back. "You don't want to go there with me, Juliana. If I remember correctly, you were the one who—"

"What is going on back here?" Goldie comes in, her eyes wide.

"I should've known better than to bring desserts for you!" Juju shouts as she walks toward the door. "You can find someone else to do your bidding, Camden Whitman!"

She says something to Goldie under her breath, and I laugh.

"May as well call a jackass a *jackass*, Juliana."

"Okay, *jackass*," she mutters before she leaves the kitchen.

Goldie rips me a new one when Juju leaves, but my sister never stays mad at me too long. One of the many things I love about her. And with this being opening night, she probably has more mercy on me than I deserve.

The night is a success.

Even more than I'd hoped it would be.

I had my family surrounding me, my best friend Jackson, and even my favorite players from the Colorado Mustangs team—Weston, Henley, Rhodes, Bowie, and Penn—along with their wives. I couldn't believe they'd all made the trip to Minnesota. My sister was thrilled to have her college room-mate, Addy, who's married to Penn, by her side. And of course, Juju was there, looking like a bombshell in a blue dress.

Speaking of the bombshell, she's lingering after everyone has left for the night. It's so late that I didn't expect anyone to be here still, but she's in the kitchen, gathering her pans, when I walk in.

It's on the tip of my tongue to apologize for being a bastard earlier when she says, "Are the rest of the desserts tucked away somewhere, or did you get rid of them all like I said you would?"

I growl, which delights her.

"You wouldn't be asking that question if you didn't already know the answer," I say.

"Oh, I know the answer. I knew the answer when I left them here. Too bad I won't be making any desserts for you again."

She carries her pans to the door, and I call after her.

"Juju, wait. Let's not—"

She whirls around. "Let's not what? Be civil to one

another? Have the common courtesy to say thank you?" Her voice cracks, and I feel like the biggest jerk. "You've got it. Let's not…ever again."

She leaves, and I slump against the island, every earlier feeling of victory squashed with her words.

CHAPTER TWO

TROUBLE WALKS IN

JULIANA

It's been weeks since the fight with Camden at his restaurant opening, and I still feel off. I survived a tense yet fun Thanksgiving, where we all celebrated together, and it was only fun because I avoided Camden like my life depended on it.

I've nearly burned the scones every morning, and that just does not happen.

The raspberry filling hasn't set the way it should, and the lemon glaze tastes flat.

I've thrown away more than I want to admit.

I keep thinking of his face before I walked out that night. Pained, angry, confused. He looked like how I feel every time I'm around him.

It wasn't always like this. I think that's why it's so hard.

It's been so long, but I miss the boy who sampled everything I baked, encouraging me with his praise and requests for more of whatever I gave him. I miss the friend who knew I hated everything grape-flavored, even though I loved grapes, and always gave me the strawberry or cherry. It was a long time before I ever knew he didn't like anything grape-flavored very much either. I miss the version of us that doesn't end with raised voices and slammed doors.

But this is our new normal, has been for years now, and I think it's time I accept it.

Besides Goldie and Jackson, Camden was always the person who got it…got me. Sometimes it felt like he got me more than anyone else. I guess that's just what I wanted to believe.

We may as well be strangers now.

Anyway.

I don't have time to stay in this headspace another second. I can't afford to ruin any more desserts.

The cinnamon rolls are in the oven, the third batch of scones is ready to go in next, and the blueberry muffins are cooling. The pies are already almost sold out for the day, and I won't have time to make more until I close. I cut the toffee bars and put them in the display case before going back to the kitchen.

The phone rings while I'm wiping flour off my cheek.

Papa Hector.

I wipe my hands and answer. "Hi, Papa!"

He doesn't bother with hello. "Your uncle Hal and I are coming tomorrow. Surprise!"

I gasp. "Really? You're coming here? That's great!"

Papa and his twin brother Hal are the life of any gathering. The age of the crowd doesn't matter—if Papa and Uncle Hal are around, everyone is having a good time. Hal is technically my great-uncle, but I always just call him Uncle Hal.

"We're missing our girl…and her banana cream pies." Papa Hector laughs and I grin, already feeling happier just hearing his voice. "Hey—I heard there's a handsome chef in town who's making waves with his delicious food. You know anything about that?"

I roll my eyes. "No, I wouldn't know anything about that."

He laughs again, not fully realizing the buttons he's pushing.

"You sound tired, sweetheart."

I glance at my reflection in the mirror we keep by the back door. My cheeks are flushed, my updo is messy, and I have dark smudges under my eyes.

"I can't remember the last time I wasn't," I admit.

"Well, Uncle Hal and I can help you. We can help at the shop, help around the house…your mom said you've sounded a little lonesome lately, and we can help with that too."

I smile. His offer of helping around the shop sounds more like a disaster waiting to happen, but I'll be happily proven wrong if that's not the case. But I'm all for everything else he said.

"I'm doing all right, but I'll be better when you're here. I can't wait to see you and Uncle Hal."

He makes a quiet sound of approval. "Can't wait to see you, sweetheart."

"I'll get your rooms ready. Hurry up and get here. But be careful," I add.

"Don't go to any trouble. We're old men. We're not particular, and we know how to change sheets and whatnot."

"I won't go to any trouble…much."

"Ahhh, my little perfectionist. I shouldn't have given you any warning!"

"I'm glad you did."

We both laugh.

"I'll see you tomorrow, sweetheart."

"Bye, Papa. I'm so excited."

When we hang up, I feel a little less hollow. I told myself the solitude would be good when I first moved to Windy Harbor. And it is, mostly. I have my best friends, Erin, who runs Cox Trading Post with her parents, and Goldie, who's now living in Windy Harbor full-time too, and I couldn't be happier to have more time with them. But after a day at the cafe, it's almost always nice to come home to the stillness.

From the time we moved to Summit Avenue and our family met the Whitmans, our families have been close. My parents still own their home in St. Paul and plan to retire here before too long. As for me, I needed the quieter pace of Windy Harbor a little sooner.

After the hectic day, I don't want to people another second. Bosco, one of the crankier regulars at The Kitty-Corner Cafe, was in rare form today. He was extra grumpy. If I hadn't offered him free coffee, I think he would've chased everyone off.

I'm exhausted. My shoulders are tight and my brain is tired. If I don't distract myself, I will go pick another fight with Camden, and that's just unnecessary.

We're already deep in a constant fight.

The sooner I can get past this, the sooner I can get rid of this tight feeling in my chest.

This is who we are now.

It was easier when he wasn't in Windy Harbor. I still thought of him often when he lived in Colorado, but it wasn't like a scab being constantly picked, the way it is now that I have to see him all the time.

I go home, get the bedrooms ready, clean for a bit, and watch something mind-numbing. The cold makes the wooden balcony off my bedroom pop, and the loud sounds make me jump every time, interrupting my relaxation. This is one of my favorite places to be in all the world, but the house has never felt bigger or emptier than it does tonight.

When my parents bought a lake home, they didn't go the usual route with a cute little cabin. They went big, like they do with everything else. The house sprawls out on Wildbriar Lane, Windy Harbor's main drag through town, and the place is a showstopper. A yellow Victorian with an updated wing at the back of the house and a cozy addition above the garage, the place is tucked into the trees, Lake Superior framing it perfectly. The Kitty-Corner Cafe is next door, situated closer to the street.

If the cafe hadn't taken off, I'd considered running a bed-and-breakfast here, but I'd decided I wanted a place to decompress after work, not have people in my space at home too.

There's only one room that hasn't been remodeled, and it's my fault. The bathroom off my bedroom is horribly outdated, and not the good kind. The rest of the house has a lot of character, original woodwork and all, but my bathroom has an eighties vibe with dusty blue everything. Toilet, sinks, and a chunky blue tub that juts out of the wall like a ship that's lost its way, stretching out into the middle of the room in the least efficient use of space ever.

I thought for sure I'd trip over the tub all the time, but I quickly got used to it, and once I'd finally taken a bath in the thing, I fell in love.

Mildred—that's what I've named this hunk of cast-iron goodness—perfectly encases my body. She slants at the back, allowing me to lounge at just the right elevation. I can look out the window while I bathe or read in there for hours. Mildred has comforted me during many a tear session and soothed my tired feet after a long day, and, since she's four hundred pounds soaking wet, she's not going anywhere.

I sink into the water and practically purr. This is often the best part of my day.

But then I toss and turn all night, my mind too full of all the things.

The next day, the anticipation of seeing my grandpa and uncle is high. Midafternoon, I see them roll in, hauling a trailer with their Harleys behind the SUV. I watch them park at the house and then stroll over, walking in sync.

The bell above the door jangles as I rush to meet them. They walk in wearing cute cable-knit sweaters with jeans, sunglasses, and wide smiles. Having been around them most of my life, I know that they did not plan to match. It just always happens.

"Papa," I say, opening my arms wide.

He hugs me tight. "There you are. It's so good to see you, sweetheart."

"You too." I sigh into his teddy-bear hold.

"Okay, my turn," Uncle Hal says.

He's grinning when I turn and barrel into him.

It's crazy how alike they look, but I can pick them out a mile apart. Papa is sweet and reserved, and Uncle Hal is pure mischief. Their personalities show in their eyes and smiles, but once they speak, their differences are more evident to everyone.

"You ready to put us to work?" Uncle Hal asks. "I can be the taste tester."

"Hmm. We'll see." I laugh. "I promise to keep you supplied with sweets for sure."

"I knew it was the right thing to come here," he teases.

"The place looks wonderful, Juju," Papa says.

I look around, and that's when I realize how quiet the cafe

is. Goldie's grandmas, Grandma Donna and Grandma Nancy, are in the shop, which is a rarity. I've known them almost as long as I've known the Whitman family, and I love them dearly. Most of the town has taken to calling them Grandma Donna and Grandma Nancy.

They're in their soft sweaters—Grandma Donna with pants and boots, Grandma Nancy with a skirt and heels that are brave to wear around here in December. Both are frozen as they stare at us. Grandma Donna's holding a pale pink flyer and a clipboard that looks like a sign-up sheet. Goldie showed me the flyer already and asked if it'd be okay if they put it on my bulletin board.

It says:

Friendship Bench
Available to anyone who needs a friend.
Come sit. I'll listen. A warm beverage is optional.
~Grandma Donna

When she realizes our attention is on her, she shyly turns and pins it up. Grandma Nancy blinks slowly but doesn't turn away.

Papa pauses.

"Well, well," he murmurs. "Windy Harbor has some surprises. Donna, is that you?"

She turns and swallows, nodding slowly.

"Hello, Hector," she says.

He moves forward and clasps her hand in his. "You haven't changed a bit."

He smiles at Grandma Donna, who blushes.

"Neither have you." Her eyes lower to the floor and then shoot back up to Papa's.

Is this a moment? It sure feels like it. I so wish Goldie could be here to witness this.

Uncle Hal lowers his sunglasses halfway. He stares at Grandma Nancy and whistles low. "Are we in heaven?"

Okay, yes, definitely a moment.

Grandma Nancy's back straightens, and she gives Uncle Hal a look that would make most men falter.

Not Uncle Hal.

"You look like trouble," she says, setting her cup down with a purposeful clink.

Uncle Hal smiles proudly. "Only on Mondays. You free?"

Nancy gasps. "Absolutely not."

I cough into my arm to avoid laughing out loud.

Papa gives a slight bow, looking very distinguished. "Forgive my brother. What he's trying to say is that he's happy to be in Windy Harbor."

"I was saying a lot more than that, and she knows it." Uncle Hal winks at Grandma Nancy. "A heavenly view," he adds.

Grandma Nancy crosses her arms, staring defiantly at Uncle Hal, and her lips twitch when she says, "I suppose you think that line works on women you want to razzle-dazzle?"

Uncle Hal pulls off his sunglasses smoothly and folds them. "Razzle-dazzle." He points at her. "That's the perfect expression for what you do, my dear."

My mouth drops. This is gold. The whole cafe is watching the exchange back and forth like we're at Wimbledon.

"Oh, I do a lot more than that, I assure you." Grandma Nancy points at Uncle Hal. "And don't call me your dear. A man like you couldn't possibly handle someone like me."

I barely hide my gasp.

"Darlin', I am up for the task," Uncle Hal says, standing taller.

"Hal, don't be scaring these beautiful ladies before we've even settled in town," Papa says.

I decide to jump in before Uncle Hal gets any bolder. "Thanks for bringing the flyer over, Grandma Donna."

She smiles sweetly at me.

"What have you got there?" Papa asks her.

Donna's cheeks flush again. "It's a little something I'm…" She waves her hand. "It's nothing really."

I reach out and touch her arm. "It's not nothing. I can't tell you how much I love this idea." I look at Papa. "She's dedicating a bench on the Whitmans' new property for anyone who needs a friend to listen. The Friendship Bench."

Papa's eyes soften. "That's really lovely."

Donna looks flustered. "We all need someone to talk to at times…it doesn't cost me a thing to listen."

Papa nods. "That's beautiful."

"I got the idea from a news program," she says, like that diminishes her part in this.

"Not everyone would take it to heart like you are," he says.

"Well. Thank you." She gives him a soft smile.

It does my sad heart some good to see genuine kindness between two people I love very much. Grandma Donna has had a difficult year, losing her husband.

Meanwhile, I hear Grandma Nancy huff and shake her head at Uncle Hal.

"You are something else," she says, tsking.

"Something good, I hope," he says, undeterred.

I lean closer to Papa and mutter, "I had no idea you and Uncle Hal were such flirts."

He smiles. "Me? No. Your uncle, yes."

"Um, you were working some of your magic too." My eyes widen. *And I think it worked*, I mouth.

He chuckles and pats my back. "She has kind eyes. And a kind heart." He leans in and whispers, "And she's as pretty as she always was."

I point at him. "See? You were flirting!"

He laughs, and we continue watching Uncle Hal and Grandma Nancy spar.

"I'll be ready if you ever need to get out and razzle-dazzle me even more," Uncle Hal says.

She raises one sculpted, perfectly penciled brow. "Keep dreaming."

I lose it. I have to move behind the counter and make it look like I'm cleaning something because I'm cracking up.

The grandmas gather their things with quiet dignity. Grandma Donna says something about picking up knitting needles.

As they pass, Uncle Hal tips his head. "We'll be seeing you lovely ladies soon."

Grandma Nancy walks by and sniffs. "Only if you're lucky."

Oh my God. What is happening right now?

There was no concealing my snort with that zinger.

"Well, put us to work," Uncle Hal says once they're gone.

"Oh, I think you've done enough, Casanova," I say.

He beams and bows. "Why, thank you."

I groan. "You're going to be a pain in my neck, aren't you?" As much as I try to sound annoyed, it comes out fondly.

Uncle Hal stretches and bops my nose. "Oh, sweetheart. You have no idea."

"Ignore him. I'll keep him in line," Papa says.

Uncle Hal gives me a deadpan look. "He's spent a lifetime trying. Hasn't worked yet."

Papa lets out a long-suffering sigh. "He does keep me busy."

I laugh, and when the timer goes off, I lift my thumb toward the kitchen. "I've gotta get that out, but you're welcome to get settled at the house whenever you want. It's open."

Papa frowns. "You don't keep your door locked?"

"It's Windy Harbor," I say. "Not necessary here."

He blows out a breath. "It's such a good thing I'm here."

CHAPTER THREE

THE GOODS

CAMDEN

Dad's humming along to an old Billy Joel song, his fingers tapping in time to the music as we drive down the winding, snowy road toward Duluth. The lake is frozen in places, and yet the waves still crash along the shore.

He looks better.

Not like the man he was before the diagnosis, but not like he did a couple of months ago in the thick of chemo either.

"You nervous?" I ask.

"Yeah. I guess I am a little worried they'll say something I don't want to hear."

I nod. "That's fair. We need some good news."

The appointment takes a while, and I sit in the corner paying attention to every detail so I can relay it all to my siblings. Dad hasn't let us come to his appointments. He's been very stubborn about it, and I'm not sure why he had me come today, but I'm glad he did.

I spent all morning at the restaurant prepping for my day off. I've only worked with my team for a short time, and it's too soon to be taking a day off, but I trust that they've got things under control. Bobby is invaluable, and so is Marilyn, the line cook. Katie and Bentley have already proven to be excellent bartenders. I was most concerned about how Annie and Hannah, Lorraine's twin daughters from The Loon, would be because they're young and distracted by Joey, Bob and Helen's son from The Hungry Walleye, but they're all doing great. It's ironic that they're working for me instead of their parents, but I think all parties involved are enjoying a little break from one another. They know the restaurant business, and it seems like they're not afraid of hard work...when Joey's not flirting with the twins, that is. And actually, that's pretty much all the time...but he's still getting the job done.

The only weak link is the pastry chef. Britney started this week, and so far, it seems like she's just in the way and with very little to show for her efforts. If only she put more time into her baking than her flirting. Every time she's in the kitchen, she's staring at me, and it's annoying as hell. If she could produce excellence, it would be different, but her desserts haven't blown me away so far. We'll see how it goes.

Dad smiles at me when the nurse leaves. "Not what you signed up for, is it? Do you regret leaving Colorado for all this?"

"Regret time with you? Hell no. I would do it again a hundred times over. No restaurant matters more than this right here...you."

He blinks slowly, his eyes welling with tears. He's become a lot more sentimental since the diagnosis.

There's a quiet knock on the door, and the doctor steps in. He says hello to my dad and then shakes my hand.

"Dr. Randolph," he says.

"This is my son, Camden," Dad says.

"Nice to meet you." I tip my head slightly. "Thank you for taking such good care of my dad, Dr. Randolph."

"He makes it easy," the doctor says, smiling at my dad. "You're doing well, Everett," he adds. "Blood counts are up. There are still a few markers we'll continue to track, but I'm encouraged."

Dad's expression doesn't change, but I feel the breath he lets out.

"We'll keep watching, but keep doing what you've been doing," the doctor says. "You seem more relaxed…happier."

Dad's mouth twitches. "I've got my kids back. Well, they're not all back full-time, but I'm getting more visits from the ones who are out of state." He points at me and grins. "This one even moved back from Colorado."

"Oh, that's great," the doctor says. "I've been hearing good things about your new restaurant in Windy Harbor. I'll have to make my way there to try it out sometime."

"That'd be great," I say.

My dad squeezes my shoulder. "It's worth the drive, I promise you that."

"Says my dad," I tease.

"Your dad's not the only one," Dr. Randolph says, chuckling. "My wife and I are foodies, and we've heard your name floating around town quite a bit. We'd actually hoped to get out to your restaurant in Colorado one of these days too, but this is much more convenient."

"I'm flattered, thank you. Whitman's will still be there, should you get out that way, but yeah, come to Windy Harbor when you get a chance. Let me or my staff know when you do, and the meal will be covered every time."

"I couldn't," he protests, and I hold up my hand.

"It's the least I can do. You've helped my dad so much. My family and I are so grateful."

"Well, like I said, Everett makes it easy. I don't think there's a more likable guy out there."

He smiles at my dad, and after my dad makes his rounds thanking everyone in the office, we leave with an appointment to follow up in six weeks.

When I pull onto the highway, Dad leans his head back and lets out a small sigh.

"What a beautiful day," he says. "You know, when your mother died, I wasn't sure I could live without her. I didn't *want* to live without her." He glances at me apologetically. "It was you kids who kept me going. I don't think I ever thanked you properly for that."

I swallow the lump in my throat. "You don't need to thank me for that, Dad. None of us could've gotten through losing Mom without each other."

"Not so long ago, I wasn't sure I'd be around to experience much more. I don't know how much time I have left, but I intend on enjoying every second. I want to be around for whatever comes, but no one lives forever, so when I go, you kids stick together."

I sigh and glance at him. "I hate it when you talk like this."

He grins. "I know, I know, but some things just have to be said."

"Okay, Dad, I promise we'll stick together. It helps that we all love each other."

He chuckles. "Yes, it does."

By the time we pull into our driveway, the trees have that sun-dappled glow, and the sky is a combination of pinks and golds over the lake. Dad stares out at the view like he's drinking it in.

"Looks like everyone's here," I say as I park.

Kevin, the Havanese Goldie brought home a few months ago, yaps at the door like he's been waiting for Dad all day. He has a hard time deciding who he's most obsessed with—Goldie or Dad. Since Dad is the one who named him and Kevin seemed to know Dad needed the extra love while he was going through chemo, I think he leans slightly more toward Dad.

He twirls so fast and his tail wags so hard that it throws off his balance. When I open the door, he launches himself at Dad, whose laugh barrels through the entryway.

I should've told the doctor about Kevin. I'd say he's had as much to do with Dad's happiness as my siblings and I have.

Inside, the house smells like pot roast and freshly baked bread. There's music playing and voices rising above the song, proof that all the Whitmans are under one roof. We're a noisy bunch.

Goldie rounds the corner and looks at Dad anxiously. "How did it go?"

"All good," Dad says, shrugging out of his coat. "They said I should be able to start training for a marathon soon."

Goldie's eyes go wide. "They did?"

"No," Dad deadpans. "But I think it'd probably be all right."

Dylan and Tully come out next. Dylan hugs us first and then Tully.

"You look awfully happy, Dylan," Dad says. "Did you have a good flight?"

"I actually had the best flight I can ever remember having," Dylan says, lifting his eyebrows cryptically.

My eyes narrow. "Sounds like you met someone."

He grins. "You could say that."

Tully studies Dad. "Did he think everything looked good for real? Your coloring is so much better."

"Yes, he's feeling optimistic about everything, so I think we should too," Dad says. He pats Tully's face. "Between the chemo and all the resort stuff, your games have gotten neglected. Watching them on TV just isn't the same. I've missed coming to all the games so much. You'll be seeing this mug there a lot more often."

Tully grins. "Sounds good to me, Pops. We've got a great lineup coming up, so the timing is perfect."

My nephew Grayson realizes we're in the room and comes running over, hugging Dad first before barreling into me. He holds his arms out, and I pick him up. We say "Crusher" at the same time, and then I flip him over. After I set him back on the ground, we high-five and fist-bump. This has been our customary greeting since the day my brother Noah first okayed the roughhousing.

Grandma Nancy and Grandma Donna descend on Dad the second they spot him. Grandma Nancy has a basket of freshly baked bread in hand, which she sets down to hug her son. Grandma Donna rushes over to get the afghan she knitted for Dad and drapes it around his shoulders.

"You look chilly. Are you okay? Your coloring is off," she says.

"Tully just told me my coloring was better." Dad laughs.

"I bet you're just hungry," Grandma Nancy says. She picks up the basket and lifts the cloth to reveal warm, buttered bread. "Here you go. This will give you some energy."

Dad takes a slice and finishes hugging everyone before saying, "I'm going to sit down before everyone kills me with kindness."

"No killing language," Grandma Nancy tsks, which

makes all of us laugh, so she eventually does too. "And dinner is ready, so march yourself right over there to that table instead of your recliner."

"So bossy," Dad grumbles as he gets up and goes to the table. "Grayson is the three-and-a-half-year-old around here, not me."

Grandma Nancy pinches his cheek and grins. "You'll always be my little boy, you know."

He laughs. "I know, I know. That's how I feel about the kiddos at this table and they're grown, so I guess it's only fair that I get that treatment too."

She laughs and piles roast onto his plate. He chuckles but doesn't try to argue with her. When she's not looking, he slides some of it onto my plate.

"There's no way I can eat all that," he whispers.

There's so much food—the grandmas have clearly gone overboard. Pot roast with mashed potatoes and gravy, the bread from heaven, several salads…oh shit, the Lutheran Jell-O is there—the lime and cottage cheese one. My siblings and I all eye each other warily as we try to come up with inventive ways to avoid it.

Goldie is closest to Grandma Donna, and my sister stares at me aghast when our grandma manages to scoop some onto Goldie's already full plate. She squeaks when Grandma Donna pulls out the squeezy mayo, all poised to give Goldie's Jell-O salad a dollop.

"No mayo for me, thanks, Grandma," Goldie rushes out.

She clears her throat and doesn't look up when my brothers and I snort, trying to hold back from laughing.

"Come on, Golds," Tully says. "It's always better with the mayo!"

"*You* try it with the mayo," she snaps. "I don't see it on

yours." Her head tilts. "Wait a minute. Grandma Donna, Tully needs some of that."

"Oh dear, I didn't realize it hadn't gotten to you yet," Grandma Donna says, reaching over to give Tully a huge helping.

He scowls at Goldie.

I choke back a laugh and then can't hold it in. Our grandmas turn, smiling to see what's so funny.

"Tully made a funny face," I say weakly to Grandma Donna.

Tully gives me the finger when Grandma Donna isn't looking, but Dad sees.

"Maybe some of us *are* still three-and-a-half years old," he says under his breath.

"Here, I need some, Grandma Donna," Goldie's fiancé Milo says, holding up his plate.

We all turn to him, mouths gaping.

"Kiss ass." Tully coughs in his fist.

Grandma Donna puts a pile on his plate, and he takes his fork and gets a huge clump of it on there. He pales when she adds the mayo at the last second, but then he gives us a defiant look as he puts it in his mouth.

"Mmm," he says.

He then proceeds to gag and then tries to cover it up, hitting his fist on his chest.

"Took too big of a bite," he says weakly.

"That's my man," Goldie says as she tries not to cackle.

Over all the laughing and chatter, Kevin decides to jump into the conversation. He hops onto his little stool beside the table and yips three times.

"Show them, Kevin," Goldie says.

"Who's the best dog in the whole world?" Dad asks.

Kevin spins in a circle, sits, then holds one paw in the air.

We all cheer, and it's so loud, it scares him. He runs under the table between Dad's and Goldie's feet.

After dinner, I make mulled wine for everyone, and we play a game of gin rummy. The warmth of the brandy in my chest, mixed with the warm fuzzies of being near my family again, leaves me feeling happier than I've been in a long time. I was content in Colorado, happy even, but I missed my family more than I thought possible. It feels right to be back.

I'm about to leave to check on the restaurant when headlights sweep across the driveway. Goldie hops up before the doorbell rings so it doesn't set Kevin off and then walks back with Ava.

She pauses just behind Goldie, holding a pie. Since discovering we have a sister we didn't know about, we've had a lot of awkward and emotional moments. Our mother had Ava when she was a teenager in high school, and her boyfriend at the time, Bruce Granger, whose family has a long-standing hatred of my dad's family, wanted her to have an abortion. She went away for a while instead, letting him think she'd had an abortion, but she'd given the baby up for adoption. When she started dating my dad and they got serious, she let him know about the baby.

Ava didn't know about us right away either, since it was a closed adoption, but with 23andMe, she was able to find her birth dad. She had no idea she had so many siblings, and I can't imagine how that must have felt to go from being an only child to having a huge family. When she came to town, she was so resentful that we'd had a great life and she hadn't that she wreaked havoc at first. She also had Bruce in her ear, bad-mouthing us, but his true colors showed early on. Once my dad realized who she was, and we found out she existed, Dad told us that our mom had never gotten over giving her baby up.

It breaks our hearts knowing Mom dealt with that secret for all those years and never got to meet Ava before she died.

As for Ava, she's trying hard to make up for our rough start, and every time she shows up, she brings something— flowers, a cake, or her favorite coffee beans. And we're all trying to make her feel welcome and comfortable, but we're still getting to know each other, so it's not going to be seamless right away.

"Hey," she says, her voice quiet but steady.

Everyone says hello.

It's jarring how much she looks like Mom. I don't know how we didn't all know she was related immediately.

"I heard you like banana cream pie," she says to Dad.

"I love it," he says, beaming at her. "I'll always say yes to banana cream pie."

"Noted." She laughs.

Goldie clears a spot for her at the table. "We just finished a game of gin rummy. Do you play?"

Ava shakes her head. "I've never played it."

"Wanna learn? It's fun and easy," I say.

"Sure."

We show her the game, and soon, she's laughing along with us, her shoulders loosening a little more.

"This has been so fun," she says later, as she gets up to leave. "Thanks for the game. I needed that. I really appreciate…you guys being so welcoming." She bites the inside of her cheek. "I still haven't met my other sister." She makes a face. "I'm not sure my dad has even told her about me."

Dylan curses, and everyone turns to look at him. He rubs a hand down his face.

"Sorry, that's just so…" He shakes his head and doesn't say anything else.

Goldie leans over and hugs Ava. "Well, hurry back. We love having you with us."

Ava swallows hard. "Thank you. I will."

———

The next day I'm talking to Joey at the host station when I hear a voice I haven't heard in a long time.

I turn around and see Hector and Hal Fair dressed in jeans and the same sweaters and jackets but in different colors. They have identical amused expressions.

"Camden Whitman, the man of the hour," Hector says, just as Hal yells, "Surprise!"

I reach Hector first, and he pulls me into a hug. Hal pounds my back, and when I'm done hugging Hector, he holds his arms wide.

"I can't believe Jackson didn't tell me you were in town," I say.

"We just pulled in yesterday," Hector says. "Saw our girl right off the bat." His eyes meet mine, and I feel instant guilt.

I'm positive he knows how things are between me and Juju now, but did she tell him about our last fight?

"It's been a long time," I say, looking between them. "You look the same."

They both laugh.

"You were always way more diplomatic than my grandson," Hector says.

"Flattery will get you everywhere." Hal winks.

"And yes, it's been a long time," Hector says. "Way too long. But just look at you. This place is gorgeous. Your mom would be so proud. *I'm* so proud." He squeezes my shoulder.

"Thank you. That means a lot. It's been really great to be

back with my family. I can handle the crazy winters as long as we're together."

Hal laughs. "It's gonna take a while for my blood to adjust back to the cold tundra."

"Oh, haven't you heard? We're having a mild winter." I laugh at their expressions.

"It's all we heard at Kitty-Corner," Hal says. "A mild winter to us is the sixty-degree days we just left in Vegas."

"Well, now you're just bragging. I bet you didn't get to wear those cool jackets in Vegas."

Hector nods, his smile wide. "Good point. And I missed the seasons. Not sure I need these extremes, but I do appreciate the milder year. It'll ease us back into this weather."

"Let me get you seated." I motion for them to follow me. "It's perfect timing. This is the table with the best view."

Hector looks out the window and sighs. "I've missed that view."

"How long are you staying?"

"Indefinitely," Hal says.

My eyebrows lift. "Really? I thought you were settled in Vegas."

Hector's nose scrunches. "It's just not for me." He points at his brother. "It's more his speed, but I think even he is ready for the quieter life. And like you said, I can handle the cold as long as I get to see my family. We saw Jackson briefly yesterday. He was at his parents' place in St. Paul when we stopped by."

"How are John and Margaret?"

"They're doing well. They've joined the pickleball craze and are trying to talk Hal and me into driving into the Cities at least once a week to play with them." He shakes his head. "I told them I'll save my chances of breaking my wrist with my Harley. I think they'll be coming up this weekend." He points at his brother. "Remind me to tell Juju that if she hasn't heard by tonight."

Hal nods. "Will do. Speaking of Juju," he says as he waves his menu, "which of her desserts should we try today?"

They both look at me expectantly.

"Uh, I'm not…we don't have Juju's desserts. Britney is the pastry chef here and—"

A sharp voice cuts in behind me. "He's already got my Brussels sprouts on his menu. I wouldn't give Camden Whitman my baked goods if he were the last man alive."

I turn slowly.

Juliana's standing behind me, arms crossed, and wearing a bright red lipstick that shoots straight to my dick. Her eyes are full of fire and maybe a bit of panic now that she realizes everyone in the restaurant heard her.

I fold my arms and stare her down. "Well, well. Someone's true wishes are coming out."

"Excuse me?" Eyes narrowed, lasers fired.

"You heard me." I lean close to her and lower my voice just enough that only she can hear me. "You want me to eat your goods. I heard your favorite is pound cake…"

She makes a noise I've never heard from her. Something between a gasp and a shriek. When I step back, her face is bright red.

"You are—" she hisses. "I can't—"

She turns on her heels and walks away, straight into the glass door that's so clean it's transparent. She holds a hand to her head, arm flinging out in frustration.

I rush toward her to see if she's okay, that old instinct taking over, but she glares at me and yanks the door open before storming toward her car.

And then she shocks me by turning around and walking back into the restaurant.

She marches past me to Hector and Hal's table, never making eye contact with me, and hands her grandpa something.

"Thank you, dear. Sorry you came all this way. Are you okay?" he asks gently.

"I'm fine," she says softly.

And she's gone as quickly as she stormed in.

I walk back to their table, a bit shaken by all that anger.

"I've never seen her like that," Hal says.

"Me either," Hector admits.

And then his eyes meet mine.

"Want to tell me what that's all about?" he asks.

I sigh. "It's a long story."

"Well, when you've got time, I'll listen."

I nod and step away to give them time to look at the menu…and to regain my footing.

CHAPTER FOUR

ON BRAND

JULIANA

The nerve of that guy!

The way he just expects women to drop at his feet. Well, from what I've seen the few times I've been at his restaurant, there are always a few women who are doing just that, so I suppose he's used to it.

He's got another thing coming if he thinks that'll ever be me.

I fume, my hands shaking with my fury.

I should go back to the bakery and work out my frustration there.

Instead, I pull out my phone and text the girls.

> Any chance you two are free for a drink? Dinner? People watching at The Loon? My place? I'm not picky.

Okay, that might've sounded desperate, but I don't care. My phone buzzes.

> **GOLDIE**
>
> I'm in! I vote The Loon because I need Lorraine's seven-layer bars desperately.
>
> **ERIN**
>
> Same. The Tater Tot hotdish is a'callin'.
>
> Yay! Thanks, you guys. I'll head over there now and get a table. Come whenever you want.

The plus of living in a small town is that it takes between one and five minutes to get everywhere. Unless it's tourist season, but even that isn't what it used to be, ever since the resort closed. But living in Windy Harbor has many advantages. It's magical. The town is quaint, with that nostalgic Main Street vibe, but inside the colorful storefronts, you'll find classy shops and restaurants. And Lake Superior will always be the star of the show, the vast water stretching out as far as the eye can see.

The Hungry Walleye serves the best fish and chips, but they can also pull out the fine dining with popovers and the best steak I've ever eaten. The Loon is a bit of a dive, but it's a *cute* dive. What the Book? is an adorable bookstore that I could live in, and The Rusty Trunk has antiques and refinished furniture. And we can't forget Cox Trading Post, where you'll find things you never knew you wanted.

The old resort's land is next to the Whitmans' property, and when it went on the market, Everett snatched it up. They're doing a complete overhaul of the place, building on and remodeling. Windhaven will be much more upscale. It's where

Camden's new restaurant is, and the whole property will be a dream once it's complete. It will level up Windy Harbor in such a huge way. As much as I loathe thinking anything positive when it comes to Camden Whitman, I have to admit that already with Elm & Echo opening, a lot more tourists have been coming through to experience the Michelin-starred chef's cooking…which means all of us in the service industry are thriving.

Our favorite table is open, so I head back there, waving at Lorraine as I go. She finishes with a customer and walks over.

"How ya doin', Juju?" She props her hand on her hip and assesses me for a second. "You're workin' too hard. I oughta know, I am too."

"Yeah, I have a love/hate relationship with being so busy," I say.

"I hear ya. Is it just you tonight or will you have company?"

"Goldie and Erin will be here any minute. I think we're all wanting Tater Tot hotdish and seven-layer bars. Can I add a Juicy Lucy to the mix too? I need one of your burgers to make this day better." I hold up a finger. "And a bottle of wine too, please. Whatever you think is good with this combo."

She knocks on the table. "You've got it. Want me to bring it all out as it's ready or wait until the girls get here?"

"Bring it out as it's ready. I'm starving."

She grins. "You've got it."

Lorraine is bringing out the Tater Tot hotdish and Juicy Lucy when the girls arrive. We all hug and I swear, I already feel better.

Erin's in her trademark red lipstick and combat boots, her black hair with a streak of blue making her look like the perfect edgy pinup girl. She shrugs off her coat, and I nod when I see her T-shirt.

Red Lip Rebellion.

"So fitting," I say.

She sticks her chest out, eyeing her shirt proudly. "I thought so. Made it myself. Clothing art at its finest."

"*You* are the finest," I tell her.

"I'm on brand," she says, smirking as she lifts a shoulder. And then she leans in and says, "But this is what I've really been wearing today." She lifts the shirt over her head, and underneath is a shirt that says *The Big O*, and there's a picture of a bull's-eye.

Goldie and I lose it.

"This one is even better," Goldie says.

"I need one in every color," I say. "Or better yet, the real thing would do. I wouldn't even have to get the shirt."

"How 'bout both?" Erin smirks. "We need to manifest getting laid." She lifts her fist for me to bump.

I snort and meet her bump.

Goldie has a messy braid, and her pink sweater looks so soft. So does her expression—that dreamy, just-engaged glow.

"You're unusually happy," I tease.

"Figures. She's enjoying the O on the regular," Erin says.

Goldie makes a face. "I am annoyingly happy, aren't I? Sorry, I'll scale it back. Milo is just so…"

"Perfect," Erin finishes. "Yeah, we know. You guys are a rom-com in real life. It's disgusting and so damn cute."

Goldie stares at her ring and sighs again. When she catches us watching, she makes another face. "Sorry, sorry. Who am I?" She laughs.

"If Goldie is living a rom-com, I'm living a sitcom. The

way my grandpa and uncle flirted with your grandmas, Goldie…" I shake my head and crack up. "It was obscene."

"I cannot believe I missed that." She laughs. "Next time, you have to text me while it's happening so I can rush over instead of after the fact!"

"Count me in on that too. I'll gladly close the shop to witness lovin' between the elderly," Erin says.

I make a face. "I'm not sure I'm ready to go that far. Flirting was okay, but…" I shudder. "I don't want to think of any sex going on there."

"Old people love sex too!" Erin argues. "Haven't you heard about all the action in the nursing homes?"

"That's all great. For old people that I don't *know*," I say emphatically. "I mean, I'd rather not know about it at all, but it's much better knowing that it's strangers I will never meet."

I cut the burger into thirds, watching the cheese ooze out of the center of the meat, and put it on plates for all of us. We pile the hotdish on our plates, and Lorraine opens the bottle of wine, pouring each of us a glass.

"Can I get you anything else to eat?" she asks. "I don't suppose you want a vegetable…"

"As if," Erin says, and we all laugh.

"There's lettuce on this burger," Goldie says. "I'm good. But I think we'll need another order of this hotdish. It's extra good tonight."

"I'm glad one of us has found her match." Erin groans when Lorraine walks away. "Meanwhile, I matched with someone who used the word *moist* in her bio."

I nearly spit out my wine. "Was it related to dessert?"

"She did mention cupcakes, which should have made it a little more acceptable, but she had to go and ruin it. She said, and I quote: 'I plan to make you as moist as my cupcakes.'"

My jaw drops. "No."

"That is all kinds of wrong," Goldie says.

"I'm afraid it made me dry forever." Erin sighs.

I giggle. "Hopefully not. They say you just need the right person. Isn't that right, Goldie?"

Goldie's laughing and nods. "I can attest to my cupcake being m—" She cringes and shakes her head. "No, I can't say it, not even joking. But yes, the right person can make it *all* work."

"Noted." Erin grins. "I don't want to say I only want dry people…but definitely not the m-word."

We crack up, but Erin's laugh dies quickly, her eyes widening. We turn in slow motion to see where she's looking.

Percy Williams.

They're wearing paint-spattered overalls, black boots, and a smile that is directed at Erin.

"Breathe," I whisper.

She inhales. "Okay." She blows out her exhale. "Okay."

Percy walks to our table. "Hey."

Goldie and I beam at Percy, while Erin continues to look frozen.

"Hi, Percy. It's good to see you," I say. "Are you happy to be back in Windy Harbor?"

"I am. I enjoyed traveling, but I missed home and… everyone here." Their eyes crinkle in the corners when they look at Erin, and Erin's lips lift slightly.

I knew she had it bad for Percy Williams, but wow. My bold girl, who's not afraid of anyone or shy about anything, *typically*, looks like she can't remember how to speak.

"Love the shirt, Erin," Percy says.

"You—oh—bull's-eye!" Erin blurts. "Rebellion. Uh…yep."

Percy's head tilts, clearly amused. "Iconic as always. It's good to see you all."

They turn and head to the bar.

"You too!" I call out.

Erin groans and drops her forehead into her hand. "Did I just say 'Bull's-eye…rebellion'? *What?*"

"You're fine," Goldie says, patting her arm.

"I need to disappear," she says.

"You need to go order a drink and try again. Get back on that horse," I say.

Erin peeks at the bar through her fingers. "My horse has run off."

My ribs hurt from laughing.

"I have a better idea." Erin sighs. "Let's talk about you."

Her attention turns to me.

I'm already shaking my head. "Let's not."

"I really want to." She grins, and my nervy friend is back.

I turn and look at the bar. "Should I call Percy over and see if they want to join us?"

"Hush," Erin says, laughing. "A little birdie told me about some tension over at Elm & Echo this afternoon."

I roll my eyes.

"Ooo, I didn't hear about this," Goldie says, rubber-necking at me. "What happened?"

"Want to tell us about your little confrontation with Camden?" Erin tilts her head and crosses her arms over her chest.

Goldie leans forward, her shoulders dropping slightly. "Don't tell me you guys fought again."

"I wouldn't call it a fight exactly. It was an…*argument* with someone who has no concept of boundaries or communication or *manners* or—" I stop myself and take a sip of my drink. "Anyway. No big deal."

Goldie reaches over and squeezes my hand. "Are you sure? It seems like it might've been a big deal."

"Have you ever resolved the issues you had at the resort opening?" Erin asks.

"Nope," I say too fast.

"It just makes me so sad to see you guys this way," Goldie says. "You were so close for such a long time."

"And now we *haven't* been for a long time." I pick at my napkin.

"Don't you miss him?" she asks.

I stare at her in shock. This is the first time she's asked me this. I think we've both avoided ever going there since I'm her best friend and he's her brother...and my brother's best friend. There are too many layers of complication with Camden and me.

"Yes," I say softly. "But I miss who he *used* to be. Maybe he's still the same guy to you, but I think the guy I was close to is long gone."

She looks at me sympathetically, her eyes full of concern, which is the last thing I want. I'd hate to put her in the middle of my problems with Camden.

"Didn't you say that women are coming out of the woodwork to see Camden in his element?" Erin asks Goldie.

My eyes widen, and then I try to act cool when Goldie glances at me, almost cautiously.

"Yeah," she says, wincing. "Women all over the Midwest are happy Camden Whitman is back in Minnesota. He's hot shit, I guess." She sighs.

"How's your dad?" I ask, very obviously changing the subject.

Her face brightens. "He's doing really well."

The next morning, I know something's up when I walk into the cafe and smell Lysol instead of sweetness.

And then I hear humming.

I go into the kitchen and find Papa on a stool in front of the large island, about to spray a harsh chemical on my wood-block baker's table.

"Wait, Papa!"

He jumps and turns, laughing. "You gave me a fright!"

He waves the bottle of spray, and I shake my head.

"No, don't use this?" he clarifies.

"No. It'll strip the oils." I show him what I use to clean and oil it. "And then for any stains, I use lemon, vinegar, or baking soda."

"Ah, okay. Sorry 'bout that. I thought maybe I could make your job a little easier, and I just about botched things up!"

"No worries," I tell him. "It was sweet of you."

Uncle Hal pops out of the pantry, holding a clipboard. "Did you know you're low on baking powder?"

My lips twitch. "You two are awake awfully early. It's still dark out. You shouldn't torture yourselves this way."

"We want to help," Papa says. "It seems like you're over-whelmed."

"Really? I mean, I'm often overwhelmed or running low on sleep, but I don't feel especially so right now."

"You yelled at Camden," Uncle Hal says. "We've never heard you even slightly raise your voice at anyone, so we drew the logical conclusion that you must be exhausted and need help."

"I'm touched that you're concerned about me, but I really am okay. Camden and I...we just don't see eye to eye on anything. We haven't for a long time."

"But you were so close!" Papa says.

"Things change."

He moves in front of me and puts his hands on my arms.

"Are you sure you're okay?" he asks.

I nod. "I am."

A little voice inside screams that I'm not being one hundred percent honest here, but I ignore it.

"We'd still enjoy helping," Uncle Hal says, grinning. "Put us to work."

I shrug. "Okay, you asked for it."

For the next couple of hours, it's a miracle that I'm able to get anything done. Uncle Hal spills flour everywhere, and Papa used baking powder instead of powdered sugar in the cream cheese frosting.

"Oh, I see the difference now," he says when he puts his glasses on.

I expect them to call it a day once Suzanne arrives for her shift, or maybe when the cafe opens, but they're still going strong.

That saying *Too many cooks in the kitchen…*

I'm seeing it firsthand.

Papa and Uncle Hal are everywhere.

Goldie and Erin come in and light up when they see them. There are hugs all around, and then Goldie leans in.

"How *are* you this morning?" she asks.

"I'm great. Why does everyone keep asking me that?"

"No reason," she says quickly. "It's so good to see Papa Hector and Uncle Hal."

"They look great," Erin says.

"I'm so happy they're in town. But I'm having to watch them like a hawk. They want to help, but baking isn't really their specialty."

We laugh.

"I'm being loved to death," I add.

WHAT IT TAKES   53

"I'm so glad our talk about getting laid is on your mind," Erin teases.

"Uh, that was too close to me talking about my grandpa and uncle." I shudder.

"Eek, you're right. Maybe it's *my* mind that's on getting laid…all the time. Percy looked so good," she whines.

"Do something about it," Goldie says. "Go over to The Cozy Palette today and pull a Papa Hector and Uncle Hal and be helpful."

Erin snorts. "If I didn't have to go to work, I would go help Percy, all right. I'd get on my knees and—" She snaps and points at me. "I've got a good idea. Maybe if you got on your knees for Camden, he'd never argue with you again."

My mouth drops and my face burns. I know without looking that it's bright red.

"My, my," Beverly says. "The things young women talk about these days." She moves up to the counter, and Goldie and Erin shuffle out of the way so she can place her order.

Sorry, Erin mouths, backing away.

I glare at her, annoyed that she'd say such a thing. And for taking my mind to being on my knees in front of Camden.

It also takes every ounce of my willpower not to laugh.

I lift my hand to say bye as Goldie and Erin start to walk to the door and focus on Beverly.

But my mind is on Camden and what it would feel like to finally shut him up.

I fan my face.

Papa and Uncle Hal must be right—I am overwhelmed.

If I were okay, I'd never think these thoughts.

That little voice rears up again, calling me out for my lack of honesty.

Camden's not the only one who needs to shut up.

CHAPTER FIVE

HIDEAWAY

CAMDEN

Past: Camden, age 13, Juju, age 11

The tree house finally looked right.

We'd gotten a lake home in Windy Harbor, a few hours from St. Paul, and after we talked about how much we loved it there, the Fairs got a vacation home there too. Now our summers were spent by the lake, swimming and fishing and exploring the woods. I loved it there. We all did.

We'd spent the summer working on the tree house, between our property and the old cabins and resort next to us, and getting it how we wanted had taken us weeks. We scrubbed the floor, fixed the door, and strung up battery-powered lights that Juju insisted we needed. Jackson and I pretended the lights were silly, but I secretly thought they were cool. Dad let us take his old Bluetooth speaker when he got a new one, and we rigged it to the rafters. Tully and I carried up sleeping bags, along with playing cards and board games, and a plastic tub filled with candy. Juju and Goldie cut up material and hung it on either side of the window, makeshift curtains that Juju held back with a little rope. They looked good.

The place felt like ours.

No parents calling us down to help carry groceries or work in the yard. Just us, stretched out on mismatched pillows in our little hideaway, drinking cold Cokes out of the bottle.

And no siblings, not today anyway.

I loved my little sister and my brothers, but there were times I didn't want the responsibility of making sure everyone was okay. Noah was out with his girlfriend all the time these days, so I was the oldest when it came time to play, and sometimes I just needed to do what I wanted for a while.

Whenever I wanted to go to the Fairs' house, Goldie was usually glued to my side. She and Juju were together anytime Goldie wasn't with Tully. If Juju was in charge, they baked, and if Goldie was, they worked on art projects.

After working so hard, the quiet was nice.

Sometimes I had the tree house to myself, and I liked that.

It felt great to have something we'd worked on with our own hands. My brother Noah helped some. He wanted to build houses in the future, and he already knew way more than I did about construction. Even though it was technically our tree house, I knew Jackson and Juju would be spending a lot of time there.

Later that night, after we'd roasted marshmallows and then went inside to watch a movie, Jackson fell asleep while the credits were rolling. I looked around for my notebook, the only thing I'd brought with me, and realized I'd left it in the tree house.

I slipped outside barefoot, the grass cool against my feet,

and heard the sound of the waves crashing against the rocks. Windy Harbor's lighthouse was a little more visible from Jackson's house than mine, but when the light turned toward our yard, it was brighter. I was still glad we had the lights at the tree house. They lit my path and the ladder when I climbed up.

When I pushed the door open, I froze.

Juju was in there, sitting cross-legged on one of the sleeping bags with a flashlight tucked between her knees, flipping through my notebook.

She looked up and dropped the flashlight. It took her a second of fumbling to pick it up again, and I blinked at her. She had on a tank top and these tiny cut-off shorts that she hadn't been wearing earlier. I couldn't remember ever seeing her wear anything like this. She looked older. Her legs went on forever. I felt my face and neck get warm.

"Uh, what are you doing?" I asked, motioning for her to hand me my notebook.

She gave it to me. "You're always guarding this like a hawk, and I wanted to see what was so important."

"Well? What do you think?"

She grinned. "I think I'd really like to try that steak wrapped in the puff pastry."

My cheeks flamed hotter. "You don't think it's stupid?"

Her smile dropped. "What's stupid?"

"That I make up recipes that I think sound good?"

She leaned up on her knees. "I think it's awesome. And you don't just write them down—you make them. I saw the recipe for that macaroni and cheese you made." She pretended she was locking her lips. "I won't tell a soul the secret ingredient."

I grinned. "You better not. One day I'm going to make

that in my restaurant, and you and I will be the only ones who know."

Her smile was huge. She liked that. I stood a little taller, my chest tight with that heated buzz I'd been getting around her a lot lately. I loved making her light up. Ever since the day we met and I saw those sad eyes looking up at me, I'd been trying to make her happy. It wasn't hard to do. She was funny, and I was never bored with her.

I'd never admit this to anyone, but sometimes I even preferred her company over Jackson's.

"You know what would be delicious with this one?" she asked, pointing to a recipe I'd made up for a pasta with chicken and mushrooms.

I moved closer and sat down beside her, our shoulders brushing against each other.

"What?"

"My caramelized Brussels sprouts." She grinned.

"Mmm, for sure."

Juju and I were the only kids we knew who liked Brussels sprouts. And we *really* liked them. Juju made them the best. I could probably eat them every day.

"*And* that raspberry cream pie I made a few weeks ago."

I groaned. "I loved that pie. Anything would be good with that, but you're right, it would be the *best* with that pasta dish."

She nodded, her smile huge again.

"When are you making it again?" I asked.

She lifted a shoulder. "I could make it anytime you want."

I smiled. "How about you come over tomorrow? I'll make that pasta, and you can make the Brussels sprouts and pie."

"Yes!" She handed me the notebook and grinned over at me. "I wish it was tomorrow right now."

My stomach growled, and we both laughed.

"Me too."

The next day, when my mom took my brothers and sister swimming, I stayed back, saying I was too tired. She came back to my room afterward, checking to see if I was okay. Since I could never seem to lie to her, I told her the truth.

"I want to fine-tune that pasta dish I made recently, and Juju's going to bring over Brussels sprouts and a pie that we think will be perfect with it."

She smiled, knowing how much cooking meant to me and also that I needed time for more quietness than my family sometimes allowed.

"Okay, just as long as you save a little bit for me," she said. "And have Juju make sure it's okay with her parents that she's here with you. Better if Jackson came over too."

"But she's here all the time." I frowned. "And Jackson doesn't get why we're so into cooking."

"I think it's wonderful that you're both so gifted in the kitchen, and I love that you're doing this together. But everyone else is usually around when she's over here. You're at an age where it'd be good to have others around."

"But why?"

"You're getting older and going through some changes, right?" She smiled at me and I flushed. "It can be a confusing time."

"*Mom*," I groaned.

"I know, I know. We don't like to talk about things like puberty." She made a face, trying to get me to smile, but I was too grossed out. "It's nothing to be embarrassed about, love. It's part of life, and you need to be aware of it. Sometimes our hormones can make things complicated." When she saw the disgust on my face, she laughed, and then she paused and her eyes lit up. "You know what? Grandma Donna said she was stopping by later with a few things. I could see if she'd hang out with you two for a while."

I grumbled under my breath while she called Grandma Donna. I loved Grandma Donna so much, but I didn't see why my mom was making such a big deal about this. It wasn't like anything weird would happen.

And then I remembered how I'd felt the night before when I saw Juju in those shorts. Her long legs. Her skin looked so soft.

I swallowed hard and avoided looking at my mom. It was terrifying how she could always read my mind.

She got off the phone and clasped her hands together. "Okay, it's perfect. She doesn't mind hanging out until we get home. She says she'll stay out of your way too." She winked.

Then why is she coming at all? I wanted to ask, but I was too shaken up by my mom's sixth sense to argue.

Mom kissed my cheek and rubbed her hand over the hair by my neck like she always did. Just like that, my annoyance with her disappeared.

"Love you, Cam," she said.

"I love you too."

Grandma Donna came a few minutes before Juju. She stood on her tiptoes and kissed both of my cheeks.

"I can't get over how fast you're growing. You're as tall as your dad!" She smiled up at me.

"He doesn't love that his boys are passing him up," I said, laughing. "Well, Noah already has, and Tully and Dylan aren't far behind."

"You boys are all growing way too fast. Knock it off!"

"Can't." I grinned and lifted my shoulder in a shrug.

When Juju got there, we couldn't stop smiling at each other.

"You kids have fun. I'll be watching my stories over here in the den," Grandma Donna said.

I didn't know why I was so into creating things in the kitchen, but I always had been, and so had Juju. No one in my family liked cooking as much as me, not even Grandma Nancy, who really enjoyed it. Juju had more special family recipes than we did, but even at her house, she'd already taken over the baking for holidays and family dinners. Sometimes when I was at their house, we would try to figure out what we all wanted to watch, and Juju and I would vote for a cooking show. Jackson griped about it, but he'd play with his Switch if we insisted on watching one. We'd make it up to him later by letting him pick what we made to eat.

I turned on the music, and we lined up our ingredients on the island. Before long, the kitchen smelled like olive oil, garlic, and sugar. Juju put graham crackers in a plastic bag, so they wouldn't make a mess, and pounded them with the bottom of a glass.

Eventually, she pounded so hard that she made a hole, and graham crackers went flying in her face.

"So you wanted to wear the graham crackers, huh?" I said, throwing a towel at her so she could wipe them off.

She pretended to be annoyed and crumbled another small piece of graham cracker in the mixing bowl with the end of a knife. When she leaned over to grab the powdered sugar, I caught the scent of her strawberry shampoo. She always smelled like either sugar or berries.

We worked, sometimes chatting and sometimes humming along with the music. I asked Grandma Donna if she wanted any food, and she said she'd let us enjoy it first, while she worked up an appetite. I thought maybe her soap opera wasn't over yet.

When we plated everything and sat down at the table, we looked at each other and grinned.

"I'm so hungry," I said.

"I can't wait to eat it. This pasta looks so good." She took a bite, and she tilted her head from side to side. "Oh, that is delicious." She covered her mouth and said it with her mouth full. "That little bit of lemon…" She nodded. "I love it."

I felt a surge of pride. I liked feeding Juju more than just about anyone. She always appreciated what it took to make something delicious, and she wasn't one of those picky eaters like most of the girls at school. Jackson liked good food, but he didn't always want to try everything.

We talked about what we wanted to do with the rest of the summer, and then we put huge slices of pie on our plates. My eyes practically rolled back when I took the first bite.

"That's even better than the last time," I said.

"Thank you," Juju said, her cheeks pink.

I was thinking about taking a second piece of pie when the back door swung open.

Jackson stepped inside, his hair plastered to his forehead from the bike ride over. He stopped in the doorway, looking between us. We were so shocked that he'd stormed in, we just stared back at him.

"What's going on?" he asked.

"We're—" Juju started.

"We made some food," I said. "Want some?"

Juju held up the pie proudly. "I made that raspberry cream—"

"*This* is where you guys have been all day?" Jackson said, cutting her off.

"Not all day, just a couple hours," I said.

He looked at me, his eyes narrowing. "Dude, it's weird."

"What's weird?" I asked, instantly defensive.

"That you want to hang out with my little sister? I don't know. It's just weird, okay? Why do you want to hang out with her all the time?"

"You like to hang out with her too. She's—" I paused.

His words hit harder than I expected, and not because I thought he was right—until my thoughts last night and the earlier conversation today with Mom came racing back. With Jackson's voice layered over hers, all I could hear was the warning.

Suddenly, everything felt off.

I looked at Juju, and a wave of sadness hit me. I picked up my plate and carried it to the sink.

"Yeah, you're right," I said. "It is weird for us to hang out without you."

I glanced at Juju and wished I hadn't because I saw her face fall. She blinked at me, confused and hurt, like she was trying to figure out who I was and what had just happened.

That was what I wanted to know too—what had happened in the past two days to change everything?

And then she was moving. She was at the door before I knew it.

"Take the rest of the pie," I said.

"Jackson can bring it," she said as she walked out.

He gave me another look, this time an angry one for hurting his sister's feelings.

I'd recognize that look anywhere because I'd given it plenty of times to people bugging Goldie.

I stood there with a messy kitchen and an ache in my gut that had nothing to do with the food.

CHAPTER SIX

HOLLY JOLLY

JULIANA

Present

"I know what we have to do as soon as Mom and Dad get here," Jackson says before he's even in the door all the way.

The facts out there about women talking more than men do not apply to my brother and me. For every one word I say, he says twenty.

"It's too late for a card since it's Christmas freaking Eve, but we can post it on the socials and give everyone a laugh." Jackson hugs Uncle Hal, who's closest to him. Papa is next, and when he reaches me, he's pulled up an old picture on his phone.

"Hello, Jackson." I laugh, giving him a playful shove when he holds the phone in my face.

"Hi…hey," he says, still grinning at his phone. "Wait till you see this. It's gonna be hilarious."

I bump him with my hip, and he grumbles but waves his phone. I begrudgingly take it from him.

"It wouldn't hurt you to hug your sister," I say.

"You sound just like Mom. *Hello, Juju*," he says, mocking me. He hugs me, lifting me off the ground. When he sets me down, he leans down so we're at eye level. "Satisfied?"

"Yes."

"Good. Now look at this picture."

I start laughing as soon as I see it. My dad is on all fours, and my mom, my brother, and I are on his back. I think I'm around four years old, old enough to remember doing this. Jackson would've been around six. We're all laughing so hard —my head has fallen back on Jackson's shoulder, and his smile is so wide. Jackson's in the middle, and Mom is in the back, looking at us to make sure we're not going to fall off. Dad's expression is very similar to Uncle Hal's—pure mischief.

"It is a great idea," I admit.

The second Mom and Dad pull into the driveway, Jackson and I run out to meet them. I practically fall into Mom's arms, laughing as we squeeze each other like we haven't seen each other in years instead of just a month ago.

"We've got to see more of each other," she says. "It's not that far, but when it's hectic, those few hours feel like an eternity. I've got an assistant who's taking a lot off my plate, though." She squeezes my arm and smooths back my hair. "I'll do better at getting to Windy Harbor. I miss you too much to go a month at a time not seeing you."

"I'd love that. The cafe has me stretched pretty thin or I'd come see you more often." I make a face.

My parents have been nothing but supportive of my business. Initially, they weren't thrilled that I was opening a cafe in Windy Harbor instead of St. Paul, since they weren't able to be here full-time, but once they saw how I was thriving here, they never brought it up again. They plan to be here once they retire, so I think they're a bit envious that I'm getting an earlier start.

I'm not sure if or when Jackson will leave Minneapolis. He has a beautiful condo downtown and isn't too far from the house we grew up in. Maybe if he ever settles down with someone, he'll move here. I don't see that happening anytime soon, but he loves it in Windy Harbor as much as I do. My family has been addicted to the town ever since we first came to visit the Whitmans at their lake home. My parents and Goldie's became instant friends when they met, and it wasn't long before we got a lake home here too, our families enjoying time together both in St. Paul and Windy Harbor.

"Come here, pretty girl," Dad says.

His hug is warm and solid, and I bury my face in his shoulder before Jackson claps him on the back.

We've barely finished hugging when Jackson says, "Okay, picture time. I have a plan for us." He points at Mom and Dad and then between me and him. "Remember this picture?"

He holds up his phone, and my parents laugh.

"Oh my gosh. That was such a fun day," Mom says.

"We need to reenact this," Jackson says.

"You think my back is strong enough for that?" Dad asks. "I mean, not because of you two," he adds, backtracking as he points at my mom and me. "It's this six-two man of muscle right here." He pats Jackson's bicep.

"I won't put all my weight on you," Jackson says, grinning.

I roll my eyes. "He's determined to do this, so we better figure it out or he'll bug us about it all night."

"Damn straight. And you already admitted it was a great idea, so don't go acting like you're not dying to do this too." Jackson holds his arms out, waiting for us to chime in.

"I don't know if I'd say *dying to*, but it does sound fun." I grin. "I won't put all my weight on you either, Dad," I add.

He laughs. "I guess we're doing this." He looks at Jackson. "Same place as this?" He points at the picture.

"Yep, to the Cozy Daisy," Jackson says.

When we moved into this house, I insisted on naming the "important" rooms. The family room was the Cozy Daisy, the living room was the Yellow Rose, and the kitchen was super creative—Chicken Lickin'. Not sure why the Cozy Daisy is the only one that stuck, but it's what we all call the family room, even our friends.

Dad looks at Jackson like *You're really gonna make me do this?* Jackson just gives him a cheesy grin that makes him look like his six-year-old self instead of twenty-eight. He has a nice camera and sets it on the tripod, checking to make sure he gets the right angle. Then he points at the floor where he wants Dad to go. Dad groans as he gets on his knees.

"Okay, Papa, you okay doing this photoshoot?" Jackson motions for Papa to come over. "Make sure we look like this." He sets his phone on the mantel next to Papa.

"I think I can handle it." Papa winks.

Papa is the one who took the original picture and also the one who taught Jackson and me how to use his Nikon.

"I'm not as nimble as I was twenty-plus years ago," Dad mutters. "Are we sure this is a good idea?"

"John, don't hurt yourself," Mom says.

He snorts. "Too late. I'm down here. Let's hurry this up, or I might get stuck this way."

"We'll just have to make it look like we're on your back," I say as I get in place first.

It's a struggle to stay steady.

Everyone's already cracking up.

"Don't make me laugh," I say, barely getting the words out. "Dad's right, we've gotta do this fast. I haven't been exercising enough to do squats here for very long."

That makes everyone but Dad and me laugh harder. I wave at Jackson and Mom, trying to hurry them up. My legs are feeling the burn as I hover over Dad's back. Jackson gets on next, and Mom wipes the tears from her eyes.

"You're so big now, there's no more room on his back!" she says, pointing at Dad's backside.

That sends us into another wave of laughter, and I'm so unsteady, I fall into Dad, who weaves, caught off guard. Jackson steadies me and waves for Mom to come on.

"Just get behind me, and don't forget to look at us like you're making sure we won't fall," he tells her.

"Mm-hmm," she says through her laughter. "On this half-inch of booty that's left for me."

"Who you callin' a half-inch booty?" Dad quips, sending us all into another round.

"No jokes," Jackson yells, trying to rein us in but laughing too hard himself.

"Okay, okay, everyone in position," Papa says after a long wheezing laugh. "Juju, tilt your head back a little, to your left. Jackson, your hand should be on Juju's right arm. Margaret, come forward a tiny bit so I can see you over your son's enormous head."

"Hey!" Jackson protests. "My head is normal for my size."

"You've had an enormous head since the day you were born," Mom says.

I lose it and have to get resituated, clearing my throat and wiping my eyes before settling into a calmer smile. It's hard to taper into a calmer smile when you're laughing too hard.

"Now is not the time to talk about my head," Jackson says.

Papa cackles and shakes out his hands, trying to steady himself. "Okay, everyone, hold still."

The click of the camera finally comes, and Papa barks out instructions for us to adjust here and there until he's happy. When we get up, we have to help Dad to his feet, and he stretches, his back letting out a loud crack as he does.

"I'm sending you my chiropractor bill," he says, pointing at Jackson.

"Let's see." Jackson is already next to Papa, checking out the photos. He puts his fist to his mouth and snorts. "Oh, these are golden," he says.

———

The fun continues throughout our Christmas Eve dinner. The prime rib is delicious, and according to Mom, my homemade rolls are to die for. Rich, buttery smells waft in the air, Christmas music is playing in the background, and I'm content. It's so good to have my family here, to sit down and *breathe*.

And there's nonstop entertainment. Jackson has had three generous fingers of Jameson, which means his filter is nonexistent.

"So, Jackson," Mom says sweetly, "how's…what was her name again?"

Jackson's fork freezes halfway to his mouth. "Which one?"

I nearly choke on my wine. "Which one?" I repeat, leaning forward. "Do you hear yourself?"

"Hey, I'm single. It's okay to mingle." He tries to look serious, but his grin ruins it. "And let me tell you, I'm mingling."

I groan. "Gross."

"It'd be selfish to only let one person get close to this," he says, pointing his hands toward his chest.

My eyes narrow. "How did we come from the same genetic pool?"

Dad chuckles. "Son, is this why you never bring anyone around us? Unable to pick one person who can enjoy all this? Or afraid we'll scare them off?"

Jackson raises his eyebrows. "Oh, I can assure you—no one scares them off." He leans in. "These girls are bold. Did I tell you about the one I couldn't get to leave? She spent the night and the next morning woke up with an outline of all the things she wanted to do…in my condo. And might I add, I didn't want her to spend the night in the first place."

"Yeah, no…I didn't need to hear that," I say.

"You act like it's scandalous. It's not," Jackson insists, pointing at me with his fork. "You just think anything involving sex is scandalous."

"Okay, ew." I put my hands over my ears. "And not true. But we're eating. And okay, maybe a little bit true when it comes to *your* sex life."

Mom's laughing so hard she's blotting her eyes with a napkin. "Can we *please* get through one holiday without turning dinner into a tabloid headline?"

"No," I say at the same time Jackson says, "Absolutely not."

The next morning is present time. Wrapping paper is everywhere, and we have hot cocoa and the cinnamon rolls I made last night for breakfast.

It's perfect—until Mom says, "Don't forget, dinner with the Whitmans at Elm & Echo tonight!"

Cue my stomach doing that twisty thing.

Goldie will be there, which is great. I love Goldie. But Camden will also be there, and I've been *very* successfully avoiding him ever since my blowup at his restaurant a couple of weeks ago. My record is flawless. I'd like to keep it that way.

Except…apparently Camden's in rare form tonight.

From the second I walk in, it's like he's made it his mission to be *in my space*. Leaning too close when he asks if I want water. Sliding a plate in front of me like he's my personal waiter. Catching my eye from across the room like he knows I hate it.

I focus on Goldie. I laugh at her jokes, braid her hair, and make a big show of not even looking at Camden.

It works…until later in the night.

The mulled wine is strong. Warm. Delicious. And way too easy to keep refilling when everyone's laughing and talking and passing around more cookies than any human should eat in one sitting.

At some point, I excuse myself to the bathroom, splash a little cold water on my face, and tell myself I'm *perfectly fine*.

When I come back out, I hear clattering from the kitchen, so I figure I'll help clean up. It's the least I can do after inhaling approximately six pounds of food.

I push through the swinging door, already rolling up my sleeves. "All right, what can I—"

I stop.

The room is quiet. Everyone's gone. No laughing, no

music, just the low hum of the fridge and the faint smell of roasted vegetables. And, standing at the sink, sleeves shoved up, rinsing plates, is Camden.

Of course.

He glances over his shoulder when he hears me, and that slow grin spreads across his face like he's been waiting for me to wander in. "Juliana. I was beginning to think you were hiding."

My brain says, *Turn around, abort mission*. My feet…do not listen.

"I didn't realize everyone had cleared out," I say, grabbing a dish towel just so I have something to hold on to.

"Mm-hmm." He stacks another plate, like I'm not fooling him for a second. "Guess it's just you and me."

And suddenly the kitchen feels too small. My head is still pleasantly fuzzy from the wine, but my pulse is sharp and fast. He's just standing there, sleeves damp, hair falling into his eyes, looking like he owns the place. Actually, he *does* own the place.

I should walk out. I should *definitely* walk out.

I don't.

Camden smirks, rinsing another plate. "And now you're stuck with me. Tragic."

"I'm sure you'll survive."

He sets the plate down, turns the water off, and wipes his hands on a towel. "You've been avoiding me."

I scoff, instantly on the defensive. "I have *not*."

His eyebrows lift. "Juju, you practically dove behind the dessert table when I walked in earlier."

"That was…strategic snacking."

"Hmm." He steps a little closer, just enough that I have to tip my chin up to look at him. "You smell like mulled wine and oranges."

I make a face. "Wow, thanks. That's…charming."

"I didn't say it was bad."

His voice drops just slightly, the corners of his mouth twitching like he's enjoying this way too much.

I roll my eyes, but the warmth pooling low in my stomach has nothing to do with the wine. "But I can tell you always mean something negative, even if you don't say it."

The smirk drops. "Is that what you really think?"

"It's been your pattern for a long time, yes."

His jaw clenches. "I could say the same about you."

"Why don't we just go back to avoiding each other? This town is too small and our families too involved with one another for us to do anything but pretend the other doesn't exist."

He leans one hand on the counter beside me, close enough that I catch the faint smell of his soap and something sharper, woodsy and spicy. "You don't mean it."

I should make a joke. Walk out. *Something.* But my brain has apparently clocked out for the night.

"I do mean it," I say finally, aiming for flippant but hearing the waver in my voice. "But I'm too nice to make you do all these dishes alone. I can't believe everyone left. And left *me*!"

"I told them it was one of my gifts to them, and I think everyone was exhausted and intoxicated enough to take me up on it." He chuckles. "So you're off the hook. I also told them I'd bring you home."

The kitchen feels smaller by the second, like the walls are caving in on us. He's still got one hand braced on the counter, his body angled toward mine, and I can't tell if he's going to shove a plate into my hands or tell me to get out.

His eyes narrow, but there's something else there too—

like the air between us has just shifted. "Why do you do this?" he asks.

I blink. "Do what?"

"This." He gestures vaguely between us, his voice rougher now. "Why do you make me feel this way?"

My heart kicks hard against my ribs. "Feel what way?"

"You know what I think?" His jaw tightens. "I think it's because you want me."

It's like the floor drops out from under me. My face goes hot—not from embarrassment, but from pure, white-hot fury. "You've got it backwards."

His mouth quirks, but it's not a smile—it's more like a challenge. "Do I?"

"Yeah," I snap, gripping the dish towel so tight it twists in my hands. "You're the one who can't stay out of *my* space, Camden. Not the other way around."

"And yet, here you are, in my kitchen."

The silence that follows crackles, thick and heavy.

We're staring each other down, and neither of us moves. His jaw's set, mine probably is too, and the air between us feels like it could shatter if one of us breathes too hard.

He takes a slow step closer. I don't back up.

Another step.

The heat rolling off him is impossible to ignore now. I can see the flecks of gold in his eyes, the tiny muscle flexing in his cheek. His gaze drops—just for a second—to my mouth, and my heart stutters so loud I'm sure he hears it.

My voice is gone, stolen by the way he's looking at me.

"Tell me you don't feel it," he murmurs.

I open my mouth, but nothing comes out. My back finds the edge of the counter, and he's right there, so close I can feel the whisper of his breath against my cheek.

The moment stretches, electric. If either of us leans forward even an inch, it will be over—no going back.

My hands twitch at my sides, and I hate that part of me wants to reach for him.

And then—

I blink, my eyes snapping open.

It's dark. I'm tangled in my sheets, the faint taste of mulled wine still in my mouth and my heart hammering like I ran the whole way here.

For a long minute, I just lie there, staring at the ceiling, trying to piece it together. The kitchen. Camden. That almost…

I press my hands over my face.

Did that actually happen? Or did I just dream it?

Wait a minute. This isn't my bed.

CHAPTER SEVEN

ALL IN MY HEAD

CAMDEN

It's hard not to laugh as I drive Juju home. Her head lolls to the side as she drifts off, even in the minuscule distance it takes us to get from the restaurant to her place. But honestly, my mood has everything to do with the moment we just had in the kitchen.

I shouldn't be, in any way, excited.

I'm not really.

Okay, I am, a little, but I shouldn't be.

She's still my best friend's sister.

He's never liked us being close—he's the reason all of this weirdness started in the first place.

And as if that isn't enough, *she hates me*. Just because her eyes softened in the kitchen and it seemed like she was leaning in to maybe kiss me doesn't mean she really wanted to. In the next second, she blinked and stepped back, nearly stumbling into the open cooler.

I don't blame her for hating me. I've been awful to her. For a long time. Once I knew how Jackson felt about our friendship, I backed way off and I knew it hurt Juju. She became sullen and short with me, which drove me crazy, but I didn't do anything to change things. It took years before I started reacting to her the way I do now…acting like I hate her right back.

I've had times I've wondered if it's true, times when I haven't seen her in a long time and think maybe I've gotten past caring. But the second I see those green eyes staring back at me, even if they're laced with disgust, I know that what I feel is not hate for Juliana Fair.

I pull into her driveway, and when she doesn't budge, I sit there for a second, wondering what to do.

"Juju," I say softly.

Nothing.

She's looked so exhausted every time I've seen her lately. I hate to wake her up. I could try to carry her inside, but what if the door isn't unlocked? I don't want to wake up the whole house.

I back up and drive to my place.

I've been staying in the walk-out basement at the lake house since I moved back. It's huge, so even with my family living here, it's not too crowded. My old bedroom is upstairs with the rest of the family, but I figured with my late nights, the lower level would be best for everyone. Milo and Goldie need their rest. They're working on their house in what little spare time they have with the resort renovations. And my grandmas and dad are light sleepers. My grandmas can bounce back with little sleep, but my dad needs all the rest he can get.

I've got a great setup in the basement—it's technically a mother-in-law apartment, though neither grandma stays down there—but I'd still like my own place. It's been years since I've lived at home, and it's been an adjustment to be back as an adult. My siblings and I each have a large plot of land on the new property. I'd love to be further along on the plans for that, but opening the restaurant has taken all of my headspace.

I get out of the SUV and walk around to Juju's side. When I open the door, I say her name again. She keeps sleeping.

"I'm going to carry you inside now, okay?"

Still nothing.

I lift her in my arms, and fuck me, she smells good. I said it without thinking earlier, and she assumed I meant the worst…probably because of all the other times I've been a jackass to her. But the mulled wine and citrus mixed with her berry shampoo is something I want to sink my nose into and never come up for air.

I walk into my dimly lit apartment, past the couch, and set her carefully on the bed. She's out. I remove her shoes and tug the covers up to her shoulders, giving her one last glance before I leave the room.

I take a quick shower and then drag a pillow and blanket to the couch. It takes forever to fall asleep. I think about the way she looked at me in the kitchen and wonder if she'll be soft like that in the morning or hate me for letting her crash here.

When I wake up, there's daylight streaking through the windows. I sit up and stretch, my back cracking in protest. Movement in the doorway catches my attention, and I turn to see Juju standing there. Her hair is a mess and there's a pillow crease on her cheek, but she looks beautiful. Her eyes are wide.

"Morning," I say, my voice rough.

I turn so my feet are on the floor and gradually stand. "You okay?"

She doesn't answer right away. And suddenly I forget to breathe.

When I speak, the words rush out. "I couldn't wake you and you were sleeping so peacefully. I didn't know if your house was unlocked and I didn't want to wake anyone up, so I brought you here."

She nods, rubbing her arms like she's still shaking off a dream.

"Thanks," she says softly.

We're quiet for a second, the silence getting heavier the longer it drags on. Her hair falls into her face and she lets it stay there, blinking at me with the one eye showing.

"I should get going."

"Oh, okay." I try not to sound disappointed, but my chest twists anyway.

And then I wonder why the hell it would. It's not like we hang out and talk. We'd probably end up fighting as usual.

She's walking past me and out the door faster than I can blink. I just stare after her for a second.

By the time I drag myself to the coffeepot to start the day, that weird heaviness in my chest is nagging.

I spend the whole day hanging out with the family before I go to the restaurant. I have a busy night, but I spend most of it trying to shake that feeling off.

It's a feeling I have way too often around Juju.

And I don't know why now—if it's because I could tuck her away as a memory when I lived in Colorado and now she's in front of me all the time, front and center—but I just can't stand for it to be this way between us anymore.

As long as I'm being honest with myself, I should admit that she's always been front and center for me.

That's been the root of the problem all along.

I don't know how to change things or if I even can.

It might be too late.

More than a week later, I still haven't seen Juju.

It's been busier than ever, out-of-towners coming in to try out the restaurant and to get a glimpse of the gorgeous resort that everyone in Minnesota is talking about.

Windhaven is impressive. My dad had a vision for a mini Rivendell straight out of the pages of *The Lord of the Rings*, and he's accomplished just that. It's spectacular, and the inside is shaping up to be just as exceptional.

We're doing a soft opening of the lodge in May, which will give us a couple of weeks to adjust before our busy season starts. It looks as if some of the cabins will be ready by then as well. My brother Noah has had contractors from all over the state coming in to help get this project done. My dad worked in real estate for ages and had established relationships with so many contractors through the years that when they found out Everett Whitman had cancer and wanted to do this new endeavor, they were eager to jump on board. It's been a labor of love for everyone involved, even though my dad has insisted on paying very well.

I have plenty to do at the restaurant, but somehow I end up at The Kitty-Corner Cafe. I'm sure it's a bad decision before I ever step inside, but since I'm here, I go on in. Loud singing catches me off guard when I open the door. Hector and Hal are flanking Juju behind the counter and half singing, half shouting an old Motown song. Juju's gaze ping-pongs between the two, her expression both amused and exasperated. I feel her pain—it'd be hard for me to focus on the job at hand with all this commotion, and yet, the customers are eating it up.

Her hair is pulled back. She's gorgeous—an effortless beauty no matter what she's wearing, whether she has makeup on or not, and whose smile can light up any room she's in.

I miss the way her smile would light up whenever she saw me.

My chest tightens the second her eyes catch mine. I brace myself for whatever sharp jab she'll have for me and tell myself not to bite back quite so hard this time.

But it doesn't come.

Instead, the corners of her lips lift slightly, and even though it doesn't reach her eyes, it's almost a smile.

"Hey, Camden," she says, like I'm just another customer.

I blink, thrown off-balance.

It's what I wanted, but it still surprises me.

"Hey," I manage, waiting for the spice under the sugar.

"I have a bear claw with your name on it. If you want it, it's yours." She sounds almost pleasant.

"Uh, yeah, that sounds great. Thank you. And a coffee, please."

"Sure thing. Coming right up. Would you like it for here or to go?"

"I might sit down for a minute."

She nods and goes to grab the pastry.

Okay, now I'm freaking out. We haven't gone this long without throwing out a barb in over a decade.

Is she messing with me?

Hector winks at me. "Good to see you, Camden," he says.

Hal sings out with a rich baritone, "There's our man Cam, who's a ham, but he's like fam so we don't give a damn."

I laugh. "Seems like someone else is the ham around here," I tell him.

He just grins and sings to the next customer walking in the door.

Juju hands me the plate and mug of coffee. "Have a good one," she says.

"I haven't paid yet."

"It's on the house." She waves me off and looks at the woman behind me.

What the hell? Have I stepped into an alternate universe? I thought I wanted her to smile at me, but this nonchalant, distant thing where she's acting like I'm no one to her is even more torturous.

This isn't how we work.

She's supposed to push back.

Throw sparks.

Is she mad that we almost kissed? If that's what it even was.

I turn and nearly run into Ava.

"Sorry, I wasn't looking where I was going," I say.

"No worries. I was distracted too," she says.

Hector and Hal start singing "Pretty Woman." Ava turns to look at the door, and Erin has walked in as well. She's steadying her arms against the door in a dramatic way, her head falling back as she shimmies.

"*Finally*, someone sees my worth," she says.

I laugh and so does Ava. Erin's head pops up and she grins when she sees us. She walks over, and Ava laughs harder.

"Nice shirt," she says.

Erin's wearing a shirt that says **Come closer and I'll bite** in bold black letters. And then in a smaller red font it says, *And you WILL like it.*

Erin winks at Ava. "Do you need a nibble?"

Ava's cheeks flame and her mouth parts. "Uh, ha, yes. No! I mean. Ha. You're so funny." She laughs again.

Erin's own cheeks turn a little pink, but she lifts an eyebrow as she smirks at Ava. "Why, thank you," she says.

Ava nods, smiling as she looks down at her feet.

Erin's gaze turns to me. "Hey, good-lookin', surprised to see you here. You giving my friend over there grief?" Her head tilts toward Juju.

"What? No!" I say, a little too forcefully.

She points at me. "Good. I've been meaning to box you upside the ears about a few things." She shakes her head. "That Caribou comment, for one. Pfft. That was so uncalled for."

I grimace and run my hand down my face. "Yeah, I don't know why I said that."

"I have a few theories, but I'll keep them to myself for now." Her eyes narrow.

"Good. I better be going," I say, backing up.

I'm starting to feel sweaty.

"But you haven't eaten your bear claw yet," Ava says.

"Oh…yeah, I should probably take it to go after all."

I rush to the little bar and get a to-go cup, sloshing some coffee as I pour. I wipe it up, cursing under my breath the whole time, and jump when Hector and Hal burst into another song.

Without another glance toward the counter, I leave. My heart is racing when I reach my SUV. What the hell is wrong with me?

My phone buzzes, and it's the family thread.

DAD

Proof of life requested, please. <Photo of
Kevin lying boneless in his little bed>

DYLAN

That's proof of Kevin's life. Where are you,
pray tell? <Photo of him and his rescued
mini dachshund, Bill>

My family has ridiculous tastes in pet names.

<Photo of me holding The Kitty-Corner
Cafe cup>

My photo choice is a big mistake. It starts a slew of
messages.

GOLDIE

I hope you played nice with Juju! <Photo of
her gazing lovingly at Milo>

NOAH

Yeah, what's with you guys? You're either
glaring at each other or blowing up. <Photo
of his hammer>

That's what they think? We're not always glaring at each
other. And yes, we blow up sometimes, but...I didn't think
we were that obvious.

DYLAN

I'm sensing some sexual tension there.

I get a text from the sibling thread. It's titled "Four Men
and a Baby," which Goldie changes every single time a text is
sent. Sure enough, she changes it to "One Woman and Four
Babies." It's changed back immediately, I suspect either by
Dylan or Tully.

TULLY

Dylan! Go delete that comment in the fam thread. Dad's in there!

DYLAN

You think Dad doesn't know what sexual tension is?!

TULLY

Of course he does. He just doesn't need to hear about ours.

DYLAN

Are you having some sexual tension, Tully? Is that what you're saying?

TULLY

My sexual tension is handled just fine, thank you very much.

GOLDIE

Ew! Should I tell you all about how Milo and I are working out any hints of sexual tension we might have? Every. Single. Night.

TULLY

I am scarred for life. No, you should not breathe another word of this, Goldie.

GOLDIE

Thought so. Goes both ways, fellas.

NOAH

Camden, you're being awfully quiet.

I notice that you are as well, Noah. Why is that?

NOAH

My hand works just fine.

GOLDIE

Milo's hand works better than any hand I've ever had.

DYLAN

That's going too far!

TULLY

I just threw up

NOAH

Sorry. I guess I asked for that.

GOLDIE

That's what she said

This is going downhill fast.

"Camden, oh my God, I can't believe how great this place is!"

I look up from my phone and see a woman with black hair and a tight red dress.

She pouts. "It's me. *Kimberly*." She puts her hand on my arm and laughs. "We hung out on the roof of The Hewing Hotel a few years ago."

"Hi…Kimberly." I'm trying really hard to place her, but it's not coming back to me.

I feel bad about it, but then she says, "Well, I was there with Jackson, but"—she leans in, and her chest hits my arm —"I wished I could've gone home with you."

I take a step back. "Good to see you, Kimberly. I have to take this and then get back to work." I wave my phone. "Take care."

She pokes her lips out again, and I nearly jog back to the kitchen.

Meanwhile, Dad's blowing up the other text thread.

> DAD
>
> I've sensed some sexual tension there myself.

I look up to remind myself what he's talking about. Oh fuck. He's still on Juju.

> DAD
>
> There's an answer for that, you know.

> DAD
>
> Ask her out, son. You know you want to.

> DAD
>
> Hello? Camden? Don't ignore me.

> DAD
>
> And Tully, what's got you so quiet?

> TULLY
>
> Forgive me. I'm over here scrubbing my brain. <Photo of a brain on the internet>

> DAD
>
> There's nothing to be ashamed of. We have all dealt with sexual tension. Some of us more than others. ;) I remember the time your mom and I...

> DYLAN
>
> For the love of all that is holy, don't tell us about the time.

> DAD
>
> 😂 You guys make it too easy.

In the other thread:

TULLY

I hope you're happy, Dylan. Look what
you've done.

DYLAN

Might be the only thing I've ever done
wrong. Sorry, guys.

CHAPTER EIGHT

BRO

JULIANA

"Hey, Juliana."

I glance up to see Bentley, a guy who moved here recently from Texas to be the bartender at Elm & Echo. People have moved here from all over the country to work for Camden. He's come in a couple of times and is always nice. Flirty, even. He's cute. Sandy-colored hair, brown eyes, and a great smile.

"Hi, Bentley. How's it going?"

"It's going better now that I've seen you," he says, his smile wide.

Uncle Hal sings, "'Amarillo by morning…'" and when I look at him, he shoots me innocent eyes. "You know that old George Strait song…"

"Can't say that I do."

Every time Bentley comes in, Uncle Hal sings a somewhat negative song, usually one about Texas. I don't know what he has against Bentley, but he gets a little saucy every time he sees him.

Bentley sings the rest of the lyrics in a high, sweet voice. He looks at me, eyebrows lifted, and I clap.

"I didn't know you could sing like that," I say.

"There's a lot about me you don't know," he says. He leans in. "I'd like to change that, if you're willing."

"Oh." I stare at him and then laugh awkwardly.

"'All my exes live in Texas,'" Uncle Hal sings.

"What do you say?" Bentley says. "You and me, dinner tonight?"

I press my lips together, my fingers fidgeting with my apron.

"Say yes," he presses.

"Okay, sure. Why not?" I say.

Erin is right. Not that I'm planning to get laid like Erin really wants me to, but she'd be all about me going on a date. And Bentley seems great.

He taps on the counter. "Excellent. How about I pick you up at seven?"

"Okay." I point in the direction of my house, even though he can't really see much of it from the cafe's windows. "I live in that house next door."

"That's what I've heard," he says, winking again.

I'm not sure how I feel about a man who winks. It kind of grates, actually.

"I'll see you tonight," he says before he walks out.

For a second, I wonder what Camden would think if he knew I was going on a date with Bentley, but in the next second, I'm pushing that thought away. Camden might be the hottest man on the planet, but he's not nice. To me anyway. Or at least, most of the time he isn't.

I don't know what to make of the way he's been acting lately.

It was so weird waking up in his bed. I still don't know what happened on Christmas night.

Which is making it hella awkward for me to be around him.

I want to ask him about it, but maybe I don't even want to know how I acted.

I need something to distract me, and Bentley feels like the perfect distraction.

When Bentley walks out of the cafe, I overhear Uncle Hal telling Papa, "This yahoo comes gallivanting into town from Texas, singing in falsetto, and Juju got all swoony."

I cover my mouth so I don't laugh out loud.

Uncle Hal's not done. "Who sings in falsetto anyway?"

"Turn on a pop station and you'll hear a whole slew of heartthrobs singing in falsetto," Papa says.

Uncle Hal snorts. "Juju needs a man who sings in full voice."

"Times are changing, little brother," Papa says.

He's all of thirty-nine minutes older than Uncle Hal.

"I have a date tonight," I say, walking up to them.

Papa startles and then puts his arm around my shoulder.

"That's wonderful, sweetheart." He looks at the clock. "Why don't you let us close up when it's time? I think we've got the system down. You could leave pretty soon even. Take your time getting ready."

"Oh, I don't want to leave you guys with all this." I pat his back.

"Nonsense. We've got it. You could use the break, and what's the worst that could happen?" He laughs. "Don't answer that. Really. We can always call or come get you if anything goes wrong."

"Are you so sure?" It's a few hours before Bentley is picking me up, but I could use a catnap. And the thought of taking my time to get ready sounds lovely…

"Go on," Uncle Hal says. "We've got this."

"Okay," I say, hugging them both. "Thank you! Are you sure?"

"Positive," they say at the same time.

I take them up on it, and it's blissful. By the time Bentley picks me up, I've napped, washed my hair, taken a long bath in Mildred, curled my hair, touched up my nails, and paced the house a few times. At the last second, I text Goldie and Erin.

> Wish me luck. I have a date tonight.

GOLDIE

WHAT! WHO?

ERIN

Attagirl. Do everything I would do.

> lol I will NOT be doing everything you would do, Erin. Even if I wish I could. 😅 It's with Bentley, the guy from Texas.

GOLDIE

The bartender at Elm & Echo?

> That's the one.

GOLDIE

He's cute! :D Oh, this is gonna be so fun. Hahahaha

> What's so funny?

ERIN

Where's he taking you?

I have no idea.

ERIN

Well, let us know when you get there. I don't
want to have to send a search party out
for you.

GOLDIE

Do not put that out there. Hold on. Let me
ask Camden about him.

No! Do not ask Camden about him.

GOLDIE

😬 Too late.

I curse under my breath.

GOLDIE

He hasn't answered yet, but I'll keep you
posted. Erin's right. Let us know where he
takes you. If possible, send a picture of his
license plate before you get in the car
with him.

You can't be serious.

GOLDIE

I'm entirely serious! He might be working for
Camden, but we don't know what he's like
with women! His dark side might come out,
for all we know.

You guys are making me nervous now. The
doorbell just rang. He's here.

ERIN

Have fun. In the sheets.

You're too much, both of you.

GOLDIE

That's why you love us.

ERIN

What she said.

I open the door, and Bentley looks me over appreciatively. "You look beautiful," he says.

"You look great too," I tell him.

He's wearing a button-down shirt and a leather jacket with jeans. I'm glad I went with a pretty sweater and jeans instead of a dress.

He holds out his arm for me to take as we walk on the sidewalk. We've put salt down, so it's not slippery at all, but it's a sweet gesture.

"I thought we could go to Elm & Echo, if that's okay with you," he says when we reach his car.

"Oh." I swallow and nod. "You're not sick of it from working there?"

"Not at all. I love the atmosphere *and* the food."

"Okay, sure. Sounds good."

Inside, I'm cringing because I don't want to spend an evening on the alert for Camden.

But Bentley doesn't see my reluctance. He smiles as he opens my car door. "Great. I had a sample of tonight's specials, and they were so delicious, it made me excited to be at work on my day off." He shuts my door and walks around.

The second we pull into the parking lot of Elm & Echo, I

know this is a bad idea. Bentley has the kind of confidence that makes him easy to be around, sweet and sure without being too cocky. It's not him that's making my stomach twist. It's the fact that we're going into Camden's orbit.

The last time I saw him wasn't a disaster. Awkward, sure. But I can handle awkward.

Elm & Echo looks gorgeous. Soft lights spill out the windows, and the glisten of the moon bouncing off the water beyond the lights on the deck is enticing. My eyes scan every corner when we walk inside, preparing myself for the moment Camden appears.

"I'm so glad you agreed to go out with me," Bentley says once we're seated. He leans in conspiratorially. "I created a drink last week that is delicious, if you like oranges and pomegranates…and vodka." He laughs.

I smile. "I do like those things."

He waves at Katie, the bartender working tonight, and she waves back.

Bentley tells me about the dish he tried and a bourbon that just came in, but my head keeps snapping toward the kitchen entrance, the bar, the hallway to the office…

Nicole, our waitress, brings a bread basket and takes our drink order, and we go ahead and tell her what we'd like to eat too. I order the special that Bentley said was the best—the pistachio-crusted halibut with truffle-pureed cauliflower and asparagus. Bentley orders the bourbon pork chops, and we decide to share a pear-berry salad.

Our drinks come, and Bentley is right—the drink is delicious. I tell myself to sip it slowly, and I'm in the middle of my third tiny sip when Camden comes out of the kitchen.

The air in the whole room changes.

He's walking with that Camden Whitman swagger that I swear he's had since the day I met him. And then he sees me.

And he freezes. For a moment, I don't know how long, we stare at each other across the room. Then he looks at Bentley, and his face hardens. His expression shifts to a scowl, and not a subtle one either.

It reminds me of the time I went out with Mitch Williams, who was friends with Jackson and Camden. The look on Camden's face cut through me like a newly sharpened knife.

Back then it gave me a thrill, but it was short-lived, once I realized he wasn't jealous at all—he was just irritated with me over something I could never figure out.

That's how I feel now. Like our brief window of a peace treaty is over.

I close him out. I lean in and listen to Bentley. I ask questions and laugh at his stories. When he teases me about finishing my drink already, I tease him back, saying he must have put a magic potion in there. Slowly, the nerves melt off of me. The next time I catch Camden's gaze from across the restaurant, still watching and glowering, I get a hit of adrenaline. I get another drink and feel warm all over. It's easy to laugh, and Bentley's right—the food is delicious.

Bentley reaches his hand out, and I take it.

"I'm having such a good time," he says.

"I am too," I say, and it's true.

I'm just not sure it's because of Bentley.

But then I see a gorgeous woman I don't recognize walk up to Camden. She's definitely not a local. He smiles politely at her, and her head falls back in laughter like he's just said something hilarious.

I look away because I don't want to see anymore, and before long, a dark shadow falls over the table. I glance up to see Camden standing there, his arms folded across his chest.

"Bentley, Juliana," he says formally.

"Camden," I say in a low voice like his.

"The food is delicious, boss," Bentley says.

"Thank you," he says, nodding but looking at me. "Juliana, can I speak with you for a moment?"

I falter for a second and then giggle. "I suppose, Mr. Whitman." Again, in that low voice, mocking him.

I stand up and walk toward the bar, but Camden points toward the hallway, so I go to the hall.

When we get there, he crosses his arms and stares at me.

"What?" I ask.

"Have you had too much to drink?"

"What?"

"I'm just making sure because the last time you had several drinks, you ended up in my bed."

My eyebrows lift, and my hands move to my hips. "Because *you* put me there."

"Because *you* couldn't walk in a straight line." He shifts closer, his face lowering to get in mine.

"Well, I'm walking in a straight line tonight, as you can see."

He takes another step closer, and I back into the wall. He puts his arm on the wall next to my face and leans in until I can smell citrus on his breath. Maybe he's had one of the drinks I'm having.

"We don't know Bentley well enough for you to get drunk around, Juliana."

"I'm not drunk, Camden. And it's not your business whether I am or not. And you hired Bentley, so I think you must trust him enough to be a decent human being."

"You have an answer for everything, don't you?"

"When it comes to the decisions I make about my life, *yes*, I do." I stare at him defiantly.

He puts his other hand on the wall, blocking me in, and my heart kicks into overdrive. Our chests are rising and falling so hard and fast that they bump into each other. My nerves are standing at attention.

"I'll be sure to let Jackson know you're being irresponsible," he says, his voice hoarse.

"You do that," I whisper.

His eyes drop to my mouth, and Christmas night comes flooding back. I didn't dream it. We almost kissed that night. And I think he wants to kiss me now!

What is this?

His hands drop, and he takes a large step back.

"You better get back to your date," he says.

"I will," I say with as much indignation as I can muster.

But my legs are shaky as I walk back to the table.

"Everything okay?" Bentley asks.

"Just Camden being his annoying self." I try to laugh it off, but it sounds forced. "He's my brother's best friend," I say, as if that should explain everything.

"Ah, so he's super protective of you, I take it. Like a big brother." He nods.

He is absolutely nothing like a brother to me.

"I have a younger sister, and I wouldn't let any guy near her," he continues.

"Ugh. You're one of those."

He laughs. "It's just because we love our sisters so much."

I sigh. All love was lost between Camden and me a long time ago.

CHAPTER NINE

SOCK IT TO HIM

CAMDEN

Well, I fucked that up royally.

I've always thought of myself as a calm, collected, clear-headed man. Unlike my brother Tully, who plays professional hockey, I've never gotten into a fist fight with anyone.

Actually, not true.

I did throw a punch at Mitch Williams when he and Juju made out in high school.

I haven't thought about Mitch in years.

Fuck, what is my deal with Juju dating?

And I don't want to think about the implications of it happening now.

Mitch was an asswad. He knew Juju was off-limits, and he went for her anyway.

When my sister texted earlier, asking about Bentley because Juju was going out with him, I'm embarrassed to say I didn't react very well.

I saw red.

I wanted to hit a wall.

I nearly called Juju to ask her what the hell she was thinking.

I did none of those things, and yet, I still blew it.

Who is this unreasonable, fly-off-the-handle guy?

I don't recognize myself. Don't know this version of me. Don't want to.

Bentley is a nice guy, maybe even great. I certainly haven't seen anything that I didn't like. Until tonight. He looked at Juju like he wanted to put her on a plate and devour her. On their first date! What a fucking animal.

I feel bad about overreacting to all of it. And that near-kiss in the hallway—God help me. I nearly crossed a line I swore I'd never cross. *Again.*

Why does she have this effect on me?

"When will it end?" I mutter to myself as I lace my boots the next morning.

When will I stop acting like a lunatic around her?

When will I stop wishing things were different between us?

When I went upstairs earlier to get coffee, Grandma Donna and Grandma Nancy were excited about Juju making stroopwafels this week. I swear, there's no getting away from Juju Fair. But I need those stroopwafels desperately.

I remember the first time I saw her making them, how impressed I was with her skill. Always had been. And she just got better all the time. I was probably seventeen and she was fifteen when she started making the thin, round waffle cookies held together by caramel. A Dutch delicacy that, once I tried, I craved them. Juju stood at her kitchen counter with an old iron press, so focused and sure of herself. I was supposed to be grabbing Gatorade for Jackson and me and rushing back outside, but instead, I stood staring at her. Caramel oozed out of the sides when she sandwiched the cookies, then scraped it away with precision.

She was wearing leggings and a fitted tank, and both showed way too much of her body than I needed to be seeing. I wanted to simultaneously thank the heavens for this experience and to run over and cover her up so no one else could.

Yeah, the age-old dilemma where Juliana is concerned.

One I've been battling a long, long time.

Britney, my pastry chef at Elm & Echo, isn't cutting it. She's messy and unfocused, and even her dinner rolls aren't consistent. She seems more interested in being in my way than in doing her job. Her advances have gotten out of hand. Last night, she cornered me against the counter and said she'd dreamed about me the night before.

This afternoon I'm meeting with Sammi, a chef from Chicago who's interviewing for the position.

I'll be surprised if she has Juju's expertise.

No one does.

The Kitty-Corner's bell jingles when I walk in, and the smell of coffee, freshly baked bread, and sugar wraps around me.

There she is. Behind the counter, head tipped back, laughing at something Bentley just said.

For Christ's sake.

The dude's got his elbows on the counter like Juju has nothing better to do than listen to him yammer on about nothing. He's leaning in close, and Juju's cheeks are pink, her eyes sparkling as she laughs.

My stomach knots with that twist of jealousy. My temper spikes, but I bite down on the inside of my cheek. No scenes. Not here. Not ever again.

I walk to the counter and get a small bit of satisfaction in seeing Juju's gaze tear away from Bentley as she stares up at me.

"I'll take all the stroopwafels you've got."

She blinks at me, stunned. "All of them?"

"Every last one." My voice comes out clipped. "Box them up. Please."

"Yes, sir." Her lips tilt up on one side, and she turns before quickly stacking the golden rounds into a bakery box.

When they reach the very top, she grabs another box.

Bentley bumps my elbow. "Have I just discovered your weakness?"

I guess everyone can see the way I look at Juju.

His smile dims when I look at him.

"Your love for stroopwafels…" he adds.

I swallow. "Right. Yes. My grandmas do too, so I'll be taking some home for them."

"Oh, that's funny. I think they're still here." He points behind me. "Right over there."

My gaze flickers over to see Grandma Nancy and Grandma Donna at the corner table, closing their eyes in bliss as they take bites of their stroopwafels.

God Almighty. I can't win.

Hector and Hal catch my attention when they walk out of the kitchen side by side. Hector is wearing a fedora with an apron and exudes class in every setting. Hal is wearing a bandana like a hat on his head of white hair. The level of his energy and confidence is apparent with every step.

I don't think they even notice I'm here—their eyes are on my grandmas, of all people. My mouth drops when they saunter over there, Hal winking at Grandma Nancy, and Hector taking Grandma Donna's hand and bowing over it.

"Donna, you look radiant today. That sweater brings out the color in your eyes."

Grandma Donna's cheeks flame, and she ducks her head. What the fuck?

"Thank you, Hector. That's awfully nice of you to say."

"How's the Friendship Bench going?" he asks.

She looks up at him, excitement making her bolder. "I have my first appointments this afternoon!"

"Wonderful! You'll have to let me know how it goes."

She nods shyly. "I will."

Meanwhile, Hal has taken a seat next to Grandma Nancy and has his elbow on the table, his face leaning into his hand, as he grins at her. I had no idea I was walking into *The Golden Bachelor* times two.

I stand there, fascinated, the whole scene so bizarre I nearly forget my own drama.

"You're a sight for sore eyes, Nancy. If I'd known I was seeing you today, I would have cleaned up a bit more," Hal says.

"There's no cleaning you up, I'm afraid," Grandma Nancy says. "An attitude like yours will always come to the surface…like an oily spot on silk."

He puts his hand to his chest. "I'm so honored that you see me."

A laugh bursts out of me, and all four look back to see who made the commotion. I step closer to their table.

"Um, hello. Good morning," I say.

"Hello, dear!" Grandma Donna perks up. "We didn't know we'd be seeing you here this morning."

Hector tilts his head toward Bentley. "That guy's been coming over constantly," he mutters under his breath. "Can't you give him more hours at the restaurant?"

I chuckle. "He's already full-time, but yeah, I'll see what I can do."

Grandma Nancy pats the seat next to her. "Join us, Cammie."

"Here you go, *Cammie*," Juju calls.

I turn to look at the counter, where Juju is smirking. If you can smirk while also giving someone the stink eye. She slides the boxes across the counter and rattles off the total.

I pay and nod my thanks, certain I shouldn't speak because I will most certainly blow it again.

I stop by my grandmas' table again and grin. "I can't stay, but it looks like you're enjoying yourselves. Carry on."

Grandma Nancy rolls her eyes in Hal's direction but smiles at me, and Grandma Donna flushes.

"We won't be long," Grandma Donna says.

"I'll put these stroopwafels in the kitchen so everyone can enjoy them," I say as I lift the boxes.

Their eyes go wide, and Grandma Nancy flashes a knowing smile at me, which I ignore.

I turn to leave, with Hector asking if he can bring Grandma Donna tea.

"You deserve to be waited on," he says.

"Oh, you don't have to—" Grandma Donna says.

"I insist," Hector says gallantly.

Hal says, "How 'bout we split a stroopwafel, Nancy? Lady and the Tramp style. You take one end, I take the other…"

"And I choke you with it? Tempting," Grandma Nancy says, cutting him off.

The people around them laugh as they entertain the whole shop.

I wait until I'm outside to let out my bottled-up laugh and all the tension from seeing Juju.

Once I'm at the restaurant a little later, I call Jackson.

"Hey, man, it's been a while," he says.

"I know. It's been crazy here. Sorry I've gone quiet."

"No, I get it. You've got a lot going on. How's the restaurant?"

I grin. "Great. I can't believe how well, actually. I thought it might be a slow starter, but people are driving in from all over."

"I love it."

"How are things with you?"

"Can't complain. I actually can't talk long. I've got a woman here."

"Oh, really? Why does that not surprise me?" I laugh. "Anyone I know?"

He chuckles. "I doubt it. I don't even know her all that well."

I swipe my hand over my face and shake my head. "I should've known. Hey, I can let you go."

"Wait. I'm glad you called. I miss you, man."

"I miss you too." I nearly don't say anything, but I can't help myself. "Juju's been seeing a guy who works for me—his name is Bentley."

"Do we not like him?" He sounds gruff already, and inwardly, I feel bad for doing this to Juju. But it's for her own good. And maybe mine a little.

"I like him fine, but I don't know him well. He's from Texas."

He grumbles.

"Very polite," I add.

"The worst ones are."

"I tried to look out for her the other night. She was drinking, and I know she doesn't know him well."

"Dammit. She's oblivious to what these jerks want. Watch out for her, okay? And I'll talk to her."

"No, I don't want her to know I told you. I just—" I sigh

at the ceiling. What did I want out of this? And why does it feel so wrong? "You know what, she's a big girl. She can take care of herself."

"She's naive sometimes, though, you know she is. She believes the best in everyone. Except you," he says, laughing. "I miss the days when you guys annoyed me with how close you were."

"You do?" I freeze.

"Yeah. I was jealous when we were younger, but it beats you wanting to strangle each other."

"Huh." I could not be more surprised by this.

"Anyway. Promise you'll watch out for her, even if you end up fighting with her in doing so."

"Okay, yeah, I will." I exhale. "Take care. And come to Windy Harbor soon. Your visit at Christmas wasn't long enough."

"Will do. Take care, man."

Throughout the night while I'm working, I'm divided. I finally have permission from Jackson to be involved with Juju. But he has no idea of the ways I think about being involved with her.

If he knew, he'd be the one throwing punches.

CHAPTER TEN

LITTLE SIS

JULIANA

Past: Juju, age 15, Camden, age 17

Caramel dripped down the side of the bowl, and I caught it with my thumb, then tasted it.

"Oh, that's good," I said to myself.

A noise in the doorway made me look, and it was Camden.

I sighed. He wasn't so bad when he was alone, but around my brother was another story. I looked up again, and it was just him. I was glad I'd worn this outfit and not my Strawberry Shortcake pajamas that I'd almost kept on. Not that I cared what he thought, but at least I knew I looked cute.

"What are you making?" he asked softly.

"Stroopwafels."

He stepped closer. "I've never had one."

"Try it. They have caramel inside."

"I like how they look." He came over to the island and towered over me.

My dad asked him how tall he was the last time he came over, and when he said he was six four, I couldn't believe it. Jackson wished he were as tall as Camden, but he was still tall too.

He picked up a stroopwafel and took a bite. He chewed slowly, nodding slightly, like he was taking in all the flavors. As much as he frustrated me, I enjoyed the way he appreciated food.

"Delicious," he said.

I glanced at him to see if he was joking at all. I could never tell anymore.

"Thank you," I said when he seemed genuine.

"Hey, shorty." Jackson walked in and put his arm around my shoulder. He grabbed a stroopwafel without asking. "I like these!" he said. "Two thumbs up." He frowned when he looked down at me.

"What?" I asked.

"What are you wearing?" he asked.

I made a face. "Leggings?"

"Has Dad seen you in those?"

"No, and I don't see what the big deal is."

"At least they're not as thin as Devyn's." He looked at Camden and laughed. "I saw her ass crack the other day, man." He looked at me again and narrowed his eyes. "It's a good thing you don't have boobs. Dad would never let you leave the house if you did."

"Jackson!" I elbowed him, and he doubled over, laughing.

"Ow! It's true," he yelled. "Right, Camden?"

Camden's head tilted, and he didn't look at me when he lifted his shoulder. "If you say so. How would I know? It's not like I'm checking out your little sister."

My cheeks flamed even hotter. He always acted like I was still five instead of fifteen.

Jackson held his fist out, and they did a fist-bump.

"Right. Because we agreed a long time ago to never date each other's sister. Goldie's hot, but she is off-limits. And so are you." Jackson looked at me and rubbed some caramel on the tip of my nose.

I was already close to boiling.

"Ugh." I rolled my eyes and wiped it off. "You are *so* annoying." I moved to the sink and washed my hands, then turned around and glared at both of them. "And Goldie would never date you, so it wouldn't matter if she's off-limits or not," I told Jackson. And then I pointed at Camden. "And I wouldn't date you, even if you were the last boy standing on a deserted island and we had to forage for our food and I needed someone tall to reach things."

He stared at me for a minute, and the room was silent before Jackson burst out laughing, and Camden eventually did too.

"Good thing we'll never be the last people on the planet, and we won't be on a deserted island together either." Camden leaned down so he was at eye level. "Because I wouldn't touch your flat chest with a ten-foot pole."

I swallowed hard. *Do not cry. DO NOT CRY.*

I crossed my arms over my flat chest and narrowed my eyes at him. "I know that's right. Because there is no way I'd ever let you come near them."

He looked like he was ready to keep arguing and then realized there was nowhere to go with that.

Jackson pounded his hand on the island. "Well, now that that's settled, we've gotta go if we wanna make the party."

Camden nodded, and they walked out.

Later that night, I couldn't stop replaying the whole thing

in the kitchen. Finally, I got out of bed and threw a sweatshirt on over my tank. I was glad we were at the lake house—I always had more freedom there. Goldie and I could hang out with Erin, a local whose family owned Cox Trading Post, and she was so much fun. It had been the perfect summer…as long as I was nowhere near Camden. Which seemed impossible, since he was *always* around.

I sighed, feeling restless. My parents were watching a movie, and I'd already told them good night. I walked down to the Whitmans' yard with my book and climbed up the stairs to the tree house. It took a few minutes for me to get comfortable, but once I had the light right and the pillows piled under my head, I leaned back and started reading. Or tried to anyway.

But I kept hearing Camden's words. *I wouldn't touch your flat chest with a ten-foot pole.*

I started crying, and at first I tried to ignore the tears, but then I gave in and turned to my side and let it all out. Once the tears had dried up, I was mad that I'd wasted my time on that. It didn't make me feel any better. I sat up and looked for the stash of makeup I kept tucked away in a box out here. The boys still came here sometimes, but not as much anymore, and I knew they wouldn't be here tonight. I did my makeup with the light from my phone and the twinkle lights around the tree house.

Jackson and Camden's friend Mitch had told me about the party. I hadn't wanted to go because Goldie had plans with her dad, but maybe I could talk Erin into going with me. Mitch had always been nice to me.

My parents were in bed when I left, and since I'd never snuck out before—or done anything else they wouldn't approve of, for that matter—I knew they'd never suspect that

I'd go to a party. I'd feel bad about it later. Or maybe not, if I didn't get caught.

The bonfire was huge, the music blasting, and the beach-front was filled with people. I could hear the noise of laughing and shouting over the music and waves.

"It's a banger," Erin said. "And I am here for it." She linked her arm through mine. "What got into you, Ms. Juliana? You're usually in bed by eight thirty."

I nudged her, laughing. "My rags will still appear at midnight, just like Cinderella."

"If you last until midnight, I won't know what has happened to my best friend."

"You make me sound ancient."

She tilted her head back and forth like she wasn't going to argue that.

Mitch spotted me before we'd made it all the way to the food. He swaggered over with an easy grin, his sun-bleached hair looking blonder in the evening light and tiki torches.

"I didn't know I'd convinced you to come," he said. He turned, looking over the crowd. "And I'm shocked your brother was okay with this."

"My brother doesn't get to tell me what to do."

His grin expanded, all sparkly-white teeth, and he handed me a plastic red cup.

"Thank you." I took the cup and sipped from it, wrinkling my nose when I tasted it.

He laughed. "Not a fan of beer?"

"I guess not."

Erin grabbed a cup too and winked at me, pointing out where she was going. "You okay?" she asked.

I nodded.

Mitch moved closer. "You look so hot," he said.

His arm brushed mine, which felt nice. He kept saying

things to make me laugh, and it was working. The more sips of beer I took, the warmer and lighter I felt. Mitch looked cuter and said funnier things, and when he kissed me, it felt nicer than I remembered a kiss feeling.

It wasn't like when Brady Lawrence kissed me at summer camp two years ago. That had been clumsy, a peck and then a hide-and-seek of tongues. Neither one of us knew what we were doing. I had since talked to Goldie and Erin and knew how to do it better, and Mitch definitely knew what he was doing.

His hand slid around my waist, tugging me closer. My heart hammered with excitement and the rush of being at this party with beer and older boys and my streak of rebellion at doing something I knew my parents and brother...and Camden...wouldn't approve of.

When one of his hands moved down to my backside and the other moved over my breast, I squeaked and tried to push him back, but he only pressed harder.

Until suddenly, he was gone.

I blinked in shock as Mitch staggered back when someone punched him in the nose. Blood ran down his face immediately. And, standing in front of me, his fists clenched and his eyes burning with fury, was Camden.

For a second, all I could do was stare.

He looked like an avenging angel with his fist still propped up as he breathed hard, his eyes locked on Mitch as if daring him to move.

My first thought was relief, sharp and undeniable. Why, I wasn't sure. That Camden had seen me. That he'd stopped Mitch from going any further. But then the relief twisted to fury.

How dare he?

"Are you kidding me?" I snapped.

I stepped between Camden and Mitch before Camden could swing again.

Camden's head whipped toward me. His jaw clenched. "He was all over you. You didn't want that."

The worst part was, he was right. I hadn't wanted things to go that far. But that didn't mean he got to swoop in like some kind of self-righteous bodyguard.

Behind me, Mitch cursed.

"So what?" I shot back, heat making my cheeks hot. "You think you get to just punch whoever you want? You don't even care about me, remember?"

"I do care," he growled, low enough that only I could hear it.

I clenched my fists to keep from shaking.

"Ten-foot pole, remember?" I muttered as I shoved past him.

My stomach tightened with every step. I wanted to scream at him and…something else entirely. I could feel his stare burning into my back all the way across the sand.

I stormed away from the fire, my feet sinking into the cool sand as I went. Erin got in step next to me.

"Are you okay?" she asked.

"Yeah. This is the reason I go to bed at eight thirty."

We both laughed.

"Juju," Camden called, his voice rough.

I turned before he could catch up, my hair flying into my face. "Don't bother, Camden."

He slowed, but he didn't stop. His expression was angry and worried, and for some reason, that only made me madder.

"Come on, Juju. You didn't want that."

Erin squeezed my arm and stepped back. I shook my head at Camden, forcing the lump in my throat down.

"You don't get to decide what I want," I whispered.

He stared at me, and for one breathless moment, neither of us moved. The distant firelight flickered against his face, and it felt like we were on a tightrope, barely hanging on.

"You…" My voice cracked, but I pushed through it. "I'm not a child, Camden. I can make my own mistakes, with or without your interference."

"I don't think you're a child, Juju."

His eyes locked on mine.

He stepped closer, his jaw tight, and added, "That's the whole fucking problem. You're not a child anymore. You're not my friend anymore. I don't even know you. And you're… making me lose my mind."

The world tilted. I couldn't move, couldn't speak. Hearing him say that…I didn't even know how to feel about it. I had so many questions.

We just stood there, staring at each other. His chest rose and fell like he'd just run a mile, and my heart threatened to pound out of my chest.

His jaw flexed, his mouth opening to speak.

"Juju? Camden? What's going on? I just saw Mitch, and someone said you hit him?" Jackson barreled toward us.

Camden's mouth shut, fists clenched at his sides.

"Yeah," he said finally. "He deserved it."

Jackson glared at me then. "What are you even doing here?"

I rolled my eyes. "Both of you need to get out of my way. I don't have the patience for either one of you tonight."

I turned and motioned to Erin that I was ready to go, and we left.

When Camden came to the house the next time, we ignored each other. I preferred to pretend he didn't exist, even though that was impossible, because he was all I could ever think about.

CHAPTER ELEVEN

CHANCE ENCOUNTERS

CAMDEN

Present

It's been a long week of interviews. Sammi was no better than Britney. The next person I interview is Olivette. She comes in with a low-cut blouse, and the only reason I notice that is because she drops a mint down her shirt and then giggles and makes a production out of digging it out. When I ask for a little more detail about her resume, she says "How about we get to know each other first?" as she slides her cell number across the table.

I don't bother tasting her profiteroles.

And then Virginia walks in, an elderly woman with a kind smile.

"How are you today?" she asks after she's introduced herself.

"I'm great. How about you?"

"I'm excellent. I'm alive and have my wits about me. Life

is good." Her smile is wide. "I brought some tiramisu with me, but I suspect you might want to see me at work."

She slides the plate of tiramisu toward me, and I have to admit, it looks impressive. When I taste it, I'm blown away. The flavors, the consistency…it's perfect.

"This is the best tiramisu I've ever had."

She beams, pleased. "Thank you. My husband thinks so too. I love to make cakes and macarons, tortes, pies, you name it."

She reminds me of my grandmothers, and I like her instantly. I'd been tempted to call in Grandma Nancy until I could find the right person, but I wasn't sure she'd be able to handle not being the one in charge. And I was almost desperate enough to call on Grandma Donna, but she's been busy with the Friendship Bench. She's booked every day from one to six. Any time we have a thirty-degree day, she's out there on the bench with a blanket and the outdoor heaters going full blast. On the cold tundra days, she takes the session into the glass pavilion. I had no idea people in a small town would need to talk so much, but Grandma Donna is a hot commodity. She knits while she listens, so I'm seeing her scarves and hats and gloves all over town. It's just as well that she couldn't work in the kitchen—she would've tried to pull out her Lutheran Jell-O salad, and that's a hard pass.

Virginia gets right to work preparing an apple rose tart that is as beautiful as it is delicious, and a lemon cake with lavender glaze that I didn't even know I'd been missing. She knows how to do amazing things with chocolate and comes to life in the kitchen without being in the way. I've found the right person.

"How soon can you start?" I ask.

She wipes her hand on her apron and shakes my hand. "Right now, if you'd like. Arthur will be glad that I'm out of the house for a while. We're driving each other crazy." She laughs.

"Yes, please." I show her around the rest of the restaurant, and when we return to the kitchen, she gets to work.

It's a weight off my mind.

The following day, I have to go to a restaurant supply store in the Twin Cities. I haven't missed living near the city like I thought I would, but driving into St. Paul, I get nostalgic. My dad still owns the house on Summit Avenue, but he's spent less and less time there since buying the land next to the lake house and working on the resort. I meet Tully for lunch and then head to the restaurant supply place near his condo.

The supply warehouse has more people in one room than I've seen in a long time. I think the last time was at a Colorado Mustangs game. Carts are everywhere, boxes are stacked like leaning Jenga towers, and people are rushing through like they're on one of those supermarket sweep reality shows. I want to march back out to my car and get back to the solitude of Windy Harbor, but we need another industrial mixer at the restaurant. Britney managed to strip the gears on ours right before I fired her.

I'm halfway down the stainless steel section when someone whips around the corner at full speed with a dolly.

I collide into the stacked crates of produce, sending the boxes careening across the floor, and I bend over, rubbing my hip where the corner of the dolly nailed me. I grit my teeth, holding back every curse word I've ever heard because dammit, that hurt.

Somewhere in there, I hear a gasp.

"Oh my goodness," a woman says. "I'm so sorry!"

It registers who it is before she pulls a large strip of kale from my head.

"Camden?"

"Yep, it's me."

Juju reaches out and plucks a leaf from my shirt, but my stomach dips like she's touching my nipple or something. "What are you doing here?" she asks.

"Same reason as you, I suspect. We own restaurants. This is where we get our toys." I nod at her dolly. "Kale shopping spree? Not exactly my idea of a good time."

Her mouth twitches like she's fighting a smile, and I feel a sense of accomplishment like I did in fifth grade when I won a blue ribbon in a relay race.

"You don't get your produce here?" she asks.

"No, you know we're growing a lot in the greenhouse, right? Tomatoes, herbs, and lettuces…we've even had some luck with vegetables."

"That's great."

"You should come by and get what you need there. Can't get any more local than that. It's practically your backyard."

There's that almost-smile again. Damn. Whatever is happening today needs to stick.

"It does feel that close sometimes, doesn't it? Small-town living is an adjustment."

I nod. "Like living in a fishbowl."

Now she does smile, and it warms my chest.

"I didn't know you were into gardening," she says. "But I guess there's a ton I don't know about you, right?"

"No, I'm still not all that great. Dad's teaching me some things. He's enjoyed taking care of the plants. It's given him something to do, and he actually likes it."

She starts to speak and then hesitates. "Maybe I *will* come shop in your greenhouse. I like supporting small growers."

"Now that you know it's not me growing it, huh."

That gets her. She laughs, a genuine laugh, and it hits me hard, because I don't hear it often when I'm around, not like this. When she stops, she grins down at the kale in her hands.

"Maybe," she says softly.

"Mm-hmm." It's fun to tease her without things blowing up. "My basil could put this place out of business."

"Your *dad's* basil," she corrects.

I snort, and there's a beat where we just look at each other. Maybe she's as relieved as I am that we're not at each other's throats.

"I wanted to see the ice sculptures in Stillwater before I head back to Windy Harbor." My voice is tentative, but I straighten my shoulders and keep going. "Would you want to—"

"I've been thinking about going to see those too," she says in surprise.

"Remember when—" we both say at the same time.

We then laugh awkwardly.

"Yes," both of us say again, and then we really laugh.

"You go first," I say.

"Remember when we were making our own ice sculptures, and we were so sad when they melted?" She looks away and smiles.

"Yeah, we had that crazy warm day in January…that is so the opposite of today, by the way."

She rubs her arms. Today's a cold one.

"We spent so many hours on those," I say. "It's the only time I've ever been sad for a warm day during the winter like I was then."

She laughs. "Same."

"So, what do you think? Would you wanna go out there?" I try again.

"Sure, I could do that," she says, her expression shy.

"Okay, we can finish up here and then head out."

She nods. I can't tell if she's still unsure.

I can't believe she said yes.

"Wait. This won't last in our cars. It's too cold out there," she says.

"Right. Didn't think of that. Where the fuck is my head?" I laugh awkwardly. "I'll see if they can set it aside for us."

"Good idea."

I go check, and they're happy to hold it.

The whole drive to Stillwater, I think about Juju and tell myself not to mess things up. Keep the peace. See if we can get through a day without fighting.

When I pull up to the parking lot overlooking the St. Croix River, I wait to take in all the ice sculptures until Juju pulls up next to me. I get out of the car and slide my hands together.

"It's brutal out here," I say.

She nods briskly, wrapping her coat around her tighter.

"I mean, it's good for the ice sculptures, but not so great for us…" I say, trailing off. "How 'bout we grab a warm drink before we start looking?"

"Good idea."

We find a place that serves hot chocolate and coffee, and we both get hot chocolate.

"Our eyelashes might be clumping with tiny icicles right now, but our mouths and bellies are warm," Juju says as we walk toward the frozen river.

I can't remember how many years the International Snow Sculpture Championships have been happening, not too many, but I've only been one other time. It's shocked me both times how skilled these artists are.

When she finally pays attention to the sculptures out on the river, she gasps. It's mind-blowing to see what people from all different countries have created out of ice, and in these painfully cold conditions no less.

We slowly walk by each one. There's a Native American woman holding a child. Lovers sitting on a swing. Another depicts an old couple walking away hand in hand. The level of detail is incredible. Finland has won first place, and the sculpture's deserving, though we equally love Spain's, a profile of a woman with long, flowing hair leaning on a crescent moon.

Things are going so well that after we've walked around the sculptures several times, I turn to her. "I'm hungry. How about you?"

"Yes. There's a restaurant I've been wanting to try. It's been open for a while, but I've been too busy in Windy Harbor to get over here very often."

"It's been a few years since I've been to Stillwater. I missed all my favorite places when I lived in Colorado... although there were plenty of beautiful places to see there."

"Do you miss it?" she asks.

"I do. I love the mountains, and I'm missing those, but it's too good to be around family to think about the things I miss. I'm glad to be home."

"I know everyone missed you. Or maybe just Jackson," she adds, smiling.

"Not you, of course."

Her cheeks flush, and she shakes her head.

"Why would I?" She laughs to kind of make up for the sharp tone, which did sting, not gonna lie.

I also know I deserve it.

"Right. Exactly," I say, going for playful.

What felt like a short walk to the restaurant feels like an eternity in the –10 degree weather. Juju's teeth are chattering before a minute has passed.

I hold my arms out and say, "Here, let me help."

She surprises me by taking me up on it, stepping into my hold gratefully. We huddle together the rest of the way.

"Thank you," she says when we step inside the warmth.

I'm reluctant to let her go—no one wants to be cold, after all—but I don't want to make it weird. The restaurant has a full bar and tables with low light, giving it a cool, vibey ambiance.

"They have a lot of new restaurants now, compared to when I was growing up here," I say, still looking around.

"I'm glad this town is thriving. Gives me hope for Windy Harbor. Things have already moved in the right direction. People are excited about the changes coming. It was sad for a while when things started shutting down a few years ago—it was a risky time for me to start a new business there, but it's all worked out."

Looking across the table at her, I'm struck by how beautiful she is. Her cheeks are rosy from the cold, her eyes luminous in the candlelight. The day is cloudy and a bit dark, but the light coming through the window shines around her like a halo.

It knocks me speechless for a moment.

"What is it?" she asks.

Her hand moves to her cheek.

"Do I have something on my face?"

"This is just nice," I say finally.

She bites her lower lip.

"I've felt bad for how things seem to go wrong between us at some point in every conversation. I don't mean for it to be that way," I confess.

"Really?" Her head tilts as she studies me. "I've gotten the impression at times that you enjoy fighting with me."

"Well, for the longest time, you ignored me. So any reaction is better than none."

Her lips part when I say that, and we stare at each other for a long moment.

The server comes up, and we order drinks and the specials. Once she leaves, we're quiet, and I wonder if maybe I said too much and made things awkward.

But then she says, "You know, at Christmas…"

When she doesn't say anything else, I lean in.

"What about Christmas?" I ask.

"I've remembered bits and pieces."

"There are parts you don't remember?"

I lean back, wondering if my pride should be hurt that she doesn't remember the electricity between us that night.

"Will you fill in the blanks?" she asks.

"It was nothing major." I shake my head slightly and see a flash of something cross Juju's face.

It's gone the next second, and I'm relieved when our server interrupts the moment to place our drinks and a large bread basket on the table.

CHAPTER TWELVE

HUMAN FREEZER

JULIANA

And here I thought we were finally getting somewhere.

Nope.

Back to square one.

Camden has been so sweet today, but I shouldn't have expected him to clarify things for me. He's never made things easy. His being so nice today has taken me by surprise, and I really enjoyed being with him more than I could have anticipated, but I'm embarrassed that I thought he felt anything at Christmas. Now I know that either I did imagine everything or he didn't feel like it was "anything major."

Talk about a blow to the ego. He's been good at doing that for years now. Why would I think anything had changed? Our food comes, and I can tell that Camden is a little bit uncomfortable. Our conversation has become stilted, mostly because I'm barely responding anymore. I think I've checked out. It reminds me of how things were when I was a kid and looking for his approval so much of the time.

I'm over that.

"Juju," he says, "I can't help but feel like I've messed things up."

"Hmm? No." I pretend to be interested in the people around us as I eat my delicious meal, and he gives up trying after a few failed attempts of getting me to talk.

I jump when he says, "So, what's the story between you and Bentley?"

"There's not much of a story, really. We're just getting to know each other. He's a nice guy. We've become friends."

"You're not dating?" His brows crease in the center, and his mouth parts as his eyes drop to my lips.

"Um. I think he'd like to, but I don't know…so far, it's more in the friend zone."

"And that's the way you want it?"

My eyes narrow. "Why do you ask?"

His shoulder lifts. "Just curious."

"Did Jackson tell you to check up on me?"

He swallows hard.

"That's what all this is, isn't it?" Anger flares. I can't believe he's still playing these old games. "My love life is none of your business…*or* Jackson's! We're adults, for crying out loud."

He nods slightly. "You're right. Just want you to be careful, that's all."

"Why? So you can be the only one to bully me? Is that it?"

He looks hurt, which I feel a little bad about, but not enough to take it back.

The meal really is enjoyable, and being distracted by that helps. Keeps me from wanting to cry or from popping

Camden Whitman over the head, so I'm going to call that a win.

When the check comes, we argue about who's gonna pay for it, and Camden gets his credit card to our server faster than I do, so he wins.

I excuse myself to go to the bathroom and give myself a pep talk. This has been a good day, a positive one. We didn't kill each other. We didn't even argue all that much.

So why do I feel dead inside?

I step into the hall and come to a stop when I see Camden straighten from the wall.

"Are we making a habit of hallway meetings?" I tilt my head when he doesn't answer.

He moves toward me, and I freeze.

"Juju, do you ever miss the days when we were friends?" His expression is tentative and vulnerable.

I swallow hard. "Do you?"

"More than I can say. All the time, every day, every day since it happened…since we stopped being friends, I've never stopped missing you."

At first I think he has to be joking to talk this way, but his eyes and voice are so intense.

I blink at him, stunned. "Then how did we get here? Why did you let it go this way?"

His face wrinkles up, and he runs his hand through his hair. "I never dreamed we'd be like this. One thing snow-balled into the other. At first, I was just trying to keep my distance because everyone was saying how weird it was for me to want to be with you, when I was older. Jackson hated it. We promised not to ever date each other's sisters, and I've kept my word."

"But you stopped being my *friend*. Dating had nothing to do with it, ever. We've never dated. Why would that even be an issue? You turned into a jerk overnight, *literally* overnight." I shake my head. "Actually, that's not true. It was from one minute to the next."

He scrubs his hand down his face. "I know, and I'm so, so sorry. At first, I just didn't know what to do. I was a kid who was trying to do the right thing, and then it just all went haywire. You started reacting to me being a jerk. I started reacting to *your* reacting." He lifts his head to the ceiling and sighs. "That sounds like I'm blaming you for the way things are, and I'm not. I know that I started this."

"Yes, you did. But I certainly haven't done anything to make it better. I'm confused ninety-nine percent of the time we have any interaction with each other, today probably more than I've been in a long time, because you flipped the script on me. You've been an asshole for years, and now suddenly you're being nice? Why? What gives?"

"We've had moments," he starts and then pauses. "Moments when I thought you might be feeling more... like me."

I frown. "What do you mean more like you?"

He exhales again and takes a deep breath. "Moments when I thought we almost kissed," he finally says. "Like maybe you had feelings for me. God, I am so out of my element right now. I don't have issues talking to women, Juju. I think you're the only woman who's ever made me nervous."

I put my hand on my cheek, still flushed from him saying he thinks we've almost kissed. *So I haven't been imagining it...*

"Why do I make you nervous?"

"Because I've always cared what you thought, whether it's trying to get a reaction out of you, making you mad to see how you'll fight back, wanting to know what you think about my cooking, wondering if you're having a good time, or if you want to kiss me as much as I want to kiss you…"

I move up to my tiptoes, put my hand on his cheek, and kiss him. In the next second, one hand goes around my waist, and the other goes to my cheek. He kisses me with everything he's got.

I've tried to imagine what kissing Camden Whitman would feel like for a very long time, and this far surpasses anything I could have imagined. For how careful he's been to say things right in the past few minutes, there's nothing careful about the way he's kissing me now. He's bold and self-assured, like he knows exactly what I need and is making sure to deliver.

My legs feel weak. My heart is racing. My hands explore his chest, his back, his hair.

He makes me feel things I've never felt.

Someone clears his throat behind us, and we break apart, both dazed as we turn to look at the person.

An older man points to the restroom that we didn't realize we were blocking.

"Hated to interrupt that, but duty calls," he says, chuckling.

We get out of the way, and then Camden leans his forehead on mine as we smile at each other.

"Holy fuck," he whispers. "Did that just happen?"

"Yes, he really had to go," I whisper back.

His lips are back on mine when he says, "That's not what I meant, and you know it."

"I'm not sure it did, so you should kiss me again…just to make sure…"

His kiss is slower this time, but when the man comes out of the bathroom a few minutes later and we're still kissing, we all three laugh. Camden pulls away and takes my hand, bringing it up to his lips.

"I don't want to stop," he says. "But I guess this isn't the place to kiss your face off."

"It was working for me." I lift my shoulder in a shrug, unable to drop my smile.

"I've stayed in town longer than I intended. Do you have to get back tonight? Could Hector and Hal cover for you?"

I make a face. "I wish, but no. I should get back, and I should probably go soon so it's not too late. Plus, we should pick up our things from the store."

"Right." He nods, but I can see the disappointment in his face. I'm disappointed too. It feels like we just opened a whole Pandora's box, and I don't like saying goodbye immediately after all that. On the other hand, maybe it's good to get some distance so I don't do anything crazy with him.

We can see how things are back in Windy Harbor…

"I really don't want to leave you, but I understand. I should get back too. I just wish…" He reaches out and runs his thumb over my cheek.

"I know. Me too," I tell him.

He smiles. "Should we go get more icicles in our noses?"

I laugh. "When you put it that way, what are we thinking? Let's never step outside again!"

He laughs and puts his arm around my shoulder. "I'll keep you warm."

The walk to our cars is much sweeter than it was before. He keeps me as warm as possible, which is to say, we're both shivering when we get to our cars. He opens my car door for me and gives me one quick kiss before shutting my door.

"Maybe I could see you tomorrow? I could come by the cafe for breakfast…"

I nod, smiling up at him. "I'd like that."

Hours later, neck deep in Mildred's hot water, I'm still smiling.

CHAPTER THIRTEEN

WHEELS TURNING

CAMDEN

I lay in bed half the night, staring at the ceiling and running through every second of yesterday on repeat. Juju's laugh, the way she looked at me like maybe she didn't hate me, her body huddled into me to keep warm, the way her lips felt against mine…

Hell yes, it happened.

We kissed, and it was perfect.

By the time the sun comes up, I'm antsy. I shower and shave, pausing over which shirt to wear. I'd like her to look at me and for those cheeks to flush like they did yesterday.

When I park in front of The Kitty-Corner Cafe, I find my pulse kicking up from just thinking about seeing her again. I push the door open, and the delicious smells waft in the air like always. Juju's behind the counter, her hair pulled back, and she's laughing. My whole chest loosens.

And then I see Jackson.

Tires come to a screeching stop in my mind.

I meet Juju's eyes over his shoulder, and she presses her lips together, the edges tilting up in a small smile before Jackson turns around and pulls me into a hug. He tries to put me in a headlock, but I have him in one in seconds.

"I didn't know you were coming to town."

"Surprise!" he says.

The room tilts a bit, my conscience at war with my heart because now I'm not just the guy who kissed Juju last night. I'm the guy who kissed my best friend's little sister…the same one I promised him I'd never date.

I force a grin, trying to match his enthusiasm. "Yeah, surprise." My voice cracks on the last syllable, and I cover it with a cough. Juju shoots me a wide-eyed look, one that suggests she's either trying not to laugh or worried I'm going to confess all my sins.

Jackson points at the table closest to the window. "I'm over there. Grab what you want and come sit with me."

I grin and nod. "Will do. How long you staying?"

"I've got a few days off, so I think I'll just hang here, spend some time with Papa Hector and Uncle Hal…Juju… you." He shakes my shoulder and grins.

A few days. Shit. I love my best friend, but his timing couldn't be worse.

He goes and sits down, and I move toward the counter. Juju's wiping down the espresso machine, but when she sees me coming, her cheeks flush. Even her ears are red.

"Morning," I say softly.

She sets down the rag and moves toward me. But then her timer goes off. She holds up her finger to me. "I'll be right back."

Suzanne, her employee, hears her and says, "I've got it."

"Thanks, Suzanne," Juju says. She looks at me tentatively.

"How are you?" I ask.

"It's been an eventful morning," she says. "An eventful couple of days, I guess."

My lips lift. "Yes, it has."

"How are you?"

"Well, I wasn't exactly expecting your brother this morning. I had plans to come in here and…"

She lifts her eyebrow when I don't finish that sentence.

"And?" she finally says.

"And not deal with him quite yet." I make a face, expecting her to laugh, but she just stares at me.

"Ahh." She nods. "What can I get you this morning?"

Shit. I'm fucking this up all over the place, but I'm not sure how to fix it. "Coffee…and whatever you recommend."

Her eyes flick to Jackson across the room, then back to me. She hesitates, then pours me a cup of coffee and hands it to me. My fingers brush over hers when I take the mug, and she glances up at me.

"Cinnamon rolls are fresh out of the oven." Her voice is stilted now, and I want to leave so I can come back and start over. "There's one serving of quiche left." She looks at the clock behind her. "Since it's eleven, you might be ready for lunch. The soup of the day is Hungarian mushroom; sandwich of the day is grilled cheese."

"I'll take it all."

She blinks. "All three things?"

"I can't think of anything better. I've been dreaming of that soup and the way you make a grilled cheese for a few years now," I admit.

"Really?" she says, looking surprised. "I don't remember you ever having this soup."

"One time when I was at your house, you'd just gotten home from school, and Jackson pulled out the leftover soup. I couldn't get enough of it."

Her eyes brighten for a second, but she's still being way more cautious than I'd like.

"Suzanne or I will bring it over in a few," she says.

"Quit hogging Juju. I need a refill," Bosco hollers from the table behind me.

Juju sighs. I turn and glare at Bosco, who gives me a surly look right back.

"I hope you're not talking to Juliana that way," I say.

His head rears back. "Juliana," he sniffs. "Who the hell calls her that around here?" He makes an exasperated sound. "Juju knows I don't mean no harm, don't you...*Juliana*?" He mimics me in a low voice.

"I know how to handle you," she tells him, which makes him laugh.

I think the only people who can get Bosco to laugh are Juju and Goldie.

When I look at Juju again, she gives me a pointed look. "Better go sit down. Jackson will be wondering what's keeping you."

Fuck. She's pissed.

"Juju," I say under my breath.

"*Cammie*," she sings.

I narrow my eyes playfully and see a tiny crack in her aloof demeanor.

"What?" she asks, sounding a helluva lot perkier than before.

"Do I need to kiss the sass off your mouth?" I say under my breath.

Her breath catches, and her eyes flash to mine. She presses her lips together, and I watch the way they plump back up when she releases them, my pants getting tight as I think about taking that bottom lip in my teeth.

"Seems like I can be as sassy as I want when my brother is around." She puts a cinnamon roll on a plate and sets it down loudly in front of me. "The soup and sandwich will be out shortly." She lifts an eyebrow, and her tone is all business again.

I sigh and turn, then walk to Jackson's table. He's got about three bites left of a three-tiered stack of pancakes, swimming in syrup.

He takes a bite and hums. "I haven't had breakfast like this in forever. A few days of this and I'll need a sugar detox when I get home."

"Or you could lay off the pancakes while you're here," I tease.

"No can do. No one makes them like my sister."

"Can't argue with you there."

"What were you guys talking about over there? I couldn't tell if I was going to have to break up a fight or if you guys were actually getting along."

"We don't *fight*," I say, frowning.

He snorts. "Right."

"We're getting along…better," I say carefully.

I take a sip of coffee and close my eyes. I don't know why I ever criticized Juju's coffee. It's fucking delicious.

His eyes round in surprise. "Well, good. What brought about this change?"

I swallow. "I…took what you said to heart. I miss the days when we got along too."

He smiles. "That's great, man. I'm really glad to hear that." He leans in. "How are things going with her and Bentley?"

"Oh, I don't think he's going to be an issue. I think they're just friends."

His expression is skeptical. "Are you sure? Papa and Uncle Hal don't seem to think so."

I turn and look around the cafe. "Where are they? Every time I've been here lately, they're entertaining the place."

He shakes his head. "I have no idea. I drove in this morning expecting to see them, but they're nowhere to be found. Juju said they told her they had an important errand to run."

"Hmm. Well, it's a lot quieter around here without them." I laugh.

"Anyway, back to you and Juju...it's a relief, man. I know you're not gonna be like best friends overnight or anything, but...it'll be nice if you can at least get along." He laughs under his breath. "Do you know that for a long time, I thought you two might end up together." He looks at me like *Isn't that the craziest thing?*

My mouth goes dry.

He shakes his head. "God, you'd be such a disaster together."

I choke on air, and his eyes narrow when I cough.

"You okay?" he asks.

"Yeah," I croak. "Just...why do you say we'd be a disaster together? Just curious," I add.

"I mean, there's the obvious." He holds out his hand and starts ticking things off. "The way you bicker. Even if you're keeping the peace for my sake, you've done nothing but set each other off for years." He leans back in his chair, looking at me like he's got it all figured out. "There's nothing about it that would work. Your schedules are completely different. You're going to bed a couple hours before she's getting up. You're both obsessed with your restaurants." He points at me. "You, especially. You barely have time for me—you think you'd have time for a woman? And then there's the little issue of you never being serious about anyone. You're a serial one-night stander."

My chest has been tightening the longer he talks. "Are you sure you're not thinking of your pattern? I've had one-night stands, sure, but it's because I don't have time to get to know people and date."

He holds his hand out. "Exactly my point."

"That doesn't mean I'm not capable of it! I've been trying to build a career here, and the timing hasn't been right. Doesn't mean it'll never happen for me."

Jackson leans forward, his elbows on the table. "Hey, I didn't mean to offend you. I know you'll have it all one day, man." His lips lift again in a cocky grin. "It just would never be with my sister, is all I was saying. None of it matters anyway, since this is all hypothetical. I know you'd never go back on your word. That's not who you are."

My stomach bottoms out. A bowl of soup appears in front of me, the sandwich coming next. I look up at Juju, who falters when she sees my expression.

"Thank you," I say, my voice sounding hollow.

She frowns but nods. "Do you need anything else?"

I need you, I think. I wish I could go back to when she was five and I was seven, and I'd ask her to play basketball with Jackson and me. Or to the time we were eleven and thirteen, and I'd stand up to Jackson and tell him there was nothing wrong with his sister and me being close. All the times I'd see her again after being in other states doing our own things, I'd hug her and ask her to fill me in on everything I'd missed.

But I didn't. And now I don't know how to undo it all.

"No, this is good, thank you," I say.

She hesitates and then nods and walks away.

I stare at all the food, wondering how I'm going to breathe, let alone eat.

The way she kissed me back last night felt like she'd been waiting for it as long as I have. Nothing about it was a disaster. When we kissed, it was like I'd been waiting to breathe for years and finally got air.

I never get serious about anyone? No, I haven't. Because I've never wanted to be serious about anyone but Juju. Not in high school or college or even in Colorado. Every time I tried, she was there at the forefront of my mind. Juju with flour on her nose, Juju's hair flying behind her as she ran by the lake, Juju's grin when she tried something new I'd made, even Juju shaking with fury at me.

I've been trying to hide how serious I am about her for so many years that I've almost convinced myself.

Yesterday felt like all our fragmented pieces were finally aligning, the fissures that had formed fitting back together. It felt miraculous and so right, and it hits me all over again: I want this.

I want her.

All of it.

More than anything.

I glance at her and wonder what she's thinking. I have no idea where she stands, what she thinks in the light of day. Maybe she regrets everything.

I get up, because if I stay planted across from Jackson much longer, I'm going to explode.

"I just remembered I need to be at the restaurant for a shipment," I tell him.

"But you didn't even eat anything," he says.

"I'll get to-go containers and take it with me."

"I know I didn't give you any warning, but I want to see you while I'm here." He points at me.

"Yeah, for sure. Come to the restaurant. I'll take a break, and we can hang out. And most mornings are good after ten."

"Okay, sounds good. I'll stop by later," he says.

I stop by the counter and only see Suzanne. She puts my food into to-go containers. When Juju comes out of the kitchen, she sees Suzanne handing me the bag of food.

"I'm heading out," I tell her.

"Okay."

"Can we…talk later?"

She nods.

"Good." I pause and lean closer. "I can't stop thinking about yesterday."

"Me either."

I smile, and when she smiles back, hope blooms in my chest.

CHAPTER FOURTEEN

THE TRUTH ABOUT MOODS

JULIANA

It's an understatement to say that my mind has been all over the place in the span of twenty-four hours.

My fingers grip the edge of the counter like it can anchor me. I need something to keep me steady.

All I can think about is Camden.

The way his lips felt on mine, the warmth of his palm cupping my jaw like I was something sacred...the kiss—slow and deliberate, like he was savoring every second and never wanted it to end.

I've been swimming in that memory all night and all morning, letting it settle into me...adjusting to the way it feels to have Camden's affection versus his annoyance.

I far prefer it.

In fact, last night, I was giddy about it. I thought it was the start of something big—the start of us.

And then he saw Jackson.

He took one look at my brother, and it was as if the entire day we'd spent together vanished. He stiffened, eyes like a caged animal, and then he ran. Not literally, but close enough.

Jackson pops into town without warning all the time. But Camden hasn't been here long enough to know that yet. And even though they've practically shared brain cells for years, he acted like seeing Jackson was a shock to his system.

God, why are men so complicated?

I press a hand to my forehead, trying to rub away the pressure. I don't have time to have a headache or to overthink everything, for that matter.

I just thought yesterday meant something. The way Camden looked at me was like he *saw* me. Like I wasn't Jackson's little sister anymore.

Maybe he's going to tell me later that the kiss was a lapse in judgment, a heat-of-the-moment kind of thing.

But if things are anything like the past, I think he's scared of Jackson. Well, not scared exactly…more like loyal. He practically bleeds honor, and my guess is that kissing your best friend's younger sister after promising to never date her checks all of his dishonor boxes.

If that's what this is about, I swear…

It was one thing when we were younger. I hated it then, that he dropped me like a dirty shirt because my brother said it was weird that we were close, but so help me, if that's still really going to be an issue…

I shouldn't get ahead of myself. It was one kiss. One great day after many horrible days. But he watches me when he thinks I'm not looking. And yesterday I remembered the guy who really knows me. I felt like I remembered who he was too.

Which is what makes all of this so frustrating.

He's infuriatingly closed off. I could always get him to

talk when he went quiet. Sometimes people accused him of being moody, but I knew it was just that he kept so much inside. He felt *everything* but said very little. When Camden's siblings or Jackson thought he was in a bad mood, it was usually because he was worried about a grade or he needed some quiet for a while…or sometimes, he was sick and didn't want to bother anyone about it.

I used to get such a thrill from thinking I knew Camden better than anyone. That's why it hurt so much when it felt like, all of a sudden, I hadn't really known him at all.

Well, guess what, Whitman? You've let me in a little bit now, and I don't plan on letting you pretend otherwise.

Unless he's a better actor than I've ever given him credit for, he wanted that kiss to happen yesterday.

When I get off work, I still haven't heard from Camden, and since he's working by now, I don't know if I will.

Jackson keeps asking if I'm okay, and I keep lying and saying I'm fine. He left a little while ago to go see Camden… another reason I don't really expect to hear from Camden.

I drag myself up the steps of the porch, exhausted. My shoulders ache from a long day of distracted work while I dissected the inner workings of Camden Whitman's mind. I can't wait to sink into Mildred. My feet are tired from all the walking I did yesterday in new boots.

I freeze before I reach the door. There's noise coming from the backyard. My eyes narrow as I try to decipher that sound.

I walk back down the porch steps and go around to the back of the house, where Papa and Uncle Hal are hard at work. On the opposite side of the yard stands a chicken coop.

Not just any old coop. Of course not. It's a big production. There's a little shed in the shape of a small barn on one side. They probably picked that up at Cox Trading Post. And then they're wrapping plastic around chicken wire on what I'm guessing is a large run where the hens can hang out. Wait. I blink. Yes, I'm seeing correctly. At least a dozen squawking chickens are inside, maybe more.

"Hey, sweetheart!" Papa Hector shouts, nearly making me drop my bag.

Uncle Hal pops his head around the opposite side of the building, and both are beaming like they're proud new parents.

"You guys have been busy," I tell them.

"I'll say." Papa steps back and puts his hands on his hips, assessing their progress.

"It's a chicken palace," Uncle Hal says as he wipes the sweat from his brow.

"It's zero degrees today. How are they supposed to survive out here?" I ask.

"It's insulated, and we put heated pads under their straw so the eggs don't freeze…and so our little ladies don't freeze their tushes off too," Uncle Hal says, grinning. "What you're seeing here is a roomy, well-ventilated, state-of-the-art insulated space that will keep the hens happy. We can take the plastic off in the summer, and they'll enjoy the weather."

One of the hens lets out a dramatic squawk, like she agrees.

"You bought chickens," I say slowly. "In *January*, our coldest month. How did you do all of this in one day?"

"We rescued them from Eugene," Papa says. "He's decided to be a snowbird in Florida. I hope it's okay that we said yes. We thought you'd be happy about it. Think of all the fresh eggs you can use at the cafe."

"People will taste the difference!" Uncle Hal adds.

"We might even have enough for Camden to use," Papa says.

He probably would be happy about that. But it's one more thing to take care of! I put my hand on top of my head.

"*Chickens*," I whisper, still unable to believe what I'm seeing. "How many are we talking?"

"Twenty," Uncle Hal says proudly.

"*Twenty*," I gasp. "Unbelievable."

"We'll take care of them, don't you worry!" Papa says.

"Look at those girls," Uncle Hal says. "They're settling in already. It's supposed to warm up tomorrow, so maybe they can wander out of the coop…get some exercise."

A handful are sitting on boards that are staggered at different heights, and a bunch are walking around clucking. It sounds like they're talking to each other.

"Don't they have enough room in there?" I point to the area they're in.

Papa nods, and Uncle Hector shakes his head at the same time.

"They do," Papa tells his brother.

"Would you want to be cooped up in there if you had the chance to roam?" Uncle Hal puts his hand on his hip. "Yes, they'll be okay in there, but I think they should be free some-times too."

"What if they try to cross the road?" I ask.

Their heads fall back as they laugh.

"To get to the other side?" Papa says once he's caught his breath.

"Just beak-cause she could," Uncle Hal adds, and they both crack up. "To bawk twaffic." He does chicken arms, which makes them laugh harder.

I sigh, and when Papa notices I'm not laughing, he sobers up.

"*Oh!*" he says, biting back his smile. "You were wondering about them crossing the street for *real*." He clears his throat, and his lips twitch. "We might have to keep an eye on them at first," he admits. "But then I think they'll get used to their parameters."

My phone buzzes in my bag, and because I've been checking it every chance I have a free moment, all day long, I pull it out. My heart flutters.

> CAMDEN
>
> Jackson got here right before I started my shift. I'm sorry—I'd planned on coming to you. Would you mind coming to the restaurant? I can take a break whenever you get here. We can talk in my office or go for a little drive. I really want to see you.

I can't read between the lines. He could want to kiss me again, or tell me it was a mistake. Flip a coin.

> CAMDEN
>
> Or we can wait until tomorrow if that's better for you.

> CAMDEN
>
> But I hope tonight is better. 😄

I smile at my phone.

> I can come to the restaurant. Maybe an hour or so?

> CAMDEN
>
> Great. See you then.

The restaurant's parking lot is packed when I arrive. I wanted to avoid the early dinner rush, but I have to be up so early tomorrow morning that I didn't want to get here too late either.

Camden is the last person I expect to see when I push open the heavy doors of Elm & Echo. He's near the entrance like he's the maître d' or something. I freeze mid-step. He's not supposed to be out here. He should be buried in the kitchen, yelling about garnishes and plating and whatever else he does on a nightly basis.

His face lights up when he sees me.

"Camden? What are you doing out here?"

Joey, the kid who's usually doing host duties with Annie or Hannah, depending on the day, perks up. "Hi, Juju!"

His eyes wander down the neckline of my fitted sweater and don't stop until they reach my feet before wandering back up.

I'm saying "Hey, Joey!" when Camden snaps his fingers in front of Joey's face.

"Eyes up here, Joey," he says, his fingers not the only thing snapping.

I laugh. "Don't you have, I don't know—food to cook?"

A slow grin spreads across his face. The next thing I know, he steps forward, catches my arm, and steers me toward the side hallway with a speed that doesn't allow for questions.

"What—"

He pushes open his office door, and we step inside. The noise from the dining room instantly muffles. My pulse trips over itself. I spin on him.

"Are we avoiding Jackson?" I ask.

He laughs, low and unguarded. He leans back against his desk, crossing his arms and giving me the same slow perusal

Joey did, except coming from this man, it makes me hot all over.

"He's busy flirting out there," he says, his eyes sparking with amusement. "And I've been waiting all day to talk to you. So yes, we're avoiding Jackson."

The way he's looking at me and the fact that he's waited all day to talk to me…it all makes my stomach swoop in a way I'd rather not acknowledge.

"You're wearing the same color you wore to prom," he says.

I glance down at my blue sweater. "You're…yeah…I never thought of that. How do you remember what I was wearing to prom?"

"I brought you home, remember?" He moves toward me.

"Yeah, but you weren't exactly looking at me that night."

"Ah, Juliana. I've always been looking at you."

CHAPTER FIFTEEN

COULD BE BETTER

CAMDEN

Past: Camden, age 20, Juju, age 18

I was excited to be home from school. I loved New York City, but I'd never want to live there. I missed the tranquility of St. Paul too much. And my family.

But fuck me, I kept getting knocked sideways by seeing Juju. She'd always been beautiful, but during my time away, she'd grown up. It shouldn't have been any surprise that she was stunning, but it was like a body slam from Bigfoot every time we ran into each other.

Today I was in some kind of fresh hell, because I was walking out of my bedroom and I ran into her…literally.

"Oof," she said.

When she looked up at me, her mouth dropped and we stared at each other for at least a minute.

"Didn't know you were here," I finally said.

Lame opener, for sure, but it had been a while since I'd

seen her, and *fuck me*, I could swear her eyes were greener, and her hair was even more vibrant than I remembered. Her chest rising and falling drew my eyes down, and despite what I'd said to her as a kid about her small tits, I thought they were the perfect handfuls. Her long legs were on display in her short shorts, and I took in a quick breath, forcing my eyes back to hers. Hard to do because I wanted to investigate every inch of her.

She motioned to Goldie's room. "I'm getting ready with Goldie. Prom," she added.

"Ah. Right. Well, I'll get out of your way."

"Yeah, you're good at that. Until you're not."

I frowned. "What do you mean by that?"

"Nothing. Just that you're good at running, hiding, etcetera…until, say…I kiss a boy you don't approve of." She leaned in, and I inhaled her berry shampoo.

My eyes closed when I smelled her. God, I'd missed her. Even though we hadn't talked in a long time, not really, it helped just to see her. I didn't have that luxury anymore, living in New York City.

"Do me a favor," she said, and I tried to focus. "Don't punch Eric while we're getting prom pictures taken."

I scowled. "Who the hell is Eric?"

"Is that all you heard from what I said?"

"No. But why do you say that? Does he *need* punching?"

"No," she snapped. "But neither did Mitch, and that didn't stop you!" Her hand went flying out when she said Mitch's name, and I took a step closer to her.

Her breath hitched, and I freaking loved that sound.

"Mitch was Jackson's friend, and he knew you were off-limits. Plus, he was a dick to girls."

"Do you hear yourself? First of all, I'm not off-limits to anyone just because they're Jackson's friend." She gave my chest a shove, but I didn't budge. "And second of all, it's none of your business who I kiss or do anything else with."

My eyes widened. "What, you're having sex now?" My chest pinched. I was too, so I didn't know why it pained me to think of her having sex.

"Yes, Camden. Not that I owe you an answer about something else that is not your business, but yes." She rolled her eyes. "I've been dating Eric for nine months."

"That doesn't mean you have to fuck him. Are you sure you were ready for that? You're only—"

"So help me, if you say I'm only eighteen, I will gut you." She was on her tiptoes now, so she wouldn't be so short, and I lowered my head until we were eye to eye.

"Just because you're eighteen doesn't mean you're ready…did he pressure you? He better not have because—"

"Ugh!" she yelled. "Get out of my way, you big baboon! You lost the right to have any say in my life a long time ago. I don't know why you think your words make any difference to me. It's not like you're even my friend."

We'd never fought. Not like this. We'd kept our distance and had edgy snippets of conversation occasionally, but the air between us was electric and raw. I couldn't shake the way my heart twisted when I looked at her now. I hated it. I hated that I felt it and I hated that *she* seemed fine.

"You're right." I took a step back and held out my arm for her to pass. "Just because I'm trying to stop you from making stupid mistakes…it doesn't mean anything."

"No, it doesn't," she said softly.

"Fine."

"Fine."

She walked past me, opened Goldie's door, and slammed it behind her.

I was by the lake, minding my own business, thank you very much, when Goldie and her date Ross came out, and behind them were Juju and Eric. I could tell he was a twat by the way he didn't help Juju when they walked toward the water. She was wearing heels and a long dress, looking incredibly beautiful, but she also moved a bit like a baby fawn trying to make her way down to the sand. All the parents were out there, snapping pictures, while I stood on the sidelines wishing Eric would take his fucking hands off of Juju.

I had to get out of there, so I went to Jackson's house. It felt safe there since Juju was at my house, but not even fifteen minutes after I got there, they all showed up to take pictures in the Fairs' yard too. Fuck my life.

When I went home later that night, I went into the kitchen to make a snack. I hadn't had much of an appetite all day. My mom turned from the pantry and smiled.

"Hey, you hungry?" she asked.

"A little bit."

She grinned and waved a box of crackers that we both loved from Trader Joe's.

"I have the perfect cheese to go with these," she said.

I nodded. "Yep, that's what I need."

"Yay." She did a little dance as she moved to the island. "I was actually hoping I'd see you before I went to bed. I wanted to talk to you about something."

"Yeah?"

"Yeah." She spread the crackers out on a plate while I cut thin slices of cheese and lined them next to the crackers.

She went to the fridge and pulled out two chilled bottles of Coke, holding them up for me to see. "Do you want?"

"Do you even have to ask?" I said, grabbing them and putting them on the island.

She laughed, and we sat on the barstools.

"Can we talk about Juju?" she said.

I sputtered on the sip of Coke I'd just taken. "I guess so? Wasn't expecting you to say that," I added.

"Well, it's something I should've said a long time ago. I guess I was just waiting to see if…" She turned to look at me and put her hand on my arm. "I've seen the way you look at her. The way you've always looked at her. And I've talked to you about how sad I am that you're not friends anymore, but I've never said what I'm about to…"

My heart thumped out of my chest.

"For you to still be thinking about her the way I know you must be, given your starry eyes whenever she's close…"

I rolled my eyes, and she laughed.

"Hear me out," she said. "I think it's the real thing. That might not be something you want to hear, but I think you need to…because I've seen the way she looks at you too." She leaned in and squeezed my arm. "Be patient, my love. Let her soar in college. Let her experience life a little bit. She'll come back, and if it's meant to be, when the timing is right, you'll be together."

"Wow. I had no idea…no idea you knew any of this. I try not to even—" I cleared my throat. "I've tried to will it away. The feelings, you know? I haven't even wanted to admit it to myself most of the time. Jackson was always so mad about how close we were, and he and I promised each other we wouldn't go there with the sisters. And…and I thought going 1,200 miles away would take care of it. I've dated, I've tried to stop thinking about her…"

"Honey, you care about her. You really do." She leaned in. "Dare I say that you might even love her."

My eyes bulged, and I swallowed hard. Shit. I knew I loved Juju like I loved my family and Jackson, but she was also different. Mom was talking about *love* love, and I couldn't believe I'd never come to this conclusion on my own. Because when she said it, everything clicked into place.

I loved Juju.

My phone buzzed on the countertop, and since it was face up, I saw that it was Juju. I grabbed it and showed Mom. Her eyes widened.

"Answer it!" she whispered.

"Hello, Juju?" I said.

"Camden," she said, her voice breaking. "I…would you…I didn't know who else to call. Can you come get me?"

I was already standing up and grabbing my keys. "Where are you? I'll be right there."

I motioned to my mom that I was going to get her, and she nodded, blowing me a kiss.

"I'm at the St. Paul Hotel." She sniffed, and the sound tugged at my chest.

I reached my car and got in. "Okay, I'm on my way. Already backing out. It'll take about twenty minutes, at most. Are you safe? Do you want to stay on the phone with me until I get there?"

"Yes, please," she said. "I'm safe, but I'd feel better talking."

"Okay, I'm right here."

I made it in fifteen minutes, and during that time, we talked about nonsense. I told her about the crackers my mom and I liked. That I hadn't played broomball since last Christmas, but that Tully had insisted we try a version of it this summer, which made her laugh. I asked him why we couldn't just play hockey like normal people.

By the time I got there, she sounded lighter, and when I

pulled up and saw her standing at the door of the lobby, my heart dipped in relief.

I got out and jogged over to help her to the car.

"Thank you," she said after I'd closed the door behind her.

I ran around, and when I got in the driver's seat and looked at her, she was glancing down at her hands, her eyes glassy and her hands shaky.

"Juju," I whispered. "What can I do?"

She glanced at me, and a tear dripped down her cheek. "You've already done enough by coming to get me."

"Can I ask what happened?"

A little sob came out, and she shook her head slightly, touching the back of her hand to her mouth. "I'm okay. I'm being ridiculous." She took a shuddering sigh. "I lied when I said Eric and I were having sex. We didn't have sex until tonight, and it was…okay, but…after…" She wiped the tears that were falling freely now. "Afterward, someone came to the door. He stepped out and I went to the bathroom, and I heard him bragging about it to his friend. But then he talked about me not being as good of a lay as Jerica Adams. I don't even know who Jerica Adams is! And it was my first time! I'll get better." A whole slew of tears came, which just about did me in.

"Son of a bitch," I muttered. "What a fucking slimeball. You deserve so much better than that, Juju."

"Anyway. We're done. He got mad when I broke up with him and refused to bring me home. He paid so much for the room and all that." She waved her hand dismissively. "I couldn't stay in there another second." Her face crumbled again. "I didn't want to ruin Goldie's night, and I really didn't want Jackson to know about this." Her eyes widened. "You can't tell him, Camden. Promise me you won't."

"I won't, I promise."

She drew in a long inhale and relaxed against the seat. When we pulled into her driveway, I came around and helped her as she was getting out of the car. We were quiet as I walked her to the door.

"You look really beautiful tonight, Juju. I hope you know that."

She sighed. "Thanks, Camden. I know we're not friends anymore, but it was really great of you to come get me tonight."

"Anytime I can help, I'm here," I said. "We may not be as close as we once were, but I care about you. I'm always here if you need me."

She gave me one last look before going inside.

And my heart whispered *I love you, I love you, I love you* the whole time.

CHAPTER SIXTEEN

HIDDEN TRUTHS

JULIANA

Present

Last night in Camden's office, when he said he's always been looking at me, I just about keeled over. My heart was pounding so hard, the intensity in his eyes, his words—it was a sensory overload.

He was on his way toward me, his eyes on my mouth, when someone knocked on the door. He looked at me with regret and apologized under his breath, then left to settle an issue in the kitchen. I ended up going home without seeing him again…early morning and all that.

Now, it's a new day and I'm wishing I could have a redo. My body is wired. I have enough adrenaline for *days*, and I need that kiss.

I know we need to have a conversation too, but…first things first. My mouth is craving his. And *then* we can talk about whatever he wanted to discuss. Now that I know he still wants—whatever we're calling this between us—I can't shove down the excitement bubbling up in me.

I don't know how many times I've heard how happy I look today, or what a great mood I'm in. I'd think I must typically be a Dour Diane if I didn't know my secret...Camden Whitman is into me!

Ahhh! I could squeal just thinking about it.

Papa Hector and Uncle Hal have been putting the finishing touches on the chicken coop and run, or else they'd probably be trying to get to the bottom of things.

Jackson bursts into the cafe, then stretches his arms out and points at me.

"Juju, you're getting off early today," he declares.

He comes over and does a drum roll on the counter.

I laugh. "Since when do you make my schedule?"

"Since we called a broomball night. Come on, you can't miss it," he says, grinning like he's already won. "All of the Whitmans are in town. Dylan's even here from California."

"Why can't it be later?"

"Okay, fine. I think it *could* be later, since Camden's staff convinced him to take a rare night off. But before he knew that was happening, we thought we'd need to do it earlier." He sighs. "Please. It's been a long day. Papa and Uncle Hal are obsessed with the chickens, and some of those ladies are aggressive! There's this one in particular..."

I snort and roll my eyes. "So you're saying you're bored."

He points at me again. "Bingo." He clasps his hands together. "Please. You're shockingly good at it. You always play with us. The rink they've built here is even bigger than the one we grew up playing on in St. Paul."

"Why is it so shocking that I'm good at it?" I cross my arms.

He grins. "It's not like you've played any other sports."

"True," I concede. "It helps that we don't have to wear skates."

He cracks up. "Yeah, you and skates are never a good idea."

I try to act exasperated, but a thrill shoots through me at the thought of playing tonight. I love broomball, always have. And the thought of seeing Camden out there seals the deal.

"Suzanne was hoping for more hours. She'd probably be happy to close up for me. Let me check."

I check with Suzanne in the kitchen.

She gives me two thumbs up. "I'd be glad to!"

"Thank you!"

When I step out of the kitchen, Jackson lifts his eyebrows. "Well?"

"Fine," I say as I toss my apron on the counter. "But only because you need me out there."

"I wouldn't really say *need*…"

I flick his arm, and he yelps.

"Okay, okay, I need you out there. Come *on*," he says, rubbing his arm.

Once we're outside, I hurry to the house and get a better coat, and we head to the rink the Whitmans built earlier this winter.

When we arrive, everyone's already on the ice. Everyone's so loud that I think maybe I heard their laughter from my house, and it's not just our crew. People from town are on the sidelines, and Tully is out there trying to convince more people to play. It's gotten dark early, but floodlights cast long shadows across the snowbanks. The cold air bites my cheeks. Goldie and Erin rush over, hugging me. Ava's not far behind, and we all hug her as well.

"I'm so glad Jackson talked you into leaving early,"

Goldie says excitedly. "We didn't want you to miss a minute out here."

Just then, Jackson waves for me to hurry up.

"He's already in full coach mode," I gripe. "Is it too late to join the Whitman team?"

Erin snorts. "Fat chance. Jackson has big plans for us." She winks. "That's right, baby. I'm on your team this time."

My eyes find Camden. He glides his feet across the ice, broom in hand, a confident smirk on his face. My stomach somersaults. He notices me right away, and his grin sharpens.

"About time, Fair," he calls, his voice carrying across the rink. "I was starting to think you were scared to face me again."

I roll my eyes, trying to sound nonchalant as I step onto the ice. "In your dreams, Whitman. I can't pass up a chance of whipping your ass."

His eyes widen and he slides my way, close enough that his shoulder brushes against mine. He dips his head, his breath fogging in the freezing air, and murmurs low enough for only me to hear, "I'd like to see you try."

The shiver that runs through me has nothing to do with the cold, and his grin tells me that he knows it.

Between Jackson and Tully, we don't waste any time. Jackson barks out what he thinks our strategy should be, and I nod, bumping his fist. Erin and her dad, Jason, are on our team, and my eyes widen when my dad hurries out on the ice.

"Dad? I didn't know you were coming into town!" I rush over to hug him really quick.

"I couldn't miss broomball!"

Once we're all in place, the game *officially* starts.

The moment the ball hits the ice, Camden is there, moving with ease, that grin never leaving his face. He swipes the ball away from Noah, cuts right past me, and then slows down—on purpose.

"You gonna stop me, Fair?" His voice is a low taunt, warm even in the sharp night air.

I dart in, steal the ball, and whoop in triumph as I skid across the ice. "Already did, Whitman."

He laughs as he chases after me, but I lose my footing on a patch of ice and stumble. Before I can hit the ground, his hand shoots out, steadying me. For a second, we're too close, my breath catching, the world narrowing to the heat of his hand on my arm.

Then Jackson yells from across the rink, "Juju, over here!"

I move away from Camden, cheeks burning, and bolt toward the goal like I meant to all along.

We go head-to-head the rest of the night. Every time I snag the ball, Camden's there, cutting me off. Every time he gets an opening, I swoop in to steal it back. Our little duels on the ice turn into a game within the game.

At one point, he leans close as we jostle for the ball. "You've gotten better since last time." His shoulder presses into mine, deliberately or not, and his eyes sparkle beneath the lights.

"I've always been good. Maybe you've gotten worse," I fire back, breathless.

His grin deepens. "Not possible. Okay…maybe I'm a little bit out of practice."

By the time the game winds down, my legs ache, my lungs burn, and I can't stop smiling. The game was close, but with the Whitmans having Tully, a professional hockey player, we rarely win. We all give each other high-fives, pretending we're a pro team like we have since we played as kids.

Everyone piles off the ice. Jackson and Dylan recount their plays, and Erin bumps my hip with hers.

"Was it my imagination, or was there a little heat between you and Camden out there tonight? And I don't mean the usual heat." She lowers her head and keeps her eyes directed on me.

I flush and am about to tell her that I have some updating to do when I see two gorgeous girls in tight ski pants and fitted jackets, every strand of long perfect hair in place, walk up to Jackson and Camden. The brunette loops her hand through Jackson's, and the redhead loops her hand through Camden's.

"They came to catch a game of broomball," Jackson says, winking at Camden.

"As if we'd be caught dead out there," the redhead laughs. "No, we just came to show our support."

"Really? Didn't notice you out there," Camden says.

She throws her head back and laughs, and my nose curls.

"Who the hell are they?" Erin mutters.

Goldie and Tully walk up to us.

"Who invited the puck bunnies?" Tully asks under his breath.

"Looks like they're friends of Jackson and Camden," I say, my voice sounding hollow.

Everyone's invited to the Whitmans' house, and I debate skipping, my earlier elation deflated by the red nails on Camden's arm. But I want to hang out with Goldie and Erin too much to miss it…and more than a little curious about the girls.

The Whitmans' house glows warm against the dark winter night, windows steaming from the heat inside. We stomp snow off our boots and leave them in the mudroom. Goldie tells us her grandmas have hot chocolate and pies ready for everyone.

As the hallway narrows, Erin moves forward first, I fall in step behind Goldie, and Milo catches up with her, putting his arm around her shoulder. I'm thinking how cute they are together when a hand catches mine and tugs me into the den. It's dark, but I can make out Camden's broad shoulders.

"What are you—?" My words die when his hand cups the side of my face, the other sliding around my waist, and he puts his mouth on mine—his lips are chilly from the cold, but his tongue is warm and insistent.

I melt into him.

The world narrows to just us. He lifts me until my feet are off the floor, kissing me soundly. When we finally break apart, I'm breathless, my forehead resting against his.

"You're keeping your redhead waiting," I whisper.

"She's not my anything," he whispers back. "Jackson thought it would be a great idea to invite some friends to keep us company tonight. Without clearing it with me first."

I smile. "You're supposed to be inside, bragging with your family," I say, my lips still tingling.

"Everyone can wait," he murmurs, his smile wicked in the dim light. "I've been waiting all day for this."

My laugh catches in my throat. "This feels like we're sneaking around."

He kisses me again, slower this time, like we have all the time in the world. When he finally pulls back, his breath is uneven, his forehead still pressed to mine. He sets me on my feet, and his hands stay on my waist.

"I don't want Jackson to find out," he says quietly, the words spilling out like he's been holding them in all night.

My stomach dips and my heart sinks. "What?"

He shakes his head, jaw tight. "Not yet. He already thinks

we'd be a disaster. He even said it was a good thing we aren't together. He wouldn't be okay with this."

"Why would he say that? And I don't understand why he gets any say." I wince at how sharp my tone is.

Camden's eyes search mine, conflicted. "I don't want him trying to shut this down before we've even had a chance to get started. And knowing your brother…he would."

I bristle, because I hate sneaking around, hate the idea that we're letting Jackson have that much power. But the part of me that's still buzzing from Camden's kiss understands what he's saying.

"So what, we're keeping this a secret?" I ask.

His thumb traces my cheek, gentle despite the tension in his shoulders. "For now?"

The way he says it, vulnerable in a way Camden Whitman never allows himself to be, knocks the wind out of me. But I can't help but let some of my walls back up. It feels necessary.

"Okay." I nod before I can talk myself out of it.

I guess I can hold this secret for now, but it won't feel real to me until everyone knows and until my brother accepts it.

Relief flashes across his face. He gives me one more kiss.

"Should we go get some hot chocolate and pie?" he asks.

"Absolutely."

He lets me leave first. When I walk into the great room beyond the kitchen, I paste on a smile, my cheeks still warm, and slide into the crowd like nothing happened.

Grayson, Noah's little boy, comes running over. Kevin's right behind him.

"Juju! Hi!" he says, wrapping his arms around my legs.

Kevin nudges his nose between us until I pet him too, which makes both of us laugh.

"It's been too long since I've seen you, buddy. How have you been?"

"I'm good. I made cookies at preschool last week."

"I wish I'd tasted those."

"They weren't as good as yours." He wrinkles his nose.

"Well, the next time your dad comes into the shop, I'll send some home with him. How 'bout that?"

"Yeah!" he says, his smile wide.

"Where the hell is Dylan?" Tully gripes. "Every time I turn around, he's disappeared."

"He has been scarce this visit," his dad agrees.

"Maybe he ran to the store…" Goldie says.

"What could he possibly need that we don't have?" Grandma Nancy sniffs.

"Maybe condoms?" Noah says under his breath.

Goldie and Tully nod in unison, wide-eyed, looking more like twins than ever.

Camden walks in. Our eyes meet for just a second, and then we look away, like it never happened at all.

CHAPTER SEVENTEEN

RESILIENT

CAMDEN

I get up early the next morning to plow the driveway to the house, a path for everyone to get to the Friendship Bench because it's still going strong for Grandma Donna, as well as the roads to the resort and the restaurant. We got a foot last night. The trees are outlined with snow, their branches droopy with the heaviness of it. A winter wonderland.

When I pull back into the driveway of the house, I see Judith Summers trekking down the path to the Friendship Bench.

One thing you've gotta say about Minnesotans is that we are hardy sons of bitches.

We don't shut down for anything.

Jackson is in my driveway, his car still running. He gets out when he sees me pull up.

"Hey," he says. He stretches and yawns, giving me a cheesy grin. "I'm exhausted."

"Yeah?"

"Yeah, you missed out, man." He wiggles his eyebrows.

"Who the hell were those two you had at broomball last night?"

He blinks, like I must be joking. "They could've been the best time of your life."

I groan, and we walk inside the house.

"Don't tell me you didn't want to…they're gorgeous! And up for *anything*."

"It was weird. Bringing them around our families, and just assuming I'd want to do anything with either one of them—"

"Aw, come on. Loosen up a little. You could use it. You're wound tighter than a drum." He squeezes my shoulders. "My man needs to get *laid*."

I hear a scoff behind me and turn to see Grandma Nancy sitting on the couch.

I glare at Jackson, who widens his eyes in apology.

"*Lemonade*," he tries to clarify. "My man needs to get *lemonade*."

Grandma Nancy quirks a brow, her lips pinching together. He goes over and kisses her cheek, and she gives him a begrudging smile when he pulls back.

"You're looking lovely today, Grandma Nancy," he says.

She pats his cheek. "You don't have to sweet-talk me just because I'm here." She waves her hand. "Pretend I'm a fly on the wall." She takes a sip of tea. "But both of you are too good for those puck bunnies."

Jackson and I both choke on our laughter.

"What? You think I'm too old to know what that is?" She winks. "One of my grandsons is a professional hockey player, remember? I've heard it all. And I've seen a few things in my day too," she adds.

"Yes, you have," I jump in, not wanting to go down this path where she might share some of those things she's seen.

Despite the facts, I prefer to keep my grandma in the virginal realm if possible.

I shoot Jackson a look, willing him to be quiet as we walk to the kitchen.

"Sorry, man," he says as soon as it's safe. His shoulders deflate, and then he shudders. "I was afraid she was going to tell us she enjoyed threesomes back in her day."

"I'm going to pretend those words didn't come out of your mouth," I mutter with a huff as I grab two mugs out of the cabinet. "Coffee?"

"Sorry. Yeah, thanks," he says.

I pour some into both mugs and hand him one. "How long are you around? You sticking around a while?"

"Yeah, I think so. I can work remotely for a while, and I just needed to get out of the city, get by the water and family. My mom's coming in later this afternoon, and I didn't want to miss out on everyone being here." He grins and leans in. "So I had to get my fix last night," he says quietly.

I chuckle and shake my head. "Look. I don't need you trying to set me up anymore. Okay?"

He cracks up. "You're telling me you don't need a little help? Come on, man, you're working crazy-ass hours at the restaurant, and you're buried in work, helping get the resort opened. When's the last time you had fun?"

Juju's lips on mine last night come to mind.

Out loud, I say, "Broomball was fun."

"With family," he argues. "You don't get to count that. I mean fun with someone who could actually rid you of some of this tension you're carrying all the time."

"I do just fine," I say tightly.

The problem is, I know exactly who I want to rid me of

this tension. It's just not someone Jackson would ever approve of.

"Not interested," I add. "Not right now."

He studies me. "Not right now? Or not ever?"

"I've got too much going on," I say. "Like you said, I'm at the restaurant a fuck-ton. We're still finding our footing. I'm trying to keep up with supply runs, payroll, the staff. And I'm trying to do my part to make sure the resort is on track to open on schedule. It's a lot."

He leans back on his heels. For once, he doesn't look like he's about to crack a joke. "That's exactly what I'm saying—you've got too much going on and need some fun. But I hear you. I just don't want you to burn out."

"I'll be okay. I don't need distractions."

What I don't add is: *except for Juju.*

And she isn't really a distraction. She's oxygen.

He shrugs. "If you're sure…"

"I'm sure."

"Okay. Guess I'll cancel the double date I'd lined up for next week."

I groan. "Immediately."

"Noted." He drains his coffee cup and sets it down, then pushes off the counter. "But time's flying by. Don't miss out on the good shit."

I'm left there with the sound of the kitchen fan and my conflicted thoughts.

I've already got what I want.

I just can't tell him yet.

Not until I can figure out how to keep everything from blowing up.

I tug my coat back on as I step onto the deck. The sun is trying to come out, which is warming things up a bit. Across the yard, Grandma Donna sits like a queen on the Friendship Bench.

She's bundled up so well that I laugh out loud. A knitted hat pulled low, her scarf wound around three times…I don't know how she can see or breathe under all her layers. Her needles click in that way that I always associate with her, since she's been knitting as far back as I can remember. Her gloves are the only lightweight thing she's wearing. She's lining black and white yarn out beside her, like she's about to start a new project.

"How's it going?" I ask, my voice breaking the quiet.

She startles, then drags her eyes from the water view up to me. "Mercy, Camden. You're quieter than your papa ever was." She shakes her head, settling. "Just got done with a session and have a little time before the next one."

"You're not freezing out here?"

"No, those heaters help so much." She points at herself. "And I'm all bundled up."

I let my laugh escape. "You look like the Abominable Snowman."

Her eyes crinkle above her scarf. "That's exactly the look I was going for."

"Is it okay if I sit down for a bit?"

Her smile spreads wide. "I'd love that."

I sit next to her. The heater hums faintly, and I'm surprised how well it works. She's right. It's not bad out here. For a second, we just sit in comfortable silence, the lake stretching gray and endless in front of us, her needles clacking away.

"Anything on your mind, honey?" she asks.

I start talking. Not about the restaurant. Not about the resort. Not about Jackson's schemes or the staff at Elm & Echo or any of the various things on my mind. No, I end up circling, hesitating, and then spilling the whole damn thing about Juju.

It comes out in staccato bursts, like I've been storing it up too long: the fights, the bickering, the way I pretended for so long that she drove me insane, when really I just wanted her attention. And then the cracks in the armor. How she smiles at me now, not just in annoyance but like maybe she's finally looking back at me and actually *sees* me too. How I've kissed her, God help me, and I don't regret it for a second. How I want our first date to be special. And then I tell her all about Jackson and why we're keeping everything quiet.

When I finally stop, Grandma Donna lowers the knitting into her lap. She studies me for a few quiet moments.

"Your mom told me to be on the lookout for this," she says finally. "She said when the time was right, I'd know, and I should give you this advice: Go for it. Don't be afraid to show her how you feel. If you still love her after loving her for a lifetime, then you will have the life of your dreams. You just have to take the next step and make sure she knows how you feel."

My throat tightens. I huff out a laugh, part nerves, part disbelief. "Wow. That sounds like Mom." I get choked up. "I think she knows how I feel…I kissed her," I remind her.

Her eyes widen. "Yes, back to that. You've kissed her but haven't taken her on a proper date?" She tsks. "I know your mother raised you better than that."

I let out a groan and rub a hand over my face. "It wasn't…the ideal way to go about it. But…it was pretty great —" I laugh.

"You're telling me you've got all this heat with her, and you're wasting it on being careful not to let anyone know?"

"You make it sound simple."

"It is simple," she says firmly, needles resuming their

clicks. "You boys like to complicate things. But honey, if you feel the way you just described, you need to show her, not just with stolen kisses."

"Jackson would never approve," I mutter.

"Jackson doesn't get a vote," she says without hesitation. "He loves his sister, yes, but this isn't about him. It's about you and Juliana."

"I don't want to screw it up," I admit, softer than I mean to. "I've wanted this for so long. Since—God, I don't even know how far back. And with how awful things got between us, I keep thinking I'll ruin it again."

She lays her knitting aside again, her gloved hand resting briefly on my arm. "You *will* ruin it, Camden, if you don't give her the chance to see the real you. Take her on a date. Make her laugh. Let her know she's worth your time and effort. That's how you honor feelings like these."

Her words hit me hard. For a second, I can picture it: Juju at a little table, candlelight flickering, her hair catching the glow. I can hear her laugh, the one that slips out before she can stop it. I can imagine holding her hand across the table, not in secret, not rushed, but because she wants me to.

"I don't even know if she wants all of this," I admit. "Yes, she likes kissing me, but—"

"She wants this," Grandma Donna says matter-of-factly. "I've been watching the two of you before you even knew what a crush was. There's a pull there. Everyone can see it."

I laugh and make a face. "Even Jackson?"

She gives me a sly look. "I bet Jackson sees it and pretends he doesn't. He thinks protecting his sister means keeping her away from trouble. But what he forgets is that love is always a little trouble. And it's worth it."

I lean back against the bench, staring at the lake. "You

make it sound like I should walk right over to Kitty-Corner and ask her out tonight."

Her eyes glint with humor. "If not tonight, soon. Don't let too many tomorrows pass."

I sit with her a while longer, listening to the steady click of needles and the lake wind whipping. My head feels quieter. Calmer.

When I finally stand, she pats my arm. "Remember—kisses are wonderful, but they're not the foundation. The two of you have built some of that with time, but now, move forward with intention."

I nod, swallowing hard. "Thanks, Grandma Donna."

She smiles up at me and holds up a swath of an intricate black-and-white knitted pattern. She studies my face and nods, looking pleased. "This will look really good on you."

I grin. "Love you."

"Oh, I love you more than I can say," she says.

I head back to the house to get ready for work, and for the first time in a while, I'm not restless.

I'm ready.

Maybe not to tell Jackson quite yet, but to show Juju the depth of what I'm feeling.

CHAPTER EIGHTEEN

THE MERRIER

JULIANA

Erin texts in our girls' thread late the next afternoon.

> **ERIN**
> Girls' night? I didn't get my fix at the broomball game.

I'm halfway through wiping down the countertop at The Kitty-Corner when I read it, and I can practically hear her voice in my head—dramatic, whiny, and always amused. Goldie's perched on a stool at the counter, hair in a messy bun, sipping a hot cocoa.

"Girls' night, huh?" She waves her phone.

"Sounds good to me," I say.

"It's perfect timing," she says, snapping her fingers. "Oh wait, can Ava come? We were supposed to hang out together tonight."

She texts the question to Erin too.

"Of course," I say before Erin can even weigh in. A second later my phone dings.

> ERIN
>
> The more the merrier. Does this mean I have to be on my best behavior, though?

Goldie and I laugh.

> GOLDIE
>
> I think she's been around you enough by now to know your vibe.

Goldie and I wait for a minute, expecting a retort from Erin, but it doesn't come right away, and when she texts again, it isn't what we're expecting.

> ERIN
>
> Should we go to The Hungry Walleye? Break tradition and show Ava something a little nicer than The Loon?

> GOLDIE
>
> But The Loon is our headquarters. It's where we go. And besides, Ava has already been to both places by now. It's not like there is a plethora of choices in Windy Harbor.

> ERIN
>
> Will she think we're not cultured if we go to The Loon?

> Since when do you care what anyone thinks?

Again, she's quiet.
And then finally...

ERIN
Okay, The Loon at 6.

———

Lorraine sees us walk in and waves like she's been expecting us all along. "Booth in the back!" she shouts, already scooping up menus. The place smells like beer and burgers, and maybe a whiff of the Tater Tot hotdish, which is exactly what I need after a long day at the cafe.

By the time we've squeezed into the booth—me and Erin on one side, Goldie and Ava on the other—Lorraine has set down four helpings of Tater Tot hotdish like she's reading our minds.

"You girls'll need more energy for all the gossip," she says, tossing a wink before disappearing again.

"Did you guys even look at the menu?" Ava asks, amused.

"We stopped pretending to a while ago," Erin says, forking into her hotdish like she hasn't eaten in weeks. "She sees us, she brings out the tots. It's a beautiful thing."

Goldie smirks. "Remember the time she tried to bring us a salad?"

"Oh my God," I groan. "You would've thought she was betraying us personally, according to that one." I point at Erin.

"Because she was," Erin says solemnly. "If I wanted greens, I'd stay home and eat the sad bagged spinach in my fridge."

That makes Ava laugh hard, and Erin's cheeks tinge pink.

Interesting.

Percy is the only one I've ever seen make Erin blush, but she also is rendered speechless whenever Percy is around.

I'm not sure that's a winning combo, when it comes right down to it.

"The only exception is a Lorraine Juicy Lucy," I tell Ava. "And I shouldn't even say *exception* because we never leave out the hotdish…it's just something in addition."

"Got it." Ava laughs. "I haven't been in Windy Harbor anywhere close to the rest of you, so I need *all* the tips."

After a few minutes of chatter about Goldie's ongoing battle with tile samples at Windhaven, and laughing about Jackson still bragging about how he did at broomball, Erin wipes her mouth with her napkin and leans in, eyes sharp.

"Okay. Now that we're fed and the hotdish-induced coma hasn't hit yet, let's get to it," she says.

"Get to what?" I ask when I realize she's looking at me.

She raises her eyebrows. "You know what. I tried to start this the other night after broomball, but with all the nosy brothers around, I couldn't get a word in. Now there's not a single brother in sight." She points a loaded fork at me. "Something was *sizzling* between you and Camden the other night. Don't even try to deny it."

Goldie sets her fork down slowly. "You know," she says, smirking, "I didn't get any of the *I'm going to claw his eyes out* vibes either. Now that you mention it, it almost seemed like"—her grin spreads wickedly—"you guys were flirting."

I nearly choke on my Coke. "We were not—"

"You were totally flirting," Erin says. "I could feel it radiating off the rink. I had to shield my eyes."

"It was…competitive energy," I say, desperate. "You know, like trash talk. Banter. Sports psychology."

Ava tilts her head, studying me. "Sports psychology?"

"Yes," I insist. "Like…keeping him off-balance."

Goldie bursts out laughing. "I got the feeling you

would've liked it if you'd caught him off-balance, right on top of you."

All three of them cackle like wicked witches.

I bury my face in my hands, but my ears are burning. They don't let up.

Erin leans closer, her red lipstick still perfect despite the hotdish, and says, "So what's really going on? Because there's definitely something."

My heart thuds. I could lie. I could deflect. But these are my best girls, and I would hate to lie to them. It's been hard enough to keep it a secret this long.

"Things have...been changing. A little," I blurt out.

The table erupts. Goldie squeals. Erin slaps the table like she's just won a prize. Ava's eyes widen with delight.

"Changing?" Erin repeats. "As in..."

"As in, we're not fighting as much anymore," I say quickly, downplaying everything. "Sometimes he actually... makes me laugh. Sometimes it feels..." I trail off, realizing I've said too much.

"Like you're into each other," Goldie says, practically glowing.

"Like sparks," Erin supplies helpfully. "Literal sparks, Juju."

Ava grins, chin propped on her hand. "I even saw it."

"I don't know about *sparks*," I groan, starting to second-guess saying anything.

"Girl, you are in denial," Erin says.

"I'm just...being realistic. He hasn't said anything about what this is, and if he wants to keep it a secret, how into me can he really be?"

That hushes them for a second.

Erin sobers, eyes narrowing. "Wait. Secret? What do you mean?"

I shrug, fiddling with my napkin. "He doesn't want Jackson to know. Or maybe anyone, I don't know. He hasn't exactly spelled it out. And if he's not willing to admit it to anyone, then maybe it's not worth as much as it feels like."

Goldie leans across the table, earnest now. "Juju. My brother is an idiot. He overthinks everything. If Camden's keeping it quiet, it's not because he doesn't care. It's because he cares too much and he's scared he'll screw it up. They were ridiculous with that whole off-limits thing. Camden's probably scared of what Jackson will do to him if he finds out."

"Camden could take Jackson…easy," I mutter.

Goldie laughs. "True, but despite the way the two of you have bickered for years, he's a lover, not a fighter."

Erin points at me. "Exactly. He looked at you like you'd hung the moon at broomball. That is not a lukewarm man. You need to pin that man to the wall like you do your favorite recipes." She points at me. "Knead him until he rises."

She tips her head and lifts her eyebrows, eyes laser-focused on me.

The table falls apart laughing.

"She's not wrong!" Ava says.

I press my lips together, trying to rein in my smile and this giddiness taking over…trying not to let their words burrow under my skin. Because I want to believe them. I want to replay every kiss over and over, the way his hand steadied me, the way he looked at me. He's so intense, and normally, I'd think he does nothing halfway, but this— keeping us a secret—it feels halfway.

So the part of me that's learned not to expect too much wins out.

"Well," I say, lifting my fork again, "until he decides to prove it, I'm not going to hang my hopes on secret sparks."

The girls exchange knowing looks. I stab a bite of hotdish with more force than necessary.

Erin grins slyly. "Denial," she singsongs.

Goldie echoes, "Big fat denial."

Even Ava joins in, her voice soft but amused. "Denial with a side of Tater Tot."

I throw my napkin at them, but my heart's not in it.

Goldie's phone buzzes, and she gives us an apologetic look.

"Sorry, I thought I'd turned my sound off." When she looks closer, she giggles. "Look."

She holds up a text from her dad.

It's a picture of Camden and Kevin. Camden is stretched out on the couch, on his side, and the dog is curled up on his hip. Both are sound asleep.

"Dad says he forgot to send this in the group thread this morning," Goldie says. "I'm gonna heart it and then put my phone away because it's going to be buzzing for a while after that."

"Not the only thing buzzing," Erin says, pointing at me. "Look at that swoony face. Mm-hmm, sparks."

I put my face in my hands and groan, which just makes them laugh harder.

CHAPTER NINETEEN

FIRSTS

CAMDEN

The idea hits me in the middle of prep at Elm & Echo. One second I'm whisking together a sauce, the next I'm staring out the kitchen window, thinking about Juju. Grandma Donna is right. Kisses are easy. Dates take intention. And I want this to mean something.

So the next morning, I duck into The Kitty-Corner Cafe before work. The bell above the door jingles, but otherwise, it's quiet in there—I chose a time when I hoped it would be. Juju's behind the counter and looks surprised to see me.

"Hey," she says, smiling at me.

I'll never get tired of that.

"I have a question," I say, lowering my voice as I lean across the counter. "Would you go on a date with me tomorrow night? I know it's Valentine's Day, so no problem if that's too much for you."

Her grin grows, her eyes lighting up. "I guess I could handle that."

Someone walks in behind me, so I straighten, but I whisper, "I really want to kiss you right now, but I'll save it for tomorrow."

"Tomorrow," she says softly.

———

The next day, I put my plan into motion. Grandma Donna's been my co-conspirator, insisting she knows the exact balance of "romantic but practical." She helps me load up a picnic basket she dug out of storage, complete with checkered napkins. I make roasted chicken sandwiches on the fresh rolls Grandma Nancy made, snuck to me by Grandma Donna, and we pack chips and cheese and crackers and nuts and fruit and anything else I can think of that will still be good after a little drive. I even tuck in a little container of the chocolate mousse I once overheard Juju say she was unable to resist. Grandma Donna throws in some cookies and peppermint candies.

I hold up the hand- and foot-warmers I'm bringing, and Grandma Donna nods her approval.

"Good. We don't want our girl getting cold," she says. "It's harder to feel the romance when you're too chilly."

"Yes, ma'am," I say, laughing.

By the time I arrive at The Kitty-Corner to pick Juju up, I'm buzzing with nerves. I told her only to dress warmly, and she listened. She's in her thickest coat, scarf looped around her neck. She looks…adorable.

I tell her so, and I add "And prepared to climb El Capitan" as I hop out to open the passenger door.

"Well, you said *warm*," she says.

I'd hoped she wouldn't glance in the back seat, and she doesn't. It helps that it's already getting dark.

"What are you up to, Whitman?" she asks.

"Thought I'd spend this Valentine's Day with the woman I'm hoping is my valentine."

I look at her once we're driving, and she's staring back at me with an unreadable expression.

"I wasn't sure you were the kind to celebrate Valentine's Day," she says.

"I haven't been in the past."

"But you want to this year…"

"You make me want to, yes, but I'd spend any day with you."

Her lips lift slightly. I hate to look away but hurry to keep my eyes on the road.

Playfully, I ask, "And don't you want to spend the day with me too?"

"Hmm. I guess you're okay to hang with."

"*Okay to hang with.*" I laugh. "Wow. Not exactly what I was hoping for, but I'll take it." I glance over and can tell she's trying not to laugh.

When I smirk, she rolls her eyes.

I don't give her the destination. Instead, I crank up the heat, put on a playlist I know she'll like—half indie, half hits from the mid-2000s—and we drive. The road winds north, trees rising tall and dark against the sky. Her curiosity builds with every mile.

"Are we going to the Boundary Waters?" she gasps when we get closer.

I just smile. "Maybe."

When I finally pull off onto a small overlook, the horizon opens up. The night sky spreads wide and infinite, stars scattered like someone tossed glitter across dark silk. And already, faint streaks of green shimmer at the edges, promising more to come.

Juju gasps again, staring out the window. "Camden."

"Yeah," I murmur, my throat tight.

I cut the engine, hop out, and open the back of the SUV. The seats are folded flat, layered with blankets and pillows. The basket sits at one end, and I line the thermoses neatly beside it. I grab her hand and help her climb in.

"This is…" she starts, then trails off, wide-eyed.

"I'll turn the heater on to warm things up if we get too cold, but I didn't want us to miss the northern lights," I say, settling in beside her. "They're supposed to be crazy tonight."

I open the basket.

"Oh my God, this looks amazing!"

"There are hand-warmers here, and feet-warmers"—I wave at them—"and about a thousand blankets, so you don't freeze."

She shakes her head, grinning. "You thought of everything."

I lean over and kiss her softly. "My grandmas would not approve of me kissing you before the date is over, but I couldn't wait."

She laughs, the sound bubbling out and making the whole night feel warmer.

I pass her a thermos, and we lean back on the pillows, the moonroof above framing the sky like a window to another world.

The first real wave of color washes across the stars—ribbons of green and pink that shift and ripple like magic. Juju sucks in a breath, hand tightening around mine. I don't look at the lights. I look at her, the glow reflecting in her eyes, her lips parted in wonder.

"Worth it?" I ask softly.

She turns her head, and her smile is the kind that makes my heart stop. "More than worth it."

We pull out the sandwiches, and she hums after she takes a bite.

"So good," she says. "You've always known how to make everything taste good."

"I've always thought that about you," I tell her truthfully.

The lights are brilliant. I've never seen such a vivid display of color across the sky. We ooh and aah like we're watching fireworks.

And then the snow comes. And it keeps on coming. Before long, the flakes are swirling hard and fast, making it feel like we're getting dumped on. I straighten.

"This looks like some serious snow." I pull out my phone. "Let me check the weather and see what's happening."

No signal.

"Shit. I forgot that it's hard to get reception up here." Fuck. I was so intent on making everything right for this date, I forgot to do one of the most important things you should do during a Minnesota winter—I forgot to check the weather forecast.

I'm suddenly aware of how remote we are. "We should probably head back before it gets worse."

She nods. "Do you think it's safe to drive?"

The pit in my stomach grows as we get out and move to the front of the vehicle. I start the engine. "If not, don't worry. We'll find a place to stay."

We creep along, my wipers working overtime, but it's not enough. Juju's quiet beside me, her hands tucked into her lap. I can feel the worry bouncing off of her. My gut makes the call. I don't want to put us at risk.

"We should stop," I say.

"I haven't seen any places," she says.

"I think there's a motel not too far." When we finally reach the motel I was thinking about, it's a lot more run-down than I was expecting.

The neon vacancy sign is flickering, and only a couple of cars are out front.

I look at Juju. "I'm really sorry about this. Not how I wanted this night to go." Snow smacks the windshield. "I hate that this is the first place we're ever spending the night," I mutter.

Her laugh breaks the tension. "You mean you didn't plan this romantic roadside motel? On our first date?" She laughs harder.

I shoot her a look, but the corner of my mouth twitches. "Nope, not the impression I was going for. I wanted a cozy picnic dinner with the northern lights, and to drive you back home like a gentleman."

She puts her hand on my shoulder. "It's fine, Camden. We'll laugh about this later." She snorts. "I'm laughing about it now."

"You're right. It's fun just being with you. I just feel bad."

"Don't. I'm having a good time." She points at me. "But if there are heart-shaped beds and champagne glass tubs, I'm out."

I snort, swiping my hand down my face.

"This is what I get for borrowing the idea from myself years ago...the last time I almost asked you out on a date..."

"What? You've never come anywhere close to asking me out...where was I?" She laughs.

CHAPTER TWENTY

SEASONS

JULIANA

Past: Juju, age 21, Camden, age 23

It felt *so* good to be home. I'd opted to go to Chicago to earn my bachelor's degree in culinary arts. Goldie was brave to go all the way to California for college, and I'd been tempted to go with her, but being that far from home felt like too much. Chicago already felt too far to me, but at least I'd be able to drive home in a day if I needed to.

Truth be told, I was a Midwest girl through and through. I could appreciate California and had enjoyed it many times during my visits to see Goldie, but there was so much that I loved about Minnesota…and Chicago too. I loved the seasons, and I loved waiting with anticipation for the leaves to change, bundling up in the winter, and feeling the awe and wonder that came when everything that had looked dry and dead and hopeless sprang back to life in the spring.

But what I loved most was when everyone was in St.

Paul…or Windy Harbor…it didn't matter which place, as long as we were together. As we got older, it had become harder for the Whitmans and Fairs to all be in one place at the same time. So when we were invited to the Whitmans' house one night while I was home for winter break, I couldn't wait to get there.

Game night at the Whitmans' had always been chaos, but it was exactly what I'd craved while I was away. Between the snacks our moms had laid out, Goldie's excited chatter, Dylan's loud storytelling, Tully's heckling of everyone before we'd even picked teams, and Noah's cuddling with his girl-friend Margo, who were stealing kisses every chance they got, the place felt like it was vibrating with energy and laughter.

I hadn't seen Camden in a long time. He had taken France by storm. He worked at a prestigious restaurant there and was gaining a lot of recognition as an up-and-coming chef. He was living a life I couldn't imagine. And yet, there he was, sitting on the arm of the couch with his sleeves rolled up and his hair falling into his eyes, looking completely down to earth. And gorgeous. Always gorgeous.

We hadn't talked about prom night since it happened, but things had been different after that. Softer edges. I no longer hated him for ditching my friendship all those years ago, though sometimes that old sting pricked if I thought about it too long. Still, he was easier to look at now without wanting to throw something at his pretty face.

Tully held up his hand to get everyone's attention. "Okay, teams. I'm gonna do the *one, two, one, two* thing, and then get in your spots."

Camden and I ended up on the same team. He came to sit beside me like it was the most natural thing in the world. My stomach gave the tiniest flip. So ridiculous. We played

Pictionary, a tradition the Whitmans always wanted to maintain—I think because they had a family full of artists. Let's just say, my skills lay elsewhere.

Jackson grabbed a marker and immediately drew something that looked like a potato with legs.

"Is that supposed to be a horse?" Goldie doubled over laughing. "That's a *horse*?"

"Shut up," Jackson said, laughing along with her. "It's obviously a horse."

"It's obviously roadkill," Tully said.

The next few minutes, I laughed so hard I had tears in my eyes. Camden leaned close enough for me to feel the warmth of his shoulder against mine.

"We've got this," he murmured.

"Don't be so sure. I haven't suddenly developed drawing skills since I last played this," I said.

His smile tugged up one corner of his mouth. "I can carry us."

I didn't know why my stomach kept diving every time he looked at me or said something, but it was dipping all over the place.

When our turn came, Camden pulled the slip from the bowl and glanced at me before crouching at the whiteboard.

"Okay, let's do it," he said under his breath.

I watched his hand move—precise, deliberate strokes, like he actually knew what he was doing. A triangle with something swirling out of it. A stick figure.

"Uh, house fire?" I guessed.

Camden pointed at me with the marker, eyes lit up. "Closer."

"Bonfire? Fireman?"

"Yes!" he crowed when I got it, slapping the marker down and looking pleased with himself.

"You got *fireman* out of that?" Jackson complained.

There were a few good-natured boos, and Dylan threw a pretzel at us.

Camden ducked, grinning. "See? We're a dream team."

I rolled my eyes but couldn't stop smiling. "Don't get cocky."

"Too late," he said, nudging my side.

Every nerve ending fired and my face heated. I was glad everyone was focused on the game.

We carried on with more bad drawings, more ridiculous guesses, and more laughter than my stomach could handle. And every time Camden leaned close to whisper a guess, or caught my eye across the board with that secret little grin, I felt it in my gut. I had no idea if it was my imagination or if there was a weird current between us that hadn't been there before.

Maybe he still felt sorry for me. Prom had been years ago, and I'd had way better boyfriends than Eric, but it was possible that that night was the memory of me that was stuck in Camden's head.

Either way, in the past, I would've hated being on a team with him, and this time, I found that I didn't mind it anymore. At all.

"No one guesses *orangutan* that fast without peeking!" Dylan yelled at Tully, and the whole room dissolved into laughter.

I slipped away to the kitchen for a glass of water. I took a minute to drink it, enjoying the quiet for a second. I was leaning against the counter when Camden walked in, head ducked, like he'd had the same idea.

"Oh—sorry," he said, stopping short.

I moved at the same time, which made us bump shoulders. My glass sloshed, dangerously close to spilling.

"Watch it," I said, half laughing, half flustered.

He reached out instinctively, steadying my wrist before I could drop it.

"Guess I'll always be crashing into you. Our origin story coming around full circle again and again," he said softly.

The heat of his hand lingered on my skin, and I pulled back reluctantly. "Some things never change."

He smiled, softer than his usual smirk, and it made my chest feel strange. "You were good out there," he said.

I raised an eyebrow. "Turns out I'm excellent at stick figures."

"That, and we seemed to know what the other person was thinking, whether the drawings were good or not." His eyes caught mine, playful. "I drew a circle and you yelled, 'Santa!' before I even got to the beard or hat!"

We laughed. I didn't know what to do with the way he was looking at me, so I filled the glass again just to have something to hold.

"We did make a pretty good team," I said.

"Pretty good." He nodded. "That's high praise from you." His voice had a teasing lilt, but it was quieter, almost thoughtful.

The noise from the living room surged—Noah shouting, Goldie cackling—and the spell snapped. Camden stepped back, running a hand through his hair. "We should probably get back."

"Right." I nodded, clutching the glass.

As we walked back into the room, I couldn't shake the awareness of his shoulder brushing mine.

He leaned in. "Hey, if you're not too busy, would you want to—"

There was a loud roar of laughter from everyone, and we glanced over, startled. Goldie waved us over.

"You've got to hear this," she said, but before she could say anything else, Stella breezed into the living room, wiping her hands on a dish towel.

Stella Whitman was one of the most beautiful humans ever...one of my favorite people on earth. Besides being gorgeous, she was warm, and kindness seeped out of her pores. She and my mom had been best friends since the time we moved into this neighborhood, and they were more like sisters at this point. Goldie and I had gone on many little getaways with our moms and always had the best time. I'd missed her almost as much as I'd missed Goldie while I'd been away at school.

"You kids are eating me out of house and home," she said, shaking her head, though her smile was full of affection. "I'm going to run to the store and grab a few more things before you empty out the pantry completely."

There was a chorus of protests and offers to go with her, but Stella waved everyone off. "I'll be quick. You won't even miss me. Keep playing. I love the sound of all my kids here." She smiled at all of us. "Love all of you people," she said, giving Everett a kiss.

"Love you!" everyone called out.

"Carefully, babe, the snow is picking up out there," Everett said.

"Okay, I will," she said, giving him one more kiss.

The door shut behind her, and the game carried on. But after a while—forty-five minutes, then an hour—Everett called her. While it was ringing, he asked, "Has anyone heard from Mom?"

They checked their phones, and no one had gotten a text or call. Thirty minutes later and still no sign of her, Noah got up. "I can go look for her."

"She probably ran into someone she knows," Goldie said, though her voice had a brittle edge.

The room's energy had shifted. Worry threaded into the sudden silence.

The knock at the door startled all of us. Dylan was the closest, and he swung it open.

Two strangers stood there—a man in uniform, and a woman holding a small folder pressed to her chest. They both had the kind of expressions you only ever see in moments when words are about to shatter someone's world. I felt like I was watching a movie, and dread bled through me.

"Mr. Whitman?" the man asked, scanning the room. "Everett Whitman?"

When he saw Camden's dad rise from his chair, his face tightened.

"I'm afraid we have some difficult news," he said.

The woman stepped forward, her voice gentle. "Your wife, Stella—there was a car accident. She didn't survive. I'm so sorry."

For a beat, everything froze. The drawings lay scattered on the table, Goldie's marker still uncapped, a pretzel perched in Tully's finger.

And then the silence cracked open. Goldie made a choking sound that didn't sound like her. Noah swore, shaking his head as if refusing to let the words in. Dylan's bravado collapsed; he folded in on himself. Tully's face went blank, but his hands clenched into fists so tight they went white.

And Camden—

I'd never seen him look small before. Not at seven, not at seventeen, or twenty-one riding in to save the day. But now he looked like a little boy. Gutted, like the ground had given way beneath him and there was nothing to grab onto.

I wanted to reach for him, to say something, anything—but the words stuck in my throat. All I could do was stand there with my own heart breaking, watching the Whitmans' world, and ours too, tilt on its axis in a way none of us could ever fix.

My mom walked in from the kitchen. "What's going on?" she asked, her face draining with color like she already felt the worst. She moved to me, and I whispered what had happened. Her face broke, and I held her up as she wept.

I didn't leave that night. None of us did. There was no way I could have walked out, not when Goldie's whole body shook against me as she sobbed into my shoulder. I held her like I'd never let go, whispering useless words that did nothing but fill the space between her gasps for air. And then just being quiet to listen.

By morning, Erin was there too. She'd driven in from Windy Harbor as soon as she heard. She looked exhausted, her hair in a messy knot, so unlike her normally perfect pinup-with-an-edge look. Her arms wrapped around both Goldie and me the second she walked through the door.

"I'm sorry I wasn't here sooner," she said, her voice thick.

The three of us stuck close, moving together through the house as casseroles and condolences started pouring in. We tried to do small things—refilling coffee cups, finding tissues, keeping track of who had eaten. But mostly, we just sat with Goldie, letting her cry, letting her talk, letting her be silent.

The Whitman house didn't sound the same anymore. I'd never heard it so quiet. The laughter was gone, swallowed by the heavy silence of grief. Every sibling wore it differently, and Camden disappeared. Not physically—he was there, always in the room, always within sight—but it was like he'd built walls overnight. He didn't sit with us, didn't let anyone touch him. When I tried—once, softly—just a hand on his arm, he jumped like I'd burned him.

Later, in the kitchen, I found him gripping the counter so hard his knuckles were white. And then he got something out of the freezer, and I heard him talking about a recipe under his breath. "I think it'll be enough for everyone," he said.

"Camden," I whispered, not even sure what I could say.

"Goldie needs you," he said, his voice raw, his eyes blazing.

I froze.

He turned away, but I saw that the tears had finally broken through.

"I can make food for everyone, if you're hungry. I'm here for you too, you know, if you need me," I whispered.

"I don't," he said.

It hit like a slap. But I didn't hold it against him.

I went back to Goldie. Back to the one thing I could do: be the friend she needed. Erin squeezed my hand tight, grounding me, as Goldie leaned against us, her sobs quieting into hiccups.

What I didn't realize that night was that whatever closeness I'd felt with Camden was gone. And it would be a long time before he'd let anyone get close again.

CHAPTER TWENTY-ONE

FIFTY SHADES OF BROWN

CAMDEN

Present

We're shivering by the time we close the door of our motel room. We both stand there, staring in shock at the most hideous room I've ever seen in my life.

Brown. There's so much brown everywhere, so even if it were new decor, which it's very much *not*, it would still look dirty. Brown carpet, brown bedspread, brown headboard, tan walls, brown table, artwork with a deer, so also brown…it's absolutely everywhere, and everything looks like it's on its last leg. I guess the only other color that would be worse in this head-to-toe lineup would be nausea green, but the brown is right up there. Speaking of up, I glance at the ceiling and see huge wet spots. The room smells damp and like the deer from the picture might've run through it and rolled on everything.

"Oh, Juju. I am so sorry. What have I gotten us into?"

She laughs. "Well, this is *something*."

"You're not lying. Can we even do this?"

"Of course we can. We can do anything," she says.

"I had such different visions of how this night would go." I reach out to take her hand and thread my fingers through hers. "Is the heater even working? It feels just as cold in here as it does outside."

"It sounds like it's working. Maybe it was just turned on right before we got here."

"Hopefully it'll kick in soon. I'm scared of what might be in that bed." I look at her with a hopeless expression. "We can safely say our first date is not going great, is it?"

"Are you kidding? I've had a great time. I've never seen such gorgeous northern lights, our picnic was delicious—"

"There's more if you're still hungry," I say, lifting the picnic basket in my other hand.

"I'm good," she says.

"What about me? How would you rate me after this date? On a scale of one to ten..."

"Hmm." She taps her chin and studies me. "The picnic wins you extra points...and so does the creativity of a drive to see the outrageous sky." She squints and puckers her lips, and I want to kiss them right off. "So I think I'd give you a solid...five."

"*Five!*" I croak.

She giggles.

"Damn. And that's with the extra points? After you've had a great time?" I set the picnic basket on the table. It looks only slightly better than any other surface in the room. Then I walk back and put my hands on her waist. "What can I do to improve my score?"

She lifts a shoulder. "How would *you* rate the date?"

"I'd say an eight, and the only thing subtracting those two points would be this dive we're in right now." I lean my face closer to hers. "Those kisses in the SUV seemed like you were enjoying yourself." She fights back a smile, and I laugh as I run my thumb over her bottom lip. "I knew it. You like me more than you're letting on."

"You're all right."

I tug her against me, and even in our wet coats, I feel heated just from being this close to her. "You're more than all right. You're incredible. You have been impressing me for as long as I've known you. And now that I know how it feels to kiss you, I'm blown away." I touch my lips to hers and then press the lightest kiss on her mouth, down her jaw, and over to her ear, where I whisper, "Admit it. You—"

Just then, the loudest wail comes from the heater next to the window, and Juju jumps in my arms.

"What just happened?" She peers around my shoulder to look at the heater. "It's not running anymore."

Sure enough, the loud rattle that's been steady since we walked in is gone. It's like the still of the snowfall outside has moved into this room.

"Fuckin' hell," I mutter, reluctantly letting her go and moving toward the heater. I flip the switch and turn the power on again. Nothing.

I move to the phone and push the button for the front desk, and it just rings and rings and rings. I hang up and try again, and after the fifth ring, there's a groggy, "Hello?"

"Hi, we're in room 104, and our heater just went out. It's not working at all."

"Sorry, sir. Everyone went home because of the storm, so I can't send anyone to look at it until the morning. If you'd like, I can move you to room 106."

"That heater's working?"

There's a pause, and then he says, "It should be."

They all should be, I think, but I keep that to myself.

"Yes, please. We'll try that room."

"Okay, great. Just come to the front desk, and I'll give you a new key."

On my way back with the new room key, I stop and grab a few of the blankets and pillows I brought for the sky-gazing. The snow hasn't let up at all, and the wind is swirling it everywhere. I tuck as much of the blankets in my jacket as I can so they won't get too wet, but there's no way to fully succeed. Still, Juju's face lights up when she sees that I'm carrying them. We walk to the new room, which is slightly warmer, but not by much, and it's not an upgrade in any other way. In fact, the smell is a little more rank.

"What do you think? Do we go for the one that's warmer or the one that smells slightly better?" I ask.

"Maybe we'll get used to the smell," Juju says.

I groan, which she seems to find comical. "Maybe we can open the window for a few minutes? Body heat and all that…"

"That's convenient," she teases.

"It's hard to argue with science."

"I guess we'll do what we have to." She laughs. "I bet Goldie would love to get her hands on this place."

"Several people in my family would see this as a wonderful challenge…I don't have that gene." I grin when she snorts. "I'll leave that to Dad, Noah, and Goldie, and they can leave the cooking up to me."

I lay the blanket out on the bed, and she helps me smooth

the other one on top of it. We fold back the top like we're making a bed.

"I'll run and get the pillows," I tell her.

She nods. "I think I'll take a shower and see if that helps me warm up."

I try not to think of her in the shower but fail.

"Sounds good," I say, getting out of there fast.

When I come back to the room, I can hear her singing "Walking on Sunshine." I can't stop smiling. The shower cuts off. For a second, I only hear my heartbeat. When Juju opens the door and steps out, steam trails behind her. Curls form where her hair is damp in places, curling at the sides and back of her topknot. Her cheeks are pink from the heat. She has her same clothes back on, not that I expected her to pull out anything else when we're stranded in this place. She's so gorgeous it hurts.

"That really helped," she says, her arms around her body like she's trying to keep the warmth from escaping. She smiles at me.

"I think I'll go get one too. Try not to make eye contact with that deer. He's a little suss."

She laughs. "What is with this place and all the brown?"

"It's taking the cabin vibe too far. You gotta break it up somewhere."

She acts impressed. "See? I knew you had at least a little of the gene."

"I mean, anyone would've been able to tell that after two seconds of walking into this room, but I'll let you believe I'm skilled in all the ways."

I step into the bathroom and shut the door. Once I've stepped into the shower for a minute, I get feeling in my hands again as I thaw. We were supposed to end tonight with me kissing her good night at her door, not under buzzing fluorescents and a heater that's barely hanging on. The whole one-bed thing too…should I have offered to get another room? Fuck, it didn't even cross my mind to do that.

I crank the water hotter and try not to overthink anything for at least the next three minutes.

When I come out, Juju is sitting cross-legged on the bed with the blanket tucked around her legs.

"Feel better?" she asks, smiling at me.

It hits me again, the way it has numerous times since things changed with Juju and me, how happy I am that she's smiling at me again. I stare at her, and it must be intense because her head tilts as she stares back.

"What are you thinking?" she asks.

"How beautiful you are. How lucky I feel to be here with you anywhere, even this trash motel."

She smiles. "You think I'm beautiful, huh?"

"Is that really a question? Yes, I've always thought you were the most beautiful girl there is."

Her cheeks flush, and she swallows. "I didn't know that."

I move toward her and sit down, facing her. "I should've told you so long ago."

"Would've made me a lot less…abrasive where you're concerned." She bites the inside of her lip as she tries to hold back her smile.

"We've had plenty to say to each other, haven't we?"

She snorts. "You could say that."

The heater lets out a loud wail, and we look at each other in horror.

When it dies, I yell, "Noooo."

I move toward the head of the bed and hold out my arms. She moves into them, and I pull the blanket over us.

"Unbelievable," I mutter. "I want to make out with you so

fucking bad, but I'm too worried you'll get frostbite if I trail my tongue…anywhere."

She gets the giggles, and I'm laughing in the next second too.

"We're just trying to survive," I say dramatically.

She burrows her face into my neck. "It's pretty fun…and hilarious. Our own little adventure. And do we really want memories of our first time doing…anything"—she peeks up at me, her cheeks flushing—"in this room?"

"I'd do…anything with you…*anywhere*. But you're right. I've gotta have it be more special for you than this."

"Wherever we are is special…but I think we'd better preserve our body heat." She holds on tightly to me.

"Here, let's lie back." I lift her and slide us both down on the bed, making sure that our heads are on my pillows and nothing gross. We lie there facing each other, our bodies locked together, and then I pull the blanket over our heads. "Our own little adventure in our very own little fort," I say.

Electricity hums under my skin when she closes that last inch and kisses me. She makes a small sound that ends me. My body is on board with doing all of this right here, right now, but then I feel how cold her hand is when she hooks it behind my neck, and then I notice how icy her nose is.

I force myself to pull back and take her hands in mine, trying to warm them up. "You're freezing."

"I'm fine," she says.

"Let me call and see if they have more blankets."

She wrinkles her nose. "Okay."

I hurry out of the blanket and smile when she pops her head out.

"Brr," she says.

I call the front desk, and a woman answers this time. "So sorry your heater's not working, sir," she says when I tell her what's going on. "I'll come take a look and bring more blankets."

"Oh, thank you," I say, surprised.

There's a knock on the door a few minutes later, and I open it to a woman almost as tall as me. She's wearing a sweater, no coat, no gloves. She hands me a pile of blankets.

"I'm Birgitta. Let me see if I can get that heater running," she says.

"Thank you," I say, opening the door wider.

She comes in and gets out a few tools, muttering under her breath the whole time. I take the blankets to Juju and lay them over her, tucking the edges around her body until no air can get in. She grins up at me.

"Okay, I'm glad we have more brown blankets," she whispers, checking to make sure Birgitta didn't hear her.

I hold back a laugh and try to be helpful to Birgitta, even though she doesn't need me—the woman is more than capable.

"I think I can get this working," she says, her voice gruff but her eyes warm.

"Really? Oh, that's good news. Thank you," I say.

And within minutes, Birgitta straightens. "I think I've fixed it for now. Let me know if it dies again or if you need more blankets."

We thank her profusely, and she tells us to have a good night.

I climb into bed next to Juju, careful at first not to undo all the tucking I did around her, but she slides her leg over, tangling it with mine.

"I'm glad you stopped," she says, her chin resting on my chest as she looks up at me. "We could've been in trouble out there. It's been a long time since I've seen a storm that bad. And it's so dark out there…"

"Good thing no one had to come tow us…"

"Jackson would've had a lot to say about that."

I wrap my arms around her. "He would never let us live it down." I sigh. "My mom would have a lot to say about this motel."

She laughs softly. "Yes, she would. I miss her," she says quietly.

"Me too. I can't decide if I miss her more when things are bad or when things are good. Both, I guess. I want to tell her about it all."

"She was the best listener," she says.

"Yes, she was. And she'd definitely approve of us not lying directly on the bedspread or sheets."

Juju laughs again, gentler now. "She'd also tell you that you're a good man for stopping and that it was worth all the germs we might be inhaling just by breathing this air."

I swallow around the lump in my throat and kiss the top of her head. "Then I'll take it."

She looks at me and sniffs. "Do you smell it anymore?"

"All I smell is your berry shampoo," I say happily. "I have always loved the way you smell."

"I'm learning all kinds of things tonight," she says softly.

Our eyes lock, and we move toward one another at the same time. Our mouths collide, and I forget why we ever stopped kissing in the first place. She tugs me tighter and lets out a soft moan when she feels how hard I am. All I have to do is look at her and I'm hard, so being this close is both sheer agony and the fucking best. I hitch her leg over my thigh and love the way she whimpers when there's better friction. She kisses the way she fights, the way she laughs, the way she cooks, the way she loves—all in. And I can't get enough. She rocks against me, and I feel like I might explode right here, right now.

I pull back, and we're both panting hard.

"Juju…I'm dying to taste you," I say, hoarsely.

"You *are*?"

I laugh against her skin at the way she squeaked.

"Is that okay with you?" I ask.

She nods, her eyes wide.

I move to her ear and whisper, "Your clit and I are gonna be best friends."

She gasps, and I fucking love it.

"Yes, please," she whispers.

"I'll keep you warm," I tell her as I duck under the covers.

As I make my way down her body, I stop to lift her sweater and kiss her breast over her bra. When I lower the lace and flick her nipple with my tongue, she hums.

"I wish I could get a better look at you. It's too dark, but you feel so good," I say against her chest. I go to the other side to play with that peak, and her hips arch against me. "Do you want me to hurry up?" I tease.

"Yes!" she says, squirming against me.

"So impatient."

I move down, lifting her sweater again to kiss the skin above her jeans. And then I slowly unbutton her jeans and lower the zipper and tug them down along with the soft material covering her up. I really do wish it was easier to see her down here because I am dying to see what every inch of Juliana Fair looks like.

First, I slide my nose along her slit and inhale. "I can't wait," I tell her. "You don't know how long I've dreamed of doing this. When we're someplace warm again, I want you to rub this pretty pussy all over me."

"I don't know how you keep managing to surprise me, but

you do," she moans. "I had no idea you were gonna be a dirty talker."

"I haven't really been before," I say. "But you're the one I've been dreaming of for a lifetime, so I wanna say it all. And I want to do it all. If you'll let me."

She lifts the blanket up so I can breathe, and I inhale, moving my head up slightly to try to look up at her. She makes me laugh when she tugs my head back down.

I press a kiss on her clit and slide my tongue over her, groaning when I get my first taste. Even better than I imagined.

I stay there for a while, taking my time, working her up and then not letting her fully get there. And then I start over, slowing things down and building, building, building, until she's whimpering. When I use my fingers and open her wider, diving my tongue in deeper, she rocks against my tongue, and one more time I take her close to the edge and then back off, starting a slow build all over again.

She's shaking with need.

Her scent and taste are *intoxicating*.

I'm hard as a rock, getting off on this without her laying a finger on me. I'm exactly where I want to be. I slide my finger inside her, while I pay attention to that little bud that's a hard peak now. When I put two fingers inside, she starts fluttering against me, crying out, and I have mercy on her this time and let her come.

The sounds she makes...good God. They're the sweetest, sexiest sounds I've ever heard. My fingers are soaked, her wetness sliding down my arm. I try to follow her body's cues of when to let up and slowly pull my fingers out, dipping my tongue back inside her gently and moving my thumb to just slightly press onto her clit.

"Oh my God, Camden!" Her hips come off the bed, and she comes even harder this time.

It's the best thing that's ever happened to me—making her fall apart like this.

When she lets out a shuddering exhale, her hands falling from the grip she's had on my hair, I emerge from the covers and take a deep breath. She giggles.

"You were under that blanket for a long time," she says.

"Worth every second." I hover over her, pushing her hair out of her eyes, and then I kiss her, slow and deep, wanting her to experience how good she tastes.

"I want to make you feel good too," she says against my mouth.

"I can't even express how good I am right now," I tell her. My dick raises its head in defiance, but I'm trying really hard to ignore the pulsing need I feel for her right now. She's finally warm and sated, and when it comes to the happiness factor, so am I. "We've got time, Juju. I plan to spend many more nights doing that and so much more."

We kiss again, and I move off of her. The room has heated up—either that or we've warmed each other up—but it's still not exactly warm in here. She cuddles up to my chest, and eventually we shed one of the blankets. The windows are fogged up.

"You're really great at that," she says sleepily. "Crazy finger and tongue coordination."

We laugh at that, and she goes quiet afterward.

"Sweet dreams, beautiful," I murmur against her hair.

"I'm not sleepy," she says.

"Such an adorable little liar."

"Shut up and hold me," she whispers, her lips lifting against my chest.

"As you wish." I tuck the blanket tighter around her, both hands splayed over her back.

The motel hums. The winds rage on. Her breath evens out.

I stare at the deer over the desk.

"I'm right where I want to be," I tell him.

It's not where I pictured our first date ending, but I like it better this way.

Our way.

CHAPTER TWENTY-TWO

A LITTLE HELP FROM MY FRIENDS

JULIANA

When I blink awake, the sunlight is blinding. The scratchy brown curtains are doing nothing to block it out. For a second, I'm not certain where I am, but then I realize my head is propped up on a broad chest, and my leg is wrapped around a thick thigh that, even through my jeans and his, feels delicious. The faint hum of the heater that rattled all night is still going strong, thank goodness.

"Morning." His voice is deep and gravelly.

"Morning," I whisper back.

I lift up and look at him. It's so strange. This man I've fought with for years, who's driven me crazy with his attitude, is looking back at me with such longing. I don't know how I didn't see it before. He looks younger, calmer. His dark hair is messy and he must be sore from this lumpy mattress, but he smiles at me like this is his happiest moment.

And I know it's mine. I feel like I'm living a dream. Last night…no one has ever made me feel like that. *Ever.*

My cheeks are suddenly hot, so I try to distract him.

"It looks like the snow stopped," I say, tilting my head toward the window.

He looks out the window. "It's pretty out there. Prettier in here."

I sit up, hugging my knees to my chest. "Yes, it is," I say shyly.

His eyes are soft when he smiles at me. He gets up and looks out the window. "It looks manageable out there."

"The roads look good?"

"A lot better than last night." He glances at me and smirks. "So…we both already told our people that we got stuck out of town last night…"

"No one knows we're together, though," I add.

He gets a funny expression. "Right," he says slowly. "And good thing we kept that to ourselves. News travels so fast in Windy Harbor—the entire town would know by the time breakfast is over. What if we…don't rush back just yet?"

I raise an eyebrow. "Don't rush back?"

He watches me carefully. "What if we continued this date?"

I bite my lip, feeling entirely too excited. "What exactly did you have in mind?"

"We could head back to Windy Harbor…hide out somewhere. Duluth…or St. Paul. I owe you something romantic after this dump." He gestures around the dingy motel room.

I laugh, shaking my head. "We had romance under the sky last night." I will always remember being out there watching the lights take over the sky, and the way his kisses left me breathless in the back of his SUV. "And amazing things happened in this dingy motel…"

His eyes light up. "Yeah? I know it was amazing for me." He moves toward me, and I hold up my hand before he can kiss me.

"I need to brush my teeth and get the smell of this room off of me before we get to…whatever we get up to." I try to give as seductive a look as I can after I've just talked about the smell of this room being on me.

God. I need to get cool, stat. I need to channel some Erin or Goldie.

"I have an idea," I say. "Just in case the roads are worse than we think, and so we're back in town for work tomorrow…what if we go to the apartment above the cafe? It's vacant right now. I actually get it cleaned once a week, just in case anyone needs it, so it's ready. I could make some food, and we could hang out there."

"I love this idea." He nods, grinning. "I'm incredibly stealthy. I can come up the back stairs and in your back door."

He freezes, and my shoulders shake with how hard I laugh.

"I mean…that's not what I meant…unless…you want me to," he says, barely getting the words out through his laughter.

"Let's see how it goes." I'm still cracking up. It feels really good to be like this with him.

"Right," he says in mock seriousness.

"And I'm not so sure you know how to be stealthy either. You're six four and walk into rooms like you're making an announcement without even trying."

He pulls back, affronted. "I will…internally announce myself."

I snort. "Okay. Sounds like a plan."

I keep Papa Hector updated on everything. Well, not

everything. He doesn't know I'm with Camden, but he knows I went out of town last night and got a room because of the weather. I let him know that I'm going to take a little rest at the apartment today. He texts back for me to get all the rest I can and to say the word if I need anything. I feel awful for not being completely honest with him.

We get on the road, only stopping for gas station coffee and two doughnuts the size of plates, and we drive south. The lake flashes through the trees, a glassy pewter sheen. The plows have been busy, and the sky is so vivid and blue, you'd never know a storm came through last night.

I text Goldie and Erin.

> I need your help.

And then I try not to be too obvious about what I'm doing while I ask them for a huge favor. When we get into town, Windy Harbor looks beautiful, with snow lining every roof and tree branch.

"You can drop me at the corner," I say.

"Should I give you an hour or two?"

"That would be perfect. I'll let you figure out your story. Alley, back stairs. If you get stopped, you're…checking our dumpster."

He nods, all business. "I have deep concerns about trash."

"Very convincing," I say

Even when we're being ridiculous, my heart trips in my chest with how right it feels.

I slip into the cafe to check on everything. The bell above the door tinkles, and it's one of the rare occasions that I'm glad for no customers. I picked a good time to come. Suzanne looks up from the counter.

"You look…like you need a nap," she says diplomatically.

"Loud heater, long night," I say. "How was the morning rush?"

"We're golden," she says. "Everything went smoothly. I got your text. Please, go upstairs and stay invisible." She grins and winks. "Goldie dropped off the groceries, and I took them upstairs already. You deserve a break! Take tomorrow off too, if you need it! I can cover."

"Oh, I'll be back tomorrow, but thank you so much, Suzanne."

She lifts her shoulder. "Let me know if you change your mind."

I blow her a kiss, and then I duck through the swinging door to the back hall and climb the narrow staircase to the apartment.

I pull the linen shade halfway over the big front window. Privacy without hiding. Once I've lit three candles in mismatched jam jars, I tuck a sprig of rosemary into one because I'm extra like that. Deep breaths.

I'm looking in the refrigerator when I hear a knock on the door.

"It's me," Erin sings. Another knock. "Juju?" She manages to sound amused and threatening all at once. Only Erin. "You alive, or are the chickens running the cafe now?

I open the door wide.

"Hi," I say, cheerful and breathless. "I'm alive."

Erin looks me over and inhales and exhales in pure exasperation. "You did not do the deed."

"Well, not yet." I hold up a finger. "But something did happen."

Her mouth drops and her eyes light up. "Do tell."

"Let's just say Camden knows what he is doing." I try to hold back my grin, but it doesn't work.

"Girl, you are not going to leave me hanging there! I assume I won't have to tell him how to find the important parts then? I mean, he looks like he would be capable, but often the prettiest ones aren't."

"He said he and my clit were going to be best friends." I cover my face and peek out, my face flaming. "And I have to say, they're already getting along *really* well."

"Ahhhh," she yells. "Attaboy, Camden! This is making my *life*. And this must be why you're here, right? To rail him against every surface?"

"Well, one can hope…but I'm just gonna make him some food, and we're going to hang out."

She waves me off. "None of that blasphemy." She winks. "This is exactly why you need this dress. It is foolproof, I swear."

"What did you bring? You were supposed to just bring that dress I left at your house…and a new razor." I laugh.

"I did you one better. I brought this pretty black dress *and* this phenomenal underwear. Thank me and Scarlett Landmark tomorrow after you ride him like your favorite horse."

"But I don't really like riding horses," I start.

"Work with me here!" she cries.

I laugh. It's so fun to provoke her.

"This dress isn't too much during the day?"

"That dress is never too much. It will be smoking with your blonde hair." She puts her fingers to her lips and kisses them. "Mwah." And then she leans into the doorjamb, eyes glittering. "Saw a very tall man in a not-so-subtle hat escaping from the alley not too long ago."

"Lots of tall men," I say. "Lots of hats."

"Uh-huh," she says, grinning. "Listen, if you need

someone to create a diversion for any reason, text me an eggplant and three water drops."

I press a hand to my chest. "What would I do without you?"

"You'd be lost without me. *Lost!*"

"Yes, I would."

She hugs me, and as she's backing away, she says, "And tell Mr. Hat, if he breaks your heart, I'll take all of his knives and scrape them over a sidewalk."

"I'll be sure to pass that along," I say.

She grins and jogs down the stairs.

I take a quick shower and get ready, feeling better already. Erin was right about the dress. It's the sexiest dress I've ever worn, and it fits perfectly.

As I start working on a late lunch, I hear three knocks on the door.

I open the door, and he's there—no hat now, pink cheeks, snow melting on his lashes. He's changed into a button-down shirt, and his hair is damp from a shower. He shrugs his coat off and hangs it on the hook next to the door.

"Hi," he says, voice hushed like someone is listening.

I yank him in and shut the door with my hip. We stare at each other for a beat, and then his lips are on mine. He backs me into the wall and kisses me senseless.

"You look beautiful," he says, when we break our kiss. "Gorgeous."

"So do you," I say.

He kisses me again, and I melt against him.

"Hungry?" I ask, because otherwise I'm going to make a sound that the downstairs customers will definitely hear through the vents.

"For…a variety of things," he says, eyes wicked, voice sexy low.

"Food first, Whitman," I boss, and he obeys so readily my knees consider buckling.

"What can I do?" he asks, rolling up his sleeves.

Forearms. Yum.

"You can pour wine and not be a chef tonight."

"I'll do my best," he says, already assessing my knives. I body-block him from the drawer. He laughs, hands raised. "I'll be good."

I make an easy pasta and a colorful lemony salad. We have a loaf of bread that Suzanne left up here, along with brioche bread pudding. I add a butter rum sauce to take our dessert to the next level.

Camden opens the wine like an expert, pours two glasses, takes a sip, and hands me a glass. I keep pinching myself over the fact that he's here. With me. Smiling at me like I'm everything he craves. The lights and the music are low—Billie Holiday sings through the little speaker, the radiator humming in the same key, and the cafe sounds busier than when I was down there. Camden leans on the counter and watches me with that soft look that knocks me off-balance.

"You're glowing," he says.

"Steam," I lie.

He just smiles like he can see right through me.

After we set the table, I slide the pasta into bowls, twisting it into cute little nests with tongs.

"Juju, I swear, your food will always be my favorite," he says after the first bite, his voice reverent.

"Seriously? After all the restaurants you've eaten in, all the chefs you've worked with…"

"I've had delicious food, you're right." He nods. "But yours is the best. You have a way of taking the simplest ingredients, and it's like sorcery, the magic you create."

He squeezes my knee under the table and leaves his hand

there, slowly going higher to rest on my thigh. After that, it's hard to focus with the meteor shower going wild behind my ribs.

When the timer goes off, I jump up to get the bread pudding out of the oven, and the apartment fills with the smells of vanilla and rum. He groans when he takes the first bite.

"Sorcery," he moans.

"Wow. That means so much, coming from you. But seriously, Camden, you're the GOAT. Come on, you know this, right? I used to watch videos people posted of you…there were a lot of you in France, but even more from Whitman's. I was so jealous that I couldn't experience your food. I saw a video of you making a pie crust, which shocked me because you always left the baking to me…"

"That's still true…I've had the worst luck with pastry chefs, but Virginia is turning things around." He takes another bite of bread pudding and looks at me with dreamy eyes. "I'd still rather have you," he says.

He leans over and kisses me and then suddenly pulls away.

"Okay, let's do these dishes so fast," he says.

"You're thinking about dishes right now?" I laugh.

He gives me the side-eye. "Juliana Fair. I know you. Dirty dishes are not in your makeup."

I laugh harder. "I think I could make an exception!"

"Be honest. If you left those dishes and happened to fall asleep or get distracted or something," he says with a smirk, "you're telling me you wouldn't wake up in the middle of the night and come in here to finish them?"

I sigh. "You do know me."

He grins with satisfaction and stands, pulling me up. He gives me another kiss once I'm upright, and when we part, he motions for me to go first and then gives my backside a little slap. I jump and laugh.

"I'm moving, I'm moving."

"I really just wanted to see this view of you in that dress."

I turn and look at him over my shoulder, and he curses under his breath.

"We're not in a dingy, freezing motel tonight," I sing.

He points at the kitchen. "You will not distract me from the dishes!" He laughs at the ridiculousness of that statement and marches to the kitchen, where he fills the dishwasher so fast it's comical.

"I didn't know you could move that fast." I put a few more things in the dishwasher and close it, giving him a flirty look over my shoulder.

He smirks and advances toward me, looking like a man on a mission.

"What would you like to do?" he asks, putting his hands on my waist and moving my hair to the side to kiss the back of my neck.

"I'd like to continue what you started last night," I say, putting my hand on the back of his head as he nuzzles me.

"There's nothing I'd love more," he whispers.

When he straightens, I hold my hand out, and he takes it as we move toward the bedroom. It's not very late, but it's dark out already, and when we move to the bedroom, the lamp is low, and the streetlamps outside give off a romantic glow.

I turn around slowly, and he's right there. His hands are still on my waist, and I put mine on his broad chest, loving that I can touch him like this now. The next thing I know, his mouth is on mine, and this kiss is slow and unhurried. But then he bites my lower lip, and there's nothing slow about what happens next. I lean on my tiptoes, and his hands move to my backside, groaning when he feels me.

"I've been dying to get my hands on your ass for a long, long time," he says between kisses.

I reach back and start to unzip my dress, and he takes over the rest. When he slides it over my shoulders and down my hips, he watches the progression, his tongue reaching out to wet his lips like he's hungry.

"Fuck," he whispers when my dress drops to the floor. "Juju."

It's the reverence in his tone that spurs me on, that and the fact that I want him so much I can hardly think straight.

I unbutton his shirt, my fingers working way better than I thought they would, given my eagerness. I have his shirt off in seconds and take a deep inhale when I see his chest. I lean forward and glide my tongue down his chest as I work on getting his pants off. The reward is so great when I do. I take a step back, my body protesting as I move away from him, but I have to see just how gorgeous he really is.

It could be intimidating, how perfect his body is, but I'm emboldened by the way his eyes are raking over every inch of me as if he can't get enough either.

He tugs off his black boxer briefs, and my knees weaken when I see all of him. My mouth goes dry and I flood between my legs, craving every part of him.

"Your turn," he says, a soft smile playing on his lips. When his hand grips his cock and he gives it a slow slide up and down, I swallow hard.

"What?" I hear myself say. I sound far away. My eyes are still glued to his cock. I don't think I've ever seen one any bigger or more perfect.

"Let me see you," he says.

"Oh," I say, biting my lower lip. "You are so distracting."

He grins and does a little sweep over his tip that has me feeling jealous of his hand. Then he points at my chest.

"Do you need help getting naked?" he asks.

It brings me out of my daze, and I reach up and undo my bra, letting it drop to the floor.

"Perfect," he says. "I've always thought everything about your body is perfect, you know. Your ass, those legs," he groans, "and your tits. What I said when we were teenagers was so far from what I thought. When I saw you in a bikini that same summer, I felt so guilty about the way I wanted you."

"Really?"

"Many times in my life, it's felt like your body was put in this universe just to drive me mad. Like the untouchable fruit, within sight, but out of my grasp at all times."

He steps closer and puts his hands on my breasts. My nipples are hard little points, and he bends down and takes them in his mouth, making me forget any insecurity I ever had about being in the itty bitty titty club. His hand is so big that when he rests it on my hip, it covers part of my stomach and back. He bends to his knees, and the sight of him down there threatens to undo me. His free hand slides my panties down my legs. He presses a kiss at my center, and then does a slow lick up my slit.

"Camden," I whisper. "I want you."

"You've got me," he says, flicking his tongue over my clit.

"I want you inside me."

In the next moment, he's on his feet. He puts his hand on my chest, and I step backward as he moves forward. His eyes are gleaming with promise, and the anticipation is more than I can take. When the backs of my legs hit the bed, I climb on and stay on my knees. He gets on, facing me, and when our bodies line up, skin to skin, it's like electricity sparking.

We kiss…and kiss and kiss…and our hands are feral and greedy. He lifts me like I weigh nothing and lays me back. I reach out and wrap my fist around his cock, squeezing him.

His eyes close and his mouth parts, and when his eyes open again, they're glazed over.

"I have condoms," I say. "From Erin," I add.

His eyebrows lift slightly.

"She gives them to me often, trying to nudge me in the direction of sex."

He laughs. "Thanks, Erin."

"And I'm also on the pill." I lift my shoulder. "And all clear."

"Me too. Condoms and all clear." His brows furrow. "Are you saying you want to—"

"I'm saying I'm good with it, if you are."

"I'm good with it," he says, eyes wide. "I've never…"

"Me either," I rush.

I pull his face down and kiss him, too impatient to wait any longer.

CHAPTER TWENTY-THREE

STEALTH MODE

CAMDEN

I don't want to even blink, in case I miss a second of this. Juju, lying back, staring up at me with those intoxicating eyes and mouth, her perfect body stretched out in front of me, saying words I never dreamed she'd say and then kissing me like she can't get enough. I have to slow down or this will be over before we've even started.

But she's tired of waiting, and fuck it, so am I.

When her hands wrap around my dick again, I can't prolong it anymore. I wrap my hand around hers.

"Show me where you want me," I tell her.

Her breath hitches, and she brings me to her slick core. She's wet and warm and feels so fucking good. When she swirls my tip around her clit, I get impossibly harder.

"Mmm," I moan.

And then she glides me along her slit, up and down, before centering me and taking in just an inch. I'm surprised when she lets go, feeling the loss immediately, but then her hands find my ass and she clenches my cheeks, driving me inside her until I'm in as deep as I can go.

I didn't want to hurt her, so I would've gone much slower, but goddamn, she was ready for me.

"*Fuck*." I draw out the word, all the blood drained from my brain and into my dick, rendering me incapable of saying anything else.

She lets out a long moan too, once I'm inside, and her mouth parts when my dick pulses. She clamps around me, and that's it, I can't be still.

"Are you okay?" I manage to grind out.

"You feel better than anything," she says.

"You do…too…the best fucking thing I've ever felt."

She arches into me, and I start a relentless pace. She takes it all, meeting me with thrusts of her own like she can't get me deep enough. The sound of us—my balls slapping against her, her wetness taking me in, and our breaths and moans—it's the most erotic thing I've ever heard.

Every part of me feels alive and hyperaware, every nerve ending firing off. All I see is her, all I feel is her, all I *want* is her, and she's finally here. *We're* finally here. I can't believe it, and at the same time, it feels so right.

"You feel so right," I say out loud.

I reach between us, needing to make her feel good in every way possible. When I rub circles over her, keeping my thrusts inside her steady, her head falls back, and I can feel her getting close.

Victorious is the only word I can think of when I feel her start to twitch around me. "That's it," I say. "God, you feel so good. Come all over me."

Her eyes squeeze shut, and the little moans she makes shoot straight to my dick. It takes everything in me not to lose my shit right then and there, but I wait it out. She looks lust-drunk when she opens her eyes again, and I grin.

She tugs my head down and kisses me hard, and our thrusts get clumsy and frantic.

"I'm so close again," she says.

She squeezes my ass, and at the same time, I feel her spasming around my dick.

"*Oh*," I moan. "Come with me."

"I am." She gasps. "*Camden*," she whimpers.

A tidal wave crashes through me, the sensation so intense I close my eyes and see spots. I come so hard, it feels endless, and we both feel the aftershocks for minutes afterward.

I stare down at her, not wanting to move, but I slowly pull out of her and turn to face her. "That was…incredible."

She turns to face me too. "It was okay."

My mouth drops, and she giggles. I reach out and tickle her, making her laugh harder.

"Tell the truth," I say between tickling her sides.

"Decent," she breathes out.

"Are you a tease, Juliana?"

"Maybe," she says with a smirk, trying to avoid my hands.

I lean in and kiss her, and she softens into me.

"Okay, it was better than okay," she says, pulling away.

"That's what I thought."

"Don't get cocky. That might've been first-timer's luck."

"Oh, little tease, you and I will only get better."

"You think so, huh?"

She gets out of bed and gives me a coy look when she turns and catches me staring at her ass as she walks to the bathroom.

"Your ass should come with a warning label," I tell her.

She laughs and rolls her eyes. "What would it say?"

"'Caution: Will bring grown men to their knees.'"

She snorts. I glance down again and curse.

"Hold on right there." I move toward her. "I'm dripping out of you," I say hoarsely.

She gasps when I reach down and swipe it off her thigh and hold my finger up to her mouth. My heart nearly shuts down when she leans forward and licks it clean. Her mouth comes off with a pop.

"Fuck *me*." I stare at her.

"Been there and done that," she says, cheekily, and then turns around and closes the bathroom door behind her. I swipe my hand down my face. It's going to take me some time to get over that image.

A few minutes later, she comes out, and I take my turn in the bathroom. When I'm done, Juju's back in bed, looking deep in thought.

"Are you okay?" I ask.

She nods. "I'm great. I think I'm in shock that we just did that."

"I get it." I crawl in bed beside her and pull her into me. She lays her head on my chest. "A good kind of shock?"

She leans her chin on my chest and grins at me. "Yes, a wonderful kind of shock."

I lean down and kiss her, and she scoots closer, her fingers diving into my hair. I pull her on top of me, and she grins against my mouth when I get hard underneath her.

"You're just wanting to prove it wasn't luck, aren't you?"

"We can call it that, if you want to," I say.

She laughs and grinds herself on me, her teeth clamping down on her bottom lip as she hisses.

"Too soon?" I ask.

"No," she says shakily. "You feel so good."

She guides me into her, and we go slower this time. I inch

into her a little bit at a time as she stretches around me. We kiss, and God, I love the way she kisses. I could spend days with her mouth and not come up for air.

She teases me by lifting just enough that I think I'm coming out before lowering onto me again, and she does this until I'm delirious with wanting her. When she sits up and I'm completely seated inside her, I'm overwhelmed by all that I feel. It's beyond the physical, way beyond.

I never imagined we could fit together so perfectly.

The high I feel watching her fall apart is something I didn't see coming. I knew it would be different with Juju, but there was no way of knowing the extent of it until I experienced it. When you have the kind of feelings I have for Juju, it takes sex to a whole different level.

I'm working with her, lifting her hips up and down as we go faster and faster.

"How have I gone this long without you?" I say, lifting up to kiss her.

Our bodies are slick, and we never look away from each other as we cross over into oblivion.

She cries out my name, and that sound alone is enough to send me flying.

We're both trembling by the time we lie back, trying to catch our breath.

"It's hard right now to remember how cold we were last night," she says.

I laugh. "I feel like I could walk out in the snow naked and still be sweating, that's how worked up you got me."

She's grinning when she looks up at me. "We could go try out that ship."

"You're not too tired?"

"Might not be a long bath, but it sounds nice right now. I'm a little sore," she admits, making a funny face.

"I'm so sorry. I was afraid we weren't going slow enough."

"It's the best kind of sore, and it's my fault for being impatient. And you can't help it that you've got a lot to work with."

That makes me laugh.

"I'll run the water," I tell her.

"Mmm, I doubt you'll get it as hot as I like."

I snort. "Do you like your baths as hot as your tea?"

"Hotter." She laughs.

"I'm getting second-degree burns in this bath, aren't I?"

We both get out of bed, and she lifts her shoulder. "I guess I can go easy on you."

I grab her waist and pull her against me. "Somehow I have a hard time imagining you ever going easy on me."

"What do you call what we just did?" She puts her arms around my neck and tugs on my hair.

"You rode me hard and fast. There was nothing easy about it. You set my body blazing."

Her face splits with a huge smile. "Erin would be so proud."

"Do I even want to know?"

She's laughing as we go into the bathroom. "Probably not."

I look at the tub again. "You do remember I'm six four, right?"

She giggles. "This should be fun."

And it is. I think more water ends up on the floor than in the tub by the time everything's all said and done.

It's one o'clock in the morning when we finally get out of the tub.

"Is it okay if I stay?" I ask. "I'll set an alarm when you get up for the bakery. It's what, two hours from now?"

"Something like that." She makes a face.

"Hat, alley, trash alibi."

"Because you're so stealthy." She laughs sleepily. "Yes, stay. It's been a long couple of days, and you need your rest. Don't worry—I'm not gonna get any ideas just because you stayed the night."

That makes me pause, but she looks so tired, I don't question it. We get in bed, and I kiss her once more before she curls into me. I trace lazy patterns on her shoulder until we're both asleep.

A couple of hours later, both of our alarms go off. We silence them, and I reach out and run my hand down her back as she gets up. We dress in whispers, stifling laughter when I pull one of her sweaters over my head by mistake. I'm exhausted but energized at the same time.

She's in the bathroom pulling her hair back when I'm ready to go. I walk over and kiss her cheek. She turns to face me, and I cup her face in my hands.

"This was…the best night I've ever had," I tell her.

"For me too," she whispers.

I steal one more kiss and put the hat on, which makes her laugh. When the door closes behind me, I laugh as I pass the dumpster and make my way home. Once I get there, I text her.

> Mission: complete. Dumpster status: contained. State of mind: captivated.

CHAPTER TWENTY-FOUR

WE THOUGHT YOU WAS A CHICKEN

JULIANA

My skin feels tired and I'm aching in the best ways, but I can't stop smiling as I make my way downstairs. I pad to the kitchen, turn on some music, and start the water for coffee before I get busy.

Suzanne set me up really well for the morning. Everything is already prepped. Veggies chopped for soups, meats sliced for sandwiches, and the dough for the bread is ready to go. I spend the next couple of hours baking, and right before the cafe is supposed to open, I spill what's left in my second mug of coffee down the front of me.

I sigh, grab my coat, and head outside. I'm surprised to see a larger path than normal shoveled between the cafe and my house. It's a little warmer than I expected and the snow doesn't look too icy, but I still take my time crossing the snow. A screeching "Ra-ra-ra-raooo!" stops me in my tracks. I turn to see what in the world that was, and one of the hens comes charging after me. I pause, thinking I'll be able to talk it down, but oh no, it does not let up. I bolt into the house and shut the door behind me, bending over to catch my breath.

I look out the window and jump when Papa Hector says, "Good morning, sweetheart."

"Good morning." Still breathless.

"You okay, dear?"

"There's a very angry chicken out there! It chased me!"

"What?" Papa laughs and looks out the window.

The chicken spots me staring at it and lets out that "Ra-ra-ra-raooo!" sound again.

"What in the world?" Papa says, frowning. "Is that…a rooster?"

"I guess it is starting to look a little different than all the rest," I say, peeking carefully from behind the curtain this time.

"Well, would you look at that," Papa says. "I believe he is a rooster."

"What's he doing out of the coop?" I put my hand on my heart, willing it to calm down.

"That is a good question," Papa says. "I'll get him back inside."

"Careful, he is out for vengeance this morning."

Papa chuckles. "Aw, nah, not these guys. They're all as gentle as can be."

I snort, eyeing the rooster warily as Papa goes out. The rotten little thing doesn't make a peep when he sees Papa. He also doesn't make it easy for Papa to catch him. I start to get worried Papa will slip on the ice trying to catch that guy, so I step outside to help.

"*Ra-ra-ra-raoooooo!*" The sound is even louder this time, and he comes charging toward me, looking like an avenging protector.

Fearing for my life, I grab the snow shovel and wave it toward him, and he lifts off the ground, his wings fluttering. With all the commotion, Papa is able to catch up to him, and while I'm saying "Watch out, don't let him hurt you," the little bastard goes right in Papa's arms without any fuss.

"I don't know what got into him," Papa says. "He was *not* happy with you!"

"Okay, Ralph," I say to the rooster. "You need to settle right on down."

He gives me the beady side-eye and somehow manages to look smug as Papa carries him to the coop.

I hurry inside to change and rush back to the cafe. By the time the shop opens, I'm ready for a nap. Papa and Uncle Hal come in around seven, already singing. Then Erin and Goldie show up a few minutes later, and they both look at me and laugh knowingly.

"What gave me away?" I ask.

"The way you're glowing like a fluorescent light," Erin says.

I wrinkle my nose. "Fluorescent lights are obnoxious."

"She meant like delicate twinkle lights," Goldie says, elbowing Erin.

Erin pretends to be annoyed, but she's grinning. "Mm-hmm, exactly what I meant."

"It was a good night then?" Goldie asks.

"It was an *amazing* night," I say under my breath.

Goldie does a little dance, and Erin crosses her arms, looking at me like a proud mama.

"Don't forget you owe us the details," Erin says, pointing at me.

"Well, not too many details because...he's my brother," Goldie says. "I mean, I want to know...because it's you, but…ugh…it's complicated." She laughs awkwardly and then gives me an apologetic smile.

"Don't worry. I'll spare you." I shake my head when Erin protests. "Both of you," I add. "If it never happens again, it'll still be a night I'll never forget."

Both of them give me sideways looks and then speak at the same time.

"What do you mean?" Erin says.

"Of course it'll happen again," Goldie says.

I lift my shoulder. "I don't know. I think it probably will, but I'm just taking it day by day…"

Goldie is frowning when she says, "Well, you need to be thinking a little more long-term than *that*."

"As long as we're keeping it a secret, I don't think so," I say. "I like him, but…will he ever let me in all the way?"

I can't think about it too much. It stings to be a secret. It feels safer to just put it in a *We'll see what happens* category.

The cafe picks up, and I say my goodbyes to the girls, promising we can catch up more later. Once the breakfast rush ends, I pour myself another cup of coffee. I'm running on fumes, but thoughts of Camden keep me moving, simply because I think of him approximately every five seconds.

I'm in the middle of adding a cake to the pastry display case when Bentley walks in.

"Hey there, gorgeous," he says with that easy grin.

He slides onto a stool at the counter.

I get a little anxious with the way he looks at me. I thought I'd been clear about the whole *We're just friends* thing, but now I'm not so sure.

I smile back, keeping it friendly but not *too* friendly.

"Hey, Bentley. What can I get for you? Coffee?"

"You know me well," he says, his smile widening.

Papa Hector and Uncle Hal come from the back with trays full of fresh scones.

"Again?" Uncle Hal mutters. "Doesn't this guy have a job?"

Heat creeps up my neck, but when I look at Bentley, he doesn't seem to have heard anything.

The bell over the door rings, and I look over, happy for anything to distract me from Bentley and my scowling grandpa and great-uncle. I don't know what they've got against Bentley, but they are *not* fans.

My stomach flips when I see Camden walk in.

But he spots Bentley staring at me and growls.

He actually growls.

It's like the cafe suddenly goes silent. Even the espresso machine pauses in mid-hiss.

Camden looks at me and gives me a look that reminds me of when he was telling me to come with him. My cheeks fire up. He clears his throat and straightens his shoulders like he'll play off that growl that just came out of him.

"Morning." His eyes flick to Bentley. "Hey, think you could do me a favor? Swing by and pick up some truffles from Duluth for the restaurant?"

Bentley blinks. "Uh…sure? If you need it."

"Great. Appreciate it." Camden claps him on the shoulder, and Bentley, looking equal parts confused and amused, drains his coffee and heads out.

I chase after him before he can hit the sidewalk. "Bentley—wait. I'm sorry about…whatever that was."

He chuckles, easygoing as ever. "It's fine, Juju. I didn't stop to consider that maybe you and Camden had…something. Guess that answers it."

I make a face. "It's—complicated."

What am I supposed to say when Camden wants to keep it a secret?

"I just…I'm really hoping we can stay friends," I add.

"Of course. I'm not going anywhere. I'll probably see you tomorrow…if he doesn't send me on another errand." He laughs. "Your coffee and blueberry muffins…*and* your Hungarian mushroom soup…and grilled cheese…all are too good to pass up." He winks. "See you later."

When I walk back into the cafe, I find Camden leaning against the counter, smug as a tomcat.

"Seriously?" I hiss. "You *growled*?"

He raises a brow. "Got the job done."

Papa Hector and Uncle Hal crack up at that. I didn't even know they were listening. I glare at both of them, and they sober up.

"You liked it," Camden says.

"I did *not.*"

He smirks and pushes off the counter, lowering his voice so only I can hear. "Your cheeks are red, little tease. Redder than your oven mitts."

My eyes narrow. "Because I'm annoyed, and I just had to go out in the cold to make sure Bentley was okay."

He scoffs. "That guy is just fine. I saved you from his relentless flirting. Besides, if anyone's going to flirt you up, it's going to be me."

My pulse skitters. "Camden—"

"Juliana," he murmurs, eyes glinting with mischief. "Did you let him know you're not into him?"

I roll my eyes. "That is none of your business."

He straightens, all teasing gone. "Really?" he asks, his voice soft.

I huff. "Yes, I told him I'd like to just be friends."

His lips quirk, and he tries not to smile.

I point at him. "Knock it out. You can't growl at someone for flirting with me. We are not—"

"You're right," he jumps in. "I'm sorry. I'll make it up to you. Dinner tonight? I can set it up in the little cove off of my office."

"You don't have to do that. I know you don't have time for that."

"I'm making time, Juju." He leans in and whispers, "You're worth it."

And damn him, because even as I mutter about his ego and the nerve he has, my heart's already saying yes.

CHAPTER TWENTY-FIVE

BLAZES

CAMDEN

Past: Camden, age 24, Juju, age 22

Ever since my mom died, I didn't know who I was. Every part of me felt unmoored, like someone had left me bobbing out in the middle of Lake Superior with no anchor in sight. My siblings and I were all floundering, trying to keep my dad afloat while barely keeping our own heads above the surface. I'd been back and forth from France, trying to convince myself that I needed to carry on—my mom would want that —but it wasn't working. It was hard to be home and even harder to leave.

This time was especially hard. It was our first trip back to Windy Harbor without Mom. She loved this place. She loved any chance to be by the water, and the view from our house was her favorite. I could hear her laughter every- where, her insistence that we go down to the water no matter what the weather was like, her humming as she brushed the sand that we'd missed off of us before letting us back inside.

Without her, Windy Harbor felt hollow.

Even though we kept things moving, stayed active, and tried to fill the spaces, the walls echoed with all that was missing—our life here with her.

We were all trying our best. But we were unraveling. Noah was going through a breakup with his long-term girl-friend, Margo, *and* she was pregnant. Tully was on a profes-sional hockey team, but he was partying too much and getting in too many fights on the ice. Goldie looked like the spark had gone out of her eyes. She had finished school and was considering taking a job in California, but I couldn't tell if she was excited about it or just trying to keep moving like I was. Dylan had just announced to the family that he wasn't going back to the U of M…he was opening a surf shop in California. Totally left field.

My poor dad. He was quieter than I'd ever seen him. He worked way too hard and was insistent that we not worry about him, but we all did. He looked haggard, but any time any of us tried to stick around to be there for him, it seemed like we just upset him more. He wanted to be together when it worked out for us, but he also wanted us to keep our commit-ments and live our lives.

None of us knew the right thing to do.

It felt like all of us were just going through the motions. When everyone finally went to bed, I felt the walls closing in on me.

I went outside and found myself walking toward one of the places I'd always felt carefree—the tree house. This place had been a refuge when I was a kid. I'd spent many days there with my brothers and sister, and with Jackson and Juju. In the early days of building it, sometimes I felt like the entire world was no bigger than the boards under us and the sound of the lake in the distance.

The ladder creaked under my weight as I climbed. When I reached the top, I pulled myself inside, feeling like a giant in the small space. And then I froze.

Because Juju was already there.

She whipped her head toward me, her eyes wide. "Camden?"

The last couple of times I'd seen her, I had been awful. She'd tried to comfort me when Mom died, and I'd shoved away any kind of sympathy. Throughout the past year, she'd tried again to show kindness to me, and I hadn't been exactly the worst, but I hadn't been warm either.

I didn't know why the thought of her comforting me made me feel like I'd break, and there'd be no fitting myself back together.

"Juju." My throat was dry. "I didn't think you guys were in town."

She looked stunning. As always. It hurt to look at her. Her hair was pulled back in a high ponytail, the ends swishing around her arms. She wore a fitted tracksuit, and I wanted to drink her in but tried really hard not to stare at her.

"My parents and I got in tonight. Jackson will be here a little later," she said. "Sorry. I know it's probably weird that I'm here. I just…still like to come out here sometimes."

"I get it."

The silence between us stretched, broken only by the faint groan of the boards under us. I didn't know whether to back out and pretend I'd never come or to make an effort.

Juju decided for me. She sat on one of the pillows, tucked her legs to the side, and asked quietly, "You've been in France?"

I nodded and sat down across from her. The tree house had so much less space now than when we were kids.

"Mostly," I said. "I'm back and forth a lot. Not quite sure where I'm sticking."

Something in her eyes flickered. Not pity so much as understanding. "I get that."

"Yeah? You're done with school, right?"

She nodded. "I'm glad to be back in St. Paul. I'm working for a family restaurant…it's not that great." She crinkled her nose. "But the experience is great…good practice. I…I'd love to open a cafe. Here…in Windy Harbor."

She looked at me shyly.

"Really? That's great. You should. You'd kill it."

Her lips parted slightly, like maybe she hadn't expected me to back her up. "You really think so?"

"I know it. You'd be incredible at it. You have everything it takes."

She let out a long exhale. "Wow. I didn't know how much I needed to hear that. Thank you."

I gave her the slightest nod.

"You know that old coffee shop that closed? It's been a lot of things—Superior Grind…Black Bear Coffee—I can't remember what all." She waved her hand. "Anyway, it's empty again, and I think I'm going to try to get in there."

"Juju. That's amazing. Really. Do it."

The boards creaked as we shifted closer. The walls seemed to shrink. Moonlight poured in through the cracks in the wood, and the twinkle lights made her face look silver. For a heartbeat, we just stared at each other. I noticed how her lashes curled against her cheeks, the cupid's bow in her top lip, her full lower lip…

Her gaze flicked to my mouth, and my chest constricted. I always felt like I was doing something wrong when I let myself imagine this, but she was here, in front of me, and this was very real.

"Camden," she whispered.

I leaned in before I could think better of it, closing the distance until I could feel the warmth of her breath. I could almost taste the promise of her lips. Her eyes fluttered shut, and my heart slammed against my ribs.

And then—POP.

We both jolted, eyes huge.

"That didn't sound good," I muttered. I stood up and held out my hand.

She took it and stood, looking at the floorboards.

The tree house groaned.

"We've gotta go. I think it's not strong enough to hold us anymore."

We hurried to the opening, and I helped Juju to the ladder, holding the top of it steady as she climbed down, and then I followed. The second my feet hit the ground, we heard another loud crack.

We spun around to see the floor of the tree house—the exact spot we'd almost kissed moments before—splinter and collapse, crashing to the ground in a heap of boards and nails. Dust puffed up around us, and Juju grabbed my arm with a gasp.

I glanced at her, and she looked crushed.

"I can't believe it," she breathed.

"I'm sorry. I should've never gone up there. I don't know what I was thinking."

"It's not your fault. I mean, neither of us probably should've been up there, since we built it years ago. The poor thing badly needed an update."

For a moment, we just stood there, both of us rattled. Then she looked at me, and her expression shifted. Regret and maybe a little bit of panic. Her grip on my arm loosened, and her hand dropped to her side.

"I'm sorry," she blurted out. "I don't know what I was thinking up there. I mean…" She swallowed, hugging her arms around herself. "Well, I have a boyfriend, and…"

The words sliced through me. Of course she did. Why wouldn't she?

I forced my jaw to unclench and tried to play it cool, even though my pulse was still going nuts from everything that had happened in the past ten minutes.

"Right," I said flatly. "It was just…" I shook my head. "Something to do. Passing time. There's not much to do in Windy Harbor…you were there."

Fuck, the more I said, the worse it got.

Her lips tightened. "Yeah. Exactly." She laughed sharply. "God knows I feel absolutely nothing for you either. It was just a lapse in judgment…on both our parts."

My brain was roaring that there'd been no lapse in judgment where I was concerned, but how emphatically she'd stated that she felt nothing for me forced me not to let that out.

"Don't worry about it. We all lose our way at one point or another."

She let out another laugh that felt more like a slap.

"*You* don't worry," she said. "I've found my way again. Won't make that mistake again."

"Guess that boyfriend isn't doing the best job if you're looking for kisses elsewhere."

"Nah, more like I was missing him, and you were there."

She walked away, leaving me standing there with the rubble. We'd not only destroyed the tree house…we'd torched our short-lived reconciliation.

CHAPTER TWENTY-SIX

FILLING THE AFTERNOON

JULIANA

Present

I get a call later in the afternoon. Camden.

I look around before I answer. It's the afternoon lull, so the cafe is quiet. Papa Hector is in the kitchen, and last time I checked, he was reading the paper at the little table back there.

"Hello?" I say.

"Hey, beautiful. So…there's been a slight change in plans," he says. "I'm sorry. I don't know if you've heard from Jackson yet because he's been here all afternoon, but he's throwing an impromptu party tonight at the restaurant…with both our families."

My phone buzzes, and I hold it out. "He's calling now."

He laughs. "I figured he wouldn't waste any time. I really tried to push it back, to say I couldn't do tonight, but you know how he gets when he's got something on the brain."

"Oh, I know how he works." I sigh. "Well, it'll be good to hang out with everyone."

"I really wanted you all to myself," he says.

My heart warms and I smile, but I try to be nonchalant when I say, "It's probably for the best. I need to get to bed earlier tonight anyway."

"I can't convince you to stay over tonight?" He sounds disappointed.

"You think we'll keep things a secret if I stay for the night?"

He groans. "I didn't have enough time with you last night…and I've been thinking about you all day."

I want to be with him too, more than anything, but I've thought about him obsessively all day, and I worry that I'm just a way for him to get all his sexual energy out. We've moved from enemies to peace to sex pretty fast, and I feel like I need to keep my wits about me, even if those wits are barely hanging on by a thread.

His pattern in the past, whether intentional or not, has always been to make me feel like we're getting closer, only for him to push me away. I don't want to think about the other shoe dropping all the time, but it *is* hanging over my head a bit. I can't let him break my heart again.

"Thinking about me is good," I say coyly.

"Mm-hmm. Little tease…I didn't realize how many ways you'd fit that name when I called you that the first time."

"Almost like you're speaking it into existence," I say, laughing.

"I want to kiss you quiet right now."

I gasp. "You don't want to hear my words?"

He groans again. "No, I always want to hear your words…less so when they're shutting me down."

I can't help the laugh that comes out.

"You're loving this, aren't you?" he says.

"A little bit. The quiet, stoic Camden Whitman has a dirty mouth *and* wants me all to himself. What's not to enjoy? If you were here, I'd pull you into the walk-in cooler and teach you a lesson—"

I hear a snort behind me, and I turn to see Everett Whitman. My face drains of color, and I have to hold on to the counter to steady myself.

Camden is saying, "Don't threaten me with a good time, Fair. Give me twenty minutes and I'll be right there."

"I've gotta go," I say.

"What? All right, I see what you're doing, little tease." He laughs. "Will I see you tonight?"

"Mm-hmm," I say before hanging up.

I meet Everett's eyes and gulp.

"Hey, Juju. How's it going?" Everett asks, unable to hold back his grin.

"It's going." I laugh awkwardly. "What can I get for you?"

"I'll have your grilled cheese with a slice of tomato…and a large mug of chamomile tea."

"Coming right up." I get his hot water and teabag right away and slide it across the counter to him, and then I get to work on his food while he sits on a stool and watches.

"Everett, I'm really, *really* sorry you had to hear that," I say.

A laugh roars out of him. "I'm not," he says. "In fact, I cannot tell you how thrilled I am to hear about this development." He leans over and squeezes my shoulder, and I pause as I'm putting cheese slices on his bread to look up, and I see his earnest expression. "Stella and I always hoped the two of you would end up together."

My breath stutters, and with a wobbly voice, I say, "You did?"

He nods. "Parents notice things, and Stella was always far more perceptive than I was, but even I always noticed the way the two of you were drawn to each other…even when things were…less than friendly," he says diplomatically. "When you went away to school, Stella said again that she thought when the time was right, you'd find your way to one another."

"It's not…I mean…we're not…" I'm a stuttery mess. "Camden would like to keep it a secret." It comes out in a rush and then hangs there.

Everett blinks and then lifts his eyebrows. "Really?"

He couldn't sound more surprised.

The weight of it lands between us.

"Well, I'm sure he has a good reason, although I can't think of any," he says before wincing.

"He thinks it's better this way…mostly because of Jackson. They have that agreement, you know."

"I always thought that was a ridiculous agreement," he says.

"And then there's the fact that our families are close. It could be weird, if…" I leave the rest unsaid.

He looks at me for a moment and then smiles. "And what do you think?"

I freeze. What *do* I think?

I can't tell him what I think…that keeping it a secret puts a bubble around us where everything is private and heady and nothing can touch it. That I see the allure there, but it also makes me want to stand outside and yell, *Mine*. That I want to kiss him out on the street and never have to explain to my brother that we're not a bad idea. That I'm afraid Camden is using Jackson as an excuse for not really being sure that I'm anything more than a good time. That I'm afraid I am more into him than he is into me. God, I hope we're on the same page.

"I don't know yet," I say honestly. "I like him. A lot. But I don't…know what we are."

Everett's eyes soften. "That's fair."

"Your family has been through a lot…Stella…your health…I don't want to make anything harder. And I'm just not sure what I really mean to him…and I don't want to push him to find out."

He sets his cup down. "Secrets can be okay for a little bit, but you don't deserve to be kept a secret for long. I'm surprised he wants to hide something that makes him smile the way he has been lately."

I pause. "He's been smiling?"

His mouth twitches, and he leans in conspiratorially. "I've caught him several times smiling at nothing." He lifts his hands up like *That settles it*, which makes me laugh. "For what it's worth, Stella would have had a fit about this being a secret. She would've been throwing a party. She liked to expose joy in the brightest light possible."

"I miss her," I say softly.

"So do I." He nods as we exchange a look. "So do I."

I hand him his sandwich. "Are you sure you don't want a sweet treat too?"

"You know I do, but I'm trying to lay off some of the sweet treats right now."

"Okay. Understood."

"If you decide not to keep it a secret and Jackson has a problem with it, send him my way. I can give him a reality check about how short life is. You've gotta live your best one while you're here."

I nod. "Thank you. I'm going with it for now, but…I'm not sure how long."

He sobers, studying me. "Understood," he says, echoing me. "In that case, I will practice selective amnesia and pretend I didn't hear any of that, unless you need me to say my piece."

"Thanks, Everett."

"Anytime."

He eats his sandwich, and we talk about the latest updates on Windhaven until he's ready to go.

"This has been fun," he says when he gets up. "I hardly ever get you all to myself. It's rather enlightening." He winks. "I think I'll have to time it out to happen again sometime… see what else I can discover."

I laugh. "You'd be surprised at the things I hear inside these four walls."

"Whew." He shakes his head. "I'm scared to even ask. We don't want to get these walls talking…"

He puts his coat on, and I go around the counter and hug him.

"You've always been so special to our family, Juju. Nothing will ever change that. Okay?"

I pull away and look up at him, nodding. "Okay. Thanks, Everett. Your family is so special to me too. That's what makes this so scary and so wonderful…"

"It's going to be okay. Trust me on this. Now that my boy has had the sense to let you in, he's not going to let you go."

I watch as he leaves the cafe, waving one more time before he opens the door, and the gust of cold comes wafting in.

I hope he's right.

CHAPTER TWENTY-SEVEN

CROSSED WIRES

CAMDEN

Elm & Echo is humming even before the festivities begin, so when the Fairs and Whitmans start piling in, it becomes a low roar. It's not even everyone yet. Noah is here with Grayson, but Tully and Dylan aren't in town. Grayson hasn't left my side since he got here.

"Uncle Camden, if I eat everything on my plate, can I have one of those?" He points at the massive lava cake at the next table.

"Absolutely."

"I'm starving," he says.

I laugh. "Okay. I can get you started on some chicken tenders and fries, if you want...or that pasta you like sometimes."

"Chicken tenders and fries!" he says.

"All right, we'll get you set up."

We go back to the kitchen, and I ask Bobby to have Hannah bring Grayson's food out when it's ready. We brought apps out already, but he wasn't really going for those. Unbeknownst to Juju, the only reason I caved with Jackson this afternoon is because her parents drove in earlier to surprise her. Once Jackson had worked out the party arrangements, John and Margaret agreed to hang out with Everett until dinner to keep it a surprise. They're seated with my family, and Hector and Hal are here too.

Everyone but Juju, Goldie, and Milo has arrived, and funny enough, neither has Jackson…the guy who insisted we do this in the first place. My eyes are on the door every few seconds.

"When are you gonna join us, son?" my dad asks. "You look like you're waiting on someone…" He smirks.

I frown, trying to figure out why he's looking at me so funny, but Annie and Hannah huff past me, so I hold up a finger to my dad and move toward the twins to figure out what's going on.

"I thought you didn't like him," Hannah says.

"I thought *you* didn't like him," Annie fires back.

Both cross their arms over their chests and glare at each other.

"Hi, ladies. What's the problem?" I ask.

It's weird how hard it's become to remember how being a teenager felt. I'm reminded daily, watching Annie, Hannah, and Joey interact with one another. From what I can tell, both girls like Joey, and Joey can't figure out which twin he likes best.

"She was just hanging out all night at the front, and I had to get the drinks for two of her tables!" Hannah tells me, flinging her arm toward her sister.

Annie's cheeks flush. "Joey was overwhelmed by the

large party, and I was just trying to help get the Whitmans in their seats," she argues.

Her eyes trail over to me like she's waiting for me to correct her, since she and I both know that I made a point to come out of the kitchen to take care of my family when they arrived.

"How about we both get where we're supposed to be. It's a good thing we don't have any surprise critics here tonight." I look around, making sure that's still true. Yep, I know everyone in the room. "Table six needs a bread basket, and table four is waiting for their drinks. Joey can handle the front. If he can't, I'll deal with him…not your responsibility."

Annie's cheeks flush again, and she mutters "Okay" quickly before dashing off to table four.

On my way to the kitchen, I overhear Hal telling Grandma Nancy, "Darlin', you look devastating…landing straight from heaven…" He taps his heart. "Right here."

Grandma Nancy does not blink. She turns her head slowly to face him. "To smite your foolishness."

His head falls back as his laughter fills the restaurant.

Juju walks in with Goldie and Milo. Her hair is down, and she's wearing tall boots and a sweater dress that hits mid-thigh. Damn, she looks so good, I'm not sure how I'll concentrate for the rest of the night. She barely gives me a glance, and for a second, I forget that we're keeping us a secret and wonder if she's mad at me. I don't like it when she walks right past me without even trying to sneak a word in or anything. It's all forgotten when she spots John and Margaret. She squeals and rushes to hug her parents. The joy on her face gives my chest a pang.

Erin and Ava walk in a few minutes later. Erin holds both arms up like *I have arrived*, and Ava looks around shyly.

"Erin asked Goldie if it was okay if we crashed," Ava says.

I hug her. "Of course—you should be here. Jackson put this little party together, and he hasn't even bothered to show yet."

I focus on the food and get everyone set up with what they want. I work with Bobby for a little while, and then he finishes up for me so I can go out there and eat with my family.

I text her with one hand under the table.

Hallway by the office in 3?

She only glances at her phone for a second and doesn't type back. She does glance my way and smirks.

I see you, little tease.

"Camden, the food is excellent," Grandma Donna says.

"This walleye is the best I've had," John says.

"So is this steak," Margaret adds, smiling at me warmly. "And this salad! Does the chef ever tell his secrets?"

My eyes flash to Juju, who's staring at her plate.

"Come on, you can give me the recipe," Margaret adds. "I won't tell anyone."

Everyone laughs.

"Only for you," I say. "And you and you," I add when my grandmas protest.

Hector leans over and whispers something in Grandma Donna's ear, and she ducks her head, her cheeks turning pink. Noah and Dad stare at them, and then at Hal and Grandma Nancy, looking like they've bitten a lemon.

"I forgot you hadn't seen all the flirtation going on," I say, chuckling. "It's a sight to see."

"You aren't kidding," Dad says. "I mean, good for them,

but…" He shakes his head like he's trying to will the images away. "It's something," he finishes weakly.

"It's wholesome in a way," Noah says quietly. "Hector and Grandma Donna, that is. Not Hal. That man wouldn't know wholesome if it hit him in the face."

Dad and I laugh.

"Mom seems to be holding her own," Dad says and then shudders. "I need to wash out my eyes with soap."

Noah and I crack up.

"I think that's the mouth usually," Noah says.

"That too." Dad laughs. "And the ears while I'm at it."

"Hello, everyone!" Jackson says.

I look up and he's in a suit, smile wide, and next to him is one of the girls he brought to broomball. I can't remember her name…or if I ever even knew it to begin with.

"Everyone, I'd like you to meet Dove…my wife."

What the fuck?

Everyone just stares at him for a long pause, and then I move to my feet and pound him on the back as I congratulate him.

"Motherfucker!" I say under my breath.

He just beams at me.

His parents get up, looking stunned, and he introduces them to Dove.

Juju is slower to move toward him, and when he sees her standing there, he looks sheepish.

"It was a sudden decision. When you know, you know."

"Apparently," she says. "Hi, Dove. I'm Juliana, Jackson's sister."

Dove opens her arms wide and hugs Juju, rocking them back and forth.

"I am so excited to have a sister!" she gushes.

"Yes!" Juju says, trying to get there with her enthusiasm. "Me too," she says softly.

She stares at me in wordless shock before excusing herself to go to the bathroom. I wait a solid minute before getting up. I've almost made it to the hallway when Jackson materializes with a fresh drink in hand.

"Hey, you need a drink?" he asks.

"I might. It sounded like you said you got married?"

He laughs. "Yeah. I know it was an impulsive decision, but look at her, man. She is unbelievable. We have had the best day."

"Did you get married before or after you asked to get the families together?"

"Right after," he said. "I thought it would be fun to surprise everyone. I'm more about the party than the wedding."

"If I'd known, I would've cleared out the restaurant, and we could've really made a party out of it."

"Nah, no need. Thanks for doing all this tonight. We won't be staying too long. Got things to do." He winks.

"Wow, you have…I can't believe you're married…"

He squeezes my shoulder. "Are you sure you don't want to see her friend again? I'd love for you to be as happy as I am with someone you love."

"I'm positive," I tell him. "Do not think of setting me up with her friend."

"Suit yourself." He grins.

Juju walks past us, and Jackson follows her back to the table. I sigh and head back myself.

"Time for dessert, Uncle Camden!" Grayson says across the table.

"You're right." I signal to Hannah, who nods before moving toward the kitchen.

Within a few minutes, the tables are filled with several helpings of every dessert on the menu.

"Virginia has outdone herself," Goldie says. "Wow, Camden, you hit the jackpot with her."

"Her desserts aren't quite as good as Juju's, but it was as close as I could get," comes out of my mouth without me thinking.

The whole table stops and turns to look at me.

I glance around and see Goldie cover her mouth with her hand. Juju's face is flushed and her eyes are wide. Jackson looks confused.

Dad clears his throat. "Well, of course. We all know Juju's desserts are superior to anyone's." He leans in like he's telling a secret. "In fact, her sandwiches and soups are better than yours too."

Everyone laughs, including me.

"Interesting," Noah says under his breath. "Very interesting."

"Shut up," I mutter.

He just laughs. "Sounds like someone's softening where Juju's concerned. Finally." He grabs his chin between his thumb and forefinger. "Or probably not softening at all…"

I kick him in the shin, and he yelps and laughs even harder. I can't be too mad. It's a challenge to make my brother laugh this hard. He used to be a lot lighter when Mom was alive. Losing her and having a son without Mom around…none of us like to think about the fact that our kids won't have her in their lives. I'm just grateful my dad's health has turned around. I can't even think about losing him.

"Oh, I'm so full," Goldie groans.

"I can't eat another bite," Grandma Donna adds.

"I'd like to propose a toast," Jackson says.

My God. This night is all over the place.

He motions to Bentley, who's been swamped at the bar all night, and Bentley comes out with glasses of champagne. Katie follows him with another tray.

"To my wife, Dove, and family. To many years of happiness," Jackson says.

We clink glasses and sip our champagne.

The round of goodbyes begins about ten minutes later, and like most Minnesota goodbyes, they linger on and on and on.

I catch Juju at the host stand.

"You keep running," I murmur. "I keep chasing."

She doesn't look at me. "Just doing what you asked."

"You okay?"

"Besides being gut-punched by my brother marrying someone he doesn't even know? Sure."

I make a face. "I don't know what the hell he was thinking."

"I have a pretty good guess," she says, rolling her eyes.

"Office?" I try. "Five minutes?"

"Five minutes," she finally agrees.

But her mom comes over then and puts her arm around Juju. "What a night." She shakes her head. "I don't even know what to think." She laughs quietly. "Are you about ready to go? Goldie said you rode with her and Milo. We can take you home."

Juju's eyes meet mine. "That sounds good, Mom."

"Good night, Camden." Margaret hugs me. "This was such a lovely night, surprise announcements and all. I know it must have just felt like work for you, taking care of us and making sure everything else was running smoothly, but we all really enjoyed the night. I know Jackson appreciates the effort you went to."

"I enjoyed the night too. Thanks, Margaret. And hopefully, it's a good beginning for Jackson and his bride, having us all wishing them well." I rub my hand down my jaw.

"Let's hope you're right. You'll have to come over while we're here," she says.

I glance at Juju. "I'll do that." I tilt my head. "Juju, would you have a minute to—"

My dad pounds my back. "Son, exceptional food."

Grayson's arms wrap around my legs. "Night, Uncle Camden."

Juju and her mom hug Grandma Nancy and Grandma Donna, and I stare after them as they walk out.

I go back to the kitchen once everyone's left, and the next time I get a break, I call her.

She answers on the second ring. "Hey, Chef."

"Hey, you home?"

"Yeah, just said good night to Mom and Dad. I'm really glad they're here."

"It was a fun surprise."

"I can't believe you knew!"

"Not until this afternoon." I pause. "Tonight felt all kinds of wrong."

"What do you mean? The surprise wedding announcement?"

"Well, yeah. That. And it felt like we were magnets that could never connect."

She doesn't say anything.

It leaves me feeling unsettled.

"I really wanted to kiss you," I say.

"I wanted to kiss you too."

"Come to the Cities with me."

"When?"

"Whenever you say? We could drive down in the afternoon, get a great dinner, spend the night, sleep in…and the next day we could go to one of Tully's games."

It's quiet for a beat.

"That sounds fun. I've just never taken this much time off work before…and I'm not sure how long my parents are staying. Probably not long, but I want to be around while they're in town."

"Of course. You can see them. We'd be right there for the game."

"Seems like it might wreck the kind of weekend you were thinking about, for me to go off for a few hours."

"I could let you out of bed for a few hours," I say.

"Oh," she says, and I can hear her smirk. "Is that the kind of trip this is?"

"I want to wine and dine you a little bit too," I tease. "Dinner, drinks, kissing you all night long…"

"Scandalous," she gasps. And then in a normal voice, she says, "It sounds fun. Let's do it."

"Okay, keep me posted on a time that seems good for you."

"I will."

"Good night, beautiful."

"Good night."

I finish closing with the crew. I step inside the cooler for a minute and let the cold chill my face. When I turn out the lights and lock the doors behind me, I wish I were going home to Juju. What would that feel like? To have her smiling up at me from bed when I got home.

She'd probably be asleep most of the time with her early mornings. But I'd pull her back to my chest and hold her all night long.

It makes me wish for things I didn't know were possible.

CHAPTER TWENTY-EIGHT

GOING ROGUE

JULIANA

My parents stay for the next few days, and we have the best time. Jackson and his new wife are the topic of many discussions, but after their surprising announcement, they left for their honeymoon, so there are still a lot of holes in knowing how this wedding happened. The only time I've seen Camden was when he came into the cafe and tried to subtly ask when he could see me again. So far I haven't worked out a time.

I'm not trying to be difficult. I just don't know how to keep our relationship a secret from my parents and the town if we're around each other.

I can only keep my lustful eyes to myself for so long.

His dad already knows, but he swore he would keep it to himself, and I trust Goldie and Erin with my life. I feel bad that I haven't exactly kept my end of the secret-keeping bargain. I'm sure he hasn't told a soul.

I just know that if we're around each other, my mom is

too perceptive not to see right through me. She already looks at me funny whenever she catches me staring dreamily into space.

During my break, I step outside, wanting to make a quick run to the house. Ralph, my nemesis, keeps sneaking out of his heated coop and going rogue. He sees me coming and starts hauling his little claws toward me as fast as he can.

"Ra-ra-ra-raooo!" he yells.

It's like he has a radar for when I'm in the vicinity. I don't know what I did to him in his past life, but the little dude has it out for me. It's a shame because he's turned into quite a beauty. He's all white with pretty red plumage or whatever it's called. I'm too bitter about his attitude toward me to find out.

I grab the broom that I keep on hand for my safety because earlier in the week I didn't have protection, and that little freak got me with his spur. It's a good thing I had jeans on, but he still drew blood.

He reaches me and does his little *Come at me, bro*, half flying, half two-stepping, and I intend on just shooing him with the broom, but he's closer than I realize, and I send him truly flying. He lands across the yard in the snow, and I rush over.

"Ralph, I'm so sorry. Are you hurt?"

He gets up and looks slightly dizzy for a second, but then he notices me standing there and rears his head back. "*Ra-ra-ra-ra-oo!*" he screeches before coming after me again.

"Ugh. So much anger, Ralph," I say, running away from him as fast as I can. "You need to take a page out of the hens' playbook." I try to pet the little one I've named Peaches as I race to the back door, but I keep it brief because Ralph is on my tail, and he's having none of it.

I make it inside and close the door, leaning against it to catch my breath.

"Did Ralph get you again?" my mom asks with concern.

"He tried. I accidentally sent him flying with the broom."

She snorts, and I laugh before walking over to kiss her on the cheek.

"Are you and Dad still planning to leave today?" I put my hands on her shoulders, facing her.

We stand about the same height, and when I see her, I can imagine what I'll look like in twenty years.

"Yeah." She sighs. "It's getting harder to leave you and Windy Harbor each time. And with Papa and Uncle Hal even living there now…"

"The only ones missing are you and Dad…and Jackson and his new…wife." I make a face. "It's gonna take some time to get used to that."

"I need some time around them together before this feels real," she says.

I hug her, lingering there for a minute before moving to the table. I plop down in the chair.

"Ah, it feels too good to sit. I can't do this for very long." I pretend to fall asleep, and she laughs.

"I don't know how you keep this schedule. You must be exhausted all the time."

"I am," I admit.

"Well…your dad and I are looking at retiring pretty soon. Maybe a little earlier than we'd planned. Seeing what Everett's been through the past year…it really brings the important things to light, doesn't it? We want to be closer to you, Dad, Uncle Hal…and the Whitmans too."

"Yes, it does. I would love it so much if you and Dad were here all the time. Would you sell the house in St. Paul?"

"It'd be hard to let that go…I'm not sure. Maybe Jackson

and his new wife would want to raise a family there. You still feel like Windy Harbor is where you want to be full-time?"

I think of Camden and how I love that we're in the same town after all these years. But if things go wrong, it could be wretched to be in Windy Harbor together. I was here first, but…I think he's here to stay too.

I nod. "It feels like home."

She pats my hand. "I'm so happy you've found a place here…it's amazing to see how much everyone loves you. That cafe is thriving. I'm so proud of you, I can hardly stand it."

"Aw, thanks, Mom."

"Are Papa and Uncle Hal driving you crazy?"

I laugh. "Not at all. At first, I wasn't sure I could handle them under my feet at the cafe, but they've actually become pretty helpful."

She grins. "They love it. Think you could use a couple more underfoot?"

"Yes! Hurry up and get here. I can't wait."

I have to return to work, so I get up and hug her again. She promises that they'll stop by the cafe on their way out of town. I peek out the window and wait until Ralph is closer to the coop and then make a run for it. He catches sight of me— of course he does—but I'm too quick for him. Maybe that flight he took earlier has slowed him down a bit.

The afternoon passes quickly. My parents come over for hugs, and once I've closed the cafe, I check outside. As always, I'm on constant alert now for Ralph, who's in the coop, so I go home. I'm exhausted from staying up late with my parents each night, so I eat with Papa Hector and Uncle Hal and then get in the bath.

I lay back and wish that Camden were in this tub with me. It's much cuter than the ship at the apartment. A teal claw-foot tub that's roomy, although probably still not spacious enough for Camden's six-four frame.

I wipe my hands on the towel and text him.

> My parents went back to St. Paul. I think I'm ready for that getaway soon, if the offer still stands.

It's about ten minutes before he replies, and I'm still in the tub.

CAMDEN

Hell yeah, the offer still stands. Tomorrow night?

> I...think I can pull that off. Yes.

CAMDEN

Can't wait. Miss you. What are you doing right now?

> I miss you too. I'm tubbing it.

CAMDEN

Was that a typo? Did you mean rubbing or tubbing?

> TUBBING. I am in the tub.

CAMDEN

Either way. What I want to know is: without me?

> I did wish you were here, yes.

The phone buzzes, and it's him FaceTiming.

I make sure the phone only shows my face when I answer.

He's in his office, looking devastatingly hot in his black button-down shirt. His expression, a smile that has his eyes all lit up, does something to me from the inside out.

"Your wish is my command. I'm here," he says. His lips quickly form into a pout. "But I thought you said we were tubbing."

I have to take a breath to tamper down my smile. "I said *I* was. But hello, welcome."

"I'm not sure I believe you. For all I know, you could be in the kitchen in an oversized onesie—for the record, I would not be opposed to that—but I just feel like I need a little proof that you are in the tub."

"Do you not believe my word, Chef Whitman?"

"You've proven that you're a little tease from time to time." He tightens the view, so it only shows his face too.

Now I'm the one pouting.

After a shuffling noise, the view shoots to black for a second. I frown, checking to see if the connection has dropped. And then he's back.

I splash the water with my free hand. "Did you hear that?"

"Could've been the kitchen sink."

"What is your fascination with the kitchen?"

He laughs at that. "Same as yours, I think." He lifts his eyes and pretends to think. "Just had a new fantasy. You and me…in the kitchen…any kitchen will do."

The lighting shifts, and it's darker behind him. I brighten my screen so I can see him better.

"We've been in the kitchen together a lot. What exactly did you have in mind?"

"You spread out on the island comes to mind."

"Chef! That's so unsanitary."

"That's what cleaning products and tablecloths are made for."

I laugh. "I don't think I've ever seen a tablecloth on either one of our islands, but okay."

"Work with me here." He smirks. "Juliana," he sings.

"Camden..." I sing back.

"Do you still leave your door unlocked?"

My forehead scrunches. "Uh, usually, yes."

"After tonight, I'm going to ask that you stop doing that. But for now, I'm really happy that you do."

I sit up in the tub. "What are you doing?"

"I'm coming over to say hello. Is that okay?"

My heart rate trips a beat. "*Yes*." I draw out the word.

"Okay," he whispers. "If you don't want me to see you naked in the tub, I'll give you five seconds..."

My eyes widen. "You're...here?"

"Three...two...one..."

The bathroom door opens, and there he stands, looking like a gorgeous giant in the doorway. He has a leather jacket on that he takes off and hangs on the hook on the back of the door.

For a moment, we just take each other in.

"Goddamn, you're beautiful," he says, his voice soft and husky.

"Hi," I whisper.

"Hi," he echoes.

"I thought you were at the restaurant."

"I was." His eyes trail down my body, and even in the hot water, my nipples pebble. "I thought you could use some help getting out of the bath."

I bite my bottom lip, anticipation surging through my veins. "I could definitely use some help."

"Did you need help washing too? Because I'd love to help with that as well."

"Nope, already done."

He grins, then reaches into the water and picks me up. He gives me a kiss that's just long enough to leave me wanting more before he sets me carefully on the floor. He wraps a towel around me and then proceeds to dry me more thoroughly than I've ever been dried before. Every crevice is carefully tended to, and my body preens under his attention.

"So beautiful," he whispers again, kissing my stomach. "So, so beautiful." He kisses me lower.

I shiver, and he notices and straightens, then wraps the towel around me and tucks it in around my chest. He bends and picks me up, and I burrow into his neck and laugh.

"Everyone asleep?" he asks.

"I think they're probably out cold."

He opens the door, carefully looking both ways before stepping out. The hallway creaks as he starts walking, and he pauses for a second before tiptoeing the rest of the way. By the time we reach my bedroom, I'm barely holding back my laughter and Camden's chest is moving with a silent laugh. The moon spills light across my room, and he pulls back the covers and lays me on the strip of light crossing the bed. I undo the towel, slide it out from under me, and toss it across the room.

His teeth flash white in the dim room, but he stands still for a moment, just looking at me. When I hold out my hand, he takes it and presses a kiss to my palm.

"I know you have an early morning, so I can let you sleep…but I'd really love to make you feel good first. I can be very quick," he adds.

I hold his hand against my cheek, leaning into it.

"I'd love to make you feel good too," I tell him.

He unbuttons his shirt and tosses it aside. Next are his pants and boxer briefs. My mouth waters when I see him stalking toward me. But his foot or knee hits the stack of books I keep next to the bed, and a small avalanche clatters to the floor.

We freeze, eyes wide, then clap our hands over our mouths as we fight back our laughter.

From down the hall, Papa Hector calls out, concerned. "Juju? Are you okay?"

I try to sound normal. "Yes, I'm okay, Papa!"

"Need some help?" Uncle Hal calls.

Camden and I laugh against each other.

"No thanks, you guys!" I say. I clear my throat because I sound like I'm crying, I'm laughing so hard. "Everything's all right. Good night, Papa. Night, Uncle Hal."

"All right. Night, sweetheart," Papa says.

"Sleep tight," Uncle Hal adds.

Camden crawls on the bed next to me and laughs in the pillow. It takes us a minute to get it out of our system. And then we face each other. He reaches out and traces a line from my neck down my chest, stopping to lightly circle my nipples. I reach out and trace his jaw with my thumb, and he turns to kiss it.

"Come here," I whisper.

Our lips collide, and our bodies don't take long to do the same. The bed complains, but we barely pause, adjusting to find a way to keep quiet. He kisses his way down my body and settles between my legs. He spreads me with his thumbs, and when his tongue makes the first contact with my skin, I arch into him, desperate for more. He doesn't make me wait. His mouth is hungry, and he sucks me and explores me with his tongue. He's relentless. My legs start trembling, and when I start to whimper, I cover my face with a pillow. I'm so close, and when his finger dips inside slowly and then deeper, his lips suctioning over my clit, I'm a goner. I hold on to his hair, gripping it tight as I ride it out. When my hands drop and I go limp, he lifts his head, his lips shiny in the dark. He crawls up my body and pauses at my breasts, licking his way around my nipple. His cock is a velvety rock against my thigh, and everything in me awakens all over again.

"You taste so good," he says. "I promised I would be quick." He grins against my skin as he kisses my other nipple. "Sweet dreams, beautiful. I will see you tomorrow."

"Come here," I say, tugging on his hair.

He looks up, and I lean up to kiss him. He shifts until his body is lined up to mine.

"Do you want more?" he asks, his voice playful.

"So much more."

Our lips meet, and he slips just barely inside me. I gasp and he's out again. His skin is heated, warming me up, and even though I've just come so hard that I should be wrung out, I ache for him. Our lips part, and when I open my eyes and look at him, he's staring back at me. He teases me by dipping inside and out again, and each time I try to hold on to him a little longer. The sound he makes deep in his chest has me clutching him even tighter, and he kisses me, swallowing my moan when he goes a little deeper. I get tunnel vision, everything around me narrowing to the rhythm we begin to make. He whispers my name against my lips and then looks down.

"I love watching you take me." He slides out and glides over my clit, so intentional and so restrained that the only sign of how it's affecting him is the slight hitch in his breath.

I don't know how he's not losing it right now.

"You feel so good, Camden," I whimper.

It feels like we're an extension of each other. Like we're in sync in every possible way.

I see some of his restraint falter when he slides out this time.

"I love how wet you are all over me." Sweat glistens on his forehead, and the muscles in his back twitch against my hands, but he doesn't stop teasing me with those slow strokes.

I want to beg him for more, and yet it feels so good, this gradual climb to devastation.

His eyes close and he squeezes them tight, cursing under his breath. He pulls out all the way, and I whimper. He's so hard against me, and when his eyes open, he looks drugged.

"I don't want this to end," he says. "But I—"

"Please, Camden," I say.

His eyes are wild, and when he thrusts into me all the way, my mouth parts in a silent scream. The spasms that take over are so strong that his head drops, and he surrenders. He drives into me, finally giving me everything, exactly what I want, and the pleasure that shoots through me is indescribable. His fall is just as intense, both of us holding on for dear life as we touch the stars.

I think I might black out for a second.

When I start to come back to earth, he brushes my hair away from my face.

"You okay?" he asks.

"More than that," I whisper. "I'm perfect."

"Yes, you are."

CHAPTER TWENTY-NINE

OBVIOUSLY

CAMDEN

DAD

It's quiet up in here. What's everyone doing?
<Picture of Kevin asleep on his back, paws in the air>

DYLAN

<Picture with bedhead, his mini Dachshund Bill, and a cup of coffee> I don't want to be awake yet. Oh, hey, I booked my ticket for two weeks from now, so get ready for the fun to begin.

GOLDIE

<Picture of her hanging curtains in the resort> Are you insinuating that we're not already having fun?

DYLAN

Not without me, you're not

GOLDIE

😌 Sigh. True.

CAMDEN

<Picture of a beautiful fish about to be filleted> Can't get more fun than this.

TULLY

Speak for yourself. <Picture of his hand holding up his ice skates> About to hit the ice.

NOAH

<Picture with Grayson, both holding huge mugs of hot chocolate> It's been a great day off so far. Wish me luck though. He's talked me into going to Nickelodeon Universe today. 😩

DAD

Have fun, you guys! Thanks for letting me know you're all alive. Speaking of fun, has anyone else noticed how happy Camden's been lately? Every time I see him, he's smiling. Whatever's got you in such a good mood, son, keep it up! 😉

I blink at the phone. What is Dad implying here? Have I really been that obvious? He can't possibly know anything, right? We haven't even been around the family very much since we got together.

I drift off, smiling as I think about last night.

Shit. I *am* being fucking obvious!

———

I park at The Hungry Walleye five minutes early. Juju's actually the one who came up with the plan. I'll go inside and get fries and a drink to go, and while I'm inside, Juju will get inside my SUV and lay low until I'm out there. Everything seems to be going as planned until Sandy walks in and asks ten thousand questions about my dad. I swear, I think she's upset that he's feeling so much better because she doesn't have an excuse to bring him hotdish anymore.

When I finally get in the car, I laugh because Juju's huddled on the floor on the passenger side.

"What are you doing down there?" I ask. "Are you freezing?"

It's so cold today.

"I wanted to maintain the secret," she grumbles. "And yes, I'm freezing. This sweater dress isn't doing very much for me right now."

"Where's your coat?"

"I wanted to look cute when you got in and accidentally put it in the back…and then I was afraid someone would see me if I tried to grab it."

I start the car and get the heat going, hurriedly pulling out onto Wildbriar Lane.

"I'm so sorry. Sandy was chatty. You look so hot in that dress. Get up here so I can get a better look at you. I love it. Please come sit by me."

She lifts up and peeks out the window. "Is it safe?"

"It's safe," I say, speeding up a little so we can get past the shops.

She sits in her seat, and I reach back and hand her the little bouquet of white roses I picked up for her earlier. She admires them and then brings them to her nose.

"Thank you," she says softly. "Are you trying to dazzle me, Whitman?"

"Is it working?" I ask.

She smirks, scraping her thumb over my knuckles when I

rest my hand on the console. The touch short-circuits me. I leave my hand there anyway, and when she plays with my knuckles again, I thread our fingers together.

We take the highway along the dark ribbon of water, Juju's playlist humming low. She points things out along the way.

"There's the bridge Uncle Hal convinced Papa Hector to climb."

"Yikes. How did that turn out?"

"He did it, but never ever wanted to do it again."

And a little later…

"That's the billboard where Erin swears she'll start a dating site. Each week will have a different starter, and whoever comes up with the best responses gets matched up with…" She pauses. "Yeah, I'm not sure how she thought that would work out. There are definitely flaws in the system."

I counter with restaurant gossip, famous chef arguments, and the many ridiculous questions I've fielded. *"Yes, ma'am, I'm positive this water doesn't have calories."*

We roll into the city in no time and decide to go straight to the restaurant, since we're so hungry. We leave the car with the valet and hurry inside. I offer my arm, and she takes it like this is a thing we do. I love being able to do this freely. Inside, the place hums—low light, dark wood, whispers of money. The host recognizes me and does that subtle double take. I put my hand on Juju's back, and we're led to a corner table.

"Champagne?" I ask.

"Absolutely," she says, and I order a bottle I love.

The first course arrives perfectly plated: shaved fennel and pear, tiny curls of pecorino, a drizzle of something that smells delicious. Juju looks at it, reverent and eager. I see her when we were kids and I see the gorgeous woman she is now, and it's like Cupid's arrow to my chest. It makes me feel drunk inside.

We take bites and quickly deconstruct the dish, listing the spices they used.

"I used to want to hate that you were a food snob," she says, "but I've always secretly liked it. And I like when you teach me things."

"*Snob* is a harsh word," I say, spearing a sliver of pear and offering it across the table. She leans forward and bites from my fork, lips closing around pear and the tip of steel, eyes on mine. I feel it in the soles of my feet. And elsewhere, where my pants are now tight. "And you've taught me just as much, if not more—trust me."

"That's sweet of you to say. Do you approve of the word *connoisseur* more?" she asks.

"That's acceptable." I grin. "And you're the connoisseur of joy. Which is much harder."

She tilts her head. "Is that how you felt when I used to bite your head off? That I'm a connoisseur of joy?"

That makes me laugh, and it takes me a second to respond. "No, I can't say that was the word that came to mind."

"Hmm. Is *irresistible* better?"

"We're getting closer to the target, yes."

She grins. "I still feel like rolling my eyes at you sometimes."

"How about we negotiate about the right words to use and kiss until we're asked to leave?"

"I don't hate the sound of that," she says, her eyes softening.

The next plates arrive—scallops in citrus, risotto, and a beautiful steak. We share everything. She narrates each bite: "Whitman goes in hard with the succulent scallops—oh! He's stunned, folks. He's stunned!" I'm laughing too hard to pretend I'm not absolutely gone for her.

Between courses, we talk about Tully's game tomorrow, how he gets in his head before games. We talk about her parents deciding to spend more time in Windy Harbor, the way it makes her feel anchored and weirdly like she's twelve again. I tell her that I still sometimes set too many plates at my dad's table out of habit, one for my mom. She slips her foot over my ankle beneath the table and leaves it there.

"My mom still does the birthday ritual they did every year for their birthdays," she says. "She goes to Cafe Latte and gets the latte and cake they always got, and then she stops at all the shops that are still around that they went to. I've tried to go with her for the past few years, since I've been living near her again. She breaks down at least once every time."

"I didn't know that," I say, touched. "Wow. They had a special bond, didn't they." I smile at her. "Our families were meant to know each other."

"Imagine if we'd moved onto another street," she says, lifting her shoulder.

"I believe we still would've met."

"I like this," she says softly. "Us. Out in the wild."

"Me too."

We enjoy our dessert and then make our way to the hotel.

"Would you like a drink before we go to our room?" I ask when we walk into the lobby.

"I think I'm good, but let's get something if you want it. You get so little time out to enjoy other restaurants."

"I'd much rather enjoy you," I tell her.

"You can enjoy me anywhere," she says, her lips lifting up.

My eyes widen as I grin and stare at her mouth. "Yeah? I

can put my head between your legs at the bar?" I say under my breath.

Her mouth parts and her cheeks flush, and I fucking love it.

"We better get to the room…fast," she says breathlessly.

My chest rumbles with my laugh, and I tug her tighter against me, kissing her hair. "Great answer. Because I'd love to see you naked against the window…or bent over the bed… or buried in the covers as I work my way up from your toes to your mouth…and everywhere in between. I've heard there are brick walls, massive showers and tubs, and the softest comforters…I've already imagined you in all the places."

I hear her breath hitch and get that rush knowing that my words affect her.

The elevator is full when we step inside. She stands in front of me, and I pull her against my chest. My hands slide to her hips. I love how my hands fit perfectly in the curve of her hips.

She leans back and tugs my head down, whispering in my ear, "We're going to be quiet, right?" she murmurs, playful. "Just in case our neighbors are nosy?"

"I can't promise anything," I say, and when the doors slide open, we almost don't make it to the room before we're kissing, laughter muffled with mouths and hands.

Inside, she lets go of me, leaving me breathless and adjusting myself as she moves through the room like she owns it. The bed is a white ocean, and she touches the comforter, nodding her approval. She walks to the window overlooking the city and traces the brick wall next to it, turning to give me a flirtatious, daring look.

I am so gone over this woman.

"Where would you like me first?" she asks.

I run my hand over my jaw, looking her over, and stalk toward her.

"Right here will do." I tug her hair back, and her face lifts for me to take her mouth. Our tongues tangle together, our hands everywhere all at once.

I break from her suddenly and get on my knees, unable to wait another second.

"Hold on, hold on," she says. "I have so many layers on, and I brought sexy things to wear for you."

I look up at her, my hands going around to squeeze her ass.

"Can I undress you now, and later you show me what you brought to wear for me?" I ask.

She bites her lips and nods.

"Such a good girl," I tell her, pulling her boots off before rolling her tights down her body. "Take your dress off. Let me see what's underneath."

She tugs her sweater dress over her head, and I take her in. Her lacy bra has an oval opening where her skin shows between her breasts, and I lean up and lick that skin.

"So beautiful," I whisper against her.

I slide the pretty lacy panties down her legs and press a kiss on her center while looking up at her.

She gasps and I grin. I'm pacing myself because I want to devour her.

"Hold on to my hair. Show me where you want me," I tell her.

She puts both hands in my hair, and I feast on her, taking my time. The desire between us is palpable. With every taste of her, I become more addicted, and the sounds she's making are sounds I want to hear her make for the rest of our lives. I feel every shudder, every pulse, every gush against my tongue, and I just crave more of her.

When she cries out my name, her fists gripping my hair tight against her body, I think I'd die a happy man if I suffocated right here. Let this be my last dying breath, buried in her pussy. True happiness.

She goes limp and I stand, lifting her in my arms. I pull back the covers and place her in the bed and get undressed. She leans up and starts helping me, pulling my pants and briefs down quickly.

"Hurry," she says, "we're not done yet."

I grin and lean over her, kissing her. She leans up, and I turn so she's on top. She grins, triumphant, and I can't stop staring at her.

"You take my breath away," I tell her.

"You take mine away too," she says. "Literally." She laughs, and then her mouth drops when I lift her and pull her down slowly on my dick. "Mmm," she shudders. "I'm so sensitive, I already feel close again."

"Take exactly what you want, Juju. I'm all yours."

She rolls her hips over me, and I'm so close too. The buildup of watching her fall apart once already was almost enough to make me come in my pants, and now, skin to skin, I'm right on the edge. And when she goes from a slow roll of her hips to gasping and bouncing up and down, chasing her high like she can't wait another second, I give in to it, clasping her hips and driving up into her like we're fused together.

A few minutes later, she's sprawled across my chest, hair everywhere, and we're still breathing hard.

"Each time, I think it can't possibly get better than the last time," she says as I trace idle patterns across her back. "And it just does."

"Did you ever think we'd be this explosive together?" I ask.

"I never let myself go there, not fully," she says. "I mean, I thought about it, but I shut it down fast. What about you?" She lifts her head up to face me. "Did you think about us like this?"

"More than I should've, given how much we fought with each other," I admit. "I did always think it'd probably be amazing, given how volatile we could make one another."

We both laugh, and then one thing leads to another, and we prove the point again about how volatile we can really be.

―――――

"Sorry, I never let you get dressed long enough to show me your pretty things," I say the next morning while we get ready for the hockey game.

"It's okay," she sighs, pretending to be more annoyed than she is. "I guess I'll have to save it for someone who cares." She lifts her shoulder, and I give her backside a little slap, making her jump.

She laughs, and I hug her to me when we get in the elevator.

"I definitely care," I tell her. "I loved every second of exactly how it happened, though. Being in the city, eating too much, sleeping…okay, *not* sleeping much, but…I can't imagine it being any better, but it'll give me something to look forward to for later." I wink and she grins. "And now, hockey?"

"You know…I don't think we've been at the same hockey game since—" Her voice trails off.

I wince. "Yeah," I say quietly.

Just the thought of that game takes me back to all the emotion, all the pain. The events that happened that day changed our lives forever, especially for my brother Noah.

"This will be a better day," she says softly.

I nod.

By the time we're at the arena, the chill has found the inside of my coat. She tucks herself close, and I pull her in, pretending it's for warmth. The mood in the stadium is exhilarating, and the melancholy that came over us as we thought about the past is swept aside for the time being.

The game starts out with a bang.

Tully is a speck in the swarm at first, and then he's cutting through so fast, reckless yet precise, going exactly where he needs to get a goal. We cheer loudly, leaning into each other. I don't think I've ever smiled this much.

Midway through the second period, Tully gets a breakaway. I watch his blades chew up the distance, and the puck leaves his stick. It clinks the post and then lands just inside the net. The red light blooms. Our section erupts.

"*Yes!*" I shout, and Juju shouts with me, and we turn to each other at exactly the same time.

We kiss—quick, hard, both laughing. Her hands are warm on my face, and my heart's a drumline. Then the sound shifts. Not just cheering. A different pitch. A ripple of voices ricochet around us.

"Hey—that's you!" someone yells, gleeful, and Juju and I pull apart, looking around.

Somehow, I don't have to look to know.

But we do. And there we are, twenty feet tall, in high definition on the Jumbotron: Juju with her eyes shining, and me looking stunned, caught in a kiss.

For a second, I get a heady rush knowing everyone just saw me kiss my girl. And in the next, reality crashes in. I hear Jackson telling me we'd be a disaster. Juju's hand finds mine and squeezes. Her shoulders square and her chin lifts. She doesn't drop my gaze. She doesn't shrink.

I take a breath and do exactly what I want. It's not like anyone we know will see this anyway. Jackson's on his honeymoon, and the chances of anyone watching and recognizing us are slim. I turn and grin at Juju. She starts laughing, and then she leans in and kisses me again, shorter this time, and our section cheers louder.

When we look again, the camera has cut away to a kid with a foam finger, doing a crazy dance.

Tully's team wins, and I feel bad for not sticking around to congratulate him, but he has a long list of obligations to fulfill after every game. And I wouldn't know how to explain why I'm with Juju. He knew I was bringing someone, but I never said who.

There will be time to brag on him later. For now, I don't want to miss a second of showing Juju just how important she is to me.

CHAPTER THIRTY

SHAKEN

JULIANA

Past: Juju, age 23, Camden, age 25

The dread I felt over the thought of seeing Camden at Tully's first professional hockey game was almost blinding. I had almost talked myself out of going so many times, but Goldie wanted me there, and I wanted to be there for her and for Tully. My entire family was going. We were all excited for him and had been talking about this game for months. I didn't want to let anyone down, and I didn't want to miss out.

But that stupid *almost* kiss. The kiss that never was.

The kiss that almost happened simply because I was a body who was there…

Every time I thought of what he'd said, I got angrier.

It was good that I could hate him a little more all the time, because softening where Camden Whitman was concerned was something I never ever needed to do again.

I couldn't believe I'd let myself go there for even a second.

I'd go to this game, and I'd look good doing it. I wouldn't show how much he'd wrecked me with the bitter pill I'd had to swallow. His honesty played on repeat in my brain around the clock, and I wasn't going to let that voice keep me from being there for my friends.

I dressed in something cute and put on a big smile, telling myself I'd do my best to stay out of his way.

The problem was that, somehow, I ended up in a car with him. Erin was in town from Windy Harbor for the game, and Jackson and Erin were laughing about something. He motioned for us to come with him and told her to get in the front seat so they could keep talking.

Which meant Camden ended up in the back seat with Goldie and me.

I didn't know how he even fit back there. When he squeezed in the back, his shoulders bunching up between me and his sister, I would've laughed if I hadn't been so disgusted with him. I was fairly certain the rage bouncing off of me melted him every time he tried to look at me. And that helped somewhat.

The ride felt like it lasted forever, and when we stopped, I hurried to get out. I wore leggings with high boots and a cropped shirt.

Some guys walked by and checked me out, and one said, "Hello, hottie, looking *good*."

Camden's eyes fluttered down to my bare stomach, and his jaw clenched. "Nice. Leaving nothing to the imagination, I see."

"Trust me, there is so much more to see than a few inches of my stomach."

He swallowed hard and chose to remain silent.

Good choice.

Goldie was bouncing with excitement to see Tully playing his first professional game, and once again, despite trying so hard, I ended up in a seat next to Camden. Goldie was on the other side of me, and Jackson was on the other side of Camden. Our parents surrounded us, and nobody seemed to notice that Camden and I were doing our best to avoid each other at all costs.

Midway through the game, Noah, who was sitting in the row right in front of us, got a call and looked past Dylan and the girl Dylan had brought, and he got his dad's attention. He looked panicked.

"She's having the baby," he said, holding up his phone.

"What?" Everett said.

"Margo's having the baby."

"It's way too soon," Everett said.

Noah nodded. "I have to get out of here." He looked around like he was stuck.

I didn't know Margo very well, even though she was at the Whitmans' almost every time I was. They were five years older than me, and ever since high school, Margo and Noah were always in their own little orbit. They'd been *relationship goals*, so I was shocked when they'd broken up. Noah had been sad ever since, but Goldie said he and Margo were still close. Both of us agreed that we didn't understand a relationship like that. How could you still be that close and not be together? We thought they'd for sure get back together once the baby came.

Goldie reached forward and put her hand on his shoulder. "We'll come with you to the hospital. I'm sure she's okay."

"Yeah, I hope so. She was crying really hard." He shook his head. "You don't need to leave the game. Stay. I don't want you to miss this. Tully needs to know we were here for him. I'm sure Dad's right. Everything will be okay. I'll catch up with you guys later."

Everett told us he'd keep us posted, and he and Noah worked their way out of the seats. We stayed and cheered our asses off. About three-quarters into the game, a vendor delivered me a drink.

I frowned and said, "What is this?" even though I could see it was canned wine.

"From that guy over there," the man said.

I looked at the row across from us, and it was the guy who'd complimented me earlier.

I lifted the can and said thank you. He winked, and he was getting up to come over when Camden stood up and looked right at the guy. I couldn't see his face because his back was to me, but whatever he did, the guy sat back down in his seat and didn't look at me for the rest of the game.

"Are you kidding me right now?" I hissed. "What did you do?"

"Jackson, deal with your sister," he said. "That punk over there is hitting on her, and she's ready to throw herself at the guy."

"I am not," I was saying as Jackson turned and told the guy to keep his eyes to himself. "You are such an idiot," I told Camden under my breath. "Some things never change. Even at twenty-five, you are the most emotionally stunted man I have ever met."

He pretended not to hear me.

Tully won. It would have been way more fun if I could've gotten out of my head about Camden and just enjoyed the game.

We'd just sat down in a booth at a nearby restaurant when Camden got a call from Everett. I had studiously avoided looking at him, but I could tell when his shoulders dropped, and then I heard his voice.

"Oh my God," he said, sounding shaken.

I looked over then to see the color drain from his face.

"What's happened?" Goldie asked.

I reached over and squeezed her hand.

"The baby's fine," Camden said, "but something's wrong with Margo. She's on a ventilator."

Over the next few days, we were in and out of the hospital, and when we weren't there, I was over at the Whitmans' house cooking for everyone, trying to keep Goldie's mind off of things, and just trying to be helpful wherever I could.

Margo died three mornings later, and Noah was left to raise a baby boy on his own.

It shook all of us to the core. Margo was beautiful and vibrant, and it was impossible to imagine that she was just gone.

Camden didn't go back to France, and suddenly, he was everywhere I turned.

I just thought we'd parted ways when I was a kid, but that was nothing compared to this.

This was the year our true animosity began.

CHAPTER THIRTY-ONE

SPIKED COFFEE

CAMDEN

Present

I haven't been able to stop smiling since I got back to Windy Harbor last night. I wanted to spend the night, but Juju said she needed her beauty sleep after this weekend. We'd barely slept at all, and I knew if we stayed together, we wouldn't get any sleep for the third night in a row.

Plus, I felt like I needed to continuously remind myself that we weren't out in the open. It had been so nice in Minneapolis not to hold back or hide anything, but now that we were back in Windy Harbor, those boundaries had to be put in place again. I didn't like it, and I wasn't sure how much longer we could keep going this way.

Sometimes I wonder if Juju might be pumping the brakes a little. It's time we tell Jackson. I can't keep hiding how I feel about Juju.

I'm getting ready to go see her at the cafe when I get a

text from Jackson. I freeze and find it hard to even swallow. It's a picture of Juju and me kissing on the Jumbotron.

JACKSON
WHAT THE FUCK IS THIS? We need to talk.

I don't respond. I take off for the cafe, wanting to talk to Juju before I say anything to Jackson, but when I walk in, I see that it's too late. Jackson is there already, looking heated, with his new wife looking worried nearby. Juju's eyes flash to me in a panic. I give her an apologetic look and rush toward her brother.

"Jackson," I say, "let's talk…please."

He whirls around, fury all over his face. He walks over to me, cocks his arm back, and punches me in the jaw. The punch's impact is the only sound for a moment, and then gasps ripple throughout the room. My hand goes to my face, and I see red.

"Jackson!" Juju yells, rushing around the counter.

Jackson's body is shaking with anger, and I'm highly tempted to hit him back. I straighten slowly, rubbing my jaw. My eyes flick from Jackson to Juju, and suddenly, I feel exhausted.

"Jackson," I say, my voice low, "I'm giving you that one hit, but you will never touch me like that again, are we clear? Take a step back before we both say things we regret. And… I'm sorry."

"Sorry?" Jackson's laugh is bitter. "How long have you been messing around with my sister?"

Juju shoves herself between us, sounding like she might do some punching of her own. "That's enough!"

Jackson is furious, and when he's like this, we both know he's almost impossible to reason with.

"He's supposed to be my best friend, Juju," Jackson yells. "He's supposed to know better. We promised each other."

"Know better than what? Liking me? Wanting me? It was a stupid promise you made when you were kids, Jackson. We're adults now. We don't need your permission!"

The cafe is so quiet you could hear a pin drop.

Hector and Hal come in, singing "New York, New York." When they assess the seriousness of the room, Hector rushes toward Juju.

"Juliana, is everything okay?"

"Ask Jackson," she says, her voice cracking. "He just punched Camden in the face."

Hector's head rears back. "Jackson!"

Jackson shakes his head, jaw clenched, and points at me. "He kissed Juju, Papa. In front of everyone."

Hector's mouth drops, and he clasps his hands together in excitement, then freezes when he catches the look on Jackson's face.

"Oh," he says softly.

Jackson slides his hand over his face and looks at Juju. "You knew how I felt about this."

"And you know I've always thought it was ridiculous," she snaps. "You don't get to throw a fit because you've decided he's off-limits." She turns to me, and the fury is buzzing through her. I stare at her, my shoulders feeling stiff. "And you…you're *sorry*?"

My brows draw together, and I know the hurt must show in my eyes. "Only that he had to find out this way. I didn't want this to explode like—"

"You didn't want to rock the boat." Her voice is raw and sharp. "You didn't want to upset Jackson. You wanted to keep me a secret and not upset anyone, not be too obvious…not claim me in front of the people who matter. I haven't been able to fully settle into us even being real because I've been kept a secret this whole time." She pauses like she's trying to keep it in, but she shakes her head and keeps going. "Well, guess what?" Her hand flings out. "Secret's out now. And half the town is here watching us like we're a soap opera."

Hector goes around the cafe and starts conversations like he's trying to distract everyone from our shit show.

I feel sick, and Jackson's fists are still balled at his sides.

"I'm mad at both of you," Juju says, voice breaking, "for making me feel like I'm something to be ashamed of." She points at Jackson. "Whoever I decide to see, or kiss, or do whatever I want with, has nothing to do with you. If you have a problem with it, that's on you." And then she turns to me, and I want to rush to her and kiss the pain out of her. "And if you're not willing to stand up for us, that's also on you, but I really do have a problem with that. I deserve to be someone's priority and to be with someone who's proud to have me by their side. I am not your dirty little secret."

Her hands are shaking, and her lip is trembling. The tears in her eyes are killing me.

"You've been choosing him since day one, and now you're choosing him again." Her voice cracks on the last word.

That hits me hard. I don't know how, but my voice is steady when I speak. I move closer and lift my hand to touch Juju's cheek, then pause when she glares at me.

"Juju. I do want to stand up for us, Juju," I say. "I choose *you*. I've always wanted you by my side. I'm so sorry for the way I've gone about all of it."

I glance at Jackson. "I just wanted to do it differently. One on one. No yelling, no fists. Just me telling you how much I love your sister."

Juju's mouth drops open. I hear several gasps in the room, one of which is hers.

"You love me?" she asks, incredulous.

I huff out a laugh, my gaze like a caress when I look at her again. "I'm surprised you even have to ask. I've been in love with you for so long, I thought everyone must know it." I feel fierce and vulnerable all at once. "I love everything about you. I always have. I want to spend the rest of my life loving you. I just needed time to convince Jackson that I deserved you…after I was sure I'd convinced *you*, that is… not that anyone deserves you. You're way too good for me. But I wanted to convince you that we belong together anyway."

I hear a couple of squeals around us that someone tries and fails to smother. Jackson is completely still, like someone's just yanked the floor out from under him.

"Camden—" Juju says, breathing out my name.

"*Have* I convinced you?" I ask her quietly.

She takes a step closer to me, and relief radiates off me when I see the love on her face.

"You have," she whispers. "I've been in love with you for a long time too."

"Yeah?" I whisper, taking a step closer.

My heart is going nuts.

"God, this is so weird," Jackson mutters.

Dove says something to him, and he mutters again under his breath.

I hear him say, "But he's never liked anyone for any length of time!"

And she says, "Because he was into your sister, you dimwit!"

All of a sudden, Juju starts laughing. It begins with a startled burst of laughter, and then she's clutching her stomach from laughing so hard. I put my arms around her and laugh with her, and it's contagious. I think everyone's probably so relieved that no more punches will be thrown today that they start laughing too, but whatever the reasons, we laugh and hold each other, and it feels like maybe everything will be okay.

CHAPTER THIRTY-TWO

ENTERTAINMENT TODAY

JULIANA

After my perfect weekend, I didn't even mind when Ralph's beak nearly took out my wrist on my run to the cafe.

I should've known something was off by the line down the street before I'd even unlocked the doors to open.

I smiled in confusion as what felt like the entire town trailed in.

Sandy…Beverly and Carol. Bosco was even beaming. He's usually here at opening, so that wasn't too unusual, but then he handed me a dried rose and gave me a little sideways almost-smile. Miss Idella and Emmy…all giggling.

A highlight was when Bosco did a low bow when he saw Miss Idella.

It was like someone had spiked the coffee, but I was the only one serving coffee so far.

Suzanne was off, and Papa Hector and Uncle Hal hadn't made it in yet.

It wasn't until noon that it all made sense.

The door slammed so hard that the bell nearly fell off. Jackson stormed in like a thundercloud, and Dove rushed behind him, looking apologetic. He was flushed red, his jaw tight. He barreled up to the counter, and the cafe went quiet.

And then he shoved the phone in my face with the picture of Camden and me in full color, kissing.

So that's why the whole town was smiling at me like they were in a cult all morning.

Fast-forward to now and Camden's declaration of love. I can hardly believe it.

But he dips me back and kisses me, to the cheers of everyone in the cafe but Jackson, and then it feels real. He loves me! And I love him. God, how I love him.

He straightens and carefully lets me go, then turns to Jackson and motions toward the back.

"Can we all talk where it's a little quieter?" he asks Jackson. He takes my hand and looks down at me. "You too, if you can?"

I nod.

"Aww, do you have to?" Beverly asks. "We want to know what happens!"

The cafe explodes in laughter.

"Don't worry, we're here to entertain you," Uncle Hal says.

Grandma Nancy and Grandma Donna walk in just then, and Uncle Hal holds his hand out with a flourish.

"See? The day has already gotten more entertaining!" he says, winking at Grandma Nancy.

She harrumphs and looks around the room suspiciously.

"What's going on in here?" she asks.

"I'll fill you in on everything," Uncle Hal says, holding out his arm.

She's so flustered, she takes it.

Jackson's been distracted like I have been, but I nudge his arm.

"Come on, let's go to my office. It's through the kitchen," I tell Dove.

Jackson grits his teeth and nods, his hand in Dove's as they follow us back.

"Is Uncle Hal making the moves on Grandma Nancy?" he asks incredulously.

"Duh, where have you been?" I snap.

I do not have the patience for him right now.

He shudders.

I close the door behind us, and for a second, we all just stare at each other. I feel a little bad that Dove has come into all this drama, but if she knows my brother, her *husband*, at all, she must know that he comes with a shitload of drama.

"I'm sorry you had to find out like this, man," Camden tells Jackson. "I was waiting until you got back from your honeymoon to talk to you."

Jackson scoffs. "Right."

"Believe it or not, it's the truth. I couldn't wait any longer, but I wanted it to be in person. I've loved your sister for a long time, but I've held it in and pushed it down deep because of my love for you and the promise we made to each other. But I can't do it anymore. She means too much to me. She deserves to be treated like a queen, and I want to be the one to do just that for the rest of my life."

"But you never stay in a relationship. Ever," Jackson argues.

"No, I haven't," Camden says. "Because my heart was already taken."

I get a lump in my throat and blink fast. I've wanted this for so long that it doesn't feel real now that it's happening.

"I've tried to fill that void, sure," Camden adds. "But you've always been more of a player than me, and look at you now, settling down. You said you wanted that for me too, and I have it. Can't you be happy for us?"

"Maybe it's the close proximity," Jackson says. "Windy Harbor is small, and it's not like there are a ton of other options out there…"

I whirl around to face him, and he flinches.

"How can you say that about her?" Camden asks. "The way we knew you'd react is what has affected our relationship more than anything. I could sense her holding back at times. We both love you so much and want your approval, but if you love either one of us, you'll get on board with this. You really think I'd ever hurt your sister?"

"You've hurt her for years," Jackson says, his voice low.

That hits me hard, and it looks like it guts Camden.

"You're right. I have," he says softly. He takes my hand and runs his fingers over mine. "And I don't know how to forgive myself for that or for the time I've wasted with her."

"We've both hurt each other," I say, barely able to see through my tears as I look at him. "If we'd just been open about our feelings all along, it would've saved us and everyone around us a lot of hurt."

Jackson sighs. "I can't believe you've loved each other all along. That's just crazy. I mean, maybe a part of me always knew you'd prefer each other over me any day, but…I didn't want to go there. Because if it didn't work out, then what would happen to our friendship? I'd always pick my sister." He makes a face at me, and my heart softens.

He's a big lug, but I love him.

"I love you both, and I don't want to jeopardize my relationship with either one of you over this." Jackson points at

Camden. "Just know that if you hurt her, I will hunt you down and make your life a living hell."

Camden laughs. "You and Erin will both make sure that I suffer forever if I hurt her." He squeezes my hand. "We're in this for the long haul, right? At least I am," he says when I don't say anything back right away.

"I am too," I say softly.

"And there are no more secrets between us." Camden faces me and puts his hands on my face. "I love you. I want to be with you for the rest of my life."

I swallow hard and then nod. "I want that too. I love you."

He leans in, his forehead against mine as we stare at each other.

Jackson shakes his head and laughs softly. "This is fucking nuts. But I can't really talk, can I? Dove has me by the balls—"

"Is there not a sweeter, more romantic way to put it?" Dove asks, crossing her arms over her chest.

I burst out laughing. "I think I really like you," I say.

Dove gives me a huge smile. "I really like you too."

"Baby, you know that you have my heart too, not just my balls," Jackson coos. "That's what I meant. You have my heart."

Dove rolls her eyes and Jackson steps closer to her, uncrossing her arms and putting them around his neck. He gives her wide doe eyes, and she softens, smiling in the next second.

He kisses her and then looks at Camden and me. "I'll make this up to you...all my assholery. I feel bad that I've held you guys back. Double date tomorrow night? My treat?"

"You're really okay about all this? Just like that?" Camden asks, then lets out a long exhale.

"You said you love her, man. And I haven't ever heard you be such a simp in all my life. So yeah, I'm gonna be okay about this. It'll take me a while to get used to it, and I didn't love seeing you dip her back out there and being all gross, but—"

"Get used to it," Camden growls, and my legs go a little weak.

Jackson's eyes widen, and he lifts his hands. "Okay, okay. Jeez."

I shake my head, laughing quietly. "This is kind of surreal."

"You're telling me," my brother says. "So tomorrow night? I'll try to wrap my head around you guys between now and then."

"How about something earlier in the day so Camden doesn't have to miss more work?" I say. "If we go after the lunch rush, I'll have enough backup to leave a little early."

Jackson frowns. "How are you guys gonna make this work? You have to get up while it's still dark out," he says to me and then points at Camden, "and you are just barely going to bed when she's getting up."

"So far, our staffs have covered for us, but during the busy seasons or when people are out sick or on vacation, it'll be challenging," Camden admits. "We'll have to put the work in to make the most of our time together."

I smile at him and put my arms around his neck, staring up at him with all the love I can finally show.

"It's worth it," I say.

"Damn straight."

Before Camden leaves for work, he grabs his phone.

> CAMDEN
>
> Proof of life incoming…

"Watch the madness unfold," he says, laughing.

He holds up his phone and kisses my temple. My head falls back on his chest, and I smile the biggest smile while closing my eyes. When I open them, he shows me the selfie he's just taken. It's perfect. He sends it and gives me a mischievous grin when he shows me what he texted.

> CAMDEN
>
> I have a girlfriend! 😃

> DYLAN
>
> Ahhh! I didn't know how bad I needed this in my life until I saw this picture! YOU AND JUJU! I am shook. This is perfect.

> DAD
>
> It is about time. I'm so happy, son. So, so happy. And it looks like the two of you are even happier about this. <3 Your mom would be beside herself.

> GOLDIE
>
> Juju will FINALLY be my sister.

"God, these people," he says, giving me a sideways look, his cheeks flushing.

I just grin and watch what he types next.

> CAMDEN
>
> Let's not get ahead of ourselves. I just got her to come around to being my girlfriend.

GOLDIE

Oh, you've had that in the bag for a while. I
don't think it'll take much convincing.

I roll my eyes. "Easy, bestie," I murmur.

NOAH

This is great, Camden. You guys are perfect
for each other.

TULLY

What they all said and a huge fucking
congratulations! But are we really going to
pretend like this is news to us, fam? We've
been talking about it for the past twenty-
four hours straight. Ace was on the bench
yesterday and sent me the picture of the
two of you kissing on the Jumbotron. We've
been taking bets on how long it would take
before you told us. I have to say, you keep it
close to the chest, dude.

GOLDIE

True confession: I actually knew before the
Jumbotron. I've known for a while...

I put my hand over my mouth when I see that part. My
eyes are wide when I look at Camden. I tap the phone to
distract him and giggle.

TULLY

WHEN WILL I EVER GET THE TWIN
BENEFITS?! You're supposed to tell me all
the things!

GOLDIE

Juju said it was a big secret! I couldn't do
that to her.

DAD

True confession: I walked in on Juju on the phone…doing some dirty talking where she mentioned your name, son…so I've actually known for a bit myself.

My head falls back.

"Someone's been keeping some secrets," Camden sings.

"Ugh. Your family is terrible at keeping secrets," I groan.

"Sounds like they're not the only ones." He chuckles.

I tap his phone again, which makes him laugh harder.

TULLY

No one tells me ANYTHING.

DYLAN

Same here. I'm offended.

CAMDEN

Same here.

He winks at me.

NOAH

No one told me, but I've been seeing the way you've looked at Juju since the day she moved into our neighborhood in St. Paul. So…I guess you could say I've known the longest.

TULLY

True. I have noticed that myself. Okay, you guys are off the hook. But next time, SHARE. Sharing is caring, dammit!

DYLAN

What Tull said.

CAMDEN

You guys are unbelievable. But I guess I love
you anyway.

He looks at me sheepishly, and I tug his head down and kiss him with everything I have in me.

When we finally break apart, he pushes my hair back and studies my face. "Are we really okay?"

"Yes," I whisper.

"I'm so sorry for all the hurt I've caused you, Juju. When we were kids. Now. That you've never known how badly I wanted you…or how much I wanted to be standing next to you, doing every part of our life together. I regret all the ways I've lashed out and tried to deflect my feelings…I'm sorry for all of it. Most of all, for how much time we've lost."

"We're here now. Clean slate. I forgive you. I'm sorry for all the times I lashed out at you too."

"I deserved it."

"Yes, you did." I laugh.

"Thank you for giving me a chance. It means every-thing…*you* mean everything to me."

CHAPTER THIRTY-THREE

TECHNICALITIES

CAMDEN

Kevin is at my feet as I get my coffee, and I stop and scoop him up. I nuzzle his face, and he pants his little dog breath all over me. I know I'm supposed to think dogs stink because they do, but I like it.

Sue me.

"There's the guy everyone's talking about," Grandma Donna says as she comes over to pat me on the arm.

Kevin wiggles to get out of my grasp, and when I set him down, he goes over to twirl by Grandma Donna's feet. She gets out his food, and after he's gotten his scratches from her, he digs in.

"Good gravy, I had no idea what we were walking into yesterday," Grandma Nancy says. She comes over, holding up a large pan of baked French toast. "Here, have some breakfast." She looks at the clock. "Okay, it's almost lunchtime, but we were up late."

"I'm supposed to meet Juju in just a few minutes."

"Oh, have her stop by here, would ya?" Grandma Donna asks. "I didn't get a chance to hug her yesterday. I want to welcome her into the family."

I wave my phone and text Juju real quick to see if they could stop by here before we go out. Then I grin at Grandma Donna.

"Well, she's always kinda been part of the family…" I say. "But she still isn't technically yet…"

"Oh, fer crying out loud," she says, her shoulders shaking with her laugh. "When are you gonna make an honest woman out of her?"

Grandma Nancy starts humming that Beyoncé song about shoulda put a ring on it, and the two of them giggle. Okay, they're not the only two.

"She says they can stop by. Jackson and Dove will be with her."

Grandma Nancy's eyes go wide. "I do not know what got into that boy. If I'd been there when he socked you, I would've gone over there and boxed his ears!"

"She's not the only one!" Grandma Donna pipes up. "I know I'm all for peace and love and whatnot, but that was out of hand." Her eyes brighten. "See if they wanna stay and eat!"

"What's all the commotion in here?" Dad walks in, smiling.

He comes over and hugs me, jabbing me in the side where he knows I'm ticklish.

"Had to hear it from the town Facebook page about my son," he says, shaking his head.

"Sounded like you heard it from the source herself," I say.

He laughs. "If you could've seen her face when she realized I was standing behind her." A loud laugh bursts out of him, and my grandmas cackle.

I swipe my hand down my face and try to hold in the laugh, but it's pointless.

"What exactly did you hear?" I ask once we've calmed down.

"Oh, something about Camden Whitman's dirty mouth and you wanting her all to yourself." Dad holds up his finger. "Oh…and the best part…she said if you were there, she'd pull you into the walk-in cooler and teach you a lesson."

"Okay, okay, that's enough," I jump in.

My grandmas trill like little birds.

"Oo-hoo-hoo," Grandma Donna says, wiping her eyes as she laughs.

"Good gravy, that sounds hot to trot!" Grandma Nancy adds.

I shake my head. "No. I can't. I cannot," I say, covering my ears. "My sweet, innocent grandmothers…"

That just makes them laugh harder.

"We are gonna have so much fun with our little Cammie and Juju being lovebirds," Grandma Donna says. "I'll have to knit you matching sweaters. With cute mittens and scarves…I can't wait. When will she be here? I'll measure her. I think I know her size pretty well without, but…"

"We've had kids. We know all about being lovebirds," Grandma Nancy says. "And the way you two are in the kitchen…oh!" She points at me. "And the way the two of you used to bicker something fierce." She waggles that finger. "Watch out, chemistry. It is going to be sizzling hot."

"Grandma!" I groan. "Uh. I—" I look at my watch helplessly, and Dad puts his arm around my shoulder.

"Don't worry. We'll settle down eventually. Give us time to celebrate, and we'll slow our roll," he says.

I smile at him. "It's okay. I'm pretty excited about all of this too."

"If we'd had the energy to stay up after you got off work last night, we would've," he says. "We tried, but since we couldn't, you're getting it all this morning."

"There's that lover boy!" Goldie sings as she comes dancing across the kitchen.

"See what I mean?" Dad chuckles.

"Everyone's so…cheery today," I say.

"Don't act like you're not," Goldie says, smirking as she points at my face.

"Couldn't if I tried," I say.

"What did I miss?" Milo asks when he walks into the room. "I miss one day at Kitty-Corner." He holds up his finger and frowns at me. "*One. Day.*"

Goldie snorts. "Maybe you could've saved my brother from getting punched in the jaw." She steps closer and studies my face. "You *look* fine."

"I am fine. It was nothing." I wave her back.

"I heard you staggered back into the tables and knocked down three shakes and two cups of coffee. It went *everywhere*," Erin says as she walks in. "Hi, fam. Your favorite child has arrived!" She holds her arms out and embraces my grandmas with huge fanfare. "I heard we're celebrating Camden losing his virginity."

I cover my eyes with my hand. "I did not knock down any food or drinks," I say grumpily. I sip some coffee because it looks like I'm gonna need an IV drip of it to get through this interrogation. "And my virginity wasn't in question," I say quietly but pointedly to Erin.

"Oooo," she sings. "Let's hope not, for our Juju's sake. You gotta know what you're doing to please our girl."

"Oh, this boy knows what he's doing, don't you worry,"

Grandma Nancy tells Erin. "When a man can slap dough around like he can, a woman can tell these things."

"*Grandma!*" I yelp.

Dad's laughing so hard he has to wipe his eyes.

"Did you lose any teeth?" Grandma Donna asks, moving around everyone to come look me over.

"No, no, all the teeth are intact."

"If I'd known you fell down in the middle of all those hot and cold beverages, I would've hustled right over to your side when I came into the cafe," she says.

"You couldn't have known," I say, giving up.

"Bosco had to help him to his feet," Erin says, winking at me. "And the two of them nearly went flying into Beverly's pancakes with maple syrup and all the whipped cream. You know how that woman likes her whipped cream."

The grandmas hum in agreement. Even I know how Beverly appreciates a little pancake with all her whipped cream.

"But fortunately, Miss Idella ran across the room and held Camden up with everything she had in her." Erin shakes her head. "Honestly, I didn't know she had that kind of brute strength."

I grumble under my breath, which makes Erin and Goldie crack up. I glare at Goldie and see that she has tears running down her face.

"Miss Idella and her brute strength," she wheezes.

"Well, I'm just glad you're okay. I'm going to have a word with that boy when I see him. He's not too old for me to give him a tongue lashing," Grandma Donna says.

"That's what she said," Grandma Nancy says tartly.

"I *cannot*," I mumble, putting my head in my hand.

For all their talk about putting Jackson in his place, all he has to do is come in and say, "Grandma Nancy, look at you, looking sexier than Dolly Parton with a new wig. And you, Grandma Donna…mmm, mmm, mmm, you get more divine every time I see you. Meet my wife, Dove Fair. Baby, these two beautiful women are who all women should aspire to be like," he says, kissing their hands one by one.

"Yeah, you knew you had to do some major ass-kissing to get in this kitchen, didn't you, Jackson Fair," Erin says under her breath.

"Every now and then I'm smarter than I look," he says with a wink when my grandmas rush to get the extra plates on the table.

CHAPTER THIRTY-FOUR

UNBEKNOWNST TO ME

JULIANA

"Thanks for hanging out with my family," Camden says as we walk to Jackson's SUV.

"They're wonderful," Dove says. "Your grandmas are the cutest! Everyone's so nice. And Milo and Goldie…dreamy. He is so…serious, and the way he looks at Goldie is—" She fans her face.

"Oh, he's got you all ready to go, does he?" Jackson says, leaning over and kissing Dove's neck. "I can go serious. If that's what you're into."

Dove laughs and pushes him back. "You're what I'm into."

"So where are we going?" I ask.

"Oh, just you wait," Jackson says.

We buckle up, and Jackson drives the not-even-a-mile distance to The Hungry Walleye.

"The Hungry Walleye? That's our big outing?" I laugh.

"Wait for it," he says, holding up his hand in mock seriousness.

"Okay," I say sarcastically.

Do siblings ever act like adults with each other? I keep waiting for it to happen with Jackson and me, but so far, it hasn't taken. I'll be shocked if it ever does.

We walk into the restaurant, and I grin at Jackson and Dove walking hand in hand in front of Camden and me.

"They're actually kind of cute together," I whisper.

He nods. "I like her more than I expected to."

"Me too. I'm relieved."

He lifts his eyebrows in agreement, and I walk under his arm when he holds the door open for me.

"Bob! Helen!" Jackson yells like he hasn't seen the owners in years.

Bob comes over and shakes Jackson's hand, and then says hello to the rest of us.

"I've got everything all set up," he says.

I frown. "Our table?" I look around, and hardly anyone is here. Since I didn't leave work until after the lunch rush and we ended up eating at Camden's house after that, The Hungry Walleye is quiet.

"Something better," Jackson says excitedly.

Bob motions for us to follow him, and we go into the room that's usually used for parties or large groups.

I've been to the party room more times than I can count over the course of my life. I've seen it with a variety of tables, different chairs and tablecloths and paint…but I have never seen it look anything close to the way it does now.

Helen comes up to stand next to me and smiles proudly.

"What…have you done?" I ask, eyes wide.

"Isn't it something?" she says.

There are two dartboards at the end of the room, and a

line of axes next to us. A cage is between the other side of the room, dividing the dartboards from each other.

"Bob saw this in the Twin Cities, and he decided to bring it to Windy Harbor. I think we can use a little excitement around here…especially in the winter. I've never been big on skiing," she explains.

"Me either," I tell her. "But I can't say I've ever tried throwing an axe either."

"You're gonna love it," Jackson says.

Dove and I look at each other doubtfully.

"Come on, Camden and I can show you how it's done, right, Cam?" Jackson smiles at Camden with that competitive gleam he's always had when it comes to the two of them. "Have you done this yet?"

"No, I haven't," Camden says. "Other than chopping wood for the fire, I haven't thrown axes." He looks at me and grins. "This should be fun."

"Mm-hmm." My voice rises at the end, and I bite my lip, wondering how the hell I'm gonna get an axe all the way over there.

Jackson shows Dove how to use the axe and lets her do a practice throw. It lands short of the dartboard by about two feet. She gets a little closer on her next throw and lifts her shoulder like *Oh well.*

"You want to go next, Juju?" he asks.

"No, it's okay. You go," I say.

"All right." He throws the axe, which hits the board…but not in any of the circles.

He curses under his breath and motions for me to go.

I look at Camden. "I've never held an axe before."

"Want me to show you the way I do it?"

I nod, and he grabs an axe and asks me to hold it.

"Does that feel okay?"

I nod.

He moves behind me and puts his arms around mine. I stick my rear end out just because it's so tempting when he's flush against me, and he groans in my ear.

"No tempting the teacher, Miss Fair," he says.

"Yes, sir, Mr. Whitman." I turn and bat my eyes up at him.

He sighs a long-suffering sigh, but I feel him get hard, and I grin.

He shakes his head. "You're evil," he sings.

"You've always known the real me," I sing back.

"What are you guys doing over there?" Jackson asks. "Is there some kind of kinky shit going on over there?"

"What?" I say in mock outrage. "Not at all."

"Evil," Camden says.

I giggle.

"Okay, watch," Camden says. "Hold it like this, and don't move any closer. You're the perfect distance away. Just throw it like this," he says, demonstrating the movement, "and you'll be golden."

"'K. Got it," I say, doubting that I, in any way, have it.

He steps back, and I take a deep breath and then do exactly what he said, and the axe lands right in the center of the bull's-eye.

"You've done this before," Jackson yells.

"Never!" I laugh happily. Camden holds up his hand and I grab it, clutching it in some kind of victory shake.

I've never been a sporty girl, so I don't know what's usually done here.

Camden goes next, and he nails it. I do a little victory dance, feeling myself now, and Jackson's eyebrows scrunch together.

"What do you guys do on your dates, play darts all night?" he asks.

"This is fun!" I say.

It continues like that, with Camden and me absolutely killing it, and Jackson getting more and more aggravated.

Helen brings back a tray of drinks, and Jackson laughs.

"Let's see if you two are as good when you've got some drinks in you."

"That doesn't sound wise," I say. "Wielding an axe and alcohol?"

"You don't know a fun time until you've had a drink and thrown an axe," Jackson says.

"I don't even want to ask," I say, holding up my hand. "You and your great ideas."

"If you take a shot and get three bull's-eyes in a row, you get to skip the Lutheran Jell-O at Easter," Jackson says, pointing at Camden, "and I'll eat it."

"Done and done," Camden says.

"And if I take a shot and get in any of the circles three times in a row, you have to eat the Jell-O *and* ask Sandy for her hotdish," Jackson says. "Goldie made me try some that one time Sandy brought it over for Everett, and that stuff is godawful."

I snort and shake my head. "How is that fair?"

Camden laughs. "It's okay. I'll take the deal." He points at Jackson. "Get ready to eat a lot of Jell-O…with mayo on top."

Jackson's eyes widen, and he looks afraid.

Camden has just taken a shot and made one bull's-eye when Mom calls.

"Ohhh, it's Mom. I hate to miss Camden beating you soundly, but I should get this. I meant to call her last night, but I fell asleep too early," I say, holding up my hand and moving where it's quieter to answer.

"Hello?" I say.

"Hello, Juliana."

"Uh-oh, you're saying my full name." I laugh.

"Is there something you want to tell me?" she asks.

"As a matter of fact there is, but it sounds like you may already know." I scrunch up my face. "Sorry, Mom. It all kind of snowballed over here."

"I'm just so excited I can't even take it," she says, her voice breaking into a sob. "I'm not sad, I'm not sad," she rushes to say. "I wish Stella could be here to know this is happening. She wanted the two of you to be together so badly." She sniffles and laughs a little, blowing her nose. "Tell me everything."

So I go back to the beginning and try to give her the abbreviated version.

We're both crying and laughing by the time I hang up.

"Who won?" I ask, walking toward the group. I wipe the tears from my face and dab my nose.

"I'm gonna need a big bottle of Tums at Easter," Jackson grumbles.

CHAPTER THIRTY-FIVE

ALIGNMENT

CAMDEN

Past: Camden, age 27, Juju, age 25

Chef Camden Whitman of Whitman's in Denver, Colorado, discusses life as a restaurant owner...a Michelin-starred restaurant owner. Tonight at ten.

I wasn't sure I could stand to watch myself on the news, even though my staff had stayed beyond their shifts to watch it with the rest of the working crew. Just because we'd gotten a star didn't mean we could stop working. The restaurant was still full; in fact, my friends from the Colorado Mustangs were sitting at a large table out there right now, feasting on every appetizer we had, our finest steaks and lobster, and the risotto that melted in your mouth.

Life was good, and I wanted to keep it that way.

My cell rang, and it was my best friend, Jackson Fair. I seldom had the time to answer my phone when I was at the restaurant, but with the extra staff here tonight, I could make an exception.

"Hey, Jackson," I said.

"My man. I heard the news. Your dad told my family about the star. Congratulations, man. I am so proud of you."

"Thank you. I can't believe it," I said, taking a deep breath. "I've barely come up for air since opening the restaurant, so it feels really good to know it's doing this well."

"Doing well," he scoffs. "You're knocking it out of the fucking park. Juju said no one has ever gotten a star so soon after opening!"

At the sound of Juju's name, I felt a flood of heat and then a chill, like actual ice in my veins. The regret with the way I'd left things with Juju the last time I saw her. The things that came out of my mouth. And hers. But still…the things I'd said had been lies. All of them. I'd wanted to kiss her for as long as I could remember. I couldn't believe that the stars might finally be aligning, like my mom had said. Maybe this was our time.

What a crock of bullshit. She didn't want me. She never had. But that didn't stop my heart from catapulting out of my chest whenever I heard her say something nice about me. It had been a long time since she'd said something nice to me, and an even longer time since I'd said anything nice about her.

"Camden? You there?" Jackson asked.

"Yeah. Yeah, I'm here."

"What are you doing to celebrate?"

"Uh, not much. I've done a lot of interviews today. We're going to watch the first of them tonight. I think it's playing now actually, but I don't really want to—"

"Are you serious? Why didn't you say so? I'll let you go. Text me where we can see it too, okay?"

"Yeah, okay. I will."

"So proud. I love you, man."

"I love you too, Jackson. Hey, thanks for calling. It means a lot."

"Of course. Don't be a stranger."

"Never."

We hung up, and I stared at my phone.

I swallowed hard and sat down in the closest chair, slumping down until my ass barely fit on the seat, I was so stretched out.

This should've been the happiest night of my life. I'd worked an insane amount of hours and was unhealthy most of the time with the way I ate and drank and barely slept. I hadn't gone the cocaine route like a lot of the friends I'd made in the food industry, but it didn't mean I was that much healthier than them.

I was proud of what I'd accomplished, but what did it even mean if I had no one special to share it with? Someone beyond the people whose paychecks I paid…

It was depressing to be so alone.

I knew I always had my family, and I felt so grateful for them, but I wanted what my parents had had. Maybe I'd set them on too high a pedestal and had held out for the unattainable, but if I couldn't have what was real and lasting, I supposed it was better to be alone. Even if it sucked sometimes.

It was a hard awakening to know that after traveling the world over, meeting hundreds of people, doing what I loved by cooking for a different crowd every night, I still only wanted to see one girl with long blonde hair.

I wanted to cook for her and see if she'd tell me what was missing.

I wanted her to fill the hollow part of me that had formed when our friendship broke.

Josue walked by and paused when he saw me. "Why are you sitting in here all alone? And where is your drink?" my sous chef asked.

He motioned for me to get up and follow him, and I joined the rest of the group where they were huddled around a TV.

"You missed the interview!" someone said.

I was handed a drink, and I took it down in one gulp and was handed another.

After four or five drinks, I stumbled to my office and shut the door.

I looked at my phone for a long time before I finally dialed Juju's number.

I had a new cell phone, new number, and all that, but I hoped Juju's number was still the same.

The phone rang twice, and when she picked up, my heart thundered so loud, I thought surely she'd hear it.

"Hello?" she said.

I swallowed, and in that pause, she said hello again. She sounded the same, yet different. I wondered if she looked different. I hadn't seen her in over a year, and the last time I'd seen her, we'd avoided each other.

"Hello?" she said one more time and then hung up.

I sat there for a long time, kicking myself for not saying hello back.

I did that for three nights in a row. Drank, called Juju, didn't say a word.

On the third night, she said, "Who is this?" And her voice broke. I wondered if she knew it was me. If I mattered enough to make her voice break like that or if I'd only imagined the sound.

On the fourth night, I didn't pick up a drink or the phone, but it didn't stop me from wishing I could hear her voice.

Whether she was mad at me or hated me or never wanted to see me again, I just wanted her back in my life. Or at least, that's what I thought.

When my dad got sick a year later, I was forced to deal with what that might look like, and I quickly realized it wasn't all I'd hoped it would be.

CHAPTER THIRTY-SIX

THE ART OF FLORALS

JULIANA

Present

I walk into the Whitman house, which is bustling with energy. Camden's grandmas insisted that neither Camden nor I lift a finger for Easter. Those were their words. Actually, more specifically, Grandma Nancy lifted her hand and said, very properly, "Neither you nor Camden shall lift a finger this Sunday. Donna and I have got it, and we don't want to hear another word about it."

It feels weird to only come in with flowers and not laden down with all the food I'd normally prepare...but kind of nice too. Camden spent the night with me last night, and we slept in this morning. I woke up to him between my legs. That was beyond nice.

He tickles my side and nuzzles my ear. "What are you thinking about? Your cheeks are all red."

I shoot him a look. "I'll give you one guess, Mr. Wonder Tongue," I whisper.

"Mr. Wonder Tongue? That is an excellent nickname."

"You deserve it," I say, lifting a shoulder.

"There you are!" Grandma Donna says. She has a stack of something knitted in her hands. "Come on back. Everyone's here."

She lifts up two sweaters. One has a bunny standing with a blue tie around its neck, and the other is a bunny with long blonde hair standing in a yellow dress. She hands Camden the one in a yellow dress and gives me the one with the blue tie. Camden and I look at each other for a beat and then have to look away because I don't want to get the giggles.

"I made these for you to wear for our Easter photo," she says.

"Wow, Grandma Donna," Camden says. "You've outdone yourself."

He pulls the sweater over his button-down shirt, grinning at me when his face pops out, hair going everywhere, and I have never loved him more.

"Amazing," I tell her. "Thank you." I put the sweater on over my dress, and Camden pushes my hair out of my eyes, kissing me softly when he's done.

"Thank you," he whispers so only I can hear.

"Oh, you two are adorable," Grandma Donna says.

My parents and Jackson and Dove walk in behind us, and hugs are exchanged all around. Grandma Donna hands them their sweaters, and I laugh when I see Jackson in his. The bunny looks just like him, complete with the attitude.

"Hello!" Uncle Hal says as he walks in. "What have we here?" He studies our sweaters and grins when Grandma Donna hands him one. "Why, thank you, dear," he says. His sweater has a Ralph the rooster look-alike, and Uncle Hal is thrilled.

She nods sweetly, and her cheeks flush when she looks past him. I turn back to see Papa Hector holding a huge bouquet of flowers.

"For you," he says as he hands them to Grandma Donna.

"They're beautiful," she says.

"As are you," he says, ducking his head.

"He's fucking flirting," Jackson hisses in my direction.

"I think you call that courting," I hiss back. "Something you wouldn't understand…"

"I call that *weird* is what I call it. They're old enough to be—"

"Our grandparents?" I supply helpfully.

He pretends to gag, and I sock him in the stomach.

He doubles over, and my mom snaps her fingers.

"Am I gonna have to separate you two?"

"Sorry, Mom." I shoot her an apologetic look, and she winks at me.

"Aww look, how sweet," she says, touching my arm.

Papa Hector is wearing his sweater, which has a very distinguished-looking bunny wearing a sweater vest and bow tie.

"Exquisite," he says as he pats the sweater down.

Jackson looks at me and mimes throwing up. I act like I'm gonna punch him again, and he stumbles as he tries to get away from me.

"Come on back," Grandma Donna says. "I've been hurrying to finish everyone's sweaters, and Nancy has been working overtime in the kitchen. I think Grayson needs the Easter egg hunt to happen before we eat, though. The little guy is so excited."

When we walk back to the kitchen and great room,

everyone is already in their sweaters. I put my hand over my mouth to cover my laugh. The sweaters have everything from bunnies to hens to eggs and carrots. It's the cutest display of knitted yarn I've ever seen.

Milo's carrot-holding-the-hand-of-a-pea sweater is almost enough to make me lose it.

"Don't," he says, pointing at me, his lips twitching.

"Aren't we cute?" Goldie says, leaning into him with her matching sweater and smiling over at me.

"The cutest," I tell her, laughing.

"Uncle Camden! Juju!" Grayson runs over and throws his arms around my legs and then Camden's. "Now we can do the Easter egg hunt! My friends are waiting outside. Come on!"

"Where's Tull?" Camden asks Goldie as we head out back.

"Oh, just you wait," she says, laughing.

Out on the grass just before the sand and water, kids are running around with their parents looking on, and someone who's dressed as a giant Easter bunny is getting his picture taken with the kids, one by one.

"No," Camden says, putting his fist over his mouth as he laughs. "How did he ever find a suit big enough?"

Dylan walks up in his emo rooster surfer sweater and shakes his head sadly. "I tried to put it on, and I was just too tall."

"Hey! You're here!" I nudge him, and he turns before giving me a huge bear hug.

Next he hugs Camden, who runs his hand over Dylan's floppy hair.

"I haven't seen you in person since I heard the good news," Dylan says. "I like it." He nods. "Have to say, I'll miss the way you insulted Camden so thoroughly, but this is really nice."

Camden puts his arm around me and leans in to kiss my hair. "Trust me, this is much, much better."

Dylan looks at his phone when it dings, smiling as he responds.

"The fam's been noticing that you smile at your phone a lot," Camden says. "I don't remember you doing that unless there was a girl on the other end. Something you want to tell us…about anyone in particular?" He lifts his eyebrows.

Dylan's mouth opens and closes, and he puts his phone in his pocket. His hand goes to the back of his neck, and he rubs it. "Just wrapping up handing everything over to Rudy. I'm going to California on Tuesday, but I'll be back in a few weeks…for good."

"I can't wait to meet Bill," Goldie says, walking up to us. "I hope he and Kevin are best buds."

"They will be," Dylan says. "Bill hasn't met a dog he doesn't like." He motions toward the house. "The bathroom's calling."

He turns and jogs to go inside, and I look at Camden. "He didn't really answer your question, did he?"

"No, he did not."

"Oh, are you talking about the girl he's always talking to?" Goldie asks.

"You know it's a girl?" Camden asks, leaning in.

Noah walks over. "Are we talking about Dylan?" he whispers. "I heard you say something about the girl he's always talking to…"

Goldie leans in, and Erin walks over, kissing everyone on the cheek.

We all lose it over her sweater: a hen with a tight red dress and red lipstick.

Once the commotion has died down, she points at Goldie. "You had gossip face when I walked up. Spill."

"We're talking about Dylan," Goldie says. "So I don't have a name, but I might've seen the contact of a long thread he had going, and it was a flower." She looks around expectantly.

"A flower," Noah says flatly.

Goldie nods excitedly. "Right? It's so obvious. Who else would he save as a flower emoji?"

"What kind of flower?" I ask.

"The cherry blossom," she says without hesitation.

"You know the names of the flower emojis?" Camden asks.

"*Yeah*," she says. "Obviously. What kind of artist would I be if I didn't know that?"

"Hmm," I say, pulling out my phone and studying the different flowers. "I'm impressed. I wouldn't have known that."

"That's our girl," Erin says. She leans in. "But I feel we're getting derailed here. Do we know who Cherry Blossom is?"

"No idea," Goldie says, shoulders falling. "And he's being so cryptic. It's not like him at all. Dylan has never been able to keep a secret to save his life. We stopped telling him about any Christmas presents we'd bought for each other because he'd spill every time."

Everett blows a whistle and the Easter egg hunt starts, so the conversation pauses as we watch the kids run in every direction.

Camden pulls my back against his chest. "I love this. Being here with you…my family. You're everything I wanted in my life, Juju."

I look back at him, and the look in his eyes is so sweet that I turn to face him. "It feels so good, doesn't it."

He nods and looks sheepish. "I went through a phase of calling you every night…a few phases of it, actually."

My eyebrows crinkle. "When? I don't remember you ever calling me every night."

"I, uh…I hung up. Every time."

"What?" I think back and remember one week in particular where it seemed like I got a call around the same time every night. "That was you? I was starting to get creeped out when it stopped."

"I started staying away from the bottle more. That helped." He laughs. "I wanted to say how sorry I was for ruining everything between us. And more than anything, I wanted to tell you that you were never just a way for me to pass the time. Being with you was the only time I wanted the moments to stand still."

"I wish I'd known."

"Me too."

"Let's not waste any more time. Okay?"

"Okay," he says.

"We say how we feel, and we don't look back with regret…at least not so much that it wrecks the right here, right now."

"I like this plan."

"And I promise when you call and breathe heavy, I'll talk dirty to you instead of hanging up."

He laughs. "Makes me want to call you right now."

CHAPTER THIRTY-SEVEN

NOT SO SOFT

CAMDEN

The time has finally come…the soft opening for Windhaven Resort is this afternoon. Our family, friends, and staff, as well as business owners from Windy Harbor and all over Minnesota and a few influencers, will all be spending the night. It's the first time we'll be showing everything Windhaven Resort has to offer.

Before the doors open, Dad stands in front of my family, as well as Juju, Milo, and Erin, who all may as well be family by now, with tears in his eyes.

"When I brought the idea of this resort to you kids, I wasn't sure I'd ever see this day. But not only have you brought what I'd envisioned to life, *and then some*, but you and the crews you've each assembled have done it in record time." He looks at Milo and wipes his eyes. "Forgive me for getting so emotional. It's been a big year." He laughs. "Cancer, beating it…" He lifts his eyes and does praying hands.

"And enlisting Milo, the most innovative architect I know… who's still living, God rest your mom's soul. She would've loved you for the way you love our daughter *and* for your work," he tells Milo. "I'm blown away by what you've made possible. What all of you have made possible."

He looks around at us and continues. "You've each contributed more than I ever thought possible. I thought it might just be me and Milo for a minute there," he laughs, "and the next thing I knew, we were all building my version of Rivendell."

He lowers his head and takes a breath. "I hope you carry a sense of pride and ownership at what you've built. This weekend is our warm-up, time to have fun and give it a practice run, but I think we've got this one in the bag, kiddos. You've already done the hardest part. There's still work ahead, but from here on out, we can enjoy everything we've put in place. It goes without saying that I'm proud of you, but I'll say it anyway: I have the best family ever, and I'm so damn proud of each and every one of you." He points at Grayson. "And as for you, my favorite grandson…"

"I'm your only grandson!" Grayson says, and we all laugh.

"You got me there." Everett chuckles. "I love seeing everything about this place through your eyes, little man. Thank you for being the sunshine for us all."

Grayson nods solemnly. "I love you too."

Grandma Nancy hands Grandma Donna a tissue, and they both blow their noses. Grandma Nancy leans in and whispers something in Dad's ear, and he nods.

"Would you like to say anything, Mom, before we open those doors?"

"I sure would." She holds out her hands on either side, and we all do the same until we're one big circle. "Get ready to change the lives of everyone who walks through those doors. I know Donna is the more positive of us two"—they share a laugh, and we all laugh too—"but she's shown me that a kind word when someone's down, or lending an ear when someone needs to talk…it does heaps in terms of turning someone's day around. In some cases, it could even be saving a life."

She looks in each of our eyes with what she says next. "All different kinds of people will come here needing to recharge, and some maybe even to find their way. I encourage you to lean in and shine as bright as that lighthouse out on the lake. You do that, and this place will be more than the beautiful resort it already is—it will be heaven on earth." She looks up to the sky. "Dear Lord, bless this place and everyone who comes through these doors. In Jesus's name. Amen."

"Amen," we echo.

"I couldn't have said it any better. Thanks, Mom," Dad says, kissing her on the cheek. "Let's open those doors."

Guests are there as soon as the doors open, mostly the locals. Each of us take a group on a tour around the place. Juju and I have two influencers, Stacy from Duluth, and Tammy from St. Paul.

Their eyes are wide as they take in the high ceilings and the intricate decor.

"I like to call it a fairy bringing her dreams indoors," Juju says, laughing. "The intricate detailing of the wood, all the arches, and the little touches of the outdoors brought inside." She points out the huge swing that fits two (or five) people in the lobby, and the moss and twisted tree trunks of the real trees that scale the walls.

"I love that," Tammy says. "It's fitting. I love that even though it's both cozy and, like you said, Juju, I could imagine a fairy popping out at any moment." We all laugh. "But all the light from the windows offsets the wood and the earth tones…" She shakes her head and points at the massive cream stone fireplace. "The carvings in that stone. It's like stepping into a movie."

Juju and I smile at each other. We show them the shop, and they decide to come back and explore more after we've given the tour. We stop by the concierge desk, where Dylan talks about all the excursions he's organized.

"There are amazing things to do around here all year long," he says. "But this seventy-degree day is perfect for what we have in mind this weekend. We'll have something for everyone—hikes, yoga, art classes, fishing, bike rides, kayaking, and so much more." He gives them a flyer with an itinerary, and we continue the tour.

"Oh my God, is that Tully Whitman?" Stacy comes to an abrupt stop.

Tully just walked in and has a few people following him already. He pauses by the fireplace, where a few girls swarm on either side of him as they take selfies.

"Are you a fan of the Minnesota Fierce?" I ask.

"A huge fan," she says. "I have season tickets and never miss a home game."

"Come on, let's go say hi," I tell her.

Her eyes bug out. "I don't know. I'm not sure I—"

"He's so nice," Juju says. "Super down to earth…and there's a drawing. Whatever name he picks gets a jersey and a meet and greet with the entire team."

"Oh my God," she whispers.

"Let's just walk over this way," I say.

I catch Tully's eye and motion for him to come over. When he starts walking toward us, Stacy grabs Juju's arm like she might go down. I make the introductions, and Tully smiles wide, looking like the hockey superstar he is…one who's been blessed with still-intact teeth.

"Hey there. Tully Whitman, nice to meet you," he says, holding out his hand.

She takes it and stares at him for at least thirty seconds before breathing and saying hi. I think we lose her concentration after that. She's lost in Tully Land as we go to the restaurant and then walk through the garden down to the pavilion filled with artwork.

"If you need to talk to anyone while you're here, Grandma Donna will listen. She keeps the Friendship Bench busy, even in the cold months," I tell them.

"That's the sweetest thing I've ever heard," Tammy says, watching as Grandma Donna hands a man she's been talking to for the past twenty minutes a knitted glasses holder.

Next to us, Noah starts a fire. Stacy sees him, and her mouth drops.

"Is everyone who works here unusually hot?" she asks Juju under her breath.

"Yes. It's the Whitman family genes," Juju says, giving me a look that makes me want to bend her over the bench, hike up that skirt, and see how fast I can make her scream my name.

Suddenly, I'm in a hurry to finish the tour.

"You okay?" Juju asks after Stacy and Tammy have gone inside the pavilion.

"You look so hot in that fucking skirt. What are you wearing underneath?" I ask.

"Wouldn't you like to know?" she says, leaning in close but not close enough.

"I really, really would."

"Hey, Erin! Ava!" Juju says, waving them over.

Ava reaches us first, and Juju points out Stacy and Tammy in the window.

"Do you think you could finish up the tour with those two girls? Really all that's left is to show them to their rooms and point out all the high points."

"Got it. We're on it," Erin says. She takes another look at Juju and then me and grins. "Mm-hmm. I see what's happening here. You two hot and horny lovebirds go get some for the rest of us."

Ava's cheeks turn red and so do Juju's, but she surprises me by hugging the girls and taking my hand, tugging me toward the resort.

"You're a lifesaver. Thank you," she calls, laughing as she pulls me inside.

CHAPTER THIRTY-EIGHT

CONVENIENCE

JULIANA

"Is everything okay?" Camden asks as I drag him into the back entrance of the resort.

"Yes," I say, moving faster. "Follow me."

We go down the hall, and I find the closest conference room. It's the smallest one, and on the side is a smaller room, a little bigger than a closet, with a computer and sound system for the times when groups are here and need to do presentations. When I lead him to the smaller room, Camden stares at me.

"Juju," he says, voice low.

"Camden," I say, just as low.

"Did you bring me back here to—"

"I brought you back here to make you deliver on that look you were giving me outside," I tell him.

"What look was that?" he asks, his husky voice sending my heart racing.

"The look that said you were imagining doing very, very naughty things to me."

His hands find my waist, and I can hear the smile in his voice.

"You have no idea how many naughty things I want to do to you," he says.

"I think I might," I say.

Our mouths collide, and when I stand on my tiptoes to reach him better, he grips my ass and presses our bodies together. Breathless, I pull away and turn to face the table, which has a computer and small sound system sitting on top of it. Then I bend over and look at him over my shoulder.

"*How did you read my mind?*" he asks. "I've been imagining lifting this skirt and doing this all afternoon."

His hands are already sliding up my skirt, and when he gets to my cheeks, he gives one side a little smack and then rubs out the sting.

"Either I can totally read your mind or you weren't as subtle as you think." I arch into his hands, and he groans when he dips under my lace and finds me wet. "We don't have long. Someone might walk in."

"You are so ready for me," he says, rubbing my wetness all over me.

"Yes, I am."

He unzips his pants and tugs my underwear until it rips apart. I gasp and then let out a long moan when he buries himself inside me.

"Ohhh," he groans. "I was so ready for you too. How are we gonna make this last?"

"We can go slow later. Fuck me hard, Camden. I need it."

"Are you so greedy?" he asks, pumping in and out, faster and faster.

"So greedy," I whimper. "Harder. Please, Camden. Don't make me wait. I want you so much. Please."

"Mmm, I love it when you tell me what you want. You feel so fucking good." He goes faster, deeper, and I slam back into him. "Taking me like such a fucking good girl."

His hand slides across my stomach and down between my legs, where he starts to rub circles over me.

I lose my rhythm, too lost in the sensations firing off everywhere, and I cry out, "I'm so close," and then in the next second, "I'm coming."

"I'm right there with you, baby. God, you know just how —" He lets out a long curse when I clench around him in tight, desperate pulses.

He gets even harder inside, and it's like time just collapses to this one stretched-out moment of bliss. He holds my back against his chest while we ride it out, whispering between staggered breaths, "I love…you…I…love you."

I can't even speak yet, but once I feel steady again, I turn my face to his, and we kiss softly.

"I love you," I whisper. "How did we get so lucky? What if we'd never gotten our act together?"

"I don't even want to think about that," he says. "I want to bury myself in you and never remember how awful it was without you."

Voices come down the hall toward us, and then the door to the conference room opens.

"This room holds about thirty," Goldie tells someone. "It'll be great for smaller meetings. This is the only room this size, and then the bigger one is next door."

We're okay, as long as no one decides to look at the sound room. Camden and I freeze, and then he slowly eases out of me and tucks himself in his pants. I pull down my skirt and look at the strip of light coming from the doorway.

I gasp and Camden stiffens. I point at the doorway, where on the floor in the strip of light are my ripped lacy panties.

"Oh!" Goldie says, a little closer. "Uh, let's take a look at that bigger one. It's even better." She sounds like she's about to start laughing, and when she gets closer to the door to the hallway, she says, "Fancy pants around here, am I right?"

I bury my head in my hands while Camden barely holds back his laugh.

CHAPTER THIRTY-NINE

IT'S REAL

CAMDEN

The resort is getting the best buzz we could've hoped for. It's been unbelievably busy the past couple of weeks, but we've got a rare day off. It'll be the last one for a while before our grand opening in a few weeks. Juju and I are in my bed down in the basement, coming down from our state of orgasm euphoria—I *love* waking up with her in the morning—when Kevin peeks his head in the door. The little dude actually smiles when he sees her and comes bounding onto the bed.

Juju laughs and leans up to pet him. He immediately rolls onto his back and throws his paws in the air, which cracks us up. Little attention slut.

"He rarely comes down to say hi to me, but he can't resist when you're here," I tell her.

"I love him so much." She laughs when Kevin lolls around on his back and then ducks his head under her hand again. "I want a dog." She sighs. "I've just always felt too busy with the cafe and couldn't have one underfoot there in the kitchen."

"You don't want your only pets to be the hens and Ralph?"

She laughs and groans. "Ralph and I do not claim each other. He is Papa Hector's through and through, and the hens are becoming mine."

"Peaches and Snowball are your girls. They don't let me hold them like they let you. And Muffin…she's come a long way."

"Aww, she has. She's finally fattening up." She sniffs and sticks her bottom lip out.

Of course I have to kiss it.

"I love them. Did I tell you I think Peaches told Ralph to knock off chasing me? Because he's not trying as hard to eat me anymore. Unless she's snoozing, and then he's his usual cray self. They all have way more personality than I realized! But I still want a dog," she coos to Kevin.

"I want one too. This guy fills the void, but it'd be nice to have one of my own sometime. You know, that's one benefit to us having different schedules. One of us will usually be around…" I lean over and kiss her shoulder.

She looks at me with playful eyes. "That's a big step, getting a dog together."

"I'm ready for all of the big steps," I tell her.

She bites her bottom lip, her eyes lighting up even more. "Me too," she says.

The inner me bangs his fists against his chest in caveman celebration. I kiss her shoulder again and go up her neck. She shivers, and I smile against her skin.

"I'm really happy to hear you say that, Juliana Fair." I plant kisses back to her shoulder and lift my head. "Are you still good to meet up in a few hours?"

"Yes," she says, her voice and eyes soft and melty. "I have a few errands to run, but two o'clock still works for me."

"Perfect."

I have a couple of errands to run too, but I keep that to myself. I take a quick shower, and when I get out, Juju and Kevin are still having their lovefest.

"Do you have time for breakfast?" I ask.

"Always," she says, hopping up. "I'll take the fastest shower and be right up."

"Hey, Juju."

She turns and looks at me.

"I love you."

She grins. "I'll never get tired of hearing you say that. I love you too."

As soon as I leave Juju, I shift gears straight into worker beast mode.

Ever since the resort opened, I've had Noah working on a side project with me. My brother's the best there is when it comes to bringing design plans to life, and it's been great to spend this time with him. We've both been too busy to hang like this, just the two of us, for a long time. I've spent every spare hour between leaving Juju and heading into my shift at the restaurant out here—sawing, hammering, and revisiting my construction skills.

Now, we're putting on the final touches.

Noah steps back first, brushing sawdust off his jeans, and gives me a satisfied grin. "She's gonna love this."

I run my hand along the smooth wood and get strangely

sentimental. That's been happening a lot lately. "I hope you're right."

"You know I am." He slings an arm around my shoulders and yanks me in for one of those classic older-brother hug-slash-chokeholds. I laugh, half gasping, and make him work to get out of my own hold on him.

While he's nailing in the last trim piece, Marilyn and Virginia pull up. It's about half an hour before I've got to pick up Juju.

"We've got it from here, boss," Virginia says, hauling food out of the truck.

"You're the best," I tell them. "Thank you. You're getting bonuses for this."

"Not necessary," Virginia says. "We're suckers for love. Now, go get your girl." She blows a kiss and waves.

I take off, buzzing with adrenaline and nerves. I jog to the door when I get to Juju's. Ralph doesn't pay any attention until Juju steps out, and then he comes trucking toward her.

"I don't think so, buddy," I say, stomping my foot when he gets close.

He halts and throws his head back. "Ra-ra-ra-raooo!" he yells.

"Ra-ra your ass back into that coop, stat," I tell him.

Juju's laugh rings out, and I grin at her when Ralph scuttles away.

"Well done," she says, still laughing when she gets in the SUV.

When we pull onto Wildbriar Lane, she looks over, eyebrows raised. "Where are we going?"

"You'll see," I say, squeezing her knee.

It's only a minute before I turn onto the dirt path that cuts through the trees and leads to my land. When Dad bought this property, he let each of us choose a parcel for ourselves. Mine has the best view of the lighthouse and the cliffs, and of course, endless water. Every window of the future house will highlight the water.

Juju gasps as we pull up, and the structure comes into view.

She turns to me, eyes wide, voice barely above a whisper. "What have you done? It's the tree house. Only so much better."

Her gaze flicks from the whimsical structure nestled among the stunning tree branches to my face and back again.

Her mouth drops open, and her hand reaches for mine.

She's quiet as I help her out of the truck, her eyes never leaving the tree house.

We walk up the ladder, sanded smooth. I ran my fingers over every inch, making sure there were no splinters. I lift her hand to the ladder, and she climbs up slowly, with me right behind her.

At the top of the stairs, I pause. "Ready?"

She nods, excitement bouncing off of her.

I push the door open, and she gasps.

The soft light spilling through the windows makes the inside look even more magical than the outside. And I have the same kind of twinkle lights that Juju insisted were in the original tree house, which makes her smile. This tree house feels like an extension of what we did to the resort. Like you might see a fairy dozing on a moss-covered tree trunk or lightning bugs slowing down to say hello. In the center is a beautiful round table Noah made, covered with an outrageous spread.

Fresh fruit sliced and shaped into a heart. Mini tarts with gold-dusted tops. Warm bread in a basket, with cheeses and figs and grapes draped on a plate next to it. Two silver domes cover the plates that I know have that pasta I made for Juju when we were kids.

"This is a dream," she says reverently. "You did all this?"

"I had lots of help. Noah did all the hard parts." I grin. "And Marilyn and Virginia brought the food over."

"It's gorgeous."

"It's yours…" I take her hand and go to the window, where we look out at the water. I point to the clearing in the trees next to us. "And a house right there, if you want it. If you want me."

I take her hands, and she turns to face me. "I want you," she whispers. "Forever."

I drop to one knee and pull a ring out of my pocket, holding it up like an offering. My heart is hammering and my palms are sweaty, but when I look up at her face—those wide, beautiful eyes and the lips I've kissed a thousand times in my dreams and finally in reality—I'm not afraid. I'm certain.

"Juliana Fair," I say, my voice steady, even though everything inside me is quaking. "I love you. I love all of you. I love the quiet times when it's just the two of us in each other's arms. I love when we talk about the little things, the big things, all the things."

Her smile grows, but a tear drips down her cheek. I reach up and grab it with my thumb.

"I love when we shake with passion, how we can't get enough of each other. I love trying to catch my breath with you." I kiss the palm of her hand. "I even love when we insulted each other, back when we pretended to hate each other, because it's made us appreciate what we have now even more. I'll love you until the day I die and then some." I take a deep breath. "Will you marry me?"

Her hand flies to her mouth, her eyes shimmering. I can see the tremor in her fingers, and the way her chest rises and falls like she's breathless. She lets out a shaky laugh and drops her hand.

"Yes," she whispers. Then louder and with certainty, "Yes, Camden. I will marry you. I cannot *wait* to marry you."

She sinks onto the floor in front of me, cupping my face in her hands. Her smile knocks the wind out of me.

"I love you," she says. "I can't wait to spend the rest of our lives together. We are more than I could've ever dreamed of…and I think we'll only get better."

I slide the ring onto her shaking hand, or is that my hand shaking? She laughs again, tears rolling down her cheeks.

"I can't believe this is real," she says.

I lay her back on the pile of blankets and pillows arranged next to the table, and we christen the new tree house.

I think it may be the only time we've ever forgotten about the food.

EPILOGUE
STOLEN MOMENTS

JULIANA

It's late afternoon, and I'm sprawled across Camden's chest, our legs tangled under the sheets in the apartment above The Kitty-Corner. His heartbeat is galloping under my cheek, and mine is still racing from what we've been doing the past hour.

If we've had any spare moments these past few weeks, we've stolen them for ourselves—against the kitchen counter, in his office at Elm & Echo, and all over this apartment we now share more often than not. We spend every night together, but the location still changes between the yellow Victorian and Camden's basement. We're busy, pulled in a hundred directions by work and family and the resort, and dreaming about the home we're going to build together, but I've never been more certain of anything. We're making this work, and life is more beautiful than I ever thought it could be.

My phone buzzes on the nightstand. Camden's fingers on my back pause when I stretch for it.

> GOLDIE
>
> You and Camden should come to Windhaven. Meet me and Ava at the rooftop bar. The weather's dreamy and it's really cozy up here.

I grin and show Camden. "She's summoning us."

He peeks at the screen, eyes still heavy-lidded. "Do we want to leave this bed?"

"No, but we probably should get some air."

He chuckles. "Okay, if you say so."

I sit up and look back at Camden, tempted to cuddle back up to him. "We won't stay long."

He grins and rolls out of bed.

I wash up quickly and throw on some clothes. He puts on jeans and a black tee, which nearly weakens my resolve, but once I've put on a soft black dress and touched up my makeup, I'm ready.

We drive over to Windhaven, Camden's hand on my thigh, and are quiet when we pull up to the resort. Neither one of us has gotten much sleep, but we're still glowing. When I look in the mirror these days, I can't believe how happy I look.

Camden threads our fingers together, and we walk inside, saying hello to the few people we pass. It takes a few minutes to get to the rooftop, and the second we step out the door, I think our hearts stop.

"Surprise!" rings out.

I clutch my hand to my chest. The rooftop is packed. Family, friends, employees, and nearly all the residents of

Windy Harbor. Everyone's grinning, holding drinks, and wearing looks of conspiratorial glee.

Camden lets out a sharp, startled laugh.

Goldie bursts out of the crowd with Erin and Ava beside her, the three of them beaming.

"Did you really think we were going to let your engagement slip by without celebrating?" Goldie asks.

My eyes sting immediately. I whirl on Camden. "Did you know about this?"

He shakes his head, looking stunned. "Not a clue."

Papa Hector appears, pressing a glass of champagne into our hands. "For my sweetheart and her man."

His eyes are shiny too, and he hugs me tight. My parents follow close behind, and my eyes keep leaking.

The rooftop buzzes with music and laughter. Candles flicker on every high-top table, with trays of hors d'oeuvres from Elm & Echo floating through the crowd.

"This is amazing," I say. "I can't believe you managed to fit this in with everything else going on."

"I had lots of help." Goldie grins. She holds out her hands when her grandmas walk up. "These two did a ton."

Grandma Donna hugs me first. "Oh, fer goodness' sake. It was the least we could do."

"You two are going to make such beautiful great-grandkids," Grandma Nancy says.

I giggle when Camden shoots me an apologetic look.

"I think so," I say, lifting a shoulder.

His eyes start smoldering, and I lift my hand, shaking my head slightly. "Not that look. Not here," I say.

The grandmas titter.

"Ohhh, we can close this party down if it means babies sooner," Grandma Nancy says.

"I can't take these two anywhere," Everett says, over-hearing the conversation.

I fan my face and shoot Camden another look, which just makes him gaze at me with that sexy smirk.

The night rolls out like a fun movie montage. People keep grabbing us, hugging us, pressing glasses into our hands. Erin twirls me around on the dance floor, her combat boots flashing in the glow of the string lights. Milo and Goldie clink glasses with us, Goldie squeezing me so tight I can barely breathe.

"We were destined to be sisters," she whispers.

I squeeze her hand, my throat tight for the hundredth time.

Jackson starts out the toasts, sharing how he's just remembered how clumsy I used to always get whenever Camden was around.

I fan my face when I laugh too hard. The Whitman siblings gather for a toast, and of course, I shed many more tears. Everyone's said such amazing things that my heart is about to burst. And then, Goldie looks around to give the mic to Dylan.

"Where is he?" She frowns.

Everyone looks around.

"He was just here," Camden says.

Uncle Hal takes over when Dylan can't be found and has us all laughing. But when Dylan's spotted sneaking back onto the rooftop, hair mussed, shirt askew, Uncle Hal calls him out on it.

"Someone's trying to blend into their surroundings, but methinks we might be hearing about more romances in the Whitman family any day now!" Uncle Hal says, and the crowd erupts.

Dylan smooths his hand over his hair and shakes his head.

"How are we unable to get to the bottom of this?" Tully asks Camden.

"I even tried following him the other day after work," Noah says. "And normally, grilling him would've had him spilling in seconds. Our little guy has grown up."

Goldie crosses her arms. "I don't like it. It was bad enough when Camden and Juju were sneaking around. Dylan doing it is going too far."

"Hey," I say, laughing and nudging her with my elbow. "You make me sound like a robber in a heist. And you knew what was going on!"

"Yeah," she says with a grin, "but they didn't." She points at her brothers.

Noah and Tully side-eye Camden and me.

"The truth's out now—let's focus on Dylan," Camden says, laughing.

But Dylan makes the best choice. He grabs a glass and lifts it. "To my brother Camden and the beautiful Juliana Fair. You make love look easy and fun and inspiring. May we all find a love like yours."

"Hear, hear," everyone says.

I cry again. I can't stop crying tonight.

The night doesn't go late—everyone knows tomorrow is going to be madness with the grand opening. But it's later than my usual evening. It's worth it, though. For these few hours, we dance and laugh and hug. The town feels knitted together tighter than ever.

When the party finally winds down and Camden and I head home, we're exhausted but giddy. We undress and fall into bed, breathing each other in. His arm wraps around me, my hand rests over his chest, and in the quiet I whisper, "I love our life."

"It's perfect," he murmurs back. "And we get to live so

much more of it just like this…with new adventures every day. You think you can handle all this goodness?"

"With you by my side, I can handle anything. We've got what it takes to face whatever comes our way."

Want more Juju and Camden?
Get the bonus scene here!
https://bookhip.com/WGSKWAN

Am I imagining things, or does Dylan keep sneaking away? Does he have a secret romance? Or is it something totally innocent? I have a feeling it might be scandalous. Find out in *All For Love*, coming April 9th, 2026! Pre Order All for Love here!
https://geni.us/AllforLove

COMING SOON

ALL FOR LOVE

Chapter 1
Right Time, Right Place
DYLAN

December

I don't like to rush, but I also don't like to be at the airport with too much time to spare. Today I rushed to get to LAX after cutting it too close and thought I might be missing my flight. I got to the gate, and as my luck would have it, my flight was delayed.

Worst of both worlds.

I shrug off the tension in my shoulders, wishing I could beam myself up to Minnesota right about now. I never knew I had the capacity to get stressed until I moved from Minnesota to LA. I grew up going to Lake Superior every summer, and when I was in high school, my family went on vacation to California. I fell in love with the ocean and surfing. In fact, I loved it so much that I moved back to ride the waves and opened a surfboard shop in Malibu that's thriving. But the traffic has threatened to take my sanity on more than one occasion. If I could just stay in my neighborhood surfing and hanging out with the peeps I meet on the beach or who come through my shop, I'd be the most chill person I know.

Contributing to the stress is the reason I'm at LAX at least once a month, if not more…my dad has cancer. And I'm doing everything I can to turn the shop over to someone who will care about it as much as I do, so I can move back home to be with Dad. He insists that I not just drop everything for his sake, and I'm trying to honor his wishes, but it's getting harder to leave him every time.

As I sit here trying to catch my breath, a pair of endless legs walk by me, and I'm ashamed to say that every other thought leaves my brain.

Fucking hell.

Who is that supermodel, and where can I follow her for life?

My eyes track up from her long legs to her ass just barely covered by a skirt that I'd love to see outside in a breeze. White tank covering a toned stomach, and tits that are the perfect handful. The prettiest hands. Long dark hair that falls down her back, splashing over that white tank like velvet. And then I reach her face.

Goddamn. That face.

Her eyes meet mine and they hold. I swallow hard, divided by staring at her full pink lips or the most mesmerizing green eyes I've ever seen.

I blink, and she's walking away.

I stand, ready to introduce myself or to just follow that sweet scent trailing in her wake. If pheromones are honey, jasmine, citrus, vanilla, orchid, peach, chocolate, and blackberry, I kid you not, that's what just walked by, blasted my senses, and woke everything up inside.

The reason I'm at the airport rushes back. Probably as the blood eventually returns to my brain.

I sit down in a stupor.

I'm at an airport and moving from LA in the next few months. I'll never see this girl again, and while that's a fucking shame, it's just the way it is. I look at the screen to see if there are any updates, and when I see that nothing has changed, we're still stuck here for at least another hour, I bury myself in my phone and don't look up again until it's time to board.

Since my legs are so long, I'm in an exit row. When the flight attendant comes by to have us state that we know what we're signing up for by sitting in this row and gets our agreement, something catches my eye.

Those sexy legs.

The girl is across the aisle and a few rows up from me. Maybe my luck is changing—she's going to Minnesota too.

Still. Doesn't mean much.

Gotta love it when you're traveling and someone finds out you live in a state that the person you're talking to is familiar with, and they say, "Oh! Maybe you know my friend John?"

Uh no, Jim. I'm sorry I don't know your friend John.

The chances might be much greater in Minnesota than California, but yeah…no.

Doesn't mean I'm not going to enjoy the hell out of being in the close vicinity of this girl for a few hours.

While I feel a bit pervy staring at her from my seat, it feels like a gift that I want to accept…*however*, my sister Goldie's voice rings out in my head. *Just because you want to look, it doesn't mean she wants you to*. Damn Goldie for sitting on my shoulder talking sense into me even when she's across the country. She's always done her best to keep me in line, as most big sisters do, I guess.

So I do the gentlemanly thing and keep my eyes to myself. Okay, maybe not entirely, certainly not every second, but more than I would've without my big sister's stern voice correcting me.

I get a drink and a snack, thinking enviously about first class. I can afford it, I just can't always excuse the expense when it's a last-minute, extra-pricy fare. I guess my parents instilled that in me—saving the dollars where I can...even though they were richer than dirt. My dad still is.

I have a row to myself, which is pretty dang nice, and I try to watch a movie, but my attention is distracted by the girl in front of me. Even more so when she stands up, her long legs drawing my eyes down them again. Her legs are bronzed and look so fucking soft. I'd give anything to reach out and touch them and see if they're as soft as they look.

I'm a tall guy—6'5" and I'd put her around 5'10" or maybe even more. She's wearing heels, and it hits me again—God, she's so hot. She can't be much more comfortable than I am in these plane seats. I glance up at her and pause when I see her expression. There's a little frown between her eyebrows. The next thing happens so fast, I'm not sure what's going on. There are gasps around us as she stumbles forward, and I reach out and catch her as she falls right into my lap, face down. It's a good thing I had the elbow rest up because her head would've hit it hard. Her left breast is in my left hand, and her ass is in my right.

I couldn't make this shit up if I tried.

Her skirt rode up when she fell, and my hands are now on her bare ass. It is as amazing as I thought it would be, and her tit is fucking perfection, but this is not the way I wanted this whole thing to go down. I sit there for a second or ten, stunned out of my mind. Then I drag my hand out from under her breast, and when my other hand shifts, I feel her lace thong and grab her skirt to cover her skin.

I'm shocked she hasn't turned around and slapped me yet for having my hands in inappropriate places, even though it was unintentional.

"Are you okay?" I ask.

She says nothing. I look at her carefully and then brush her hair back. My God, she's passed out. I push the button above me for the flight attendant, and in the meantime, feel for a pulse. The relief when I feel a pulse is massive and it only grows when she stirs in my arms and turns her head to look up at me.

"What—?" she asks, her voice groggy.

I make sure my hands are nowhere near her ass or touching anything else inappropriate, but I also don't want to let her go down again.

"I think you passed out," I say.

The flight attendant comes over and gives me a look like *What the hell are you doing with a woman on your lap?*

"She passed out," I say hurriedly. "Fell right here when she got up. I'm worried about her."

"Oh my goodness!" The flight attendant jumps into action. "Can I help you get seated?" she asks the girl.

"You can sit right here next to me," I say. "No one else is sitting here. I can go by the window if you need more air."

She nods and takes a deep breath.

"Can I just sit right there?" she asks, pointing at the seat next to me.

"Absolutely." I hold onto her arm as she lowers her legs to the ground and moves to the seat next to me.

Meanwhile, the flight attendant has called for backup to bring the medical kit, and she comes and does the girl's vitals.

"Do you have low blood sugar?" she asks.

"I don't know," the girl says.

"Can you tell us your name?"

"Dahlia," the girl says.

Dahlia, I think, running the sound of her name through my mind.

It fits her.

"I'm okay," Dahlia says. "I think I've just been…" She shakes her head. "I probably do have low blood sugar because I didn't eat enough before I left." She takes a deep breath. "I…didn't get much sleep last night and am already a nervous flyer."

The first flight attendant nods. "We'll keep an eye on you. Do you need a drink and something to eat? Maybe some juice or ginger ale?"

Dahlia nods. "That would be great. Thank you so much."

When the flight attendant hurries off, Dahlia turns and looks at me. I want to reach out and smooth the crease between her brows. She's too beautiful to look so worried.

"I'm really sorry I just completely—" Her hand flies up and she sighs. "I've never passed out before. Did I make a complete fool of myself?"

"Are you kidding? I've never seen a more graceful dive." I grin at her and she looks taken aback, which just makes me smile bigger. I hold my hand out. "Hi, I'm Dylan."

Some of the color is returning to her cheeks. She gives me a small smile and shakes my hand.

"Dahlia."

"The professional diver."

A small giggle escapes and she covers her mouth with her hand, shaking her head.

"I'm so embarrassed," she says.

I lean in slightly and lower my voice. "I'm speaking with

one hundred percent honesty when I tell you that I have never seen anyone more beautiful than you. The fact that you made faceplanting look that good…" I shake my head. "That takes an extremely high level of skill."

Her lips twitch as she tries to contain her smile. "You're flirting with me."

"Is it working?" I whisper.

She puts her hand on her forehead. "I think I must have lost some brain cells when I fainted because it—" She looks around for the flight attendant.

"You're gonna leave me hanging?" I ask incredulously.

Now she really laughs, and I feel it from head to toe. Her eyes are sparkling with playful energy, and it's good to see even more color returning to her cheeks.

"You look like a man who has no doubts about the effect he has on women."

"I only care about the effect I have on *you*."

Shit, I'm laying it on thick, but I mean it with every fiber of my being. This woman is intoxicating.

Her eyes widen and she swallows hard.

The flight attendant chooses that moment to interrupt the best moment I've ever had.

Pre Order All for Love Here!
https://geni.us/AllforLove

ACKNOWLEDGMENTS

All my thanks and love to...

Nate Sabin, my husband, you are all that's good.

Greyley and Kira Sabin, these covers are so great and they make me happy every time I look at them. I also feel that way about looking at your faces. :)

Indigo Sabin, my sonshine. Thanks for always cheering me on.

Kess Fennell, your artwork makes me so happy.

Christine Estevez, you keep me sane.

Natalie Burtner, you're always on top of all the things, and I'm so grateful.

Katie Friend, the way I look forward to those comments!

Georgie Grinstead, you are the best in every way!

To the VPR team, I'm so thankful for all of you! Thank you, Nina, Kim, Charlie, Valentine, Kelley, Christine, Sarah, Jill, Jaime, Ratula, Josette, Meagan, Tiffany, Stephanie, Megan, Emma, Olivia, Jess, and Keriann!!!

Bill Siever, it's been such a joy to work with you!

To the Lyric team, Kim Gilmour and Katie Robinson, you're so great!

Sebastian York, this is the second time you have saved me, and I just love you for it. Thank you, thank you, thank you. Rose Dioro, I am so honored to have you on this project!

Laura Pavlov, there aren't words for how big the love is.

Catherine Cowles, my fellow #1 empath, love you forever.

Claribel Contreras, I want to have endless days to chat without interruption.

Tarryn Fisher, bestie for eternity.

Erin, thanks for letting me steal your name for this series. I hope you love your namesake. ;)

My family and friends who are like family—I'm so grateful for each of you!! Tosha Khoury & Courtney Nuness, my besties through thick and thin. Christine Bowden, my bestie across the world. Savita Naik, can't do life without you. Destini, grateful you love me anyway. Terrijo Montgomery, for the hair but mostly the love! Jesse Nava, love you always! Troi & Phyllis Atkinson, love you! Stefen and Jared, proud of you both. Winston, I won't clone you, but I wish you could live by my side forever.

Anthony Colletti, you're a rock star.

I'm so grateful for anyone who has taken the time to read my books, to review it, for the beautiful graphics, the sweet messages...it means everything to know you care about my stories. Thank you so much!

XO,
Willow

ALSO BY WILLOW ASTER

The Windy Harbor Series

Take This Heart

What It Takes

All for Love

Endless Summer Nights

Now and Forever

The Single Dad Playbook Series

Mad Love

Secret Love

Reckless Love

Wicked Love

Crazy Love

Landmark Mountain Series

Unforgettable

Someday

Irresistible

Falling

Stay

Standalones with Interconnected Characters

Summertime

Autumn Nights

FOLLOW ME

JOIN MY MASTER LIST…
https://bit.ly/3CMKz5y

Website willowaster.com
Facebook @willowasterauthor
Instagram @willowaster
Amazon @willowaster
Bookbub @willow-aster
Tiktok @willowaster1
Goodreads @Willow_Aster
Asters group @Astersgroup
Pinterest @WillowAster

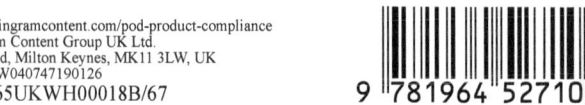
www.ingramcontent.com/pod-product-compliance
Ingram Content Group UK Ltd.
Pitfield, Milton Keynes, MK11 3LW, UK
UKHW040747190126
10165UKWH00018B/67